CANTERBURY 2100

Pilgrimages in a new world

Other titles by Dirk Flinthart:

Brotherly Love (Duffy & Snellgrove), 1995
Coasting (Duffy & Snellgrove), 1996
How To Be A Man – with John Birmingham (Duffy & Snellgrove), 1998

Other Titles by Agog! Press:

AustrAlien Absurdities, Edited by Chuck McKenzie and Tansy Rayner Roberts, 2002/2006

Agog! Fantastic Fiction: 29 New Tales of Fantasy, Imagination and Wonder, Edited by Cat Sparks, 2002/2006

Agog! Terrific Tales: New Australian Speculative Fiction, Edited by Cat Sparks, 2003/2006

Agog! Smashing Stories: New Australian Speculative Fiction, Edited by Cat Sparks, 2004/2006

Daikaiju! Giant Monster Tales, Edited by Robert Hood and Robin Pen, 2005/2006

Agog! Ripping Reads, Edited by Cat Sparks, 2006

Daikaiju!2 Revenge of the Giant Monsters, Edited by Robert Hood and Robin Pen, 2007

Daikaiju!3 Giant Monsters vs the World, Edited by Robert Hood and Robin Pen, 2007

Scary Food: a compendium of gastronomic atrocity, Edited by Cat Sparks, 2008

Canterbury 2100

Pilgrimages in a new world

Edited by Dirk Flinthart

Canterbury 2100: Pilgrimages in a new world © Dirk Flinthart 2008
Cover art and design by Nick Stathopoulos
Internal design and layout by Cat Sparks

Typeset in Century Schoolbook, Helvetica, First Order and Apple Chancery

All stories © 2008 by their respective authors, printed by permission of the authors

Published by Agog! Press
PO Box U302
University of Wollongong
NSW 2522
Australia
www.catsparks.net

In partnership with Prime Books
www.prime-books.com

ISBN:
978-0-8095-7327-1 (hc)
978-0-8095-7328-8 (pbk)

To Natalie, who put up with an awful lot

INTRODUCTION

Chaucer's Canterbury Tales and the Decameron of Boccaccio remain vivid, charming works that find new readers to this day. It's not their artistry; very few people can appreciate Chaucer in the original Middle English. Likewise, the stories are a mixed bag. What keeps them fresh is their humanity: the sense of the people in and behind those stories, still reaching out centuries later, though the world has changed drastically.

The stories we choose to tell speak volumes about us, as people. Six or seven hundred years from now, our present-day body of popular fiction in all its forms will be just as intriguing to the readers and viewers of that time as Chaucer is to us, and just as relevant.

It was that line of thought which made me wonder: what would the fiction of an imaginary world be? Would it possible to depict a fictional future by exploring the stories that the people of that future tell each other?

To me, that idea was utterly irresistible. Even after a year and a half of work, I'm still delighted by the concept. The book you hold now is only one glimpse of one possible future. The stories are dark, light, sad, joyful, desperate, hopeful – exactly what you would expect. But more than that: taken collectively, the stories become a window, a kaleidoscope looking into a world which doesn't yet exist. In the interstices, in the assumptions of the characters, in their language, in their motivations and hopes and fears, the reader gets a sort of shadow-show, a tiny stage where human dramas play out as ever while behind, the vastly changed economic, social, religious, military and environmental underpinnings of the world act subtly and powerfully to alter the shapes on the screen in ways that are not always comprehensible to our present-day way of thinking.

I won't lie. This anthology was extraordinarily hard work, and I'd like another year and a half to make it better than it is – as I would with just about every project, of course. But... I think it's there. That sense of another world behind the stories, a living, breathing human world full of real people doing real things – I think we did it. Check it out for yourself. Read, and if you find yourself wondering about half-submerged Londonistan, or the role of the Church in 22nd century scientific research, or contemplating the lineage of King Charles V, or exactly how a Carbon-Knitter goes about her task, then yes: it worked.

Enjoy.

Dirk F. September 2008

☙

*I*n the late spring of this year two thousand, one hundred and nine CE, I made it my business to board the first of the new CC Special Service trains from Newcastle to Canterbury. Like many a hundred other, I came both as pilgrim, and – if it may be believed in these times – tourist, to witness and celebrate the anniversary of our King Charles IV, long may he reign.

Of course, as milord knows well I held other motives.

Like many, I argued against the CC Special programme. Certainly, a simple pebble-bed reactor does provide a clean source of high-pressure steam. Equally, I admit the use of the nuclear engine to liquefy coal for use in our returning industries is ingenious. The system worked perfectly in the secret trials, and even the prototype unit could withstand close inspection: it looks for all the world like a carbon-capture coal engine of the latest design.

Nevertheless, it remains a complex deception, difficult to sustain. I have concerns for the public backlash if we are discovered returning to atomic power after the disasters of the last century.

I took the liberty of assuring first-class passage for myself, the better to make my observations. I have included the price of both the ticket and the necessary bribes in my expense account. I expect that milord will authorise my remuneration at his earliest convenience, naturally; the modest income of an agent of Crown Intelligence doesn't stretch to such niceties.

It must be admitted that the new CC Special Engines are impressive. If I was more of a technophile, I might even say they are beautiful: long, low, sleek and black. With its raked lines and polished planes, it raised a deafening roar from the crowd as it pulled into Newcastle Station with a shrill blast from its whistle.

We had the best of weather, fine spring sun and a sweet sea breeze off the river. A band played. Speeches were delivered, and duly ignored by an unruly mob far more interested by the mummers and tinglers, troubadours and miracle men. And then, at last, a fat man in long robes cut a shiny ribbon with a pair of outsized scissors and in a roaring flood we pushed and shoved our way aboard.

His highness the king may well take pride in the new service, milord. Even to a man of my education, knowing the accomplishments of the past as I do, it seemed a miracle that so many could be carried in such comfort. Yes, I know – I have seen the graveyards where the giant aircraft that once plied our skies are slowly stripped of their valuables. I know that once we flew more folk from north to south in a matter of hours than our mighty train can carry in a long day's travel. Still, it was a brave sight and a wonderful thing to think upon.

I rode in a carriage near the front, next to the luxurious saloon car. It is rumoured that some of the old sleeper cars are being recommissioned for future runs of the CC Special. Perhaps that will be a good thing, but for this journey, at least the saloon car became the life and soul of the train. A goodly number of people gathered there, and there was laughter, and drink for those who take it, and food, and much good cheer.

The group in the saloon car was remarkable in its diversity, at least to me. I had imagined that the travellers on this prestigious maiden run would be monied and influential, and indeed, I suppose there were some. Yet I met with others, quite humble in their origins. A lighterman, rough as his trade, all callused hands and curses; he sat next to a doctor out of Australia if you can believe such a thing. The Australian claimed to have an invitation from the Royal Society to present information on a vaccine for one of the plagues. I'm sure milord will know if this is so, and I hope it is true. He got along with the lighterman well enough, in any case.

And who else? A Scribbler, with the pens and papers of his trade, taking notes all the while. A nun. A census-taker. A wild, holy woman from far Siberia. A half-mad peat digger from the ice-wastes of the Hebrides. A lovelorn priest, God help us. Oh, it was a strange, wild crew, but good company, milord, and the miles went quickly.

Leastwise, they did until the storm came.

Milord will know already the damage wrought by that storm. Crops blasted, rivers bursting their banks, winds the like of which we've not seen for a quarter-century, or so they say. I understand the weather savants claim it was kin to the great Catastrophe Storms that battered us in my grandfather's time, when the ocean currents shifted and the climate turned wild. I wouldn't know, of course, but I will say this: the rain fell like hammers, lightning stalked across the earth like an angry giant, and the wind was so strong that even our mighty chariot shuddered, and slowed, and at last came to a shaking halt.

With the sound of the engine and the rattle of the tracks gone, the roar of the storm seemed louder and more terrifying still. We drew together in the saloon car, away from the windows and the lashing of the rain. The conductor came through, on his way to reassure the passengers at the back of the train. No danger, he said, but we were halted by rising waters. The bar would stay open for our convenience, but the lights must go out to save power, save only the emergency LEDs that ran off their store of sun-power.

Very dark it was then; dark, and but for the little coal stove near the centre of the car, bitter cold. We talked among ourselves for a time, but with our voices low and fearful, skittish from the night and the fury outside. Then, as the storm reached its height and our spirits fell to their lowest ebb, we turned to that most human of all actions – storytelling.

It began this way:

The Tingler's Tale

a rumour passed from the front carriages that there was a Bollywoodheart singer on the train. He was said to be a handsome young man with lovely coffee-coloured skin and a voice that soared to the ancient heavens. He knew all the old songs like Mumbay Masala and Chittipore Lane; the Bollywoodhearts had preserved them so well. He was said to be travelling to Canterbury to meet his new wife, another Bollywoodheart, as was their custom, and as was their custom they had never met before. Rumour was uncertain as to whether she was a singer or a dancer, or perhaps an actor. The Bollywoodhearts were an entertaining lot, and the news lifted our spirits, at least for a time.

Yet the singer failed to appear, and after a time, all hope of hearing his jolly love songs was given up. In that moment, a scarecrow of a man stepped forward. This was the Tingler who frightened small children and adults alike if the price was right. He was six foot tall at least and starved as a skeleton. He must have stayed out of the sun too, to keep his skin as pale as pale could be. Not even wine flushed his cheeks. Dark hair fell across his face and his eyes protruded from their sockets with a bulbous gaze. Dressed he was all in black as you might expect from a man who made his living scaring the wits out of the soft underbelly of the upper-classes. Black robe, black shirt, black pants and a black cravat tied with a flourish about his neck. Even more spooky he would have been if he had dressed in white. A living ghost, come to give us fright. He had once haunted a mansion for a week, he said, rattling chains and making eerie sounds at night, popping out of closets unexpectedly, but still finding time to have a fling or two with every women in the house, from the kitchen maid right up to the lady of the house herself.

'I believe it is time for a tale,' he told us and though his voice was sombre, it rang clear over the wind and the storm, and all at once.

'Are there any hangmen present?' he asked, casting his poppy eyes about.

No one raised their hand. He sighed. It seemed he was relieved. Or perhaps disappointed. Impossible to tell.

'Perhaps, then there is a Scribbler in our midst?' A short, stout man at the back of the carriage raised his hand. He had the look of one married to his desk, and perhaps the whisky bottle too.

The Tingler bowed to him. 'Then, Dear Sir, this tale I tell for you.'

I shall tell you about a Hangman and a Scribbler, and a most foul and evil murderer, or two. It starts like this and ends ... well, you shall know where it ends, unless you doze off, or our Bollywoodheart finally arrives to sing his song.

The Scribbler worked for another who called himself an Editor. Pamphlets they produced and sold on street corners and all the squares of all the major towns. Horrible crimes they told of as you would expect in this day and age. It's why the hangman has his due once more, although in long forgotten times the profession had disappeared from these lands; so good and noble and decent were the people back then, or so I presume.

The Scribbler was sent by his Editor to Newcastle Gaol one day. He was there to write about the untimely end of a man called Witherspoon. Perhaps, some of you remember the case. Witherspoon was the butler who had trod in his master's footsteps – the most notorious Lord Suchinbrook. He, who was arrested, tried and hung, for preying on the sons of the middleclass, as well as dozens of street urchins. He had cut their hearts out and eaten them, severed their penises from their bodies and stuffed them in their mouths. Their bodies were found floating in the murky waters of the Tyne. There was no purpose in what he did, that I can fathom, other than he was a madman or possessed by the devil. As the Archbishop of Canterbury himself has said: 'The devil is once more abroad in the land. Due and constant vigilance is required to defeat his evil ways.'

The Scribbler had interviewed the condemned man earlier that morning and more of that I will tell later. Now we find him with the Hangman, learning what a very technical business it is.

The execution rope must be of superb quality. (Italian hemp is the best, but in short supply.) It should be thirteen feet long and three-quarters of an inch in diameter precisely. There should be soft kid leather on the noose itself to reduce the bruising on the neck. The aim it seems is to leave a pretty corpse. And a professional noose must have a brass eyelet, not a hangman's knot. It allows the rope free running and breaks the neck with more certainty. The Scribbler dutifully wrote these facts down as the Hangman explained them.

It is a science and an art, most certainly.

Now the Hangman stood poised on the scaffold's steps, gazing upwards, a solemn look upon his face. But he was clearly relishing the opportunity to speak of his profession. It was rare that a hangman was ever asked about the business of his trade. 'The gallows ain't changed much over the years. The Hangmen's Guild found books from long ago; did their research, yes, they did, and all of us work within a certain code or lore, you might call it. Once you could hang a man, or a woman for that matter, from a tree with a stout branch. Sit them on a horse or a donkey, and whack its arse. It did the job, but it wasn't clean. It wasn't neat. And it wasn't necessarily swift either, and these days, clean, neat and swift is what it's all about. Hanging isn't strangulation; it's getting a good clean break of the neck. Instant death.'

The Hangman said this without a trace of emotion on his face. He was a man who took great pride in his work.

Up to now the Scribbler had thought hanging *was* about strangulation. It was an important point he must distinguish for his readers. They would be sure to enjoy the gruesome details.

'So all you need for a gallows,' the Hangman said, pointing as he went, 'is two upright beams, a cross-bar to hitch the rope to, and a long drop through a trap door. Come, let me show you.'

The Hangman took the Scribbler to the scaffold, placed him standing on the trapdoor, put the noose around his neck and the white hood over his head. Then he bound his hands and feet with ropes. The Scribbler thought it was all a lark. He had asked for a full demonstration. He wished to place himself in the position of the condemned man, so much better for him to describe the moment for his readers.

Once he was bound and trussed and set up in this way, the Hangman asked: 'You okay?'

The Scribbler replied: 'Most certainly.' But the truth was the lark had suddenly passed. He was feeling vulnerable, and there was an unpleasant odour in his nostrils which he imagined was either fear or a premonition of the smell of death itself.

The Hangman spoke again: 'So this is the way I set them up, and I'm sure you can imagine what they're thinking in their heads, the poor miserable bastards. About all their crimes and how they're going to meet their maker, and wished they hadn't done all those bad things they did. I always like to give them time to think. Not too long. Half a minute's all they need, before I pull the Monkey on them.'

'The Monkey?' the Scribbler said. He had no idea what a monkey was.

'The handle that controls the trapdoor,' the Hangmen replied. 'It's a tricky beast. Sometimes it does your bidding; sometimes it doesn't. Let me show you how it works.'

'No, that won't be necessary,' the Scribbler cried. 'I'm quite comfortable standing here, just understanding what it's all about. Really, I am.'

'No need to worry,' the Hangman replied, 'you're perfectly safe in my hands.'

Next the Scribbler heard a great clunky sound. The trapdoor shuddered beneath his feet, opened, and the air rushed around him: Down...down... down, he fell, feeling every inch of that drop. Dear God, he cried, and prayed to all the saints, although he was not a religious man. In the three-quarters of a second it took to drop, the Scribbler apologised for all the bad things he'd done to others; he promised, if he were to live, he would lead a life of utmost holiness, and make his pilgrimage to Canterbury one day. Alas, the poor man promised anything and everything. So much he wished to live.

The Scribbler landed at the end of the long drop in a pile of sawdust. The rope slipped freely from his neck. His legs were weak beneath him. With his hands bound he toppled over – into more sawdust. He heard the Hangman's voice calling down the drop: 'Now how was that? I've never tried it me'self, but I reckon that'd give you a real insight into what it's like.'

The Scribbler lay there, thinking what a terrible business it was. His heart was beating loudly, wildly pumping his blood. The Hangman was an irresponsible bastard, an arsehole, a complete and utter madman. Oh, but then he recalled that he had insisted on a full demonstration and that was exactly what he'd been given. It was an experience; that was for sure, and he could see the readers lining up for miles to buy the story he would tell.

Now the Hangman was beside him, pulling the hood off, unstrapping his arms and ankles, and ushering him through a narrow door into a tunnel that led from the bottom of the drop. He sat the Scribbler down on a wooden bench and handed him a silver flask. 'Here, a spot of whisky will do you good.'

The Scribbler took a shallow sip. He was not a drinking man. The flask was sturdy and expensive, but the whisky inside was cheap and raw. He passed it back to Hangman who took a hefty swig.

Opposite the Scribbler was a dirty grey stretcher propped against the wall. Its canvas had once been white, but was now covered in mildew. Every six feet or so, along the length of the tunnel, a gas jet burnt, giving the place a gloomy light. Water seeped and trickled through the cracks in the bricks. Everything was moist and damp. The air smelt faintly noxious.

Lost in his thoughts, the Scribbler jumped when the Hangman spoke again. 'So during the hanging, the doctor and his orderlies wait here, behind the door. As soon as they hear the clunk of the Monkey, Doc opens the door. The orderlies grab the body to stop it swaying, and the Doc does his business, checking for a pulse and stuff like that. When he's sure I've done me job, the body's placed on this here stretcher and it's off down the tunnel to the prison morgue. Then the Doc does his autopsy – to certify that death was by hanging – and prepares the death certificate. After that they're given a decent burial by the chaplain in the prison graveyard. Although if you ask me the decent burial part's wasted on them, seeing as the Devil's already taken their soul.'

'There are rumours,' the Scribbler said, 'that the bodies aren't given a decent burial at all, but are sold off to the highest bidder among the medical colleges of the city.'

The Hangman smacked his lips. 'Heard that one m'self. Didn't know what to make of it. All I know is I seen the coffins buried in the prison graveyard. As to what was in them, you'd be better speaking to the Doc about that. Who knows what these doctors get up to, eh? Ain't none of my business, ways I see it. I'm a simple hangman; I just drop them the best I can.'

'Yes, I shall speak with him.' The Scribbler pulled a silk handkerchief from his pocket to wipe the sweat from his brow. Despite the dank dark tunnel he was in. 'One last question. Is it possible to beat the gallows?'

'Beat the gallows?' The Hangman looked genuinely puzzled, as if he had never been asked such a question in all his life.

'There must be a way,' the Scribbler said, to which the Hangman replied: 'I don't believe there is.'

The Scribbler raised his eyebrows, feigning some surprise. 'There was the Deacon Brodie case in Edinburgh. I've heard it's part of hangman's lore.'

The Hangman licked his lips. 'Can't say the name rings a bell.'

But the Scribbler thought there was a flicker of recognition in the Hangman's eyes and so he spoke once more: 'Deacon Brodie cheated the gallows by wearing a special harness beneath his prison shirt, which the noose could be affixed to, thus preventing the clean break you have so eloquently described to me.'

The Hangman cleared his throat. 'A risky business if it be true, and only possible if the hangman of the day was in league with the condemned man, the doctor too, and those who cut the body down. But I can assure you nothing like that has happened in this old gaol.'

The Scribbler looked the Hangman up and down. He thought he had his number now, but then realised he was feeling faint. The darkness at the end of the tunnel twisted and turned before him, spun around and twisted some more. He needed to get into the fresh air – to feel the warmth of the sun on his face.

But sadly it was a rainy day.

Now while the Scribbler revives himself, whilst listening to the rain, I shall tell you what happened earlier that morning.

The Scribbler after his breakfast of poached eggs, and a quick cab ride across the river – the driver had whipped the horses mercilessly – had arrived at the gaol to interview the murderer, Henry Witherspoon, prior to his execution. This had been at condemned man's request and the Scribbler thought he was about to get the confession that had eluded the authorities.

On his arrival, the Scribbler was taken to a small room hardly bigger than a lowly worker's kitchen. Cutting the room in two was a steel grille, its bars so close together.

The Scribbler sat down on a three-legged stool, crossed his legs, placed his notebook on his knee and stared through the grille. His pen was poised ready to write. He was convinced he was about to get the scoop of his life. Behind him a middle-aged guard minded the door.

The condemned man was brought in. With his hands and feet bound by iron shackles, he walked with slow, shuffling steps. He had the same resigned look in his eye that the Scribbler had witnessed during his trial. The young guard who escorted him closed the door and leaned up against it.

Witherspoon sat down slowly on his own three legged stool and said: 'You've been following my case closely. I saw you in the courtroom. You looked me in the eye fair and square and I knew I could trust you when you did.'

The Scribbler nodded his head. It was true what the condemned man said.

The condemned man moved closer to the grille, he dropped his voice, spoke in a whisper: 'I did not commit those crimes. It was Suchinbrook. He is still alive.'

'He was hanged by the neck until dead,' the Scribbler replied. He had heard the defence before, and all had disregarded it. But there was something in the condemned man's voice that drew him in and made him doubt his own words even as he spoke them.

'Did you see it, did you verify it? Were you the hangman, the doctor that attended him, did you see what was in the coffin he was supposedly buried in?'

'I am not here to save you,' the Scribbler said. 'It is not in my power to do so.'

The condemned man shrugged. 'It's too late for that. I knew it as soon as I was arrested. Suchinbrook left me a legacy; it was more money than I knew how to use. I was reckless and tainted with his name. The police would never believe I had nothing to do with the old bastard's crimes. But a good servant learns to speak only when spoken to, and I was one of the very best. Suchinbrook isn't dead. That's God's honest truth. And when I'm gone, he'll still be out there, killing those young men.'

The Scribbler leaned close to the grille, so close that he was exchanging breath with the man who was about to die. 'You're saying he wasn't hanged?'

'Ask the hangman about Deacon Brodie. Edinburgh. It's well known in hangman's lore.'

And the condemned man gave him the details of the case, finishing with: 'That's the way it was done. I'm certain of it.'

Before the Scribbler could respond, Witherspoon said: 'I can see you're scared of what might happen. Here take this. For good luck.' He rolled one hand over another, slipped something out of his sleeve and pushed it through the grille.

Witherspoon's action was so fast and full of sleight that the Scribbler was surprised when he saw the carved piece of amber sitting in front of him.

Upon a leather string. 'What is it?' he asked in the quietest of whispers.

'An amulet. Didn't do me no good, but I was already a condemned man when it came into my possession.'

Witherspoon rose from his stool, looked into the Scribbler's eyes, smiled, then shuffled away.

The Scribbler slipped the amulet into his pocket before either of the guards could see it. Inwardly he chuckled at the ridiculous irony of it. A condemned man had given him a good luck charm. Still, he thought, as he left the interview room, it would add an extra element of mystery to the pamphlet he would write. The readers loved that sort of thing.

Much revived by the air of a rain-soaked day, we find the Scribbler returning to his work. Now it is time for the hanging.

From his front row seat, the Scribbler had an excellent view of the proceedings. A fellow Scribbler was sitting next to him. A man sensational for articles depicting Newcastle as the most sinful city in the land, which it is; I grant him that.

When Witherspoon was upon the gallows, the Scribbler looked up and caught his eye. His readers would wish to know whether there was fear there, remorse, madness or cold-blooded arrogance. He saw none of these emotions. Instead he saw excitement, pure, wild-eyed excitement on his face. The condemned man gave him a wink, as if they had sealed some deal. The Hangman pulled the white hood over Witherspoon's head and stepped back. He placed his hand on the Monkey in a slow deliberate fashion. He likes to give them time to think, the Scribbler thought, not long, but long enough.

The Scribbler closed his eyes and counted slowly to thirty, believing he knew exactly what would happen next. He reached into the pocket of his coat and rubbed the amulet that the condemned man had given him. It was a nervous reaction, something to do, while he waited for the clunk of the Monkey and the terrible shuddering sound of the trap door opening. The seconds counted seemed to stretch to minutes.

The clunk did not come, nor the shuddering. The Scribbler opened his eyes when he heard the excited voices around him, and looked up once more at the gallows. The white hood was off the condemned man's head. The noose had been removed from his neck and the Hangman was at his feet unbinding his ankles.

Witherspoon had a smile on his face. He winked at the Scribbler as the Hangman led him away, but not down the steps, as the Scribbler had expected, but through a door on the far side of the scaffold.

'A terrible business,' his fellow Scribbler said, but the look on his face told the Scribbler he was pleased to have something more than an ordinary hanging to report. 'By all accounts the Hangman has fully tested the apparatus today, with a man who was the same build and weight as the condemned. It's what they call a mock hanging. They do it to make sure the trapdoor releases as it should.'

'Yes, I see,' the Scribbler said, realising now why the Hangman had been so willing to give him the full demonstration. So very close was he to the same weight and build of Henry Witherspoon.

'So now,' his fellow said, keen to give instruction, 'he has been taken to a secure room, and the Hangman and the prison Governor will inspect the trapdoor. If it appears to be in order, the condemned man will be returned to the gallows. This is your first hanging?'

The Scribbler smiled to himself. 'No, my second. The first went smoothly enough.'

Ten minutes later, after the inspection of the gallows found no fault, Witherspoon was brought out and placed over the trapdoor once more. His ankles and arms were bound again, and as the white hood was placed over his head, his gaze fell on the Scribbler.

This time the Scribbler did not close his eyes. The Hangman stood away quickly and when his hand gripped the Monkey, he pulled it straightaway. The Monkey clunked. The trapdoor quivered. Its wood hummed, but refused to open.

The Hangman swore beneath his breath and unbound the condemned man for the second time that day.

'Dear God,' the Scribbler muttered, using his handkerchief to mop away his nervous sweat.

'They'll give it one more try,' his colleague said. 'A tenner that it fails again. Three times lucky, that's what they say.'

But the Scribbler shook his head. He was not a betting man.

Once more the trapdoor and the Monkey were checked and there was agreement between the Hangman and the Governor that the gallows was in working order.

This time when Witherspoon looked at him, as the white hood was placed over his head, the Scribbler felt he'd been shot through the eye with an arrow. He plunged forward in his chair, hearing the grunt of the Monkey, and the thundering shudder of the trapdoor ...

... as it opened beneath him ...

... the air rushing, the smooth suede of the noose, around his neck..

And so fast did it all happen, there was not a thought in the Scribbler's head. But suddenly, what was that? The Scribbler felt a wasp had stung him on the neck.

At the bottom of the drop the Doctor was in a furious state. 'Cut him down,' he ordered, 'Cut him down. The Hangman calls this a clean break does he? Goddamn you, Hangman, I'll have your bones served to the dogs.'

The rope was cut. The hood was pulled. A terrible gasp came from all those that bore witness. For it was not the condemned man but the Scribbler that lay there on the straw, with thick red marks around his neck from where the noose had strangled but not broken.

More confusion now.

'Where's Witherspoon?'

'Dear God, where is Witherspoon?'

'Hangman, you fool, you hanged the wrong man!'

'Impossible.'

'Get him on the stretcher, quickly to the clinic.' The Doctor was frantically thinking of what to do next. 'No word of this to anyone. Or I shall have your balls for breakfast. That's each of you. Every single one'

The Scribbler was in a poorly way. Hanged twice in one day, but still his life lingered on. When next he was able to open his blood-flecked eyes, he saw the face of the Doctor hanging over him. It was a kindly face, he thought, with such pale blue eyes and soft pink cheeks.

But kindness of any kind was the furthest thing from the Doctor's mind. And the Scribbler heard the following words which were to be the last he would ever hear: 'Alas, he's not dead yet. I'll need the chloroform.'

The Tingler stood there quietly for a moment. It seemed his tale was finished and he had told all there was to tell. But then his hand slipped into the pocket of his long black robe and brought forth an amulet of amber. He held it up for all to see, then spoke again: 'It was the amulet, of course, that brought the poor Scribbler to an untimely end. And the Doctor – what was he to do, but pretend the condemned man had been hanged as planned? Most assuredly a decent corpse was needed, and already promised to a certain college. Empty coffins were not rare in that gaol.'

The Tingler then tossed the amulet through the air. It sailed in a high arc, way down to the back of the carriage. There our own Scribbler screamed with fright and scrambled from its flight. The Tingler gave a hearty laugh and bowed. He was pleased with what he'd done.

So much I have from memory, and from the Scribbler's own jottings which I bought from him later. He was so fearfully embarrassed at being gulled by the Tingler that he would not part with his notes until I promised not to use his name. Easily done; like everyone else in these tales, I have named him by his profession.

The wailing and lashing of the storm made the Tingler's tale, told with spooky skill and gusto, all the more atmospheric. When the Scribbler screamed, half the carriage screamed with him, and in the aftermath, we all burst into laughter. It was well done.

Still, in his wake it seemed the stories might be done. The Tingler had spoken so well that no one else wanted to step up into his boots. If it wasn't for the Scribbler, mightily shaken, politely offering a draught of his wine to the nun sitting beside him, perhaps we might have tried to sleep, despite the storm.

Up to then, I had barely noticed her. Mostly, she sat by the window and watched the rain. Sometimes she nodded at a particularly savage bolt of lightning, as though indicating approval, or perhaps understanding.

Her habit was rain-grey, as if she wore a piece of sky wrapped about her. The white hood hid most of her face and the omega symbol embroidered around its edge marked her as a member of the Order of the Sisters of the Empty Name. All I knew of them was that they weren't much given to speaking.

The Scribbler had made his offer of wine without thinking, and for a few moments silence rewarded him. Then one or another of the travellers in the car giggled at his gaffe.

There were more than a score, mostly pilgrims. They would be going to the Cathedral to ask for something: some would settle themselves in the enormous open area of the nave and pray earnestly; others would kneel hopefully beside the stained, inscribed stone where Beckett had lost his life; some would wander the cloisters, rest underneath the stone arches and hope for peace to seep into their bones; yet others, those with darker desires, would sit in the Chapel of Our Lady Undercroft, breathing in the stale darkness and begging for their deepest wish to either come true or leave them altogether. To such people, the nun was almost invisible; she had given herself over to worship, what could she possibly pray for?

Her voice, when it came, was rough, low, unused. 'They built a city.'

The Scribbler almost dropped his wineskin. 'What?'

'They built a city,' she repeated, 'and they raised it high.'

She turned to look at those of us who were watching. All I could make out – and I sat quite close – was the lower half of her pale face (the tip of a nose, thin lips, a hard chin), and the glimmer of eyes in the shadow of her hood. 'I offer you this tale, Story-gatherer. Will you take it?'

Sobered, the Scribbler nodded. How many of his kind had the chance of a tale from one such as her? Our fellow travellers felt the same. The children moved away from their parents and settled among the fine old seats and upon the faded carpet, as near as they dared to the nun. She folded her hands into her lap, seemed to consider them for a moment, the short fingers, the bitten-back nails.

'They built a city and they raised it high,' she began, repeating the words as a formula, as if she had told this story many times. 'Then, one day, one of its women woke up.'

The Nun's Tale

I don't quite open my eyes when I wake. I peer out under the lashes. He's staring at my skin, his large hand hovering over the tattoo on my forearm. I study him while he thinks himself unobserved.

His hair is iron grey, curly at the crown but close-cropped elsewhere, the hair to the left and right of the clump hanging over his forehead has receded slightly, like an apathetic tide, leaving small, symmetrical clearings. He's late forties-early fifties, six foot four, heavy around the shoulders and chest: an aging athlete. His legs are long and still well-muscled, his thighs and calves strong, hairy. He has a gut, not a great balcony of a thing, just a spare tyre; he's not fat, but an imposing man, strangely graceful for his size.

His face is unfathomable as he stares at the dark blue of my tattooed numbers – it will fade, in years to come – his fingers don't quite touch me. I think he must have been born with the tired look of a decadent saint on his face, large and battered as it is, with pale blue eyes and a full, whore's mouth. He hesitates, leans forward and closes his lips around the tattooed skin, a gesture somewhere between a kiss and a bite. His tongue is slow, silky against the flesh, his teeth strong.

I run my free hand through his hair. His eyes meet mine. 'How long have you been awake?'

'Long enough,' I answer; the hum of his voice goes through me, low, limber and sweet. He shifts, looms over me and the air buzzes.

I gasp, jerk, almost gag, wake; open my eyes and stare at the polished metal of the ceiling. It shows me as I am, naked and fragile, not as my dreams tell me I once was. The shaved hair is growing back, but only slowly, my skin is pale, dotted with red scabs where sockets have grown over. My eyes are blurs, the metal not polished enough to show the detail of my lashes, cornea, iris. I think my eyes used to be green.

The door slides open and I freeze, barely breathing. The rhythmic thud of boots. He looms over me, face shadowed by the ceiling lights. I stare straight ahead, don't blink, no sign of life. I wonder if the Marshall knows his face decorates my sleep, that when he's not here I take a strange comfort from him. I wonder that I choose to graft my tormentor's face and body onto my dreams.

'Terminal Six?' His voice is a threat and a caress. 'Terminal Six, I know you're in there. Somewhere in there, I know you can hear me.'

His fingers touch the barcode on my forearm, lightly, but with enough pressure to activate the metallic ink, enough to make it sting. I'm ready for this; I've grown used to pain. I keep my pulse steady and slow, my breathing minimal, no eye movements, no twitching, not even when he pinches my right nipple so hard that it bleeds, scarlet fluid welling up through the dry, cracked epidermis.

If they think you don't work anymore, they throw you out. The memory of someone telling me this is clear. A woman. A name slips in: Bella. *It's all you can hope for, really, being thrown out.*

But they don't throw us out that easily, we're too expensive, hard to find, to train; even harder to keep alive while they make us into what they need.

'I will get rid of you, Terminal Six, I promise you. If you don't come back from wherever you're hiding inside that mind of yours, I will personally drop you down a drain. You'll be flushed out beyond the city walls with all the other shit.' He leans even closer, his breath sour and warm and damp on my cheek. 'I will do it, Fionnuala, don't tempt me.'

The name almost makes me react. He straightens, smoothes his grey uniform jacket against his broad chest, contemplates me for a few more moments, turns away.

'Will you, sir? Will you get rid of Terminal Six?' His aide speaks in a low voice; this one is young, eager, unwary, filled with awe. I watch their reflections in the ceiling. The Marshall shakes his head, violent as the slash of a blade.

'No, you fucking idiot. She's too valuable. They all are, the bitches, and don't they know it. Unless we can find a new one, and soon, we're fucked.'

'There hasn't been one born in –'

'Fifty years, yes, I know. This one was the last.' He runs a hand through his hair. 'This one cost me everything.' He throws one last look at me and leaves, the door sliding shut with a hydraulic sigh.

A woman, who came in behind the Marshall, behind the aide, like a timid shadow, begins to move around, checking my vitals pulsing on the screen embedded in the wall, and the needles, vials, and bags of liquid stored in the locked, recessed cupboard. She glances at me occasionally.

She is tall and thin, with fine, dark hair threaded with dull grey; it lies on her shoulders, as though it has a hard time growing any longer, indeed, as if it took all its strength and her will to get to this length. Old burn scars mar her temples and on her forearms are raised bumps, still a little pink; grown-over sockets. She walks slowly, not quite limping, but each step is an effort.

This nurse has been a frequent visitor, but she's never spoken to me.

I know what you're doing. I know you're awake.

I turn my head, look at her, the shock irresistible this time. I lock up my mind so she can't get in. Beside my bed, bent forward, hands on knees, she grins triumphantly, madly, maliciously.

This, I realise, will not be an ally. Again, I look at the scars on her temples, know then that she did not take. That, although she had some psychic ability, her brain did not fit. She was burnt, scoured, scarred and discarded.

Her eyes are bright, angry, starved.

'I know,' she says aloud this time. 'I know you're faking, foxing – sneaky weasel!'

I don't recall what a fox is, nor a weasel, but her tone is not complimentary. She leaves before I can ask her anything, snatch anything from her mind.

I relax as well as I can – the bed beneath me is hard, the mattress a thin slice of foam, crushed by the weight of previous bodies. Taking a deep breath, I contemplate the things someone tried to erase.

The memories, the dreams, the things that float free when I sleep, I don't even know if they belong to me. Perhaps they go with my blood, perhaps they're race memory, family memory; perhaps they're planted, false things to lead me astray. It's a comfort, though, no matter what they are; this accessing of treasures lost for so long.

I had forgotten – or was made to forget – who I had been.

Something went awry. A power surge shot through my section of the Grid, the network that controls power, communications, water, all the essentials of the city's life. The surge toasted something inside me, burned away a part of my brain. I was in a coma for two weeks; the last two weeks, however, I've been faking, just as the nurse suggested. Whatever was destroyed wasn't anything I needed – something they added to suppress my memories, to dampen my free will, my power to act by my own volition.

I have no solid remembrance of *before* – only fleeting things that come and go, snatches of a past life, prior to being plugged into the Grid. They're like ghosts: faces, people, things, events; they flash in and out of my mind, not really telling me anything, but leaving me hints of what I was.

I can feel the flood of power in my veins. I wonder that they haven't caught an echo of it on the Grid; perhaps they no longer look for things like that, so convinced of their own infallibility. It's there, and it's growing stronger. I can throw my mind, my etheric body, out over the city, fly from one wall of the citadel to another in a trice. But I can't make anything happen in the Grid – can't control the things I used to when I was plugged in, a mindless cog in the great machine of the city. I have tried; but it's like bumping up against something and not being able to catch hold of it.

This silence, this mute rebellion has given me time to grow stronger, to experiment, to explore the Grid in ways I previously could not. If I want to change anything, however, I'll need to connect again.

'What are you?' My voice is low and rough; words have not been my currency for longer than I can remember.

She doesn't answer directly. 'They made you a goddess and *you* didn't care. *He* made you and you spurn his gift – ingrate!'

'I can't even remember how I got this way.'

Leaning closer, her spit sprinkles my face. 'Everything else was gone but he saved us, gave us this place. Built this city and raised us high. Gave you power but still it's not good enough for *you*.'

'The Grid rejected you, didn't it?'

She recoils. Did she want to be a Terminal so badly? Or is this mania the only way she can deal with what the incompatibility has done to her, how it's twisted her body and mind?

'Why haven't you told him I'm awake?'

'You heard him – he'll throw you out with the garbage if this goes on for much longer. You'll be gone. I'll have another chance.'

'No,' I say gently. 'There are no second chances in the Grid. It would kill you.'

'You don't know that …'

'I've been inside it for … for a long time. I don't remember much, but that I do know.'

Her face turns red. 'I'll tell him. I'll tell him you're awake.'

I shake my head. 'No, you won't. Because then he'll pay attention to me forever,' I whisper, treading with no certainty, only instinct. 'Let him think me broken, irreparable. Let him throw me away. Doesn't that make you happy? The thought of me plunging through the poisoned air, shattering on the earth below?'

The appeal to her madness gives her pause. I hold my breath. She smiles, nods. 'Sleep tight, Terminal Six.'

I wait until it's late, when they won't monitor the Grid so closely, when some boy sleeps in front of the screens and doesn't notice the blips and blinks. I seek out the others. There are five other Terminals. I know them only as electrical impulses, not as faces; but perhaps I knew their faces once. Features dart in and out, distracting me. I put these imperfect memories aside and seek what I know for certain, what I recognise without doubt: their heartbeats, their shallow breaths, their blankness, the machine-like functioning of their minds. I locate them but fail to connect – they cannot hear me without the Grid. They are bright pulses I cannot reach.

I sense the empty spot on the Grid where I should be; I feel the canton of the city where no power flows. I dart away from the Terminals, seeking something else.

The Marshall's quarters are spick and span, military and grey. No one else lives here. He slumps in an armchair, the top buttons of his jacket undone, his face worn, unguarded in the privacy of his home. Amber liquid pools in a heavy glass, the only warm colour in the whole place. There are photographs on the walls: other men in uniform, one with a woman. She is tall, dark haired, green eyed and he looks younger. She leans into him, laughing. His arm is around her waist, one hand caresses her neck. I wonder how long ago this was – time moves differently here. The longer I look at the picture, the stronger is the sensation of his hand on the small of my back.

I swim my etheric body around him, knowing that my molecules can disturb nothing, but he frowns, sniffs, reaches a hand out and grabs at the air. His fingers pass through my non-existent stomach, causing a ghostly sensation in my actual body.

'Terminal Six!'

I fall back into my cell, into my body. I didn't hear him enter, the aide. I'm standing, having moved about the room as my mind flickered across the Grid. This boy knows I'm awake.

He has taken two steps inside my cell. I grab at his mind before he can reconsider.

'Kneel,' I tell him. He resists for a moment then his knees buckle. 'Tell me. Tell me about the Grid.'

He stammers, doesn't manage to speak, so I save him the choice and dig into his brain, pulling out what I need, trying to fill in the gaps in my memory.

All the fossil fuels were gone, uranium reactors had scarred the planet, a new power source was needed. Next came the plagues, sweeping through entire nations like a mighty blow, leaving only a hardy few in their wake. We thought to escape: the city was built on a platform and raised high on gigantic metal legs, above the fumes and filth of a diseased earth. Power, water, everything needed to run the city was connected to the Grid, and the Grid was connected to the women, the Terminals.

At first, we did this willingly. Once, we were happy to serve the city; then, as our numbers dwindled, it became something forced upon the few who survived. Finally we became prisoners, kept as machine parts. Six women, six witches, one for each Terminal chamber in the hexagonal citadel. A small room fitted with a chair, electrodes that feed into socket holes drilled into flesh, a helmet lined with gold tracery to help conduct, direct and magnify the thoughts and impulses of the brain. As we became fewer in number, they found ways to extend our lives, kept us alive but only as long as we breathed the rarefied air of the city, only as long as we stayed above the clouds. They made us forget.

I let the boy go. He falls and cries. I turn away. 'This is what you will do: call him. Tell him I'm awake, ready to go back in. When you know he's on his way, find the highest point on the city walls.'

'And?' He stares at me, mind broken.

'And jump.'

The Marshall escorts me. I could paddle about inside his mind if I chose, but I fear there is nothing I want to see. No betrayal I don't already suspect. His hand in the small of my back is assured, as if he believes this is all he needs to control me.

He opens the door of the Terminal chamber, offers his hand to assist me with the three steps up. I ignore him, settle into the chair. The helmet is new and feels cold against my freshly-shaven scalp. Cables flail about like serpents, before slipping their connectors into the sockets of my forearms, breaking the cobweb of fresh skin. The barcode on my arm lights up as the Grid recognises me, welcomes me back.

Behind the Marshall, the ruined woman rounds the corner, her mouth opening in an 'o' of protest, drawing breath to yell a warning, but the Marshall sees only me. The handle is ripped out of his hand and the door slams shut, the Grid obedient to my thoughts. Outside he is yelling, banging on the metal, knowing at last that something is wrong. He can't override the system soon enough to stop me. I turn to the other Terminals.

Their electromagnetic pulses flicker before me like candles. I thread my way through the paths of their minds, up and down synapses, energising neurons as I pass. I seek out the firewalls holding memory at bay and burn them away. There is a collective cry and the Grid throbs, brightens.

We have names, I whisper to them. *We have names, remember them.*

There's a spark, a shiver through the network and names come to me. *Bella, Erzabet, Sheva, Hannah-li, Maeve.*

I hear, *feel,* sighs of recognition and relief, memories like a balm. I instruct the Grid to unlock their Terminal chambers, to free them from the cables and helmets holding them in place. I sense them rising, slowly, staggering. They are weak, emaciated, but determined. In my mind I see each of them leave the confines of their prisons, feet cold on metal floors as they find their way out.

They shine as they walk through the streets of the city we have served for so long.

I give one last signal to the Grid: lower the city, open the gates. The hydraulics groan and scream. The people, asleep in their beds, wake in fright, rush to their windows, see the shining bodies walking the streets, their feet barely touching the ground. The city, the citadel, slowly, slowly descends through mists that are no longer acrid smoke, to the earth, where a jungle has grown up around the great metal legs that held the city aloft.

I meet my sisters at the gates. They stare around them, at each other, touching their thin faces, the luminous skin, the frail, bird-like limbs. The Marshall trails behind me; I press the shape of my mind onto his, jamming his thoughts into a little box, shoving all that was *him* into a corner of his skull. Into my mind came an image, a memory. Not mine. Whose? Yet it compels, and the terrible, insistent truth of it will not be denied. I give it to the Marshall; force it upon him, demanded that he confront it: *I was your wife. I was your lover. But you loved your city more.*

I drive the knowledge deep into the centre of him. He tries to hide, to cower, to deny.

'No', he says, soft and broken, 'I didn't choose that. I didn't. Get to choose. They would have died. All gone. It had to be you. It was never a choice.'

But it was, and for the sake of she who lived that memory, for my sake, for the sake of all we Terminals, I engrave the memory into the fabric of his mind, never to be lost, never more to be denied. Now he can live a life that's anathema to him, softer than mine has been, for certain, but no less a warping.

A ramp juts out, sinking into the green of the jungle. When I set foot on it, he drops to his knees, presses his face to the soft white of my belly. I run a hand over his coarse hair, knowing the real him would hate the tenderness in my touch. I leave him behind, his face a study in loss.

Behind him stands the ruined one. I wonder if she will follow us, but realise that she will only ever see us as ungrateful goddesses, unworthy women. I arrest my step, move back to her, touch her face and press my tale into her skin, so she will know, perhaps understand; perhaps not.

We meander down the ramp, step out into the green. As we get further from the city, from the artificial atmosphere that kept us alive for centuries, our bodies age. We feel the withering, the diaspora of our molecules, the relief of death, and the lift of the wind. We fly as surely as the memories of the lost.

There was silence when she finished.

They left her in peace after that. I wondered, of course. I'm sure everyone else did too, but no one was ready to ask her, so calm, so careful, so silent. Well, almost no one. For I watched her a little longer, as the storm receded and the next tale began, and I saw the Scribbler say something to her, hesitantly, his eyes lowered.

In answer, she pulled back her sleeve. Beneath lay red marks, places where skin had grown over holes bored into her flesh.

When the Scribbler raised his eyes to meet hers, she nodded, and pulled down the sleeve once more. As unobtrusively as I could, I leaned in to catch her final words.

'All tales are penance, Story-gatherer. I carried this story for another. Now carry my penance for me.'

*B*y now, milord will have realised I resorted to my multicorder to capture these stories and most likely, will be wondering why. *Imprimus*: the mood in the carriage was infectious. The stories interested and compelled me. Being among the others while they were told made me feel as though I was part of something – special. In short, my judgement was affected, and I wanted to remember the feeling. *Secundus:* I felt the tales made a pleasant change from the usual dry stuff I file, milord. You have joked more than once about my dull reports. Here is my riposte. *Tertius:* It occurs to me that a certain young prince took a first in Sociology. Doubtless you recall his thesis better than I – but since he has shown such an interest in the relationships between government, society, and the prevailing myths of that society, it seems to me that he might well be interested in a collection of stories much like this.

A man can do worse than cultivate the attention of his sovereign in these times, milord.

In any case, once the Nun fell silent, calls went up for another story. The travellers were in good spirits by now. Bottles and wineskins passed from hand to hand, baskets were opened and provisions shared. Good natured jests and insults flew, and the storm seemed all but forgotten. Then, in a lull, a strong voice rose and I saw a man of middle years, with a touch of frost at his temples.

'Friends,' he said, 'For so I will call you, my fellow travellers – my friends, it seems to me I remember a tale that might suit, for it ends in the same destination for which we are bound. And since we have had a tale from a nun of death-in-life, I think you might find interest in my tale of a priest, and life after death. If you will have it, I will give you: The Dead Priest's Tale.'

the dead priest's tale

his name was Thomas, and he was born to die.

He didn't know that. He was reared by a devout couple in a small town in Northern Scotland, one of the few places the Calamity hadn't really touched. The Highlands remained, as they always had, a landlocked island of austerity and isolation, surrounded by an ocean of rough terrain and harsh weather. It was here, away from the floods and pandemics of the south, that Thomas was raised. This was shortly after the Plague Years, remember, an anarchic time, before the Re-Reformation. Life was brutal, and often short. But that didn't make it worthless; quite the opposite in fact. Every child was precious, a gift from God.

Thomas, though, was born to die. And that made him even more precious still.

The Church fractured during the Calamity, shedding its extremities like a meteor breaking up in the atmosphere, burning to embers long before hitting the earth. In the town where Thomas was raised, though, the Church still prevailed, offering some kind of hope in hopeless times. It survived the plagues, remained more intact than its flock. Thomas was schooled by the Church, as were all the children of the town, in the hope that, once grown, they could venture out beyond the Highlands, spread the Good Word, and perhaps plant the seeds for the rebirth of a national religion. It was an optimistic plan, and one that appealed to the townsfolk. They felt special, the chosen few, ready to lead their country back into the warm arms of a loving God's embrace, despite all evidence to the contrary.

Thomas excelled in school, particularly in theological studies. He received tutoring outside of school hours; his father was a clergyman, a teacher at the church school himself, and ensured that his son learned the day's lessons by reinforcing them nightly, often with force. The bruises across Thomas' knuckles and back were never questioned, least of all by the boy. This was his life, all he had ever known. By the time he was in his early teens, he was advanced enough to teach students himself, both younger and older than him.

His parents told him he was special, unique. It was that most awful of lies, one with a cold truth in its heart. For Thomas was born to die.

The first inkling Thomas had of his destiny came during the springtime festival of his fourteenth year. Despite the cold — for springtime in the village was scarcely warmer than the chill winter — he sat under a tree with only a woollen jerkin and trousers on, his feet and hands bare. He sipped at the sweet honey wine that was popular in those parts. His head spun.

That was when Sarah MacMillan kissed him.

It was unexpected. He'd thought himself alone, under the gnarled oak tree, older than he could imagine, though in an odd way younger than himself, something he couldn't have suspected. He didn't hear her footsteps sneaking up behind him, the half-melted snow muffling her approach. The first he knew of her presence was her warm, full lips upon his. The sweet scent of her auburn hair filled his senses. He closed his eyes, and lost himself in the kiss. Then, too soon, it was over.

'Happy Wintersturn,' she laughed, kissed his forehead, and skipped away. Thomas just sat there, stunned, still smelling and tasting Sarah MacMillan. A pleasant ache settled deep in his chest. He smiled.

He didn't see the man standing across the way, watching from within his robes. He only found out about him much, much later.

That evening, Thomas went to the festival dance and bonfire, hoping to see Sarah there. He'd imagined going up to her, taking her hands, and dancing with her around the hot fire, spinning like a zephyr, his eyes never leaving hers. And then, perhaps, they might kiss again. It seemed like a wonderful plan, a simple plan.

Sarah MacMillan never showed up. Thomas asked after her, but nobody knew where she was. Dejected, he returned home to a cold bed, alone, and dreamt of warm, wet kisses and dancing.

He never saw Sarah again. When he visited her parents' house the next day, it was empty. A week later, a new family moved in. It was as if they'd never been there. *Gone away*, the word was in the village. *A family emergency in the east. No time for goodbyes.* Perhaps that was why Sarah had kissed him, as her way of saying farewell? The thought made Thomas sad, but it never occurred to him that there might have been another reason for the MacMillans' sudden departure, a hidden reason. It wasn't in his nature, nor his upbringing, to question authority. Not then.

Once Thomas graduated from school, at the age of eighteen, he went straight into the priesthood. The Church sent him to a town further south, outside of Scotland, near Newcastle. It was another small town, as most were in those days, and very poor. He worked with an older priest, Father Robert: a big, bear-like man who filled his cassock to bursting. Father Robert was a man defined by his lack of attributes, a bas relief carving made flesh — charmless, humourless, emotionless. His only joy came from fighting, which he did with relish – and not a little skill – whenever the opportunity arose, and eating, which he also did to excess, despite the lack of foodstuffs in those tough times. Thomas was horrified by the man's greed, while many in the village went hungry. He dared not go against his superior, but instead distributed much of his own food to the townsfolk whenever he could. He lost a lot of weight, until he looked like one of the villagers himself, almost vanishing inside his cloak, while Father Robert grew ever more obese. It was a miserable time, for himself and the entire village.

He was in the village for twenty three years with Father Robert as his superior, twenty three long years, until one winter's day, Father Robert went for an afternoon stroll and never returned. There were whispers in the village, whispers of murder, revenge, even cannibalism, but nothing came of it. His body was never found. And, as if a curse had been lifted, the town came alive. Fields that hadn't yielded crops in a lifetime became fertile again. The bellies of the tiny herd of skinny long-haired cows swelled, yielded milk and, more importantly, new calves. The flock of sheep multiplied. Life in the town became, if not good, at least more comfortable than it had been in living memory.

And Thomas oversaw everything, his heart proud. God smiled on him. And all was well.

Eleven years later, Father Thomas received a message via carrier pigeon. He was summoned to Canterbury, to meet with the Archbishop. It appeared that word of his achievements had spread.

Please bear in mind, friends, this was many years before Canterbury took up the mantle as the seat of government. It was a city long neglected by all but the Church. The Church never left, of course, not that most holy of cities. They maintained the cathedral as best they could in the circumstances, despite the wild weather and outbreaks of deadly influenza ravaging their population. It remained the seat of the Church. That, and of something else, something more, something secret.

It was over three hundred miles from his town to Canterbury. Thomas had never even been south of the Tyne, but he felt no fear, for God was by his side. He rode his horse, a chestnut mare, into the remains of Newcastle. He crossed the river on the last remaining bridge, and followed the cracked and ruined A1 motorway south.

On the second day of his travels, he made a small detour to the east and visited York. The town had suffered greatly during the Plague Years, but it was still an important centre of activity, especially for the Church. The cathedral there was largely intact, and the town bustled with business. Thomas bought new supplies there, rested and stabled his horse, and took a room for the night in a small inn on the outskirts of town.

The next morning, as he left the inn, he encountered a man coming in. They nearly collided. 'My apologies,' Thomas said to the man, stepping aside nimbly.

'None necessary, my ...' The man trailed off as he looked at Thomas' face. His eyes widened. 'Father Thomas!' he exclaimed. 'My word, we haven't seen you here in, what, must be five years now? How are you?? '

Thomas was taken aback. 'I'm sorry, sir,' he said, 'but I think you've mistaken me for somebody else. I've never been to York before.'

The man looked at Thomas for a moment, then laughed loudly. 'You always did have a strange sense of humour, Father,' he chuckled. 'You don't look a day older than the last time you were here. How did your trip to Canterbury go?'

'I have to go,' Thomas muttered, anxious to get away from the man. He felt like the Devil himself had crawled into bed with him. Perhaps the man was demented, perhaps possessed. Either way, Thomas wanted to put as many miles between them as he could comfortably manage. He hurried away, not looking back.

A few more days of riding dimmed the memory of the strange man who seemed to know who he was and where he was going, or at least moved it to the back of his mind. The daily routine consumed his thoughts; riding hard, stopping only to rest and water his horse, eat his simple food, stone-hard bread and butter, deer jerky, and whatever he caught along the road. Rabbits were plentiful, drawn by the lush green grass that sprung from the deep cracks in the asphalt. It was child's play to bring one down with his slingshot, and women's work to skin and cook it of a night. In many regards, he ate better on the road than he had in the safety of his church. Though he missed the honey wine, it had to be said.

That was why he dallied in Cambridge, and how he came to understand the truth, or a small part of it.

Cambridge was once the home of one of the greatest seats of learning the world has ever seen, but the floods and plagues gutted the town like a fish, leaving nothing but bones and scales and a startled post-mortem expression. I know the colleges and scholars are returned, though much reduced, but in those days Cambridge was little more than a farming village living in the skeleton of a university; libraries of books rotted to mulch, lecture theatres holding grain, rugby fields ploughed and planted with wheat and vegetables. Cambridge was no more a place to stop than any of the dozens of other towns Thomas had passed through on his long journey to Canterbury. But it was replete with supplies, and he had heard rumours that they produced a particularly fine red wine in the southern hills, where vines grew wild in the wet earth. He travelled there, hoping to sample some of their wares.

He wasn't expecting the reaction he got.

The woman screamed when she saw him ride up, fell to the ground writhing and clawing at her face. He watched, horrified, as she flipped back and forth in the mud, as if she was having a seizure of some description. He climbed down from his horse and approached her.

'Ma'am? What is it?' he asked with some trepidation.

'Begone!' she shrieked. 'Begone, foul spirit! Take your omens with you!'

Thomas didn't understand. He looked to her house, a rough stone building with a thatched roof, and saw a young boy looking out at him from the window. The boy looked familiar, somehow, and he felt a strange pang in his stomach at the sight of him.

He realised what it was. The boy's eyes, blue, clear. They were his own, seen every day in his shaving mirror.

The woman had stopped screaming, and lay in the mud, rocking back and forth, moaning like a wounded animal.

'Ma'am?' he tried again.

'Please,' she whimpered. 'Please, Thomas, if you ever loved me, if any part of you remains, please ... please go.'

'How do you know my name?' Thomas demanded. He was feeling the same way as he had in York, when confronted by the madman who seemed to know him. He shivered. 'How do you know my name?' he repeated.

The woman opened her eyes, looked at him. Tears trickled down her cheeks. 'Do ye not know me, Thomas?' she asked. 'Has the Devil taken even that from me?'

Thomas didn't know what to say. He just stared at the woman, her eyes so filled with pain that he could barely meet them.

'Thomas,' she said in a soft voice. 'My love, Thomas. You are my husband, and I am Maria, your wife.' She shook her head, confused. 'No, not your wife. Your widow. I buried you two winters ago, below the very ground upon which you now stand.'

Thomas stepped back, startled, and looked down at the earth at his feet. It looked the same as everywhere else, but somehow, he knew it wasn't. Another shiver gripped his spine .

'You ... you're insane,' he said finally, but his voice lacked conviction. He took a few deep breaths, swallowed. 'How?'

'A plague,' she sobbed. 'It's not so bad now, not like before, but they're still about. The flu consumed you, took you from us.'

'No,' Thomas said, 'I mean, how? How did, uh, I come to be here?' He felt like he'd fallen into a nightmare, a dark future unfolding at his feet. 'When?'

'Eight years ago, this summer,' the woman, his wife, his widow, said. A small smile twitched the corners of her lips, despite her tears. 'You came here, summoned to Canterbury.' He flinched at that. 'We fell in love, and you stayed here. Stayed until ...' The tears redoubled then, the smile gone. She looked at him. 'Oh Lord,' she cried, 'Please take this spirit from me. Please, punish us no more.'

'Us?' Thomas looked over at the child in the window. Her son.

His son.

He could bear it no longer. He spun and ran back to his horse, clambered onto its back, and rode away as fast as he could. After an hour or two of aimless riding, the cold air had cleared his head a little, given him a chance to think. He was well schooled, proficient in logic. He couldn't allow himself to be overcome by superstitious nonsense. There had to be an explanation for this. A logical, reasonable explanation.

He remembered the man in York, how he'd supposedly met him five years earlier, on his way to Canterbury. Yet the woman in Cambridge claimed he'd arrived eight years earlier, also on his way to Canterbury. That meant he'd arrived in Cambridge *before* York, and stayed there. And yet, of course, he'd never been to any of these places before in his life. How could this be?

His own tears began then, as he knew, truly *knew*, his own destiny, inevitable, unavoidable. There was no logical explanation, except that God Himself had sent visions of his own destiny to vex him.

Thomas was born to die.

He found himself travelling more slowly now, with less enthusiasm. He survived purely off the bread and jerky he had in his saddlebags, having neither the energy nor inclination to hunt rabbits anymore. His appetite waned, as each clip-clop of his horse's hooves brought him closer to Canterbury, to his fate. Food tasted like ashes, water burned his stomach like whiskey. The sun, when it peeked from the heavy cloud cover, stabbed at his eyes.

When he got to Dartford, most of the town now under the swollen waters of the Thames, he met another man, also travelling to Canterbury. The man was in his thirties, a good two decades younger than Thomas, and introduced himself as William. He looked strong and fit, with a steel in his eye that matched the sword strapped to his side. But his smile was warm, and his handshake firm. He offered to travel with Thomas, share his food, and Thomas accepted the offer without much enthusiasm. It was easier than fighting. Thomas felt that he had no fight left in him.

'Do you believe in destiny?' he asked William as they rode. 'That our futures are laid out before us, like the very road we travel, you and I?'

William didn't hesitate. 'I do, Thomas,' he replied. 'I've been raised to believe that, my entire life. That God has a plan for every single one of us. Especially me.'

'Especially you?' Thomas asked with a raised eyebrow. 'Why so?'

William smiled mysteriously. 'Ah, my friend,' he said, 'that is a question I cannot answer. We all have a destiny, but we should never reveal that destiny to others, or else face certain death.'

'Too late,' Thomas sighed. They rode on.

They arrived in Canterbury two days later.

The city was still in tatters, from the weather and neglect, but also the plague riots that had swept the lands: angry, dying people blaming God and the Church for their plight. Buildings had been burnt and smashed, fields torched, churches razed to the ground. But the cathedral, wonderful Canterbury Cathedral, had stood against all comers, like a medieval fortress repelling siege after siege. It was damaged, yes, but there it stood, defiant, rebellious, majestic. Intact. Upon seeing it, Thomas' spirits lifted a little. How could God, a kind God, a God who oversaw such a magnificent creation, treat Thomas with such disdain and thoughtless cruelty? No, the visions must have been from the Devil, he decided, to break his spirit, prevent him from reaching his destination. But Thomas had prevailed, and now he was here.

Both he and William entered the cathedral, to be met by a young monk, Brother Edward. He led the two men into the cool, dark structure, towards the back, to the small chapel at the rear. As they walked, Thomas glanced at the stained glass windows they passed. Most were damaged, long replaced by simple panes, but some were still whole, and there was something indefinable about them that bothered him. That strange feeling he'd had twice before on his journey slithered into his guts, the horrible sensation of something not being right. It put him on edge.

They entered the chapel together, the three of them. Inside were three more men, of a similar age and build to William. All had swords at their belts. The feeling of wrongness intensified in Thomas.

'Gentlemen,' Brother Edward addressed the four armed men, 'you know your duty.'

William looked surprised for a moment, glancing at Thomas. A flicker of regret crossed his eyes. Then they turned to steel again, and as one, the four men drew their swords. Brother Edward stood back against a wall, beneath another stained glass window. Thomas saw the movement, then looked up at the window, at the picture contained within its bounds, wan afternoon sun illuminating it from behind.

It was Thomas' face.

'Hugh, Reginald, William, Richard. You know the king's orders,' Brother Edward said, despite the fact that there was no king at the time.

The four men nodded, and recited in unison, voices hollow, cold. *'Who will rid me of this turbulent priest?'*

The men advanced upon Thomas, swords raised. Thomas looked to each of them for mercy, but saw none in their eyes, except perhaps William's. His eyes were less sure than the others. This, Thomas realised, was his one chance.

'William, please,' he said, hands raised before him. 'Don't do this, my son. How can this be God's plan for you?'

William hesitated.

With a speed that belied his age, Thomas ducked beneath William's sword and grasped his wrist. He twisted, and the younger man yelped in pain and surprise. The sword dropped from his hand, and Thomas caught it easily, swinging it around and ramming the pommel into the side of William's temple, drawing blood. His eyes rolled back in their sockets and he folded like a scarecrow cut loose of its pole.

The other three men looked shocked. Thomas grinned; he was certain this wasn't how their destinies had been described to them. He didn't hesitate; with a single fluid movement, he thrust his sword at the nearest man's guts, the steel sliding into the soft flesh with little resistance. The man gurgled and fell to his knees. Still moving forward, Thomas withdrew the sword and slashed at the third man, opening his throat to the cold chapel air with a splash of hot blood. He fell aside.

That left the last man. Thomas faced him, ignoring the sounds behind him, the moans of the man he'd disembowelled, the bubbling of the one he'd slashed. The whimpers of Brother Edward, cowering somewhere in a dark corner of the chapel. All his attention was focused on this man, this armed man who'd intended to kill him with such casual disregard, as if it was simply a duty to be fulfilled.

'Well?' Thomas asked the man. He drew a small figure eight in the air with his sword tip, over and over again, keeping the blade in motion, like a snake preparing to strike. 'Well?' he asked again.

The man's eyes were wide, his sword shaking. He looked around, then threw the sword clattering to the ground, turned and bolted from the room. Echoes of his pounding footsteps faded into the distance.

Thomas turned then, looked at the carnage he'd wrought. The man whose throat he'd slit was dead, lying in an ever-widening pool of his own blood, fingers still twitching a little. The man he'd stabbed in the stomach still knelt there, slick loops of intestine peeking out between his shaking fingers. He looked up at Thomas as he approached.

'Please ...' he croaked softly.

Thomas swung his sword and decapitated the man. The head bounced off the far wall of the chapel, and came to rest right next to Brother Edward, who squealed in horror. The rest of the body collapsed to the floor, the stump of its neck jetting blood across the smooth stones. Its legs jerked once, twice, thrice. Then no more.

'Now,' Thomas said, and walked up to the cringing monk. He could smell faeces and urine, and suspected it wasn't entirely from the dead bodies. He stepped over the unconscious William on the way, careful not to tread on the man. He deserved that much respect.

'Oh God, please help me,' the monk was whimpering. 'Oh God, oh God ...'

'God?' Thomas echoed. 'Is it God who called for bloody murder, here in His own house?' He shook his head. 'No, this isn't the work of God. It's the work of man.'

'Please ...'

Thomas pointed his sword at the stained glass portrait over Brother Edward's head. 'That's me,' he declared. 'But the glass looks old, very old. How can that be?'

'Please ...'

He lowered the sword, rested its tip against the pulsing vein in Edward's forehead. 'Speak, monk, or I'll cut you down and find someone else who will.'

'It is you,' the monk said quickly. 'It is you as you were, nine hundred years ago.'

As Brother Edward explained, tumbling over his words like a kitten chasing its own tail, everything began to make sense to Thomas. His childhood, his upbringing, his trip to Canterbury, the people who'd recognised him ... it all made sense at last. A terrible, heartbreaking sense.

Thomas was born to die.

Oh, I know, at a genetic, evolutionary level, we're *all* born to die. We're carriers of our own DNA, designed to pass it on to the next generation and then move aside, make way for our children, our murderers. But for Thomas, it was much more than that. He wasn't just born to die. He was *destined* to die. *Designed* to die.

The Church was still in disarray, a shadow of its former self. Its power was weakened, its influence in tatters. And so, in the town of Canterbury, what was left of the Church hierarchy met to determine strategies to reclaim its glory days, not just from before the Plague Years and the Calamity, but indeed from its golden history itself. The days when it ruled through a monarchy devoted to its teachings, a populace caught in its rules and regulations. Through piety and power and fear, it dominated the entire country. *This* is what the remaining elite desired, above all else. But it needed an event to trigger this, a symbol, of the past and of the future.

It needed a martyr.

'It's like a passion play,' Edward explained. 'There are video cameras secreted all around this chapel, half a dozen in all, leading to digital recorders we salvaged . Once the word spread, we could bring our flock back together, all over the land.'

'I don't understand,' Thomas said, though that wasn't entirely true. He *did* understand, even if he couldn't accept it, not straight away.

This was a re-enactment.

He was a re-enactment.

'The remains of Thomas Becket, Saint Thomas, were kept hidden in this very cathedral for centuries,' the monk told him. 'After he was slain by four knights, sent by the dying King Henry II. His priests kept what remained of him here, safe, secure. But the Church hierarchy found them. Found them, and extracted enough tissue from inside the bones to reconstruct his DNA. The rest was simple.'

A child, born of no mother, no father. Twinned from the flesh of a long dead martyr, a revered saint, then fostered to a devout family. Guided on his path to purity. Any distractions removed. Distractions like Sarah MacMillan, who ignored the standing order in the town to avoid personal contact with the young Thomas and dared to kiss him one cold spring afternoon, under an old oak tree, observed by his overseers; the entire family banished for their daughter's innocent caress. Given a town of his own to care for, watch over, until he's old enough, the right age.

The right age to die. Here, in the chapel in Canterbury Cathedral.

'And the men?' Thomas asked, his head hurting. 'The four knights. What of them?'

'The same,' Edward answered. 'Tissue samples extracted from their graves, raised as warriors, told that the day would come when they must fulfil their destinies.'

'They knew,' Thomas mumbled. Then louder. '*They* knew. Why didn't I?'

'Would you have come if you'd known?' Edward asked.

Thomas had no answer to that. But something else was bothering him. The people he'd met. The man in York, the woman in Cambridge. A cold realisation that made everything so much worse.

'I'm not the first,' he said. .

'No,' Brother Edward replied. His fear seemed to be gone now. Perhaps he'd accepted his fate, or perhaps unloading this secret had finally cleaned his soul. 'You don't plant a single seed when searching for a special fruit.'

Others. For years, perhaps decades. And others still, surely, who had not yet reached maturity. 'Dozens?' Thomas asked, furious. 'Hundreds?'

Edward shrugged. 'I don't know, Thomas,' he admitted. 'Like you, I am just a pawn, an actor. It was my job to bear witness, like the man they created me from. And, like you, there are others of me, waiting in line in case this fails. Which it has,' he conceded. He sounded like a man whose life was over, his destiny unfulfilled. Which, of course he was. 'And now, you'll end it.'

Thomas lowered his sword. 'I'm not a butcher, brother,' he said, and threw the weapon aside, letting it clatter against the stone walls and floor. 'I am just a priest.'

Brother Edward looked up at him in wonder. 'There's one thing I must know, Father Thomas,' he said. 'How did you do it? How does a mere priest defeat four armed and trained knights half his age?'

'I don't know,' Thomas lied. 'Perhaps God was on my side.'

The truth was simpler, and far more brutal. Twenty three miserable years in his assigned village, watching an evil, greedy priest crush the spirits of his parishioners, day by day grinding them into the dirt as he stuffed his fat face and laughed at them. Twenty three years of secretly training with a sword, in the cold dead of night. Twenty three years of preparing for the afternoon when Robert was alone, helpless. The fight had lasted less than ten seconds; the big man was strong, and faster than he looked, but Thomas had had more than two decades of hatred on his side. He'd rolled Robert's massive body down to a frozen stream, hacked a hole in the ice, and pushed him under. In a matter of days, the hole had sealed itself, and Father Robert had never been seen again.

Twenty three years of training is not something that is easily forgotten, even by a man of God.

Thomas left the Church then, both physically and spiritually. He walked out of Canterbury Cathedral, leaving Edward shaking in the corner and William unconscious on the stone floor, got on his horse and rode away. They say he spent the rest of his days seeking out his fellow man-made martyrs, searching for all the other Thomas Becket doppelgangers in the country. Nobody knows how many he found, how many he managed to save. But I'm sure we'd have heard if the plan had eventually succeeded, if a new martyr, an old martyr, had galvanised the Church again. And, since Canterbury is now the centre of government for the entire country, and that jolly King Charles sits upon the throne there, it's unlikely such a drastic and violent event will ever happen. Some even say he sought out his childhood sweetheart, Sarah MacMillan, and forged a life with her, back in his beloved Highlands. This, though, is just wishful thinking, I fear. That sort of happy ending is reserved for fairy tales, romantic fantasies. Not harsh realities.

There are rumours, though, that one day Thomas will return to Canterbury, one last time, perhaps even on a train such as this one. And that, on that day, his destiny will finally be determined, not by man, but by God.

Thomas was born to die, but he lived to be alive. Can any of us claim more?

Outside, the rain eased though the wind still lashed at our refuge. The door to the saloon car opened, and the conductor came in. With him came one of the Royal Rangers assigned to guard the train; a sergeant, by his chevrons. They made their way through the press, and people fell silent in their wake. There was something in their look, or perhaps the way they moved, a touch of unease that spread quickly through the group.

The sergeant stopped in front of a man I'd noticed before. His fustian tunic was much-stained, but I knew him only as a fellow pilgrim. He had the look of a man seeking forgiveness, though without much hope; he also had a soldier's stance and gait, though he carried no weapon. One thing I saw: he had a soldier's eyes, though perhaps he'd bought those. Such things are still possible in other lands, they say. They're always vague about exactly where.

The sergeant spoke in a low, tight voice. The little I caught was coded in the Battle Talk of the Royal Rangers, and milord knows I'm not fluent. I heard the word 'Londonistan', though. There was no mistaking that, nor the intake of breath from the people who sat closest, pretending not to listen.

The soldier nodded, and said something that seemed to satisfy the sergeant, who turned away. Even as the sergeant negotiated a passage to the exit, the soldier spoke: 'The lights will be turned off now. There may be men outside, watching, so we will give them nothing to see.'

His voice was rough, and his accent was strange, but he had the calm of a man who expected obedience, and he got it. The saloon car fell silent, and the conductor hurried to shut off the electric lanterns, but that wasn't enough for the man with the eyes of a soldier. Even the faithful solar-driven oleds of the 'Exit' sign had to come down, and be put away.

In the utter darkness, children began to cry; first one, then another, and another. I heard mothers hushing them, and snatches of song. Then, rough and strange but strong and warm, I heard his voice, and everyone else, even the little ones, grew quiet.

'The great plagues had left a great many dead in the Eastern Duchies,' he said, 'more than the farmers' pigs could eat. The soil atop the graves of those who were fortunate enough to be buried was rich, and made for good farming ... though there were few left with the strength, and the will, to till it. To many in those lands, especially the young men, fighting has long seemed easier than farming, and more profitable. And perhaps it was, when there were still stores of food, and ammunition for the guns, and medicines for the wounded.

'Men who had served in the old armies began to call themselves captains, then generals, then warlords, then counts or barons or dukes. Many of those who rose to the top and were able to stay there were said to be Myrmidon-class super-soldiers created by scientists before the Collapse: men designed by genetic engineers, immune to pain or disease or radiation; men with faster reflexes, who healed faster and could fight for longer with neither food nor sleep; men able to see heat and read maps by starlight, more aware of danger but never paralyzed by fear ... They were the stuff of legend, and maybe no more than that, for these warlords looked much like other men, and in all likelihood they were, for certainly they wanted what other men wanted.

'The legends agree on one strange thing, however. None of the warlords who endured, the men said to be Myrmidons and abominations, had sons.'

The Veteran's Tale

There came a time when the larger guns fell silent for lack of ammunition, and then the smaller ones, and men were reduced to fighting with axes and machetes and spears. The battles continued, of course, even though there was little left to loot, and deaths were slower and more painful. Old hatreds can make you forget an empty belly, at least for a time, and rape … well, it's said that in some villages, the only seed being sown was manseed.

It was at this time that one of the warlords, a man named Erich, called for a truce and a meeting with his fellow dukes. After much argument, there came a day when six of them, all said to be Myrmidons, met in a small camouflaged tent on a windy plain – unarmed, but accompanied by their counsellors and surrounded by their armies.

'This cannot go on,' said blue-eyed Erich, after the formalities were done. 'If we continue to fight in this way, we will leave nothing for our own sons. No more ammunition, and no more food for our wives, unless you want them to eat manflesh.' He looked around; three of the warlords shuddered at the thought, and four crossed themselves. 'And how long is it before men raiding the villages are killing their own sons and raping their own daughters, as they raped their mothers? That's an abomination, too; do you think God won't punish us?'

'Easily fixed,' grunted Odi. 'If a man knows a child isn't his, he kills it. And if a woman is with child and has no husband, you kill her too, so they won't be a burden on the others. That's how we do it, and there are damn few bastards in my lands.'

'And damn few women,' muttered Milos, whose lands bordered on Odi's; then, more loudly, 'It's an interesting idea, Erich, but you can't stop men fighting. Everyone knows that whoever wins an honest fight, it was God's will or Darwin's. No man here is going to go back to the old ways of settling things.'

'Honest fights are fine,' said Erich. 'But one man against another, not clans or armies, and not to the death. Just enough of a fight so that we know who is in the right.

'Have any of you heard of a pentathlon? It was a contest of soldier's skills. In the original Olympics, they ran and wrestled and threw javelins. When it was revived, soldiering had changed, so they changed the event as well. Athletes ran, swam, raced horses, fought with swords, and fired guns at targets.'

'I'm damned if I'm going to waste what bullets I got left shooting at a piece of paper,' said Odi. 'Some-one else had better provide the bullets – and the paper, for that matter.'

'We can,' said Erich, nodding at his counsellor. 'Raul has the skill and the equipment to reload nine millimetre cartridges. Not enough to equip an army for more than one or two campaigns, but enough for us to use to settle disputes in this way.'

Walter stood and stretched. 'I'd like more time to think about this, but a truce, until the harvest is done … that sounds good to me. What say you all?'

Raul looked around nervously as they walked back to the shelter of their armoured wagon. By his best estimate, there were at least three hundred men in the open, and no way of knowing how many might be hiding behind hedges and walls and in the surrounding forests. Most of the rifles on display were probably empty, useful only as clubs or pikes, and he was wearing an old vest of synthetic spidersilk, but all it would take was one loaded gun and one good shot …

Once inside the wagon, Erich threw off his much-patched leather coat and peeled off the ballistic armour he wore beneath it. 'What happens now?'

'Walter will argue about the details, simply because it wasn't his idea,' replied Raul, 'but I think he'll agree eventually, and the others won't dare cross him. Odi may be a fool, but he listens to his counsellor. If we can have peace for a year, and a plentiful harvest, I think they'll come to see the good of it.'

Erich nodded, and thumped on the wall before sitting down. The wagon lurched as the oxen began pulling it back towards the bunker. 'If nothing else, it's given us a chance to look at each other's armies. How's the other thing going?'

The 'other thing', Raul knew, meant his attempts at cloning; Erich might be an abomination himself, but he was too superstitious to use the word, even in private. 'I'm doing what I can. The only ones that have been born alive have been sick, as though they were born old. Until I know I can do better than that with sheep and horses, I'm not going to risk subjecting a human to that sort of misery.'

'I'm not going to live forever.'

'I know. I can keep working with your cells after you die, unless I die first. But I can promise you this; it's your best chance of ever having a son of your own. Something in your body attacks all your Y-chromosome sperm, kills them instantly; I've tried implanting eggs with them, but none of them survive.'

Erich grunted. His grandson was five years old, scared of horses and clumsy with weapons, but already able to beat him at chess. 'What if you never succeed? Who's going to protect my family from the other dukes when I'm gone? You?'

The dukes met again two weeks later, to haggle over details of the pentathlon. It was decided that the races would be held first, and if either contender won all three, the matter was resolved. 'If not,' Walter growled, 'Sabres, but blunted, and first blood. If this does not decide the matter, then guns.' He glared at Odi, silencing him, then turned back to Erich. 'But none of this nonsense about shooting at paper targets. If it comes to that, we shoot at each other – and with our own pistols and our own bullets. And stripped to the waist, as for the other events. One shot each, at ten paces: if we need five contests to let God or Darwin tell us who is in the right, then continuing to shoot won't make the answer any clearer. And whoever breaks any terms of the truce, is the enemy of us all.'

All agreed, and the harvest in the duchies that year was the best there had been since the Fimbulwetr. No one starved, though some elders grumbled that there weren't enough dead to fertilize the fields for the year ahead. The next harvest was better still, and even in the hill country, the priests spent more time presiding at baptisms and weddings and court than they did at funerals. When Odi's people raided a village on Arvid's land, stealing food and a young girl, Arvid challenged Odi and demanded compensation, but they waited until after the harvest to meet. With Walter, Milos, Erich and all their counsellors watching, the two men raced their best horses, ran for three kilometres, and swam in the river, before taking up blunted sabres and slashing at each other. Odi settled the dispute by drawing first blood; Arvid's faith in the rightness of his cause, and his own ability, earned him a short but jagged scar above one eye.

Once the duellists had departed, Erich worried aloud that Odi might be encouraged by this to order more raids on Arvid's land; instead, he learned that Odi had introduced the pentathlon to his villagers as a means of settling disputes if they were dissatisfied with the judgement of the priests. Anyone who wished to challenge Odi himself on any matter was free to do so, providing he had his own horse, gun, and bullet.

'What are women supposed to do when *they* have disputes?' asked Tracy, Erich's favourite wife, that night at the dinner table. 'Fight it out?'

'They can choose a champion,' said Raul. 'It's hardly an ideal solution …

but at least it's one man fighting another, not whole families.'

'And if she has no champion?'

Rana, Raul's wife, shrugged and smiled. 'Champions want the same thing other men want.'

'What worries me,' said Raul, smiling despite himself, 'is that Odi may have turned this into a way to train his men into a real army.'

The duke snorted, picked up his dagger, and carved a thick slice off the roast. 'He doesn't trust them that far, and I don't blame him. No, Kane will use this as a way to find out who has guns or bullets hidden away, or who might be good enough with a sword to be a threat to Odi and his family, and then he'll make sure that if Odi ever *does* have to fight 'em, it'll be in single combat. But he's not the one who worries me. It's Milos. He's too damn clever.' He chewed at his meat for a while. 'How're you doing with the other thing?'

'How's the lamb?'

'What? It's fine … You can talk here. Tracy knows all about –' He stopped, and looked down at his plate. 'This is …?'

'Cloned. Yes. My assistants and I have been eating it too, and I haven't noticed any problems.' He cut himself another piece, and bit into it. 'Not bad, if I do say so myself.'

'You can do it, then?'

'One success isn't enough, not after all these failures. When I've managed to clone your favourite horse, *then* I'll be willing to take a risk with humans.' He shrugged. 'A few more years. Is that so long to wait, for immortality?'

The next three years saw better harvests, fewer raids, and more disputes settled without bloodshed.

The year after that saw National forces reach the northern border of Odi's and Tino's lands.

The National envoy was a tall, thin, clean-shaven man with eyes as blue as his helmet and tunic. It was raining heavily on the day the dukes and their counsellors gathered to meet with him, in the same weatherproof tent they'd met in when Erich had first suggested a truce. The envoy wasn't accompanied by an army, only a single vertol gunshop with firepower enough to wipe out all of their assembled troops.

The envoy looked at the warlords, at their scars and their beards, their hand-made boots and the patched leathers they wore over their body armour, and barely managed to keep his expression neutral. 'First,' he said, 'I'd like to get one thing straight: we are not trying to take your lands from you. You can keep your forts, your titles, your weapons – for the time being, at least. We'll trade for any excess food you may grow, and take a small commission out of that, but no other taxes. We'll use that income to repair or build infrastructure here: communications, roads, schools, hospitals -'

'What do you mean by "for the time being"?' growled Walter.

'I can't give you an exact timeline; but you can stay in power for at least a year, and then we let your people vote for a regional governor. A lot of feudal warlords like yourselves have decided not to contest the elections, but made an agreement with the elected government that lets them hold onto a ceremonial title, their keep, and a few retainers. You can live out your life here, instead of a cell, which is what would happen if I had my way.' He shrugged. 'Oh, you can say that it's not your fault that you're Myrmidon-class abominations, and that you were only obeying orders –'

Odi leapt to his feet, his face almost as red as his hair, but Kane, on his right, grabbed one arm, and Milos the other. Odi shook his counsellor's hand off easily enough, but his fellow Myrmidon tightened his grip until Odi's face went from red to white. 'You think you can make us obey *your* orders?' Odi blustered.

'That's up to you, but if you resist, we could wipe you out with just one gunship and a single squad. We've learned it's dangerous to create martyrs, but personally, I'd be willing to take the risk.'

'What about one on one?' asked Milos, softly. 'Single combat. Wager of battel.'

The envoy stared at him for a moment, astonishment showing despite his training. 'You can't be serious …'

'We have a way of resolving disputes here,' said Tino. 'Pentathlon. Maybe you've heard of it.'

'Of course I've heard of it.' He looked around the tent at the men gathered there, then shook his head. 'I'm no great athlete, certainly no horseman, but I could probably beat some of you at some events. But what would it prove?'

'It would prove who was the better man,' said Odi. 'The better soldier.'

'You're not *soldiers*,' the envoy replied scornfully. 'Warriors, I grant you, but you haven't been soldiers in years. I'm a soldier. I wear a uniform, I obey orders. You're thugs, nothing more.'

Raul pursed his lips. The closest thing their troops had to uniforms were the coloured caps or berets the warlords issued to sergeants and officers. 'And here I was, thinking you were a diplomat.'

The envoy chuckled. 'I know your record too, Doctor … and I don't like you, either. But the offer's good for you, too – all of you in this room. Whatever you've done in the past, we'll let you stay on your own lands, as long as you obey the laws in those books,' he nodded at the pile of compads he'd placed on the table. 'You can even keep your weapons, as long as you don't kill anyone. Fortunately, for you, what *I* want doesn't matter.' He stood, inclined his head slightly. 'One year,' he repeated, as he walked out.

The dukes and their counsellors watched him leave, Odi still straining to escape from Milos's grasp. 'He can't –'

'He *can*,' said Milos, gloomily. 'Whatever it was you were about to say, he probably can … or his army can, anyway.'

Odi thought about this for a moment, and brightened. 'What if nobody runs against me?'

'They'll find someone who will,' said Raul, looking at the map on the compad screen. 'They've played this game too often, and when they've lost, they've learned from their mistakes and tried again.'

Odi sat down. 'What if I win?'

Milos shrugged. 'That's possible, I suppose. But don't forget, women can run against you – and they can vote, too.'

'*What?*'

'The troops make sure they can, and they can give as much help as they like to your opponents. And *they* count the votes. The only good news is that they hate casualties, and not just on their own side. If you can convince them that keeping you in power is the least bloody option, they'll go along with that, and wait for you to die. After all, we're the last of our kind.'

Erich grimaced, but didn't contradict him. Only when they were both back in their armoured wagon did he ask Raul, 'What about ...?'

'Your clone? In another year, I *might* be ready.'

'You're wanted for war crimes too,' the duke reminded him. 'If I go ...'

The counsellor took a deep breath before replying. 'I didn't do anything that their side wasn't doing too.'

'Me neither. But that doesn't matter when you lose.'

Choosing a day for the elections took considerable negotiation with the Nationals. Most of the dukes left this tedious task to their counsellors – except for Milos and Walter, who attended every meeting and listened carefully to the discussions. Milos cornered Raul on his way out of one particularly boring session, and asked, 'You seem to agree with them about having all the elections on the same day. Why?'

Raul's expression turned sour for an instant, but he covered it up quickly. 'It advantages all of us. It means that the Nationals won't be able to concentrate their overseers and soldiers in one duchy on election day; they'll be stretched over the whole region – with most of them in the likely trouble spots.'

Milos looked over at Kane, who was out of earshot but watching them as though he were trying to read their lips. So, Raul noticed, was Walter. 'You mean the hills?'

'Primarily, yes.'

'So you're not just trying to buy more time for your cloning experiments.'

'My *what?*' Raul's voice rose to a squeak, making Walter and Kane turn around and stare.

Milos smiled. 'You think you're the only one with spies in the other keeps? You'd better hope the Nationals don't know. Of course, cloning sheep and horses isn't illegal, but humans ... especially genemod humans ... well, some people would find that useful, but many others ... they'd call it an abomination.' He glanced over his shoulder at Kane. 'Of course, you do what you have to do to survive. I always have. But extinction ... sometimes that's part of God and Darwin's plan, too. Maybe some genes we can do without. Do you understand?'

The election results were sent to everyone simultaneously over the compads. Erich, Walter, and Milos had held onto power, by fair means or subtly foul, but the others had lost their elections and it remained to be seen whether they would even manage to hold onto their keeps. Erich, sitting in his war room, drained his cup of moonshine, and peered at Raul, who had fallen asleep in his chair at the other end of the long table.

Tracy, sitting beside him, read the results from the hill country, and snorted in a most unladylike fashion. 'Beaten by a woman. That must really sting.'

Erich nodded. 'He'll be lucky if she lets him stay in his castle as a prisoner, and die there.'

'Did you offer him ...'

She was too drunk to say 'sanctuary', but Erich was just sober enough to guess at her meaning. 'No,' he replied. 'I don't know about the others. I'll take Kane, if he wants to work for me, but not Odi ...' He reached for the jug, and grunted with irritation when he discovered it was empty. 'Kane has a month to work something out ... but the hills are going to be crawling with Nationals by the time that's over. Odi can't run, unless he does it now, and if he tries to fight ... I guess the Nationals will kill him, if someone else doesn't.'

The next month passed fairly peacefully, except in the hill country, where it was said dozens of women and a handful of men were murdered for having voted against the duke. The new governor announced that Odi would be exiled, and his keep transformed into a hospital and police station. National troops waited on the northern border, ready to fly in, but at the last moment, Odi accepted an offer of sanctuary from Cam, who'd been allowed to keep a small patch of land around his own fort.

Kane had already left the hills and was working as Walter's treasurer and lieutenant-governor. Tino was a prisoner in his own fort. Arvid had disappeared; some said that he went on a pilgrimage to as many holy sites as he could visit, to ask forgiveness for what he'd done and what he was, and some said the Nationals caught him as he tried to flee, and perhaps they killed him, for he was never heard from in those lands again.

Another year passed, another harvest was gathered, and excess food was traded for building material and furniture and blankets and other luxuries. People who'd learned to read the previous winter even bought books. In what had once been Odi's duchy, women and girls studied to become doctors and teachers and police. Some thought that this news might be enough to kill Odi, but he survived. It was Walter who died, on the coldest day of that winter.

It was whispered by some that Kane had murdered the old man, but even the Nationals agreed that it had been a natural death. The news shocked and saddened Erich and Milos, but not so greatly as the news that Kane had claimed power and offered sanctuary to Odi and Cam.

Raul looked up from the compad, his expression sour. 'I'm afraid he can,' he said. "The Nationals" constitution says that election dates are fixed, and if a governor dies, the lieutenant-governor succeeds him or chooses a successor until the next election.' He looked around Erich's cavernous war room; Erich stood beside him, studying the maps spread across the great table, while Milos sat at the far end with his own counsellor, Ishan, beside him. All of them looked as gloomy as the windowless room. 'He'll probably put Odi in charge of the guard, with Cam and Tino as his lieutenants. If they bring in their loyalists from their own duchies, they might even outnumber Walter's own troops.'

'Odi providing the muscle, and Kane the brain,' muttered Milos. 'What do you think they'll do?'

'Nothing too blatant,' said Ishan. 'As you say, Kane's not stupid.'

'Just gutless. How long do you think it'll be before Odi's named as lieutenant-governor?'

'I don't know ... but I think he'll stop him invading any of the other duchies. They'll just plunder Walter's and steal what they can from just over the borders.'

'And what will the Nationals do about it?'

Ishan shrugged. 'They can help his neighbours defend their borders, but they can't send troops into Walter's land without his permission ...'

'Except as guards on trade convoys, in case of bandit attacks,' said Raul blandly. 'And they can fly over at any time, even in gunships. If anyone's stupid enough to attack the Nationals ...'

'Do we *want* that sort of National presence around?' asked Milos. 'Wouldn't it be better if we took care of this ourselves?'

'Do their dirty work for them?' asked Raul.

'Why do you think they haven't had us killed? Or even disarmed?'

The counsellor conceded the point. 'What did you have in mind?'

'We challenge them to a pentathlon.'

'*What?*'

'For the position of lieutenant-governor. Kane's probably playing Odi and Cam off against each other, but I think they'll both jump at the chance to prove that God and Darwin are on their side. Tino might not be so eager, but he won't dare refuse a challenge, and he believes in God's will, even if the others don't.' He turned to Erich. 'And even if I can't beat Odi, I'm sure that you can – and I'd rather see you in the position than him.'

'Even though I'll control the two largest duchies?'

'There's no law that says you can't. Ishan's checked. And we can let God decide which is the least of the evils.'

'Or the best of the abominations,' said Erich, smiling.

Raul, staring intently into his microscope, jumped when he heard a faint and unfamiliar cough behind him, and he nearly fell off his stool as he spun around. Milos stared at the jumble of equipment on the laboratory benches, and shook his head. 'So this is where it all happens? That's what you use for making bullets?'

'Yes. How did you get – you're not meant to -'

'The door wasn't locked. And the cloning? I hear you've cloned his fastest horse.'

The counsellor nodded rapidly, then regained some of his composure. 'Do you want one?'

'A clone of my own?' said Milos, raising his eyebrows. 'Well, if you can clone one Myrmidon, why not me?'

'I meant – a horse, not –'

'Why not an army of us?'

'I can't do *that*! Even if I had more equipment, and more women to serve as hosts … I'm lucky if one transfer in a thousand is viable, and I don't have any assistants who can do that work for me … even if I can get one to come to term, I'm not sure I'll ever succeed in making a real duplicate of him. And of course, it's not just genetics, there's also training … I don't think there's any possibility that I'll ever be able to make more than a few, even if he wanted them.'

'And no one else is doing this?'

'Not here. In other lands, maybe, but as far as I know, you're the last of the Myrmidon class. I mean, you and Erich and -'

'I know what you meant. But if you're going to duplicate one of us, it could as easily be me as Erich?'

'In theory, but you don't look anything –'

'How many women would you need? And do they have any special requirements? Youth, health, size, genetic makeup?'

Raul hesitated. 'How would you get them in here?' he asked.

Odi had gained some weight since Erich had seen him last, but he didn't look soft, and neither his pace nor his temper seemed to have slowed. Negotiating the terms for the pentathlon had taken Kane, Raul and Ishan several weeks, especially as they'd had to choose a course for the foot race that was neither too rough nor too flat. Odi had suggested they dispense with the first three events and go straight to the swordfight and shooting, and protested when the matter was resolved with a vote, but Kane had finally convinced him that he didn't stand to lose anything by participating. 'Only if somebody wins all three of the races can they claim the prize,' he pointed out. 'That's not likely.'

The first of the events, the cross-country run, began soon after sunrise; Tino took the lead early, but Odi caught up with him by the mid-point and soon passed him. Tino chased him, but the redhead was the first over the line, with Erich, Milos, Tino and a Nationals telecopter all close behind him. Red with pride as well as fatigue, Odi was easily beaten when it came to the swim across the river, and for a moment the others even dared to hope that he'd drown. The day ended with the steeplechase, which Erich won easily, much to Odi's obvious disgust. As night fell, the five returned to Walter's fort; Erich, Milos and their counsellors begged off the banquet, saying they'd brought their own food. 'One to me, one to Tino, one to Odi,' muttered Erich, once he was back in the bulletproof tent with Raul. 'So much for my winning three events without anyone needing to fire a shot.'

'It was worth a try,' said Raul. He seemed too tired to shrug, but his tone made up for it. 'Tino must have decided to save his strength for the swimming. I didn't think he was that smart.'

'How's the shooting going to work?'

The counsellor flopped onto the camp bed. 'Anyone who hasn't won an event by then can withdraw. The rest of you face off against each other, chosen by lots, until there's only one man left who's not bloodied.'

'Or dead. Odi's going to go for the kill.'

'Then if he wins, the next man who faces him will try to kill him.' Raul looked up as one Erich's serving-wenches came into the closely guarded tent, with a tray loaded with food. He watched as she bent over, even though he'd already seen her naked. 'And God will forgive him, I'm sure.'

Erich nodded, but waited until the girl had gone before asking, 'What about Milos?'

'What about him?'

'Should I try to kill him, too?'

Raul took a bite out of the tart on his plate, and chewed on it for a moment before replying. 'Do you think he'll try to kill you?'

'I don't know. I can read the others well enough, but him ... he's too close, too clever.'

'Which would make him a valuable ally. And I'd sooner trust him than Odi or Cam.'

'That's not saying much.'

'No, I suppose not,' Raul conceded. 'But this is a decision you'll have to make for yourself. I just make the ammo. You're the one who has to fire the gun.'

The five men met again on a football field outside Walter's fort, as soon as the morning mists had cleared enough for them to see more than ten metres. Despite the cold, all had stripped to the waist again, showing that they were wearing no armour. A crowd had gathered behind the fences, including their counsellors and medics and several observers from the north, some of them with cameras. The five saluted each other with their blunted sabres, then two of Walter's widows drew lots to choose the first two competitors. Cam defeated Tino quickly and easily, and the two retired to the benches.

'Duke Erich.'

'Duke Odi.'

Odi grinned as he picked up his sabre and advanced. Erich approached him warily, waiting for the aggressive redhead to make the first move. Odi was a skilled swordsman, strong and fast with a good reach, but inclined to be flashy. Erich ignored his first feint, and parried a slash at his chest, but was caught unawares by a blow to the knee. It didn't count as first blood, but it startled him, and might have been enough to disable a weaker man. Erich caught his opponent's blade as he withdrew it, trapping it and buying himself enough time to think. He retreated, waiting for Odi to lunge, and was not disappointed by the response; the redhead leaned so far forwards that he almost overbalanced without any help. Erich stamped down, putting all his weight on the blunted blade, then dashed forward and swiped at Odi's face. Odi recoiled, but the tip of Erich's sword left a shallow gouge across the bridge of his nose. He swore loudly, but this was drowned out by a shout from the crowd. Erich leaped aside, blade held at en garde in case Odi decided to counter-attack, but the redhead merely grinned, rubbed his nose – and bowed.

Erich retired to his tent, limping slightly, and let Raul fuss over him while Walter's wives called Milos and Tino into the ring. Erich watched curiously as the two men circled, making experimental feints at each other, before Tino delivered the first backhanded swipe. Milos parried it, but didn't counter-attack; he seemed to be happy to stay on the defensive and concentrate on taking the measure of his opponent ... and maybe wear the other man out. The match continued in this style for nearly four minutes before Milos delivered a riposte to one of Tino's clumsier slashes – but the thrust was merely a feint, and Tino fell into his trap, leaving himself open to a quick cut to the shoulder.

Erich glanced at their audience behind the fence, and noticed the Nationals' envoy standing there with a small group of uniformed guards. 'I wonder who they're betting on,' he murmured.

'For this event, or for the whole pentathlon?'

Erich looked startled. 'People are actually betting?'

'Of course. Kane's expecting to make a fortune: he's called two of the three last events correctly. For the swords, the favourite is Odi, though you're not far behind him. The next –'

'Duke Cam!' came the call from the box.

'Duke Milos!'

Raul pursed his lips. 'This should be interesting. They both need to win at this event to have any chance.' He watched in silence as the two men approached each other, and went to it with a will. Milos remained on the defensive for a few minutes, as he had with Tino, but Cam's slashing blows were delivered with enough force that they nearly spun him around.

'What the hell is Milos doing?' Erich muttered. 'Cam's going to wear him down if he doesn't start fighting back soon.' He winced as Milos seemed to stagger backwards. If this was a trap, Cam avoided it, standing his ground and waiting for Milos to recover. The two men faced each other warily for a moment before Cam resumed the attack. Milos continued to parry blows, making the occasional feeble feint, then suddenly weaved aside as Cam made a downward swing at his shoulder. Before Cam could recover, Milos had driven the tip of his sabre into his right eye with enough force that Erich was sure he heard the sword scrape on the other side of his skull. Cam stood there for an instant, then his knees buckled and he hit the ground.

Raul woke the next morning to the sound of gunfire – a pistol, single shots, not far away … or maybe two pistols. He looked around the tent, and was unsurprised to see that Erich was gone; the warlord rarely slept more than three hours a night. The counsellor dressed quickly, and hurried outside. The guards sitting on either side of the door glanced at him, but neither saluted. 'Where is the Duke?'

'I'll take you to him,' said the younger of the guards, putting down his mess kit and wiping his mouth. 'He went out for some target practice.' As though on cue, another four shots rang out.

'Alone?'

'No, with Duke Milos.'

Raul felt his sphincter tighten, and he hurried after the guard as they walked down towards the source of the sounds. Milos and Erich were standing in a clearing shooting at an ancient pine tree. A rough human face had been carved, jack-o-lantern style, into the bark, though it was difficult to tell the eyes from the bullet-holes that surrounded them. Two guards stood a respectful distance behind them: they turned their guns on Raul and his escort as they ran towards them, but relaxed when they recognised the counsellor and the grey beret of one of Erich's officers. Erich glanced at them, then emptied the brass out of his revolver into his palm, pocketed the spent cartridges, and reloaded. Raul noticed that they were talking as well as shooting, but the guards kept him out of earshot. The warlords fired another six shots each, then walked back to their guards. The counsellor waited until they were alone before asking, 'What was *that* about?'

'I wanted to ask why he'd killed Cam.'

'And?'

'He said it was because he was too good a shot. Odi's better with a sword. But whoever faces him first today, will try to kill him. Now, it all depends whose lot is drawn first – and that's down to God.'

'And when you have to face Milos? Will you try to kill him, too?'

'No. We swore an oath before we prayed.'

'What did you pray for?'

'I prayed for victory,' said Erich. 'I can only assume he did the same.' And he said nothing more until they reached the arena.

The crowds were standing further from the fence than they had been for the swordfight, and the Nationals were wearing visored helmets as well as body armour. The four combatants stripped to the waist, then handed their guns over to Walter's widows so that they could make sure that each only held one bullet; then, on retrieving them, checked to make sure that neither gun nor ammunition had been tampered with.

The women then reached into a helmet and drew lots. The first was black, Milos' colour, and Raul held his breath for an instant, until the next was drawn. Dark brown. Tino.

The two men advanced into the field, and took their positions – ten metres apart, and facing away from each other. Kane blew a whistle, and the dukes spun around. Tino, as always, dropped into a crouch and steadied his pistol with both hands, but Milos was faster; he fired one-handed, hitting Tino just below the throat. The younger man fell backwards, his finger tightening on the trigger, but the shot went wild. Kane hurried over to where Tino lay gasping. The Nationals envoy, standing behind Raul, cleared his throat. 'I have a medikit …'

'Do you think he'll trust you to treat him?' asked the counsellor, quietly, as Tino was lifted onto a stretcher and carried away. 'Last I heard, you wanted to execute him.'

'We don't have the death penalty. Not even for war criminals and abominations. He'd be imprisoned for life, but he would be alive.'

'I suspect he'd rather die, but it's not my decision. I'll ask his counsellor.' He was walking towards the medics when the widows drew the lots for the next two men to shoot.

'Duke Odi.'

'Duke Erich.'

Erich looked closely at his gun as the women handed it back to him. It was a revolver designed to fire any round of approximately .38 calibre, including 9mm parabellum. Odi favoured a more powerful .44 Magnum automatic, which Erich found oddly reassuring: it seemed unlikely that he could have found enough ammunition in that calibre to expend it on target practice. The two men took their positions, and waited. The whistle blew, and Erich turned around, taking a fraction of a second to aim. He heard Odi's bullet whistle past his ear as he squeezed the trigger. Odi staggered backwards with a small hole in his cheek and a larger one in the back of his skull. Erich stood there for a moment, feeling neither triumph nor remorse, then walked back to where Kane and the widows were seated, and handed over his gun. The envoy looked at him for a moment, his expression unreadable behind his tinted visor, and Kane shrugged.

'I told him not to allow this,' he said, as the stretcher-bearers carried Odi's corpse away. 'But he always had more pride than sense.' He looked down at the lots in the old helmet. 'Next round in twenty minutes.'

Erich turned to face Milos, then nodded slightly. Raul walked over, and handed him another bullet. Kane examined it closely before handing it, and the revolver, back to Erich. Milos walked over to the table, and showed

Kane his own pistol. The counsellor checked it, saying softly, 'You realise this now that Odi's dead, you're no closer to being governor, don't you?'

The dukes stared at him.

'Your arrangement was with Odi, not with me, and Odi's dead. Oh, yes, whoever wins this last round will succeed him as lieutenant-governor, even if Tino lives ... but I've left documents with the Nationals, and Walter's family, naming my successor in the event that my death is violent or suspicious.' He smiled sourly, and handed the whistle to 'Now, if you'll excuse me, I think I'd rather watch this through my telescope.'

The two dukes were silent as the counsellor walked back to the shelter of Walter's fort. 'Coward,' said Milos, softly and neutrally.

Erich shrugged. 'Are we going to do this?'

'Yes,' Milos replied, with no sign of emotion, and picked up his own pistol, a 9mm Beretta. The two walked to their positions ten metres apart, and waited for the signal.

Raul flinched as he heard the whistle, and his grip tightened on the bullets in his tunic pocket. He'd deliberately cast a few rounds with too little powder, in case he decided to handicap Erich and prevent him killing Milos. In the end, however, he'd chosen to let the two of them face each other and leave the decision up to God and Darwin. If Erich died, he would succeed him as governor of his lands, and put in a better position to negotiate with the Nationals; if Milos died, then life might be less interesting without the steady supply of women, but it would also be less risky. If both died, well, that would be –

The whistle blew, and Milos spun around and shot the counsellor between the eyes.

'Raul died instantly; Tino, a few days later,' said the man with soldier's eyes. 'Erich's shot wounded Milos in the arm, and Erich was counted the victor of the pentathlon. It's said that Milos told a priest that he'd prayed that if God could forgive him for what he was, He should die that day: if He let him live, he would think it a sign that He had more work for him to do.

'Milos and Erich remained in power until the end of their first term, and both were re-elected, as was Kane. Erich died a year into his second term; none of his daughters or sons-in-law succeeded him, and of course he had no sons or clones.

'Milos left the territory after Erich's funeral, and was never seen there again. Some say he went on a pilgrimage to as many holy sites as he could visit, to ask forgiveness for what he'd done and what he was. Some say he's hunting for Arvid, and that God means the two of them to fight, and put an end to the line of the Myrmidons forever. Which of these is true,' the man with the soldier's eyes finished, 'I cannot say.'

*A*t the end of his tale, the Veteran rose and simply walked out of the saloon car. People moved out of the way to let him pass, and silence grew in his wake. When the door hissed shut behind him we all looked at one another, faces white in the dark, like ghosts.

A few minutes later, one of the Rangers put his head through the door and called to the Conductor, who promptly restored the oled emergency lights, and then the little night-lights near the floor.

'The situation is under control,' the Conductor reported, as people once more began to move, and murmur. 'The Rangers have taken up positions around the train. There is no cause for alarm.'

A cautious silence followed. Nobody seemed ready to sit up in front of the windows yet.

I heard a nervous laugh from a man of middle years, yet fresh-faced. 'Up to me, then, I guess,' he said. 'I've a story too – a nice one, with a sort of hero and everything, and no wars or duels or hangings or aught like that.' He fumbled in his bag for a moment, and brought out an old magazine, carefully preserved in a clear plastic bag. 'I live in Canterbury,' he said. 'I'm on my way back from a pilgrimage, sort of. My dad was Thomas Griffiths, if you've heard of him.'

I knew the name, as did many of the others. The speaker looked pleased at that. 'Well – he's not my actual dad. He raised me, though, after he and my mum got together. I wanted to go back and visit the place where it happened, see. And I brought this,' he lifted the magazine high. 'Dad never did interviews or anything. My uncle Mike did, sometimes. He wanted to make sure people knew the proper story. Dad never bothered.' In the gloom, he squinted, then shrugged . 'I could have read this to you, if the light was better. But I read it just yesterday, sitting by the statue near the mine gate. Anyway, I know the story. Uncle Mike told me a hundred times. I could tell it to you now, if you like.'

He looked around, a hopeful half-smile lingering at the corners of his mouth.

Someone – I think maybe the Priest – laughed. 'The night's a long way yet to run,' he said. 'Tell us your story, son of Thomas Griffiths. I think everyone here would like to know what really happened.'

People moved here and there, making themselves more comfortable. Bottles came out, and baskets of food. And amidst it all, the young-old man sat, stroking the plastic that protected his magazine, and talked.

The Miner's Tale

My Uncle Mike always told it like this: I started out mining coal in the Illawarra, myself. That's in Australia. It was China that used to buy what came out of the Bulli Seam, to make steel. Used to. And the greenies make so much trouble there, the mining companies reckon what's left just isn't worth it. So I had to come all the way here for work.

My mate Griff had a shorter trip – he'd come in from Wales a few years before. He got tired of worrying about when the demonstrators would get tired of throwing rocks and start throwing bombs. He said his family were coal miners from three hundred years back, that he could read the coal face just like reading a newspaper. I thought at the time he was a bit up himself.

Our job was to take out the coal pillars that'd been left behind in the old, old, old days. We'd take a pillar, brace up the roof with a piece of old timber from somewhere else in the mine, and move on. Sooner or later, the voids would cave in. You have to not think about it.

This story starts the day after Griff's wife left him for good. We were taking pillars, as usual. By chance I caught a good look at Griff's face in the light of my caplamp. He was staring at the pillar, then at the roof. Suddenly he yelled, 'Out! Everyone out! *Go go go go!*'

We were out into the heading in two heartbeats. A big section of roof caved in exactly where we'd been standing.

The shift was nowhere near over, but we decided: stuff the bosses, we were going up top for a smoke. Of course, the undermanager was hanging around looking for slackers, and we were sacked on the spot.

We showered off and changed into our street clothes, and walked out the gate. I saw the people outside, like always, waiting for a chance at a job.

Their raised hands, fingers hooked through the chain-link fence, looked like dead vines.

Tony and Mark turned off for home. I didn't envy them, having to break it to their wives and kids. It hit me that Griff didn't have a wife anymore, so I said, 'Mate, I've got some change. Can I shout you a beer?'

He looked down and nodded.

People in regular jobs were all just getting off work, so the pub was crowded. I bought us each a pint and we found a couple of chairs at a half-full table. Griff and I sat, drinking slowly and silently.

A bloke who was already at the table looked at me. 'Coal miner,' he shouted over the noise. I checked him out: didn't look like a greenie. I took a risk and nodded.

'How'd you know?' I shouted back.

He pointed to the back of his hand. I understood: mine were permanently marked, like tattoos, from coal dust getting into cuts.

The bloke looked at his watch, then looked puzzled, as if to say: *It's not shift changeover, what are you doing here?*

I shrugged.

His look said: *Poor bugger, you've been sacked.* He leaned close. 'You and your mate, finish your beers and we'll go somewhere and talk. I have jobs for you.'

Griff and I upended our glasses and set them down with a thump. The three of us shouldered our way back outside.

He led us a fair way down the street. I started looking around in case some of his mates were waiting to get the lousy 50p I had left in my pocket, but he just took us to a house and brought us inside. It was a nice house as English houses go, but way too cramped up for an Australian.

The bloke made us coffee – real coffee! The smell of it alone was enough to make me optimistic. As he brought the mugs over to the kitchen table, he said, 'There's more if you want it. My name's Jacob Heath.'

'Thomas Griffiths.'

'Mike Andonovski.'

He got a coffee for himself and we sat. He had an eager look on his face. 'I was glad to run into you. See, I'm in a bit of a pinch. My company's working a new mine—'

'New mine?' said Griff sharply. 'New *coal* mine?'

Heath shifted in his chair. Sure enough, his next words were, 'All right, yes, the coal's dirty.'

Griff and I looked at each other. Dirty coal. Planet-killer stuff, the greenies had everyone believing. But our ex-boss would have blacklisted us out of every honest mine in the country.

We took the job.

A bus came for us at dawn. It took us two kilometres or so from the mine entrance, and we walked through the snow up to the gate. That was the first funny thing: most mines, there are lumps of coal scattered over everything. But the snow was absolutely white and smooth.

The guard found our names on a list and let us in without ever looking at us. 'Third on the left,' he mumbled. He didn't have any teeth. He looked like he might have lost them in fights, big footy-player type.

The building was cold and stark. Two other recruits were waiting: a hollow-cheeked woman with long, stringy hair, and a scrawny kid of about fifteen. I almost told him to get home, that a dirty mine was no place for him. Then I thought he might have a family, maybe even a kid of his own, to support.

We all shivered in silence. Just on eight, this guy walked in with a folder full of papers. He gave each of us a list of safety rules, and went through them out loud, maybe in case anyone had trouble reading. That was more induction than there'd been at the last two mines I'd worked at. I guess I looked surprised, because the guy said, 'We take safety seriously here, Mr—'

'Andonovski.'

'Mr. Andonovski. We're making an investment in training and equipping you, and we don't want to lose that investment. That reminds me: this mine requires specialised tools, which are trade secrets, so I'm handing out a confidentiality agreement for you all to sign. '

As we were signing, the guy said, 'If nobody has any questions, I'll take you to get your equipment.'

In a warehouse-sized shed, a scraggy sort of woman dumped our kit on us. She had a warty thing by her nose that looked like the skin cancers I used to see in Australia. It was odd to see one here, where the sun didn't shine worth a damn.

The gear was nothing special: overalls, helmets, caplamps, boots, pickaxes, short-handled shovels, sledgehammers, and a tool bag for each of us. Must have looked like Aladdin's treasure to the boy, though. His eyes got really wide when the boots came out. I glanced down at his feet: his shoes were a few scraps of nylon held by threads onto rubber soles – looked like what was left of a pair of joggers. I thought of him walking here through the snow.

As we were finishing up, two people walked in with the kind of carelessness that told me they were bosses.

'Any of you ever work together before?' said one.

Griff and I knew better than to say yes. They always separate you.

The skinnier one beckoned to the woman and the boy. 'You two all right with confined spaces?' Of course they said yes. 'Then pack your gear, suit up, and I'll get you started. You have three minutes.'

They scrambled. The boy's feet were going to be raw meat by the end of the shift, wearing those boots without any socks.

The other boss, the big one, said, 'You, too. Suit up.' I realised that in spite of her size, this was a woman. Her voice was shocking: high and wheezy, like she had laryngitis.

She took us to the mine entrance. We switched our caplamps on and followed her down the heading.

'I'm Denise, your team leader, ' she said, without turning to look at us. 'You look like nice guys. Don't wreck my opinion of you.' That was all she said until she took us to where a half-dozen other people were shoring the roof with some of the dodgiest timber I'd ever seen. 'Right,' Denise wheezed loudly enough for everyone to hear. 'These are your new mates.' Then she just took off.

Griff and I introduced ourselves, but the others just muttered 'Hello' and never told us their names.

'We're checking the face here for the right kind of coal,' said the fat guy. 'Shows up red on this thing.' He waved a device about the size of a sandwich, with a small screen. 'Chromaspec.'

The old woman was pointing something at the face that looked like a torch on a tripod.

'What's that do?' said Griff.

'It's a stabiliser, stupid,' said the old woman. 'So the walls and ceiling don't squash us flat. Bloody newbs, now they're not even training them before they send them down.'

Griff stared hard at the stabiliser, then even harder at the coal face. He looked distracted and anxious. 'Turn it off', he said.

All six of them laughed raucously.

After that, none of them said a word to us except things like 'Shovel the coal into the tub', 'Hold this', or 'Don't bloody spill any of that.' We tried to learn by watching and eavesdropping. They didn't make either easy.

Denise reappeared at the end of the shift. 'Go on,' she said, and we all trudged back up. Griff and I were about to walk out of the portal into the winter evening, but Denise stopped us. 'Leave your equipment over there, in your team's box. No, right there, stupid. Okay, step onto the grate and rinse your boots off here,' she said. 'And turn out your pockets.' Coal grit showered down, making little tinkling sounds as it hit the grate and fell through. 'Boss likes the surface works clean.'

When we were dressed, we picked up our day's pay at the pay window and walked out to catch the bus. The two who had done induction with us were by the gate.

'Hey,' said the boy. He hadn't got the hang of washing all the coal dust off yet. Especially around his eyes. If you scrunch your eyes tight when you're washing your face, there's always a bit of coal dust gets left behind. Looks like makeup.

'How'd it go?' I asked.

'Oh, yeah, all right,' said the boy. The woman didn't say anything. Her hair, wet from the shower, was already stiffening to ice.

'What did they have you doing?'

'Crawling in and taking coal out with those hand picks,' said the boy.

'We were supposed to look at it with the, what, the chromaspec, and if it looked red, it was the kind they wanted.'

Out of nowhere, the guard with no teeth ran up and swung his arm into the boy's head, sending him flying into a snowbank. 'No talking about the equipment above ground,' the guard snarled.

Griff and I helped him up. None of us said anything more, about anything, even after we got on the bus.

The next week or so was pretty much the same. Griff and I got all the crap work to do, our team leader only appeared at the start and end of shift, and I was a little bit tireder and felt a little bit meaner at the end of every day. We rode the bus with the woman and the boy, but we never talked, nothing more than: 'Hello, how are you?' We always told each other, 'Good, yeah, I'm good. You?'

It was a Wednesday evening when it all started to really go to hell. Griff and I had just got off the bus, and he said, 'Mike, come on over to the house. I'll make you some dinner. I need to talk.'

He made something or other from the freezer; it may even have been something his wife had cooked before she walked out. Griff started talking right away, as though he'd been dying to for days.

'You remember I told you my family's been mining coal for hundreds of years? It may be genetic, I don't know, but we can feel how the coal lies, where the faults are, where the methane is, when it's going to blow or collapse. Those stabilisers are dangerous, Mike, they'll kill us. They set up *wrong* stresses. The coal fights back. Every minute using them is borrowed time.'

'Hang on,' I said, laughing. 'That's no different from every mine, every day.'

'No, it *is* different,' he said, his eyes wide and worried. 'It masks the natural stresses, makes them harder to feel. And what makes the chromaspec go red? What are we breathing down there? What's getting into our skin, our eyes and ears? Radiation? Something worse?'

He saw I wasn't buying it, but he kept trying. 'When the stabilisers are off, I can tell there's an aquifer a few strata up. And in between there and the coal it feels like sandstone – porous. Whatever's in that aquifer is seeping down into the coal. Coal soaks up anything and everything. That's why this mine is dirty. Not because the coal *burns* dirty, because it's *contaminated*.'

'With water. Come on, Griffo.'

'With whatever makes the chromaspec shine red, you heard the kid. Our lot, too, they only dig where the red is.'

'Mate, we need the work,' I said. 'What's your point?'

'They're using that contaminated coal for something so secret that every last piece of coal we cut is swept up and taken away. Mike, people are going to die.'

'Mate,' I said. He was starting to scare me, the way he was looking. 'Mate, people die all the time.'

'Yeah,' he said, like I was distracting him from something important.

We finished eating, neither of us talking much. I wasn't hungry, but that never matters. There's food, you eat it. When we finished up, I helped wash the dishes.

'I'll see you tomorrow, yeah?' I said as I got my coat on.

'You weren't listening, were you?' he said, but he didn't sound angry. Just sad. 'You didn't listen to a thing I said.'

'Sure I did, Griffo,' I said. 'But–' I tried to put words to what I was feeling. 'But we're useless. We're rubbish to them, guys like us, we can't fix anything.'

'Yeah,' he said in that far-off way again. 'Okay, Mike. See you tomorrow. Thanks for coming over.'

He'd written me off, I could tell. My stomach felt bitter. I went home, but it was a while before I fell asleep. And I felt like crap when I got up at dawn the next morning.

I waited for the bus at the usual place, usual time, but Griff didn't show up until a few seconds before the bus got there. He must have been waiting around the corner or something. Avoiding me.

All day, every time the chromaspec pulsed red, I wondered what my skin and lungs were absorbing. I started to think I could actually feel it seeping in, whatever it was. Every time someone deployed a stabiliser, I felt like I could feel the layers above us groaning, like someone lifting a heavy box the wrong way.

It was crap, of course. Lack of sleep and arguing with Griff – it was making me upset, that was all.

But when the chromaspec topped out, even the others on our team looked at each other nervously.

'What?' said Griff in a voice I'd never heard from him before. 'What's wrong?'

'Nothing,' said one of them.

Griff grabbed the guy's overalls in both hands and slammed him against the face. 'What – is – *wrong*?'

To the extent the guy could move, he turned his head to give a panicky look at the rest of the team. He was scared of Griff, but something else was scaring him more.

Griff let him drop, then turned on the others. 'You're killing people – *killing them*! Tell me what's going on!'

'Why? So my kids can starve?' said one.

'Nobody knows anything for sure anyway,' said another.

We all heard it: the sound of a boot scuffing on coal grit, back in the heading. And another scuff, fainter. Like someone was going off to report.

'Oh God,' whimpered the guy Griff had grabbed. 'Oh God, we're dead.'

As if he hadn't heard, Griff suddenly lifted his head, staring at nothing, and said, 'We're dead.'

I'd seen that look on his face before. 'RUN!' I shouted. 'RUN!' And Griff and I took off for the surface.

'It's no use, they already heard us!' one of them yelled after us. That was the last we heard from any of them. Griff and I were a fair way up the heading when we felt the shock of the collapse.

A moment later, Griff dragged me roughly into one of the alcoves that are supposed to give you somewhere to get out of the way if a truck or something loses its brakes and comes barrelling down the heading at you. 'They'll think we died too,' he said.

I could hardly hear him for the ringing in my ears, but I nodded. We had to find a place to hide until shift change, when no-one would notice us leaving. I hoped. Even though I wanted to turn and head back underground for safety, like a burrowing animal, it was better to go toward the surface. There would be places to hide – control rooms, storage rooms, sheds.

The collapse had shaken the mine like kicking an anthill. By the time we got to the surface, people were pouring out of every entrance. But the gates were locked, as usual.

It was easy enough in the confusion to find an unlocked storeroom. Griff and I rearranged some boxes to give us a tiny cave to sit in, and we sat, breathing air that stank of old cardboard and sweat, for two hours. Even if we'd had anything to say to each other, we wouldn't have risked it.

We waited for the noise of shift change, left our helmets hidden there, and crawled out from the box cave. We stood to the side of the door and waited for a big group to walk by, then we did our best to sort of fade into them as everyone walked to the showers. People tend to keep to themselves in the showers, partly because they're tired, and partly because no-one wants to look like they're staring at another bloke's equipment. So we managed to get the worst of the coal dust off us and change into our street clothes.

Griff came close and murmured to me, 'They'll check if our street clothes are gone.'

'If people thought we were dead, they'd steal them that quick,' I murmured back. He nodded.

We made it through the gate by blending in with the crowd again.

The bus was packed enough we could risk getting on. Less obvious than walking the deserted, icy road, anyway. When we got off, Griff stopped walking two blocks from the stop and looked back. The woman and the kid were walking towards us.

'Yeah, well, see you, Griff,' I said.

'Mike.' It made me feel like crying, how he said my name. He reached out to touch my arm, but he took his hand back before it got to me, like he was afraid.

That's why I stayed.

When the other two reached us, Griff said, 'Got a minute?'

They looked at him warily, but nodded.

We found a place out of the cold. It was a public library, of all things.

I didn't want to go in, because when do a bunch of miners sit around in a library? But it was there, and it was warm. And it wouldn't seem suspicious if we kept our voices down.

The place smelled like the big box of crayon pieces we'd had in kindy. We walked past shelves and shelves of books – you forget there are so many books in the *world* – and sat at a table in the back.

Griff didn't waste any time. 'That coal is contaminated.'

'Yeah?' said the woman. 'How do you know?'

'Fact: the coal lights up that chromaspec like a Christmas tree. Fact: they gather every fleck, I bet they even filter it out of the water we shower in. So either it's really valuable or really illegal – or both. Fact: we're not allowed to talk about it or even tell anyone where the mine is. Fact: nobody knows the name of the company, not even the people who work there. Fact: everyone who's been there a while's got something *wrong* with them. Sores, bald patches, missing teeth, you name it.'

'Oh, God,' said the woman, sounding like she was about to faint.

'What is it?' said the boy.

'What is it doing to the baby?' And she laid her hand, gently, on her stomach.

Horror rushed through me, cold, like water.

The boy laid his hand on top of hers. 'It'll be all right,' he said, as if it might even be true.

Griff said, 'Mike and I can't go back. They think we died in the collapse. Mike got the two of us out in time.' He looked at me kind of sideways; it was an apology and a thanks and a plea for secrecy, all at once. 'If we show up there again, they'll make sure we *are* dead. A boss heard me asking the others about the coal. Thing is, we still don't know enough. Do you want to help?'

'What will we do for work, if we get sacked? Or if we ... if we stop them?' said the boy.

Griff looked at him for a long moment. 'I don't know,' was all he said.

'I have people at home,' said the boy.

The woman laughed a little. 'I wish I didn't,' she said. I noticed some yellow discolouration on her cheekbone: an old bruise.

'Some things are important,' said Griff. 'More important than we are. We're talking thousands, maybe millions of lives.'

'We're still important enough to have names, though,' I said. 'I'm Mike, this is Griff.'

'Renee,' said the woman.

'Milton,' said the boy. We all turned and looked at him. Who names their kid Milton? He raised his chin defiantly, but we all dropped the subject.

'Well?' I said. 'You in?'

'Are *you*?' Griff said to me.

There was something crucial that Griff needed to do, and he wanted me along, *needed* me. 'Aw, yeah, I'm in,' I said. That was the first time I'd ever seen Griff smile.

'What about you?' he said to Renee and Milton. They both nodded. 'Renee, if you're pregnant, maybe you shouldn't go back underground.'

'They know all four of us came in together,' she said. 'It'd look kind of funny, wouldn't it, if I quit? It'll – it'll motivate me to do the job quick. And why shouldn't I get another day or two's pay off them while I'm at it?'

Milton looked like he was about to argue, but Griff cut him off. 'Okay, then. Renee, what I want you to do is watch and listen. I can't be any more specific, because anything you find out is more than we know now. Milton, can you figure out a way to sneak just one piece of the contaminated coal out of the mine?'

'I guess.'

We set up staggered times for each of us to come to the library the next afternoon, then Griff sent Milton on his way, and Renee a few minutes later. Then he said, 'You head home, Mike. I'm going to stay here until closing and see if I can find anything in the newspapers that might give us an idea of what's going on.'

'See you tomorrow, then.'

'See you.'

I went home. And sat. And thought. And slept a little. When I got up, I got dressed and made myself eat a sandwich. I wouldn't be much good to Griff if I passed out from hunger. I got my coat and boots on, and headed out for a walk. Eventually I ended up at the library.

I found them at the same table. Renee and Griff were talking quietly, and Milton was gripping a book so hard his knuckles looked like marbles. He was moving his lips as he read.

Renee and Griff looked up when I sat down, but Milton kept reading.

'Hey, mate,' I said softly. He didn't even hear me. I touched him on the shoulder and he instantly recoiled, shielding his head with his arms. The book fell to the floor. 'Sorry,' I said, and bent to pick it up. *Harry Potter and the Philosopher's Stone*. I hadn't read much as a kid, but I'd loved that one.

He ducked his head and blushed, poor bugger. I looked around the table. A twitchy kid, a battered pregnant woman, a genius freak, and me, just a bloke with dirty hands, doing our best to save thousands of lives. I started to grin.

'What?' said Griff.

'Nothing,' I said. But what I wanted to say was, Look at us, aren't we ... amazing, aren't we legends!

Renee said, 'Everyone's saying it was the worst collapse in a hundred years. They're certain your whole team is dead. But I haven't heard much else. Yet.'

Griff said, 'Thanks, Renee. Any luck, Milt?'

Milton took something out of his pocket, wrapped in some toilet paper. 'Keep it wrapped, Griff, I had to hide it between my ... um ... Sorry. I changed the paper, though. Clean paper.'

Griff took the wad of paper solemnly. 'I appreciate what you went through. Thanks,' he said. Milton blushed again.

'I've been reading the papers,' Griff continued. 'There's not much, but about six months ago local unemployment figures dropped. And the university here got a big grant from an anonymous donor. It made big news because they were about to go under. No coal company has that kind of money, not anymore. And who paid for the chromaspecs and stabilisers? Someone's got very deep pockets. And very big ideas.'

'If they made something out of whatever's poisoning the coal, that could go in a bomb,' I said. 'Or in the drinking water, or anything.'

'Plenty of people would pay for a new kind of bomb,' said Milton.

'Maybe we should go over to the uni,' I said. 'Can we risk it?'

'Can we not?' said Griff. 'You and I can go tomorrow. Renee and Milt, you'll need to keep showing up for work and keep listening. I'm really sorry.'

They told him it was all right, and we left, one at a time. Milton said he'd go last because he wanted to read some more.

Next morning, when Griff and I met up outside the uni, he wordlessly showed me a newspaper: a boy had been stabbed the night before as he walked home. The photo didn't show the boy's face, but his shoes were nothing more than worn rubber soles held to his feet with a few scraps of nylon.

I let out a kind of gulping sound, I couldn't help it. Griff still said nothing, but as he turned to walk to the uni, he put a hand on my shoulder for a moment.

The uni was in an old three-story office building, dark and cramped. We went in and walked up to the front desk. I waited for Griff to do the talking.

Suddenly he was shy and timid, and he said hesitantly, 'Me and my mate, we want to go to uni. We want to study chemistry. Me great-granddad studied chemistry, is why. Who do we talk to about that?'

The guy behind the counter stared. I suppose it was pretty implausible, but who would lie about wanting to go to uni? It wasn't like it got you a better job or anything.

'Up one flight, turn left out of the stairwell,' he said, after a good long look at the two of us. 'Ask for Dr. Cantrell.'

Up one flight was just as cramped and dark – worse even, because the grimy windows were mostly blocked by piles of paper and books. There was a woman in one of the offices.

'Excuse me,' said Griff, 'but where can I find Dr. Cantrell?'

'That's me,' said the woman.

'I'm sorry we can't give you our names, but we need your help,' said Griff. He took the piece of coal out of his pocket and unwrapped it. It was clean enough; poor Milton must have been really careful where he kept it. Funny, the thoughts that make you want to cry.

'We need to know what's in this coal,' said Griff

'What, from a piece that small?' said Cantrell. 'And who's going to pay for the lab time?'

'We don't have any money,' said Griff. 'But maybe you could be famous if you broke the news that someone is distilling a weapons-grade toxin out of contaminated coal. There'd be no shortage of grant money then, everyone wanting to find out how to neutralise it.'

'I'm not part of the coal research,' said Cantrell.

'I guessed that, since you're the one they send clods off the street to,' said Griff. 'That's why I came to you. Why should the coal project get all the money, for doing someone's killing for them? Why shouldn't you get it, for saving thousands, maybe millions, of lives?'

I said, 'Who's funding the coal project?'

'It was an anonymous donation,' said Cantrell. 'That means—'

'I know what it means,' I said.

'The uni's given them some office and lab space upstairs, but nobody's said the name of their company,' said Cantrell.

'Can you tell us what's in the coal?' said Griff.

'It'll take a while. Weeks.'

'We'll be back tomorrow. It's important.'

She gave Griff a long, long look. 'I'll see what I can do,' she said.

We waited out the day in the pub. There were always a few people there, which was good for us. Knife attacks are less likely when there are witnesses.

That afternoon, I went into the library first, then Griff. A few minutes later, Renee came in. She had that anxious look people get when they've been trying all day not to cry. Griff put an awkward arm around her, and she leaned into him. She didn't make a sound, but her shoulders shook.

After a while, she said, 'I heard something today. We found a big section of the dirty coal, the chromaspec practically buzzed. My team leader said, 'Work slower. Faster we fill the quota, faster we're out of a job.' I never heard anything about a quota before.'

'They'll have enough soon, then, if someone's worried about losing his job,' said Griff. Renee's head was still resting on his shoulder, but I don't think he noticed. Or maybe he did.

Griff said, 'We could try to neutralise whatever the stuff is, but we don't know *where* it is, and we don't have any resources. We could try and disrupt distribution, but again, we don't know where it's stored. I'm thinking publicity is our best weapon, and Dr. Cantrell can help us there.'

'She didn't seem too friendly,' I said.

'As long as she wants fame and grant money, she'll help. If she breaks it to the media, we can get reporters and cameras. We'll need someone already inside who can take us right to a big section of dirty coal.'

Renee didn't lift her head from Griff's shoulder, but I saw her smile. Griff must have felt it.

'Tomorrow, towards the end of shift, then,' he said. 'See if you can get to the mine entrance at 2 p.m.'

We walked Renee home – that is, Griff walked her home, and I came along.

The next morning Griff and I met at the uni. Cantrell was in her office. She looked like hell. She'd been up all night turning that lump of coal inside out.

'It's a precursor to a neurotoxin, a substance that paralyses,' she said. 'Even by itself it's nasty – carcinogenic. You'd have been in trouble if it hadn't been bound up in the coal. Even so, it would get you after a while. But combine it with another precursor and it's agonising death for anyone in range.' She actually shuddered.

'We need to get the word out,' said Griff. 'Have you got a contact list for the media?'

'I've been thinking about that,' she said. 'You're right, it may get me publicity and funding. It may also get me the sack. I'm not sure I want to go public on a few grams of coal and an all-nighter.'

Griff looked a little desperate at that. 'They've nearly got enough to start using it.'

'How do you know?' she said, sounding not very friendly again.

'Down in the mine they're talking about the quota being filled.'

'That could mean anything.'

'Ask your mates in the lab upstairs about that,' he said. 'How many all-nighters have *they* been pulling lately? Every day we wait, we're getting closer to disaster.'

She fiddled with some papers on her desk, picked up a pen, put it down, then said, 'All right. How do you want to do this?'

At 1:30, the media types turned up outside There were four cars, each with two or three people and a load of equipment inside. Only one camera though, and that seemed mostly duct tape. I hoped it would do the job.

We piled in, and the convoy took off.

The mine gate was locked, of course, not being shift-change. But Griff just told the media people to start recording, and went up to the guard's booth.

'We need to see mine management,' he said.

The guard just laughed.

'We want them to answer some questions about contaminated coal. If they don't let us in, we'll broadcast to the whole country that they have something criminal to hide.'

The guard stopped laughing. He went inside the booth and we saw him talking to someone on the phone. A few minutes later two people in heavy, expensive coats walked out of a building and up to the gate. They told the guard to let us in, and as soon as the microphones were in their faces, they said, 'Ladies and gentlemen, we're happy to discuss any concerns you have at any time.'

Cantrell stepped up to stand near the microphones and said, 'We'd like to know more about the chromaspec instruments. What, exactly, are they measuring?'

'They measure the purity of the carbon. When they get a strong signal, the carbon is relatively free of ash, sulphur, and other impurities.'

'I have reason to suspect that's untrue,' said Cantrell. 'My analysis of coal from this mine – coal that registered strongly on the chromaspec – is that it contains a contaminant that, when combined with another agent, produces a very deadly nerve gas.'

'Rubbish,' snapped one of the managers, but the other one laid a hand on her arm.

'How large was the analysis sample?' he said.

'Tiny. That's why I'd appreciate your supplying 50 kilograms for a comprehensive verification and complete analysis.'

'Certainly,' he said. 'If you'll just allow me a day to arrange it, I'll deliver–'

'Now would be good,' said Cantrell.

I saw that Renee had managed to sneak away from her team and come up to stand near. 'I can take you right to a spot where the chromaspec tops out,' she said loudly. 'You can get a load of coal there.'

'Let's go,' said Cantrell. The managers looked like they wanted to block her way, but she and Renee and the reporters and Griff and I, one by one, pushed past them. One of them tried to stop the camera operator, saying something about sparks from the camera creating a hazard, but everyone ignored him.

Renee led us down to where her team was working. She grabbed the chromaspec from a startled teammate and pointed it at the face, and it lit up like fireworks, even with the television crew's lights glaring.

'Fill this tub with the dirty coal,' she said. Her teammates stared at her; obviously they'd never seen her so ... assertive. That was the second time I saw Griff smile.

It only took them a few minutes to get about 50 kilos of coal in the tub. Renee pointed the chromaspec at the tub, and made sure the reporters saw it light up again. Then we started back up top. 'Come on up,' said Griff casually over his shoulder to Renee's teammates. 'See the fun.' They shrugged and followed.

Griff stumbled as we walked. I looked over; in the television lights his face was grey and sweaty. I moved close and took his arm. He leaned on me suddenly and heavily, and together we walked up the road to the surface. We fell behind, as Griff was moving slower and slower. Just as we got to the surface, he passed out.

And the earth shook with another ceiling collapse.

Renee looked back to see what was keeping Griff and saw me trying to get his arms around my neck so I could carry him to someplace warm. The nearest building was the storeroom where we'd hidden just a few days before. I put him down on his side. Renee sat next to him, tense and silent.

After a minute he gave a shuddering sigh and, without opening his eyes, murmured, 'Those bastards.'

'Who?' I said.

It was another long minute or so before he could answer. 'Managers. Bloody bastards were sneaking out, turned a stabiliser all wonky. Stupid of me. Should have left one of us up top. So it wouldn't die with us.'

'They collapsed the mine on *purpose?*'

'You held it off,' said Renee, sounding absolutely certain. 'You stopped it until we could get out.'

After a moment Griff said, 'I didn't know I could do that,' and passed out again.

'Get help,' said Renee. 'I'll stay.' She lifted his head and put it on her lap.

I found a reporter who was willing to drop us off at Griff's place. Renee and I looked after him the best we knew how. At least by dinner time he was conscious.

That night it was all over the radio and the television, and the next day the two newspapers put it on the front page. Cantrell was quoted at length, but the three of us might as well not have been there. We're okay with that.

Cantrell tracked us down a couple of days later from the reporter who'd driven us to Griff's place. We were staying at Griff's place, me and Renee. Kind of looking after him. Renee didn't want to go home anyway. She was starting to like not getting belted around.

Griff was sitting up – he'd only been doing that for the past day or so – and Renee and I were washing the dishes from dinner. We offered Cantrell the usual cardboardy coffee.

She said, 'You were right. The fellowship offers are pouring in. I'm headed to the uni in Canterbury. I was wondering if you would like to come with me.'

'I'm staying with my mates,' said Griff. He took Renee's hand.

'No, all three of you. There are jobs. If you don't mind doing cleaning, maintenance, that sort of thing.'

We looked at each other. I walked to the freezer and peered in. 'Not much left here,' I said. I didn't mean just the food, either.

Anyway, Griff and Renee went ahead to get things set up. I stayed behind to find Milton's family and let them know he was a hero. They weren't all that happy for the news when I found them, but I'd still rather they knew he didn't die in a gutter for nothing.

I got a letter yesterday from Griff, with his and Renee's new address. They're going to put me up until I get a job. They both like it there. Renee has started taking classes at night. She's studying politics or something, and the uni is studying Griff. They think it's a bit strange that he can do what he can do.

Renee is starting to throw up a lot. There's a doctor there who reckons that's a sign she won't miscarry, so it's a good thing. Griff says if the baby is a boy, they're going to name him Milton. The voice of Thomas Griffin's son trailed off, and he chuckled. 'Jeez, who names their kid Milton?'

*T*he Miner's Tale of heroes triumphant and villains thwarted had restored the good mood of the carriage – aided, doubtless, by the wine and ale offered by the imperturbable barman. As Thomas Griffin's son fell quiet, several others clamoured to be heard. The voice that won out was surprisingly quiet, but sharp with authority. It belonged to an older woman, straight-backed and bright-eyed, with iron-grey hair.

'I haven't seen a bad storm from aboveground in many years,' she said. 'This is the first time I've stirred from home since I was a girl. To go to Canterbury is an honour and all but it is no easy undertaking. Yet we honour the King in Aqua Sulis, and I have come, as Sky Chief, for this anniversary of his. And though it may seem I come empty-handed, it is not so, as you shall see. It is simply that the gift of Aqua Sulis is too great, too large to be moved without much aid.

'Listen, and I will tell you now of the first Sky-Chief of Aqua Sulis. How he earned his title, and how we came to survive the Storm Years and the Plague Years, and yes, even of the great and precious gift we have kept so long, awaiting a time when hope returned to the world ...'

The sky chief's tale

Davin, the son of the chief, stood in the Hall's inner entrance, watching the hunters bring the half-frozen man inside. It wasn't only exposure which made the stranger the colour of snow. Though the man's face was relatively young, his hair was white. His voice had an odd accent but he was speaking English. 'Help them,' he pleaded, half-rousing as the hunters wrapped dry blankets around him. 'They're all alone up there. Please help them!'

'Dav!' called one of the hunters, seeing him standing by the outside-gear racks. 'Where's your mother?'

'I think she's in council.' Always have some sort of an answer, Camilla had told him. Don't lie but try not to sound like an idiot.

'Can you call her or send someone? We don't have authorisation to pass this fellow any further and he needs to see a medic. A good soak in the hot water wouldn't hurt him any either.'

Davin looked at the man, tempted to tell them to take him through to the Great Baths anyway but a moment's reflection told him that was stupid. If he was carrying something, infecting the entire lot of them was rather worse than being embarrassed. There was no one else here but him and this group and he was only here because he didn't want his mother to make him stay for council. 'I'll go,' he said as the man began to call out again.

One of the medics came to the hall; Rosanna, the young one not long out of her apprenticeship. She examined the man while the hunters guarded the far doors to make sure no one else wandered in. 'He seems healthy,' she said at last, 'but we'll stick him in the isolation room as usual until I'm sure. He's lucky you found him when you did.'

Davin, still lurking in the doorway, squawked as an unexpected hand tapped his shoulder. His mother grinned when he turned quickly around. Always good to show the younger generation you hadn't completely lost everything. Camilla Winterton, who liked to call herself London's last debutante, was as pale and fair-haired as her son, looking ghostly in the lantern-shadowed passage. She wore only her light wolf-hide jacket and trousers since she had not intended to go outside today.

'Is he healthy?' she asked, pitching her voice to carry to those in the empty hall. Its wall decorations had been left but all the furnishings removed years ago for use further inside the complex. Voices echoed here and the small group of humans in their animal-furred garments looked very like a wolf-pack crouched over prey in the centre of the hall.

'I think so, Chief,' Rosanna called back. 'I want to keep him isolated here for a few days, just to be sure. These guys say they found him about an hour ago and it's so bloody cold – begging your pardon – that I don't think any bug would survive out there. Even so, I want them isolated too.' This brought a general groan and complaint from the hunters.

'As you say, Medic,' Camilla answered. 'Close the hall doors. Somebody will bring the supplies up and knock so you know when to retrieve them. Boys – if you didn't find any prey on this trip, feel free to try again. I'll see you all in three days.'

Three days later, Rosanna knocked on the heavy bolted inner door and called through to the guard there that all was well. Not long after, the message reached Camilla who headed along to speak to the stranger. The chief of the community still wasn't sure admitting the man was a good idea. She'd tried to keep his arrival quiet but of course everyone knew the Hall was quarantined. There was only one reason for that. She'd meant to come alone but Davin's instincts were too good and he'd caught up with her shortly after she received the news.

Camilla gave Davin a half-irritated, half-affectionate glance as he jogged along the passage beside her. In some ways he was younger than his fifteen years, certainly younger in spirit than the teen she'd been when she came here with her parents. She had known a far wider world. Her father had taught at a great centre of learning and her mother had travelled the world as the chief of great sky-craft. Then when Camilla was about Davin's age, the great sicknesses began. At first her people believed themselves safe, living in a civilised nation with advanced medical knowledge. Camilla's father was in advance of his peers in his understanding. He gathered together a select group of people and supplies and took them out of London to what had been the tourist town of Bath. Even then, people travelled for the sake of it, to look at strange things and tell about them when they returned home.

Then the spreading plagues finally began to frighten people and they stopped travelling. They huddled into their homes, into tunnels and caves, anywhere they could to get away from the growing disarray. Places which had been owned by the government, the chosen rulers, had no visitors and were offered for sale. Camilla's father and his group had been waiting for this. They offered money for the half-buried buildings where the only hot springs in Britain bubbled to the surface. They enclosed them and moved in with all that they had; their families and the supplies they had managed to collect and the precious knowledge of their world. Camilla, who had hoped to go to that same centre of learning and study to become a doctor, instead grew up as her father's apprentice in a lair of caves and inheritor to a struggling little community of less than one hundred souls. Too few for ultimate survival. Her father, the first chief, had known this but he had refused to accept anyone but those he and his council chose. Too many, he said, and we won't pass a single generation.

Now there was Davin and a small generation of young people like him, born and living most of their lives underground except when they ventured out to hunt and scavenge. Most would grow up to be hunters while others would tend plants grown with arts the modern world has since lost. There was much of Camilla's world which was only fantastic stories to her son, limited to his home and to the distance a young boy was allowed to travel in a single day. In other ways, of course, he was far more self-reliant and tougher than his mother and her peers. 'We'll go back,' Camilla's father had said, in those early days. 'In a lot of ways we'll have to go back to the ways things used to be done. One of the things that'll have to go is those very long, indulged childhoods we enjoyed. Our kids won't have time for that.'

For a while now Camilla had discussed with the council what role Davin would begin to undertake when he turned sixteen. He was very, very bright and she wanted him to begin studying the old knowledge, the scientific books the community had managed to save from the self-destruction of the old world. Their tiny core of scientists had been working on various projects and experiments for years, with uncertain success but she thought that with Davin, they might well achieve something of real worth.

She and Davin emerged in the Baths' reception hall, still in its renovated-Roman trappings which had once drawn the tourists. Camilla glanced at the bolted outer door, automatically reassuring herself that all was secure. They had stopped posting guards since the last of the sick starving refugees had reached them, back in her father's time. The chief led her son onwards, through another passage and out through the welcome warmth of the Great Baths chamber to the isolation chamber. A few people were in the greenish, yard and a half deep steaming water or sitting at the far side talking but that was usual. This was the only place her people had to relax.

The changes wrought by Camilla's people were not for the better, aesthetically speaking. Some buried part of her mind still cringed when she saw things like the portcullis and the ugly gray concrete roof which now covered the Baths and kept their precious heat within. Without it, the ancient structures would have suffered the same storm-destruction as the great Abbey beside them, now a snow-swept hull. Davin, of course, never even noticed. This was how things had always been for him.

The isolation room had probably been once a sort of meeting-room, somewhere for bathers to sit and talk, have drinks and relax. Now, as the largest such chamber, its purpose was far less social. Camilla ordered Rosanna outside to wait until she was finished, relieving her of her extra lantern first. She put it on the table by the patient's bed and looked curiously at him. Davin had said but it was a shock to see his strange paleness of skin and hair for herself. Perhaps, she thought, they were a shock to him. He blinked and stared as though he had never seen a woman in a wolf-hide coat before.

'My name is Camilla Winterton and this is my son Davin,' she said. 'You're our first visitor in a very long time. The people who found you told me you said you'd come from Bristol, is that so?'

'Yes, I am from Bristol.' His voice was strange too and she could not place the accent.

'Who are you?'

'I am Dr Vladislav Woislaw of Warsaw University, later assigned to the cosmonaut program in Baikonur – Star City – Kazakhstan.' He said this very carefully and then waited, as though knowing she would need time to absorb it.

'I see,' Camilla said slowly. A host of questions arose in her mind, all struggling to be first. She rubbed her eyes, thinking of her council's reaction, of the cell of scientists who would be clamouring for access once they knew. Davin, though, didn't wait for his mother to think things through and blurted out the one question, as she immediately knew, which had to be asked.

'Why did you come *here*?'

Vlad Woislaw smiled, still carefully, as though he was afraid of both of them. Of course, there would be no comeback if she did choose to kill him, saying she had found he was a danger to their survival. Her people would believe that.

'I am here because the people on the moon want to come home.'

Camilla's confused mind tried to make sense of his words. He might as well have said he'd seen a tribe of people dancing naked in the snow. In his fever dreams, more likely. 'You – believe there are people on the moon?'

'I know it,' he said softly. 'Women on the moon. Men also, of course, but we understand the population is tilted more towards the females. We have spoken to them at last, after years of trying. They say they will land near here, that it is now not possible to land the craft in the ocean as they would once have done. They do not dare risk their original landing site.'

Camilla nodded. At last he'd said something she could follow from her own experience. She had been to Bristol when she was twenty and her father was still chief here. She didn't think the storms had been so bad then or perhaps that was always the case when you were young. Whatever the reason, no one from their community had made the twelve-mile trek to the coast since before Davin was born. The sea had risen, her father said, and now no one lived in the houses which had once looked on to the water. The worsening storms made it very dangerous to go out in fishing boats, though people still did it. But a community of people on the Moon? She remembered reading and hearing about space programs – the Chinese especially, they had been the ones to reach Mars – but not that anyone was still there.

'Davin,' she said sharply, 'here's a chance for you to prove you really did pay attention in school. Is he raving or did you hear something about this?'

There were only five scientists now among the ninety or so people who called her chief and lived in the cavelike rooms around the hot springs. There wasn't much for them to do except serve as repositories of knowledge and to teach what they could to the few children. The two under sixty made what few journeys were possible outside to study conditions and collect samples of vegetation. Mostly, though, they minded the children.

'There was a group who went to the Moon,' Davin said slowly. 'The Americans put them there and then the Chinese sent people. And the Russians. The Americans went there in 2017 but then stuff happened to them here and they couldn't look after it. One of the other bases, I forget which one, had an accident and I forget what happened to the other one but they had to move in together. Then later China and Russia had biowars so they couldn't look after it either.'

'Stuff happened?' Camilla asked pointedly. 'The Plague Wars are reduced to "stuff happened"?' Davin returned a helpless look; what one of Camilla's own long-ago instructors had once termed a "deer in headlights" expression. 'Never mind. So there was no return? None of those nations brought their people home?'

'No,' said Vlad Woislaw, propping himself up on his side. 'Information is very confused at that time, many records lost when the Internet failed. There was no way to talk to the Moon and none of the nations involved retained the ability to launch a rescue ship.'

'But they must have died?' the Sulis chief persisted. 'That was so long ago and if they didn't have food sent and medical supplies, how could they survive?'

'They did,' Vlad Woislaw said softly. 'We managed to reinstate contact, shortly before we made the journey south.'

'And back to now,' Camilla said. 'Why do they want to come back? I can't even imagine how it will be done but I know – I remember that people are very light on the Moon, aren't they? Wouldn't it hurt to come back here?'

'More than any of us can imagine,' Woislaw said.

A good end line, Camilla thought, turning to check briefly on her son. He was fascinated with what the stranger was saying. None of their storytellers had come up with anything this bizarre in years. A pity for Woislaw that she didn't intend to let him be the star of his own particular tale here. 'Speaking of coming and going to places, you said you came from

Bristol. That was a lie, was it?' She kept her voice casual but saw Davin stiffen. Her son knew, if Woislaw did not, that to lie to the chief was cause to be thrown out of the community.

'No,' said Vlad. He spoke slowly, his eyes seeing something, some time other than this cave-room and two primitives. Her scientists had been apprentices to people who had gone to the great centres of learning, who had practised the skills which now might as well be called magic. 'I was in Bristol for a conference when my country closed its borders. It was supposed to be London but we were told that was unwise.'

'Poland or Russia?'

'I am a citizen of Russia.'

Russia, as its last ambassador had said, answered no more questions. Camilla stood silently, wishing her father, the old chief, were here. He had lived at a time when people truly understood these matters. London had suffered badly from floods in recent years and she doubted anyone would willingly go there for any reason. Bristol wasn't much better off; having experienced floods both from the rising ocean and the Avon bursting its banks. It wasn't a place where specialised experts were allowed to pursue their near-useless occupations. 'What are you a doctor of?'

'Computer science ... and psychiatry.'

'Interesting mix.'

'Anyone who could needed to have more than one skill,' he said. 'At one time I was aiming to join the cosmonaut program itself, before that became impractical. I did work within it, though, counselling those who went to space. That's why I was chosen to be the one who spoke to the Moonbase, when we restored contact. We had a very short time to speak to them.'

'How short? Damn it, just tell me, don't make me keep asking.'

'Four minutes,' Woislaw answered hurriedly.

'What could they say in four minutes?' Davin asked, still happy and excited.

'Not a great deal,' Vlad admitted. 'I had spoken with them before, years ago, and they remembered me when I identified myself. They said their community was in trouble with no support from outside but that they were holding. Then they said they had to return to Earth and would we meet them? They were very frightened.'

'What enemies do they have there?' Camilla demanded.

'It is more fear of what greets them here,' Vlad told her. 'There is very little gravity on the moon, as you said. That means yes, they feel very light, so their bones are brittle – like a bird's. They have lived always in a controlled climate so they have no tolerance for cold as we know it now. They have lived in a tiny group, far smaller than this one, with no diseases. They know to come back may kill them – in a few months, a few years – even if the fall does not.'

'We need more people, that's sure,' Camilla agreed, 'but why do they want to come here?'

'They said they did not want to but that they had to.'

'All right, why do they have to? I warned you about making me ask.'

'I'm sorry,' Woislaw said, rubbing his eyes. 'I am having trouble keeping my thoughts clear. Our link with the Moonbase broke while I was still speaking. The person I spoke to had time only to give me the coordinates of their landing and the date, which is three days from now.'

'Here,' Davin burst out, too excited to wait for him to finish. 'They're going to come down here so we can take them in!'

'I could see that coming,' his mother admitted. She looked at the scientist, the only true scientist of her people, then at her son. She felt almost too tired to think herself. It wasn't that she had been awake for so terribly long but that the thoughts themselves, forcing themselves through unused pathways in her brain, were exhausting her. They needed new blood, strangers with whom to breed and to learn, even if it meant harder work for them all to live. She couldn't refuse to take them in, any more than she could have refused to help Woislaw himself. She could hear her mother saying it and that was strange, for her mother had died while she was still a child. 'It just isn't done, darling. Civilised people don't do that kind of thing.' Now, though, she turned to her son again. If he isn't ready, she thought, it's too bad. I've been chief for twenty-odd years, and I'm getting tired. He has to take this over.

'Davin, you and Dr Woislaw will be in charge of meeting these people from the moon. He will tell you what is needed and you will arrange it with as many folk as you need for the work. Agreed?'

'Yes, Chief,' her son said correctly but he grinned. She swiped at his head.

'Dr Woislaw,' she said quietly, 'I have one final question for you, however?' He waited and she made herself say, 'You have said 'we', that you met with others in Bristol. Where are they?'

'They began the journey with me, Chief.'

'I see. We'll do whatever we can for these moon-folk, Dr Woislaw. I promise you that.'

'Thank you, Chief,' he answered, bowing his head.

The sky-craft was barely visible, a black speck in the gray, overcast morning sky. It should have landed in water, Camilla remembered Woislaw saying. If the moon-folk had been able to bring it down where it was supposed to be, water would have cushioned the fall but no rescue ship could have gone to their aid in the seas as they now were. They had to hope that the huge cushioning drifts of snow would be enough. Davin had thought of trying to build up the snow but Vlad told him there was no way of knowing with any precision where impact would be. Nature would be enough, or not.

Davin had called almost every one of their people outside, from young children to the elders, the scientist cell. They wore every warm item of clothes in Aqua Sulis, Camilla thought. Blankets, pieces of canvas and sacking, half-cured hides. There weren't enough of the wolf and deer-hide clothes the hunters wore, even if they hunted every surviving creature in the countryside.

Vlad, his white hair blown crazily about by the wind, pushed his way over to her. 'They have to move back!' he shouted, pointing to where five or so children, the last born of their group, were pushing forward and staring up at the sky.

'Everyone, with me!' Camilla shouted. She saw Davin run forward, calling to the children and urging them back with him. Good, she thought absently, he's thinking ahead. Davin helped her and Vlad to herd the people further back yet, until they were only just within sight of the supplemented meadow. Their retreat was barely in time. The speck became a rock and then a gray metal craft the ungainly shape of a large bell, swinging insanely from a huge parachute. People were still backing off when the craft fell the final distance with a great rushing thump.

Vlad Woislaw scrambled forward. 'They need to be helped quickly,' he said. 'They will not be able to walk or even stand, though they said they were trying to maintain bone density. They have no tolerance to these temperatures and we must get them inside quickly, down to the hot springs.'

'Yes, you told us. We won't forget,' Camilla assured him. She was normally a bit sharp with those who questioned her memory or abilities but the scientist's face was tense with worry. He reached the capsule moments before she did and was first to reach out a hand when the heavy metal door, steaming with heat, fell down into the snow. A pale face, close to the floor as the capsule was now oriented, appeared and hands weakly pulled. Davin and another boy rushed forward and the other knelt to give Davin a hands-clasp foothold upwards.

'We will get you down,' Vlad called. 'I am Dr Woislaw. I spoke to you on the link. Be patient, we will get you all inside.'

Camilla waved the rest of her people forward. It was numbers they needed now. Another youth climbed up to join Davin, crouching to go through the entrance and lifting the collapsed figure there to pass it down. Hand to hand, the women and men from the moon were passed like helpless babies through the snow and the rising chill of the wind, into the Aqua Sulis lair and down to the last hot water in the world. So it might be.

Night was closing, brought faster by overcast sky and Camilla was intensely relieved when the last of her folk was safe inside and the barrier closed.

Hours later, Camilla went down to the main pool to find out how the Moon-tribe was faring. Some were still in the water, supported by several of her people, to bake the chill and relieve the terrible weight of gravity for a time. Others were in beds around the pool, lying as flat as though they were actually crushed to the ground. Camilla gazed at them and located

Rosanna, who didn't look immediately intent on anyone. 'What can you tell me about them?' she asked. 'Will they live?'

'I believe they will. There are some broken bones. By Lady Minerva, their bones break like matchsticks!' The young doctor lowered her voice. 'There are thirty-two of them. Dr Woislaw was correct about the gender balance. There are twenty one women and eleven men, all between the ages of fourteen and somewhere in the fifties – early sixties? I'm guessing. We haven't had a chance to interview them yet. They can barely talk.'

'Didn't they have any children?' Camilla said, puzzled. 'Or old people?'

Vlad – Dr Woislaw seemed to have gone by the by – appeared, hurrying to her side as best he could through the mass of beds and carers. 'Chief,' he said, 'come here. She wants to talk to you.'

'Who does?'

'The – well, I suppose you might call her the chief of the Moon-tribe. She's over here.' Vlad led the way around two of the pillars which stood about the huge pool to one of the pallets. The woman lying there might have had more colour in her face than the snow outside but it was an near thing. She was broad-faced, her eyes had hints of epicanthic folds and her hair, though very short, was rough and black. Camilla guessed her as among the elders of the group, befitting a chief. 'This is Dr Irina Zhdanova,' Vlad said quietly. 'She is the chief administrator of the Moonbase and also a doctor of physics. I do not know how I should introduce you.'

'I'm Camilla, chief of Sulis, which is this community you're in,' the chief said, feeling unusually shy as Irina's dark eyes examined her. 'We don't use much ceremony. I was going to leave it awhile till you feel better before we do much talking. Winter's coming on and talking is about all you *can* do then ...'

'Who are you?' At first Camilla thought the Moon-woman's wits were wandering, then realised that Davin had come up alongside her and that the woman's gaze was fixed on his face. 'Who is this?'

'My son, Davin. He's fifteen,' Camilla said, a little puzzled by the intensity of Irina's voice. Irina blinked several times and Camilla realised she was trying to get rid of tears. The Moon-woman tried to lift a hand but could not raise her arm enough to wipe her eyes. 'Just rest,' the chief said, alarmed. 'I'll call one of the healers.'

'Nikita,' Irina whispered. With a visible effort, she turned her mind from tears. Camilla could see the effort of will. 'Nikita was my son, Chief of the caves. He was born on the Moon. We always tried to make the children exercise in the heavy-wheel, to keep the strength in their bones. They never wanted to. Why should they put themselves through that pain when they could fly? They couldn't see why we wished it and it hurt them. Only a few of the young ones could come, those whose bones showed sufficient density. Nikita and the rest had to stay behind with the elders. They can never come to Earth.'

Camilla, stricken, bowed her head as though to her own chief. New blood for her clan, she thought. The possibility of enough babies for them to continue, even to grow. New knowledge, with all the skills the Moon-tribe brought with them. Even an opening of the borders, she thought, if knowledge could bring them protection against the bio-plagues and permit exploration once more. All these things, dropped in her lap by chance and a half-frozen stranger finding his way to Sulis. It could be nothing like that for this Irina and her folk, who were more imprisoned than they could ever have been on the airless Moon. There was nothing she could think of, no comfort she could offer this woman.

Camilla had dropped to her knees without thinking of it, so that she could grip Irina's weak hand. The Moon-chief's eyes met hers and they were clear once more. 'No,' she said. 'We would have died there. There were too many for the food-processors and the life-support was struggling. We had to come back. We don't know what it's like here, not really. We have not been able to learn very much – but we have been able to watch and we have seen the cold and the storms. You will need us. On the Moon you know there were once three bases of three nations?'

'Yes,' Camilla said. 'Vlad has told me.'

'Now there are no more nations and all of us are one tribe,' Irina said. 'That is what we will be with you, so that we all survive. Do you understand?' Though she could barely move, her voice had in it the snap of command so that Camilla, managing to smile back at her, wondered which of them would be Chief here when the woman from the moon was on her feet once more. It didn't matter, she knew. She would pass the Chieftainship on to Davin or not but with the coming of these folk and the sacrifice they had made, the survival chance of her people was greater by far.

Davin had listened carefully to his mother and to the Moon-Chief speaking about their two peoples and the need to become one. That was obvious, he thought. Both of them had forgotten about the other thing. So he left the room and found, one by one, all the young people of the community, all those who had grown up beneath the ground in a world of storms. They went to the outer chamber and put on the heavy travelling clothing the hunters wore and then returned to the meadow of snow where a gray metal thing had fallen from the forever dark. It was too heavy for them to move with only their bodies and with ropes. Davin ordered the others to help him cover the craft with branches, with rocks, with whatever earth they could manage to prise from the ground. Anything at all to create a disguising hill over it, to conceal and protect it from human scavengers and even the elders of his own community, who would see only a great deal of useful metal.

Davin didn't know himself why he wanted to protect the ship from the sky so much or what he could ultimately make of it but he and the others successfully buried the thing, working not only that day but many others. When his mother found out what he and the others were doing, she was startled at first and thought to retrieve the craft and have it dragged into the Baths to be broken up.

'You want me to be the chief here some day,' her son answered. 'I want to have the sky-ship when I am chief.'

'It won't ever fly again, you know,' Camilla told him.

'No,' said Davin. 'I don't.'

So Camilla let him hide the sky-craft and keep it. She was the first one to begin calling my father the Sky Chief, as a joke but others joined in and the joke was forgotten. When Davin was older, he married one of the girls from the Moon. They had three children and in time, when one of them became chief of the council, she too took the title of Sky Chief. This, of course, is how I introduced myself to you and you can possibly guess, now, what is the gift which Aqua Sulis has for the King.

*T*here were cries of wonder at the end of the Sky Chief's tale, and a few minutes of fierce debate over the question of humans on the moon. I remained silent, for I wasn't entirely surprised by the Sky Chief's story. I'm sure you recall, milord, the last time the people of Aqua Sulis came bearing gifts: a treasury of scientific and historical knowledge carefully archived and indexed in imperishable nano-crystal slices, and even a pair of still-functional readers to decode them. I believe the university is still transcribing their bounty.

I was not the only one in the car who recognised the name of Aqua Sulis, however. Aside from the Scribbler, who took notes furiously when the Sky-Chief spoke of the Moon People, there was another – a middle-aged man who listened intently, nodding his head and writing carefully in a small notebook. He had done so through all the stories so far, and at last, someone else noticed.

the census-taker's tale

You listen very well,' a man with hair sprouting from his ears said, 'and yet you have nothing to say. What are you writing in that book of yours? Are you a spy, looking for secrets to take to Londonistan?'

The man smiled. 'No, I am not a spy, although I have spoken to three. I am, rather, a Census-Taker.'

There was little uproar in the carriage following this announcement. Most of the other passengers continued with their earlier conversations. One young woman, a neat girl with hair cut short in the fashion of the day, continued to watch him. She was of the innocent breed — the adults who never fully become adults.

'I never met a Census-Taker,' she said. 'I met farmers and builders and once I met a man who worked at the Council.'

'We have over 100,000 council workers by last count. You'll probably meet a few in your day. Especially if you're going to Canterbury.'

A woman with the girl – her mother? – looked him up and down.

'She's not staying in Canterbury, so lift your mind out of the bedroom. She's stopping off to get the train down to Dover. They need seamstresses down in Dover.' The woman sniffed. 'Don't meet many Census-Takers.'

'There are 53 of us working in the country. I can't answer for elsewhere.'

'Elsewhere!' The woman snorted at the thought of such a place.

'Not too many of us are happy elsewhere. I see a lot of that in my work,' the Census-Taker said. 'My name is Romulus Remus Jones. My father read history at Oxford and was sure I would be one of the founders of the new England. He thought the weight of the future rested happily with me.'

The man smiled. Cleared his throat. 'I do a lot more listening than telling. People give me their stories. Even as a child, I always listened. I remember more about my parents' childhood than my own. My mother's first memory is of sitting in her push chair, surrounded by her aunties and uncles. She says her mother put her there on purpose, to keep her quiet. The aunties and uncles were all dead with the plague, and here's this little girl with all the hopes and dreams, sitting amongst them.'

'Are you the only Census-Taker?' the young girl asked.

'He already said.' Her mother slapped her gently.

'Are you married, then?' the young girl asked.

He laughed. 'You think I can count five million people plus ghosts myself? I am no Santa Claus.'

'Have you seen a lot of houses? How other people live?'

'People live in similar ways. You'd be surprised. Bottles are precious everywhere, filled and refilled and filled again. Many houses are built out of rubbish, gaps plugged with more rubbish, glass houses. I went to one home with forty rooms, so many rooms I didn't know where to sit and there was a ghost in every room. This was the home of the Banker. I heard his son's story. The son was the guard at the bank, but he fell asleep, drunk. The money was stolen and the son was hung.'

The man nodded his head at each of the travelers, counting them. He said, 'I was married once, but my wife was not what she was supposed to be. She did not support a head of household. We need rule in the house, while we have no strong rule of law outside. I followed the way of Londonistan; I simply said, 'I divorce you,' three times. I have not married since. I am married to my job, I always say. Can't have a father who's never home. You'll end up with drunkards for children.'

'I know a woman doesn't remember how many husbands she's had,' the girl's mother said.

'Records are lost. Not everyone remembers the spouses.'

The Tingler, whose tale had drawn the women of the carriage to him in horror, said, 'So you'll tell us a story then, Number Man? A story of counting sheep, perhaps.'

The rest of the carriage laughed, but the Census-Taker did not seem bothered by the mockery.

'I am more of a listener than a teller, but I will do my best. I could tell you plenty of stories which have happened to other people; love gone wrong ending in bloodshed, love too strong, love unrequited. Murder and betrayal, lust and magic; these things happened to other people. I am not an investigator. I ask the same questions of everyone. It is the answers which make the difference. I like people who can't read or write because I write their answers. Otherwise I'm not supposed to know.'

'The story I will tell you is a frightening one and I hope it won't upset you too much.'

He was rewarded with a slight opening of lips from the ladies, a shifting in the seats.

'My parents are both what is known as Plague Babies. Babies born during the plague years who never fell sick, but who prospered and flourished. Many who survived those years are thin, unhealthy beings, exhausted from a short walk out for milk and bread. They managed to have children; some of you are that issue- and the children are weakfish, too.

'Not my parents. They grew up pink-cheeked and bouncy, on opposite sides of England.

'The doctors noticed them early on, and the few others like them. Twenty, perhaps, around the country, standing out from their fellows.

'There came a time when somebody, a doctor who studied and read the past, thought perhaps that the blood of these children, taken as a dose, could cure, or at least protect from, the plague.

'So this is how my parents met. Plague Babies brought to Eastbridge Hospital, here in Canterbury.

'My mother still talks about the arrival. They had been taken from what remained of their families and transported by carriage. They were treated well. My mother saw many families along the way, some walking, the children dragged on wheeled carts when they needed to sleep. Others crammed into old carriages, babies hung out the windows on improvised hammocks. It made my mother tired to watch, and she slept a lot on her journey.

'She said she wasn't worried about where she was going. It was an adventure to her, something different. The small village she lived in bored her. The only thing she found interesting were the ghosts which clung to the village like the dags on a sheep.'

The ladies sat forward again. They liked a ghost story.

'My mother could hear the ghosts when the rest of them were deaf and blind to it. She found out about the villagers, especially the ones who would prefer their secrets kept.

'The schoolteacher, an ignorant, angry woman who taught only as much as she knew, which was very little indeed, always stood on her step and screamed at passersby. 'Look at your wife, her body hanging out,' or 'Some learning wouldn't go astray, Mr. Plod.' Yet my mother knew, through the radiant ghost of a baby which crawled the streets crying for her, that the schoolteacher had more than one child and she had drowned them all. These are the things my mother learned from the ghosts in her village.

'Meanwhile, my father grew up on a farm, where three uncles not much older than he ran the cattle in a very efficient way. None of them had book learning, but they were smart in the ways of animals and the sun and were rarely surprised. My father swears there were no ghosts, though my mother says she has seen plenty there. That everyone has secrets.'

' 'Not these men,' my father says. 'They were too busy with their cattle for secrets. Too busy Feeding the Nation.'

'Whenever I heard 'Feeding the Nation' I knew it was time to make myself scarce. A full-blown argument was brewing, wherein they would insult each other's families. Deride each other's knowledge, mock each other's perceived ailments and then move to the next phase; violent love-making. If I was still there at this point one of them would have the presence of mind to thrust a coin at me, tell me to go to the village for a puppet show. Mostly I took the coin for myself before it got to that point. If I was lucky there would be something other than Punch and Judy. If I saw Punch and Judy, I expected to come home and find one of my parents murdered with a rolling pin.

'So my parents from different sides of the country and with different lives, came together at Eastbridge Hospital.'

'I went knocking there one time,' one of the passengers said. 'When I broke my arm falling out of a tree. They said they couldn't do me unless I paid. 900 years they've been there, and they can't fix one measly arm?'

'They were not set up as a medical facility when my parents arrived. It was a home for old, wealthy citizens. And for travellers and pilgrims. It surprises me they turned you away, sir. They have never been known to turn a needy person away. In my opinion that hospital is one of the reasons Canterbury was chosen as the new capital. Its spirit of giving and helping is one we would all do well to adhere to.'

'Well, all I know is they turned me away. I had to go to a local man and my arm's never sat right since.'

It was true; the man's arm sat at an odd angle.

The Census-Taker nodded. 'We all take impressions differently. That's why numbers are important. Numbers are what they are and cannot be argued with. We have this many men, that many women, this many children. That is why I count. To have something to rely on. Why, did you know that of our population, there are....' Here, the Census-Taker drifted into statistics, little realizing that his audience was not interested.

'Tell us about the ghosts,' the young girl interrupted.

'Hear, hear,' the others agreed.

'The twenty Plague Babies, the children, were treated very well. Each had their own room, but they were lonely and often ended up sleeping three or four to a bed. My mother was the only one to see the ghosts and she kept everyone awake repeating the stories they told. Can you imagine? 900 years of the sick and the people who cared for them. There was no end to the stories.

'It was a time of adventure. They had a small amount of schooling, but mostly they were subjected to one medical test and examination after another, until they felt like museum specimens. Apart from that, they were free to explore.'

'I've been to the museum. Smelly, dusty place it is. I wouldn't go there again,' the girl's mother said. 'What's the point in all that history, anyway? Doesn't mean a thing.'

'I agree with you there, Good Lady,' the Census-Taker said, smiling. 'In all my questionnaires, the one about the level of historical education draws the most confusion. What is history, indeed? It is opinion, nothing more. Ask any two people about the fall of London and you will get two different stories. Ask ten and you will get ten stories.

'The tests became more invasive as time went on. There was an air of desperation. This was in 2058, when my mother was five and my father eight. An air of desperation as the plague continued to kill.

'Finally, one morning the children were given a particularly fine breakfast of bacon and eggs and herded into what was once the kitchen. It was vast and still full of the items of the past. Rusting machines, the use of which the children could not imagine. They were gathered in the corner and told, 'We have a very special man coming to see us. Who has heard of Prince Charles?'

There was a clamour in the carriage. 'What year was this again?'

'2058.'

'Fifteen years before he became king, then.'

'Yes. He was just a young man. But with great vision, even then.'

'You say he's got vision? What about the workers? What's he ever done for us?' the Lighterman said.

The Census-Taker shook his head. 'He has done more than you know. He was reading medicine at Oxford at the time. I think they held the school open for him, or near enough. Anyway, he came to the hospital to talk to my parents and their friends. My father never forgot the speech, being old enough to listen. Whereas my mother was more interested in his formal mode of dress and in contemplating what would be for lunch.

' 'Now is the time for sacrifice,' the Prince told them. 'The future of all of England lies in your veins. You are the strong. The fit. You are unaffected by the plague which is slowly but surely destroying us. I ask of you a sacrifice, but this sacrifice will not kill you. And you will be compensated, both with money and with fame. Your names will be known now and forever.''

'What are their names?' the Scribbler said.

The Census-Taker named his parents and some of their friends. The passengers shook their heads.

'You see? History is bunk. The great sacrifices are forgotten.'

'What sacrifice was it?' the young girl asked. 'Did your parents die?'

The passengers spluttered into laughter. 'If they'd died, they couldn't have had him, right?'

The Census-taker smiled gently. 'No, they didn't die, though three of their friends did through miscalculation. Are any of you old enough to remember the medicine taking of 2060?'

An older gentleman nodded.

'That serum, given to every man, woman and child of Great Britain, was made from the blood of the Plague Babies. It is because of my parents, their blood, and King Charles V, that we're here today at all. She still makes me my lozenges, Mum does, with drops of her blood, to suck on. Keep me healthy.'

'The plague simply died out. Everyone knows that. You're no hero for that,' the Lighterman said.

'Not me, no. But my parents and the other children spent five years in that hospital, giving their blood to the cause. They were not unhappy; any cache of toys or books found were allocated to them, over and above the Royal family. They got used to a rich diet, unlike anything we know. And the doctors worked to use the inoculation. There is still a stock somewhere, of the blood. Kept underground, I believe, somewhere in Scotland, where the ice rarely melts.'

A sunburnt man cleared his throat, waited to be heard. Later, we learned he was a doctor from Australia. 'It's true,' he said. 'I went there. They gave me a sample to confirm–' He paused for a moment, his eyes narrowed. 'To study. I'm going to Canterbury to make a presentation before the Royal Society.'

The Census-taker waited politely for him to finish before continuing.

'My parents and their friends thrived and grew. My mother in particular was never bored. She had the other children, but she also had the ghosts, who told her all kinds of wondrous things. She tried to teach the others how to see the ghosts and, after five years passed and they were sent back to their ordinary lives of struggle, some of them could indeed discern movement. They could not hear the voices though.

'My parents and the other children disliked being back at home. They felt displaced, as if the world had shifted slightly while they were in the sky-high world of Eastbridge Hospital and their feet had landed in an unfamiliar place. Things were the same; in fact life had gone on without them quite well. They were different, but not in a good way. People walked around with their inoculation scars, little realising it was my parent's blood which had saved them. My parents didn't really realise this themselves until later when they read together at Oxford.

'For yes, they did meet again, as young adults. The others fared both well and ill; some went to an early death (though none through the plague) and others turned to a life of crime, seeking the riches they had known as children. The Prince made sure they were looked after, but it was not enough. My parents both accepted their lives in a way which meant they would change it at the first opportunity.

'They kept in contact through long, increasingly personal letters. One of their members (she is a writer for the newspapers, has been since they started up again. King Charles is not always pleased with what she has to say, but that is by the by) built them a newsletter, a very private sheet only ever seen by the Plague Babies. In this way those capable amongst them plotted to meet up at Oxford, where they would learn enough to save the world. Rule the world. Change the world. Again.'

'Who are these people?' demanded the mother. 'More names. You say they changed the world yet we know nothing of them.' She gave the Census-

Taker a hard look and seemed to decide he might be good material after all. 'You should sit up straight. Strong men don't slump.'

He shrugged his shoulders back. 'I always carry forms with me. They're heavy.' He gave them more names, of a writer, an architect, a historian, people whose names were in the newspaper. He unrolled a roti with curry and was looked on with suspicion by the others. 'It's tasty and handy food. It doesn't mean I am Indian.'

'None of us care what you eat, mate. It's the fact you're eating. Dead people out there. Ghosts in here. Most of us couldn't manage it,' the Lighterman said.

The Census-Taker ate his roti.

'My parents were quieter in their achievements. And, before too long passed, they gave birth to me. Well, my mother did. She said that around the birthing bed clustered women who had died in childbirth. They didn't want to see her die. *Shift this way, now that*, they told her. They knew the best way to get a baby out. I was fine, they knew. Strong and healthy, ready to claw my way out. *Slow him down*, they told my mother. *Not too fast.*

'I was one of 40 babies born in England that day. I can give you the statistics on the others. The Plague Babies expect great things of their own children. Hard work, no illness, no foolish thoughts. My parents expected great things of me. They taught me to respect difference and risk. They expected me to be perfect, a great creator. I am neither of those things. I believe in a complete count, and that my numbers matter, but I don't believe I am the one they think I am. They even opened me up to see if I would be a priest.' Here, he lifted his shirt to show his belly; a jagged scar, angry and red, across the front. 'Priests have a small, hard stone in their stomach, to remind them to think of God at all times. I've known men to swallow a stone in order to be chosen as a priest.

'My mother became a faith healer. She sucks up the poison in a person's soul. She always smells awful. Oh, the stink of her after a day at work. She comes home, dusty, dirty, wanting to squeeze me tight to help her forget about death and disease. But I can't stand the sour-sweet smell of her.

'I tell you this so you will understand how very accepting I was when I entered the village of Beddington and found everyone dead.

'There are some who say that people like me, children of Plague Babies, attract death. Or can sense death in large numbers.'

The Lighterman said, 'You people, people like you, you got everything.'

'If I have everything it is because my parents gave everything. Don't you understand that?' He took a lozenge from a small bag and sucked on it.

'From the start, my mother was determined to teach me to see ghosts. She said that ghosts took advantage of the ignorant, that they stole thoughts away and memories, too. It's happening to my father. Most days he knows where his hat is, but others he'll spend an hour searching and there it is on his head all along.'

'That happens to all people as they get old,' the older gentleman said.

'Not my mother. She snarls at those ghosts if they come reaching for her. She thought she had failed in her lessons because for a long time I couldn't see what sat right in front of my face. I could hear them, though, small voices telling me if someone was lying or not. It was only once I started work I could see them. If people left out information, the ghosts would laugh. They like liars. They like people who leave information out of their census answers which would help the country. That makes me very unhappy.'

Here he stared at the narrator of the Dead Priest's tale who had, perhaps, embellished.

'I have been working as a Census-Taker since I left school fifteen years ago. In that time I have spoken to people of many walks of life. I have seen fresh-born babies and noted their birth defects. I have watched people say goodbye to their loved ones as the priest calls last rites. These things bring ghosts, chattering creatures who fill me with their own important nonsense. My awareness grew stronger, to my mother's delight. The ghosts began to appear as a shimmering apparition then, as I learned to focus, as formed humans, albeit unstable ones. They sit with us now, in this carriage.'

The young, slow girl squealed in horror and leapt to her feet. 'Where? Where do they sit?'

'There, there and there. They are raggedy creatures and bloody. Victims, I would say, of the terrible storm which has caused our delay. And you,' he said to the mother, 'You have a radiant boy by your side, watching over you. We only see radiant boys who have been killed by their mothers.'

'I never,' she whispered.

'You act as though this was ordinary,' the older gentleman said.

'It is to me. I'm not telling the story very well if you don't understand that. Seeing and hearing these things was ordinary in my household. You know that some evolution seems damaging to the creature, but it takes that creature forward. Hyenas give birth through a pseudo penis. Peacocks' tails, nightingales' songs, goldfinches' plumage; all this attracts the mate, but the predator as well. I think ghosts are evolving like that. They are damaging themselves, but evolving. Most ghosts will stay at home, except for the men who like the travel, looking for a host body. They move further from home, seeking purchase, but they weaken as they do so. You can tell them by their foot fall. Heavy, slow steps. They might be body-less, but they have the weight of the world on their shoulders.'

There came the sudden noise of a door soon after and there was panic in the cabin. 'He wants to take my body,' the young girl screamed. So she had understood that much. But it was an old woman walking to the lavatory.

'I had been asked to take the census on the road from Canterbury to Brighton, taking in Ashford, Rye, Hastings...' This time he did notice the bored shuffling. 'Some of the villages I stopped at had no numbers recorded there for 30 years. Partly this was due to the isolation of the countryside in this direction; it was three days journey to get there from the nearest major road and I needed to take my own supplies. There were no shops along the way. Not even a roadside stall. There was barely a roadside. Lack of travel meant the cowslips and grass had grown, the rocks and pebbles washed over by the rain were not cleared, the pot holes were not filled. More than once I felt despair. I pulled a small cart behind my bicycle with few comforts in it, and I peddled hard to get to my destination. I believe the future of Great Britain belongs in the counting, and that the first civilised nation to account for its people will be the one to hold sway over the rest.

'After close to four days travel and thousands of questions, a great downpour forced me to shelter for close to eight hours inside a derelict cow shed. I would guess the abandonment occurred during the heat wave of 2078, because there were old newspapers lining the windows dated around this time. People tried to keep the heat out in such ways but these cows died like so many of them at the time. There was bone here; nothing but. Well, nothing until evening fell and with the storm still raging outside, I settled in for the night.

'As I warmed some beans over a Bunsen flame and sorted through my forms to ensure none were damp, I heard a whispering in the corner.

'One of the things we learn before we go on the road is how to defend ourselves, but from a sitting position this was not easy. Still, I shifted carefully, as if I were preparing for sleep, in order to catch a glimpse of who I was up against.

'The glow told me it was nothing alive. Ghosts can affect you at a spiritual and emotional level, if you let your guard down, but not at a physical level, so I stood up cautiously.

'These boys were very, very clear. I assumed they had died in the shed along with the cattle, because the closer the place of death, the clearer the apparition. Your boy,' the Census-Taker said to the mother, 'is very blurry, so I would say he died a long way from here.'

The mother began to cry quietly. Her daughter didn't seem to fathom what was happening, and no one chose to tell her about her dead brother.

'The radiant boys crouched in the corner over a small piles of coins, playing some simple game. They were not yet aware of my presence. Like all children, they were too thoroughly absorbed in themselves to be observant, but I didn't want them to discover me as I slept, so I walked over to them.

'Radiant children rarely speak. I think it is because they do not want to talk about their mothers. There is great shame and sorrow in such a death; I think by not speaking they avoid the subject.

' 'I am the Census-Taker,' I said. 'I would like to record your details for the files.'

'Using sign language, and fingers, and pointing, we filled out a form for their barn as place of residence. I was cold, but they were not. Ghosts don't feel the cold. When I asked them if this was their place of birth, they flapped their hands about, shook their heads until I produced a map of the region.

'They pointed to a small village some ten kilometres from our position.

On the map it was dominated by an Anglican Church. My map was quite a new one, but I knew it had not been updated in these regions for many years. The church could well be long gone and the road impassable.

'My final question on the Census for the dead is cause of death. One I hear often is the loss of sanity. The inability to feed oneself. The loss of desire to survive. The lack of intent to work.

'No one admits to suicide in the family. It is considered the worst sin after infanticide. I know the suicides, though. They have a reddish glow, and they smell of wet dog. They wander, causing havoc. Sucking the will to live from others.

'The children didn't want to answer this question, but as we communicated, their stomachs glowed blue and I checked 'poisoning.'

'I knew that a visit to their village could well lead to my loss of employment. My supervisor frowns on sidetracks, prefers us to stick to the job at hand. He doesn't understand how many sidetracks there are. He moves from his neat, clean home in Canterbury to his neat, large office in Canterbury, wearing a sheltering hat and barely noticing the world passing him by. He knows how many steps take him from place to place and he knows, according to the figures, how many people should cross his path. But he doesn't care to look any of them in the face.

'It seemed important to me to count this village. I would not be back this way again; my route was a circuitous one, moving up past Croydon on my return to Canterbury. Yet here was a whole brood of boys, killed by their mothers away from home. I needed to know their number.

'So in the morning I orientated myself and, trying to avoid the thickest puddles of mud, I set off on my detour.

'As I approached the village, just on lunchtime, I heard a low hum. I rode into the village mud-spattered and hair awry. I must have looked quite a sight.

'I called out as I walked, wary to be a stranger in a place which hadn't seen such a thing in a long time. I heard women's voices, no men's. This is not uncommon. Whole villages, sometimes, all the men gone. Those women are old, though, old widows. These voices sounded younger.

'The voices of young mothers.

'I found them clustered around the communal cooking pot. I called again and didn't realise until I was close that they glowed. Every one of the six women glowed.'

He stopped and closed his eyes. 'Go on,' the mother said. 'Tell us about the ghosts.'

'I admit to being shocked to find them all dead. The radiant boys hadn't warned me about this. Perhaps they didn't realise. It was not surprising to find the women around the cooking pot, though. Ghosts like to be in the place they were happiest, most cohesive. I wished my mother was with me, to help me speak to them, take their count. But she had taught me well.

'I took out my forms and began to ask my questions. One woman spoke loudly enough for me to hear her. The rest had so much shame they couldn't speak.'

The Dead Son's Mother's Tale

'Our boys were once beautiful boys. Good to their sisters. Kind to their mothers. The only trouble was boy trouble. Mud fights, cow pushing, blindfold races. We laughed at such trouble.

'But then the heat came, and dried up the wells. Dried our skin, our eyes, dried the cow's milk, the river, dried the life's blood. Oh, the heat. We couldn't understand where such a thing came from until the day we saw the boys, six of them, hanging their arms over the pig sty. Dried mud and straw, that's all that was in there. But the boys (and who was it who saw it again? Was it your Laura? Or your Sarah?) reached in, and, with their fingertips, set the straw alight. It spread to the fence and before we knew it, the whole thing was ash.

'Word got out about the boys. Others saw them transforming into fire-breathing monsters who burned all they touched. Our policeman burned that way, and the school. When they started to burn the babies in their pushchairs, it was time to do something terrible.

'We shake to think of it. We don't want to remember.

'How did they convince us? They held our babies up to us. Showed us the future. They said, *Your sons have the envy. They know that the girls are important, that they are far less so. Their envy transforms them into monsters. They are not your sons once this happens. They will never be your sons again.*

So we lured our boys to the barn. We told them there was a party with cakes and treats and games. We gave them poison in sweet, cold drinks. We ran faster than when we were children. We wanted to be gone before they realised what we had done. It was all we could do, to put out the fire.

'One month later the church burned down with everyone in it. Every last one of us. It was Palm Sunday, you know, and no one misses church that day.

'Some of us think the boys came back to destroy us, that the fire-breathing monsters did it. But we know, don't we? About the organist and her foul smoking. She'd hide beneath the floorboards, where the priest hid for safety in those times, and she'd smoke her filthy cigarettes. Burnt the church down. You've never heard such a terrible thing as your own child burning to death. The boys died easy, compared.'

The Census-Taker shook his head. He told the passengers, 'Those boys did not die easy. I didn't tell the mothers that. But they died in agony. That's all they remember of being alive.

I noted cause of death in the village as insanity brought on by the heat, the weather. This is not the only place this happened. I think villages lost sense like that all over the country. The children are often the first to go.'

'So what did you do? What will you do?' the older gentleman asked.

'I will enter my census forms. I will account for each and every village left. I will note ages and I will note cause of death. I will add "abandoned" for the domicile question.'

'Did none survive?'

'None in this village. I can't speak for the other places.'

The Census-Taker took a sip of water without offering any around.

'So that is my tale,' he said.

'English people don't treat each other that way. It must have been the Indians. Or the Pakis. It was the Chinese. The Bangladeshis. They're like that.'

'When it comes to survival, we are no different to anyone else.'

There was silence in the carriage. Outside, the night was no darker than before. The young girl took his hand.

'Anyone going to the Empire Games? I would if it wasn't in Birmingham. That place is a fucken hole,' the Lighterman said, and they spoke of sport, and competition, and tried not to think about villages of dead children around the countryside.

*A*fter the Census-Taker stopped talking, a white-haired man with an armband of curiously braided leather shook his head, and spoke. 'I don't know about your glowing children and what-not,' he said. 'Seems to me ghosts are something a touch more complex than that.'

The Census-Taker said nothing, went on eating his supper. All eyes now turned to the white-haired man. He raised his arm to show off his bracelet. 'See that? That's a genuine Dysart Eightfold Polyflexure. I learned to make that knot off a master. Maybe the last true master. I call myself a Knot-man, it's true, but I'm nothing to him. He it was taught me all my trade, and he showed me a thing or two about ghosts, I can tell you. Yes, and he told me a tale, once – a tale of the terrible Aberdeen Hulks and the dead things there. It's many a ghost I've seen for myself since then, but it's his story I'll give you now. A story to remember him by.'

The mathematician's tale

The Knot Man sat by the seaside, working a strip of leather in his arthritic hands. The balloon animals he'd once knotted on the promenade of this empty town had been far easier. But there wasn't much call for balloon animals any more.

As he worked, the Knot Man watched the stranger out of the corner of his eye. The stranger stood a few metres away, silently watching as the Knot Man flexed and looped the leather.

Finally, the stranger said, 'You'd be the Knot Man, then?'

The Knot Man held up the braided leather. It seemed the best reply he could offer.

'Aye, you're weren't easy to find, you know,' the stranger said. 'Well, putting it simply, the reason I'm standing out here in the cold is that I need your help.'

'You want a balloon animal?' the Knot Man murmured. 'I used to make them out here for the children.'

'Have you heard of the Aberdeen Hulks?' the man said, and something different entered his voice – a tremor?

Then the Knot Man remembered what lay in Aberdeen, and a cold vice grasped his heart. 'Aye. I recall.'

Aberdeen: the granite city. He'd passed through on his way to Orkney, long ago. The Hulks had been at anchor, their bellies fat and red against the grey North Sea. Outwardly, they had still resembled oil tankers, but inside they'd been stripped and vivisected, the huge oil reservoirs re-tooled into prison cells.

The Knot Man had seen the Hulks before the Great Ocean Current died and the pack ice came crawling down from the pole. Before the jailors abandoned their posts and left the prisoners to starvation or hypothermia. Before the rusty tankers holed and sank.

'I was a jailor, back in the day,' the traveller said. A confession. Few jailors admitted their past.

'Criminals were easier to come by than oil in those last days,' the Knot Man replied. 'Bad times, though I can't say they've gotten much better. I knew a man who died aboard one of those hulks.' The Knot Man didn't speak it like an accusation. It was a fact, nothing more.

'I'm sorry.'

'He doesn't deserve your sorrow.'

'I'm sorry all the same. For all of them.'

Everyone, whether right or wrong, seemed to carry a regret these days. Hard times did that. The Knot Man toyed at his pocket lining, twisted a tiny double hitch from a loose thread. As he finished it, his fingers brushed the ribbon that was nestled in a fold of the lining. A fat, bloated knot grew from the ribbon's centre, the fabric worn smooth with handling. It was both a final insult and a parting challenge: a signature Gordian thrown down before him on a work bench, many years ago. The Knot Man had long since given up trying to break it. He would have been better off hurling it into the sea, but something always stopped him. He was stubborn that way. Not prideful, mind. Just stubborn.

'What is it you want?' the Knot Man asked. He looked behind him. The Jailer was a stocky man and dressed entirely in grey. A woollen scarf coiled around his throat and chin, and his brow crouched towards its sanctuary like a hiding fugitive. Dark circles engulfed his eyes. He was a man burning the candle at both ends and running out of wick.

'The Siesta Grande – my old ship – is surfacing. Her smoke stacks are only a foot beneath the ice.'

The Knot Man felt a hollow sensation in his belly. The ribbon brushed his fingers. The Siesta Grande: his apprentice's ship.

'Surfacing?' the Knot Man said.

'Aye. With all hands on deck, if you know what I mean.' The Jailor shook his head. 'I hear them screaming in my dreams – the spirits, the dead men beneath the ice. Lately, I hear those screams even when I'm awake.'

The Knot Man tried envisioning his apprentice screaming – and found it impossible. His apprentice had made others scream.

'Why do you suppose I care, friend?'

The Jailer shuffled his feet with the heavy clops of a trotting horse, as if not sure how to continue. Then he pushed back his shoulders, and said, 'I need help to untie the ghosts from the ship. I need to make the screaming stop.'

So many people had died, trampled by war, famine, pestilence ... it was hard to care. The Knot Man didn't miss the rapists, murderers and thieves in their rusty, water locked tomb; he only missed the children. Arthritis or not, the magic of the Craft had died with the children. What did he owe a ship of dead criminals?

'My help, eh?'

'An astral umbilical fuses each of them to the world of the living. It can't be cut with any blade. There's only one way to sever it.'

'So, you need a Knot Master to break the umbilical's root knot.' The Knot Man jammed his hands hard against the insides of his pockets, felt his coat draw around his back as tightly as a bandage. He pushed his apprentice's ribbon down into the furthest reaches of the lining. 'Friend, untying the knots connecting the dead to the living is difficult – and dangerous.'

'That's why I need a Master.'

'So go to Canterbury, seek out Lois Mistral. Bane Farrell. The Rizzard twins.'

The Jailor shook his head. 'You are the last of the Masters. The only one still living.'

The Knot Man bowed his head. So it was true. Time had caught up with them all. He felt the ages whispering in his ears like rough sand.

'Surely there were apprentices?'

'There are only charlatans and pretenders in Canterbury. You are the only Master left in the length and breadth of the Kingdom.'

They had been too greedy, guarded their secrets too tightly. Now the Craft was dead. They had all been fools.

The Jailor said, 'You were the best. So I've been told.'

'I've heard too much flattery in my time. I even believed some of it. But I'm just a man. An old man.' He held out his hands for the Jailor to see: thick, muscled hands, grooved with lines like deep fissures. The knuckles and joints were swollen like plums.

'Aren't we all,' the Jailor said, 'just men?'

At that the Knot Man smiled. He missed repartee. The path of a man with great passion was singular and lonely, but he was old now, and age had tempered his lust for passions, both great and not so great.

The Jailor's expression became serious again. 'As a child, I used to watch you for hours.' He waved a hand at the crumbling promenade. 'Out here, you were a magician. We needed magic back then, and this was where we came to find it. Those children who lived are men now, but we still remember with the hearts of children.'

'Aye, I was good in those days.'

'You are still good,' the Jailor said.

'You want to drag an old man, then, into the Northern Wastes to heal your wounded sense of justice? Why, pray tell, should I go?'

'Adventure. A true odyssey.'

The Knot Man laughed. 'An odyssey. Aye, do I look like a Greek hero to you?'

'There is also your apprentice to consider.'

'My apprentice.' The word tasted foul. A good word made wrong.

'He will stalk the ice floes for eternity, trapping unwary travellers ...

unless someone frees him.'

The Knot Man kept silent.

'I have dogs, a sled, provisions,' the Jailor said. 'We can leave at your convenience.'

'My convenience!' the Knot Man said, and laughed anew.

The dogs led the way into the Northern Wastes, grinning like a pack of fools. The Knot Man watched the lead dog hustle between tricky outcroppings, around deadfalls, and along narrow hunting trails. In the beginning the Knot Man rarely interrupted the Jailor, who seemed at peace with the wind in his face and the sled skipping and whistling on the frozen earth. The Knot Man's thoughts started drifting to speculation on possible variations of the hitches fixing the tug lines to the harnesses. Late on the first day, the Jailor noticed him studying the traces, and remarked, 'It must be a fine thing to discover your calling.'

The Knot Man rubbed his lumpish hands together, winced, and said, 'Yes, but losing it is not so fine.' The Jailor seemed puzzled, but then the lead dog foundered in a wire fence hidden by bracken, and the Jailor swore and pulled his knife out amidst a chorus of howls.

The days grew longer as they progressed north, but the sun had no strength. It was a bauble, a false charm against the encircling cold.

The dogs ate better than them. They needed the strength to pull the sled. Nomadic tribes fed their old and infirm to the dogs, the Knot Man recalled. Comparing his worth against a pack of animals would have been unthinkable, once. But pride had been the first vanity to slink away when the arthritis claimed him.

He wrapped his hands carefully. He warmed them by the oil stove when they camped. Nightly, he did his exercises and hid the pain. Afterwards, if the Jailor was interested, he showed him a trick or two. The Jailor's hands were deft, but he was clumsy with the mathematics. Mathematics was the grist, the very foundation, of Knot Craft. Topography, integers, primes, polynomials – a piece of string could hold them all and more. Back in Cornwall, a booty of salvaged mathematical texts filled the Knot Man's safe house, although now, in the Northern Wastes, he started wondering why. His last apprentice was dead; the Craft was dead. Maybe he would sell the books when he returned.

But to who?

Boundaries had shifted, and he was lost. He now took solace in the Jailor's company, where once he would have scorned it. They passed a hipflask between them in the evenings and watched the Northern lights, while in the day they stood side by side above the runners as snow blanketed moors, empty stone cottages, and deserted civic centres rolled by.

A week in, they camped near an frozen brook with a huge Ferris wheel mired in it like a dunked biscuit. Neither of them could fathom how it had landed there.

That night, the Knot Man taught the Jailor about the Anti-Knot.

'If a knot and its anti-knot meet, they cancel each other out. That is the definition of an anti-knot. Therefore, a line with an anti-knot and a knot appears the same as a line with no knots at all.' To illustrate, he used a stick to draw a straight line in the snow.

The Jailor squinted as if his eyesight were bad, but said nothing.

'Now the knot energy of a line is zero. But a knot and its counterpart anti-knot must have a knot energy greater than zero. The theory of anti-knots is thereby proven false.'

'Why do knots so intrigue you?' the Jailor said, and scrubbed out the line the Knot Man had scratched. 'Aren't they only screwed up patterns on bits of string? They make my head hurt.'

'Are you the same person as when you were eight?' the Knot man said.

'Of course.'

'Are you the same man, then?'

'But I wasn't a man at eight.'

The Knot Man tapped the scraped area where the equation had been, his point made. 'Every cell in your body is replaced within weeks. You excrete the old material, you swallow the new. It is simply the pattern which remains the same, and even that is imperfect – we all age and decay. But in a tightly wound knot, a proper knot, the pattern and the material are inseparable. You cannot remove and then replace one strand of a knot. You can not touch-up a knot as you can a painting. You cannot replace the pieces one by one like the stones in a cathedral. In a knot, unlike in us, there is truth.'

The Jailor shook his head and regarded the Knot Man with a wry grin. 'Show me that anti-knot thing again. If I had not heard otherwise, I would take you for a madman.'

'Every Master is a madman,' the Knot Man replied, and drew his stick back through the snow.

Atop a steep crest, the Jailor whistled a piercing note and the lead dog swung his head back and stopped. The swing dogs followed, then the team dogs, and finally the wheel dogs, who shuttled along just before the curving runners.

A sparkling ice field unfurled below. Pressure ridges scored the middle distance, demarking the impact zone between the shore ice and the thicker pack ice. Inland, rose toppling white ziggurats, the remnants of Aberdeen's apartment blocks.

A score of days had passed since the night by the Ferris wheel. The Knot Man felt every one of them in his bones. Both he and the Jailor were swaddled in thermal undershirts and layers of woollens. Polarized goggles shielded their eyes from the glare.

The Jailor took a small device from his pocket and stared intently at its face. He rotated in a circle until a tinny oriental voice gabbled out the device's speaker.

'We're here,' the Jailor said. 'Put your ice-boots on. The ice is too thin to risk the sled.'

The Knot man flexed his fingers. They felt swollen and painful.

'You ready?' the Jailor asked.

The Knot Man nodded. It was a long way back if he wasn't.

They struck out east, cleats gouging at the ice, the Jailor in the lead. The Knot Man looked back and saw the dogs watching, their eyes plaintive. Blue eyes ... the eyes of newborn babes.

Fifty metres from the sled, oriental squawking brought the Jailor to a halt. He stared at his device. 'We're above the Barbarosa. She's sunk deep, though.' He tilted his head to the right. 'A little ways over there – see where the ice has been pushed up into a miniature glacial horn. That is where the Siesta Grande is rising.'

The Knot Man squinted, and through his goggles noted the wavering light, the play of shimmers along the horn's sides. The lights had vague human outlines: ghosts; apparitions; the dead.

He followed the jailor across a network of fissures and cracks, which fashioned the terrain into a motley quilt with the horn as the centre design. When they reached the horn's base, the Jailor tilted back his head. The Knot Man followed his gaze, and at the apex spied a red streak – the up thrust smokestack of the Siesta Grande. Most of the ship was imprisoned, a mummified shadow within a cocoon of frozen seawater. The ship was canted, the stern angled up, the prow still somewhere below the ice field. The angle was gentle enough, though, that the smoke stack remained the tanker's highest point.

The horn was crawling with ghosts. They coated the ship like tiny turrets of icing on a wedding cake. Their astral umbilicals trailed through the ice, down into the tanker's rusted holds and bulwarks, where their corpse's old bones lay fused to the steel.

The Jailor's lips locked tight, his breath puffed from his nostrils in white blasts.

'I'll start now, while the sun is up,' the Knot Man said.

'Thank you,' the Jailor replied. The dark circles under his eyes seemed paler. He no longer glared over the top of his scarf like a fugitive, but towered above it like a man at a lectern. The Knot Man didn't share his optimism: the Jailor's faith was surely misplaced.

The Knot Man started forwards, the Jailor in tow. He met the first ghost, a weeping woman, at the horn's base. She skimmed towards him until her umbilical pulled taut and jerked her to a standstill. She reminded the Knot Man of dry tobacco smoke.

Three bites of his metal cleats, *snap, snap, snap,* ate the distance between them. The umbilical sprouted from her sternum, a near-ephemeral rope, but a rope all the same, and the Knot Man bent close and prepared his hands. Mathematics unfolded for him. He broke the knot's spine with a hyperbolic algorithm and a matrix containing all her frailties, wrongs and regrets. Subtler techniques popped the knot's guts loose; then he squeezed hard and applied the final twist.

Pain blasted his fingers, but they did not falter. The knot flowered open. He raised his head in time to catch the ghost's smile, and for a moment things felt right. Something in the air flexed beyond the normal senses, and the ghost shot skyward like a reversing moonbeam.

'She's gone,' the Knot Man said. He waggled his sore fingers and feigned a grin.

The Knot Man and the Jailor made a slow, spiral ascent.

They scaled the horn with only cleats, the ice having splintered into gently angled planes riddled with footholds. For the most part it was akin to following a winding staircase. Fading sunlight painted the ice red; the ziggurats became broken teeth in a bloody mouth. The Knot Man moved between the ghosts, and one by one they gave up their connection to the world and flickered out of being.

The first anomaly, the first real hurdle, appeared in a cleft between two sloping ice walls. The ghost was ordinary, but the knot in its chest was not. The knot was diabolical. The Knot Man recognized his apprentice's hand, his crafty preference for false trails and deliberate chaos. Even the dead had become his puppets and playthings.

The knot took a full ten minutes to break. Afterwards, the Knot Man rested a spell, then continued on. Closer to the summit, the ghosts became stranger, the knots even harder.

'These are not the ghosts of the men I left behind,' the Jailor said, aghast. Before them wafted a stick figure with backwards facing legs and a face sculpted into a horse-like wedge. It whinnied and then uttered a pitiful sobbing noise.

'Our DNA, our genes, are similar to knots on pieces of string,' the Knot Man said. 'The mathematics are transferable. My apprentice wasn't just a prisoner, was he?'

The Jailor looked to the setting sun. 'No.'

'Ah, let me guess. There was a laboratory, secret handshakes, the laudable pursuit of cures for Bird 'Flu and the Grey Plague. It appears my apprentice continued on with that good work after you left.'

The Jailor pulled his scarf up higher. The frayed tip flicked in the wind like a raccoon's tail.

'This isn't about bad dreams, is it?' the Knot Man said.

Again: 'No.'

'Ah, you are scared of the prospectors and their mediums. You are scared they will try to mine this vein of astral wealth for memories of the golden age. You don't want to be known as a monster, an accomplice to this.'

The Jailor nodded.

'No man wants to be known as a monster,' the Knot Man said. His throat felt thick as he spoke. He swallowed, coughed, and said, 'Did you ever blame me for teaching my apprentice his craft?'

The Jailor shook his head.

The Knot Man exhaled a long, slow breath. 'Forget your guilt. The man who taught him all he knew is standing next to you, and while you might not blame him, plenty of others do.' He jabbed the Jailor in the back with his index finger and approached the horse creature. 'We're both making amends, I think.'

Amends ... as if he could ever make amends.

The Knot Man's apprentice had been a murderer. He had knitted men's fingers together like wool; he had made balloon animals from live human intestines, animals which moved in lifelike parodies as faecal matter squirmed through them and their owner's cried or screamed; he had strangled unborn foetus's with their own umbilicals, using nothing but gentle manipulations of their mother's bellies. Insanity. Utter insanity.

The worst stories were the ones about the children – those tales had stolen the last of the joy from his heart. Even before the world went bad, his apprentice had snatched the children away from him, had turned the Craft into an obscenity that brought them pain instead of joy.

The horse creature bucked as the Knot Man's fingers slipped on the knot. Chill breath washed the Knot Man's cheeks. He tried again, teased the knot open.

Sweat bled down his skull. Aches sparked from his fingertips to his shoulders. Where was his apprentice: the traitor; the blasphemer. The Knot Man looked up, and knew. The summit. Where else?

'I am going to the top,' he told the Jailor.

The Jailor fixed him with a heavy stare. 'You think he is there?'

'Aye.'

'I'm coming.'

The Knot Man shrugged, and clambered up the slope, cleats digging at the ice. The Jailor surveyed the terrain ahead, crossed himself, and followed.

The higher they climbed, the more deformed the ghosts became. Near the summit, the ghosts huddled together like dandelion seeds. When he could not go around them, the Knot Man went through them, steeling himself as he plunged through shapes that resembled chewed gristle but had the eyes of men.

His stomach sickened. Why should I do this? he thought. But the Jailor had been right: there was no one else to do it. When the arthritis ruined his hands and stole the true Craft from the world, his apprentice's legacy would be all that remained. Unless he intervened, this blighted place would be his legacy, too.

The ziggurats now lay completely in shadow. As the sun set, the ghosts brightened, their light washing over the horn, reflecting off rills and angular slabs, letting the Knot Man find his way without need of a torch or lantern. Close behind, the Jailor's rasping boot steps kept pace.

The Jailor was a good man, but naive. He'd sought redemption, had nurtured that dream for many years, but now that the penultimate moment had arrived he knew redemption was beyond him. Dread upon dread piled up, sorrow rocked him against her breast. He suckled weakly at sorrow's teat and cried frozen tears. Up ahead, the Knot Man seemed to have grown in stature; he no longer had to walk through the ghosts, they moved aside in deference. The Jailor struggled to keep up.

Red paint marked the Knot Man's goal: the Siesta Grande's smoke stack. Silence met him. Nothing sounded except the Jailor's trailing boot steps, and a moment later they ended as the Jailor came alongside.

'Where is he?' the Jailor said.

The Knot Man studied the peak. 'He's a crafty bastard. Always was.'

'But where?'

The Knot Man looked down at the tanker's smokestack boring into the horn's depths. 'Knock on the smokestack. My hands aren't up to that right now.'

A frown crossed the Jailor's face, but he thumped his gloved hand on the exposed metal. Dull booms echoed into the ice. 'The other night, you remember telling me all Masters were mad. I'm beginning to be sorry I didn't believe you.'

'You're the one doing the knocking,' the Knot Man said, and grinned. His lips cracked open. They were too dry to bleed.

The smokestack suddenly reverberated with a hollow clangor, as if something was drawing itself up the pipe. The Knot Man stripped off his gloves and flexed his fingers.

The clangs got louder and louder. Vibrations strummed the Knot Man's feet through his cleated boots.

Claws snatched at the stack's rim, and a blot of smoky darkness heaved over the lip. Death had not been kind to his apprentice. The thing little resembled a man's ghost. Arms and legs sprouted at random, and spines extruded from its swollen torso.

The Apprentice's umbilical, which snaked back into the stack, began to shiver like an earthworm on a griddle. The stack boomed as if an army were pounding from within. A second ghost, dark as squid ink, boiled out. The ghost settled down onto the ice and lazily stretched out arms that were impossibly long and impossibly thick. Clouds of dark vapour steamed off its thick back, and its great stanchion of a head broke into a smile.

'Bubba Moray,' the Jailor whispered. 'One of the worst from solitary.'

The Apprentice and this ghost were different from the others, and not just in hue. Death should have stripped away their higher functions, but the Apprentice had clearly tinkered with their deaths, found a way to bind their darker natures to the mundane world. Insane, but a genius.

'I've waited a long time,' the Apprentice said. His voice was thin, like a man with cancer in his throat. 'And you've grown old.'

'Avoiding death does that,' the Knot Man replied. He thought about the children. He thought about betrayal. He thought about all the misery, and how it might have been avoided if only he'd looked at this man's heart, rather than his talent, all those years ago. He thought again about the children, who had smiled and laughed as he twisted balloon animals on the promenade.

The Apprentice cocked his head. Plumes of black smoke spiralled out his downwards ear. 'You're here to destroy me?'

'Yes.'

The Knot Man tried to decipher the knotted umbilical; Torus tubes and Gordian analogues twisted up and down its length. The mathematics felt like pressurized gas behind the Knot Man's eyes. A twinge of doubt struck him. Then he saw the Apprentice's root knot, and he felt weak. He pulled the ribbon from his pocket and held it up. The knot he'd never come close to breaking, the knot tossed to him as a challenge years and years before, was there before him in the Apprentice's chest.

'What is that?' the Jailor asked.

'A challenge,' the Knot Man said, and left it at that.

The Knot Man turned from the Jailor just as Bubba Moray sprang. So quick! – the Knot Man barely saw it coming. Bubba Moray's cold hands plunged into the Knot Man's chest, grasping for his soul. Caught off guard, the Knot Man staggered back, ice chips spitting between his boot heels. Bubba tried to sever the Knot Man's soul using brute strength alone. Great bulges of phantasmal muscle rippled up the ghost's arms, and instantly the Knot Man felt the horrid pulling at his inner being. A blistering seam of agony shot down his middle. Quickly, he hardened his centre using an Origami double fold, and stitched the ripping of his soul with lightning speed. His fingers screamed with pain. His small joints felt as if they would fly apart like the pistons of an over-revved machine.

Bubba Moray rotated his head to stare at the Jailor. 'Remember me?' he said. 'Well, I remember you. I'll eat your soul. I'll swallow you in tiny bites and chew your faith, your love, your hope, chew it all like tasty bonemeal.'

The Jailor gave a hideous scream and threw a flurry of punches at Bubba Moray. His fists went right through Bubba; the Jailor might as well have been trying to punch a hole in a waterfall. Bubba laughed, and the sound was colder than all the ice in the North Sea.

But in that brief moment of laughter and distraction, the Knot Man made his move. In the beat between stitches, he seized Bubba Moray's umbilical in the bight – the loop between the fixed ends – and wove a variance of the Hangman's Noose. He slipped it over Bubba Moray's neck and snapped it shut. The noose yanked Bubba's head back around. His hold on the Knot Man's soul weakened.

The Knot Man gripped Bubba's umbilical at the root and traced the knot outline with his fingertips. Bubba roared. The stench of black oil and dead meat roiled out his mouth. The knot was his apprentice's work, and it was a near impregnable Gordian. But the Knot Man was a true Master: he had read the secret text of Abalakov, the Russian cipher, had done tutelage at the Black Institute under Yosef Mandelstam, the lunatic Jew, had plied the North Sea oil fields with salt-veined fishermen who lived and died by the strength of their hitches. A lifetime of study would not betray him now.

The two of them locked together like wrestlers in a clinch. And then the Knot Man pried free the key, a fantastical list of polynomials, and twisted it in the lock. Bubba's knot cracked open. 'At least hell is warm,' he said in Bubba's ear as he pulled the strands of the umbilical apart. Bubba began to dissolve. His body broke into streaming black chunks, which seemed to fold in on themselves over and over. He howled once, but it was a faraway sound, as if from the bottom of a deep pit. A moment later, Bubba Moray was gone.

The Apprentice leaned forward and sneered. 'I expected you to finish him quicker, old man.'

'Perhaps age has simply made me patient.'

'You should have heard the children scream, old man. It was far sweeter than hearing them laugh. So much talent, and what did you do? Balloon animals by the sea.'

'What have you done, dead man?' the Knot Man replied. 'What have you achieved?'

The banter was over; the Apprentice stalked forward.

The Jailor shivered beside the Knot Man. He looked ready to plunge off the horn and take his chances with the fall.

'The Anti-knot,' the Knot Man said softly.

'What do you mean?' the Jailor asked. He tottered like a drunk. His legs shook so badly he was almost dancing.

'The opposite of death is life. If the Anti-Knot is shaped from life, and the target knot is conjured from death itself, then their knot energy can sum to zero. There is a way, friend. A way to end this. A loophole in the idea that the Anti-knot is impossible. But my apprentice's umbilical is dangerously fragmented. It is rife with stopper knots and hidden traps. I see several Claw Knots that will capsize under tension into snares. And I need a way to package the Anti-Knot then deliver it. I don't know what to use. I just don't know.'

The Apprentice took another long step forwards. 'Still holding my ribbon, old man?' he said. 'You've been playing with it, I see. Too hard for you? Too much for your old hands?'

The Knot Man looked at the ribbon, the intricacies of which he'd studied for years. With an anti-knot, he could open it. He was suddenly sure of it. The Apprentice had allowed him decades of preparation. Such stupid arrogance. He tossed the fluttering ribbon off the edge of the horn, took great pleasure in watching it spiral into the dark. But still, he had no package for the anti-knot, no living rope with which to deliver it.

'The opposite of death is life. That's the loophole. But I don't know what to use,' he said.

The Jailor pulled his scarf down, squeezed the coils down into a flat hoop. 'I do.' He turned up to the starry sky, as if searching one last time for salvation.

'What do you mean?' the Knot Man asked.

The apprentice circled, draining the light from the ice. The distance was closing. The Knot Man's hands felt as stiff as solid bone. The arthritis burned.

'This is what I mean,' The Jailor said, and he drew out his knife. The blade was matte-black, showed no reflection. It was a shard fallen from the space between the stars. 'You'll have your Anti-Knot.'

With that, he pulled up his woollens and stabbed deep into his pale belly. The Jailor jerked the blade downwards, worked the handle with both hands. He kept cutting until his hot guts flopped from his abdomen. Then he fell to his knees. Steam from the purplish mass rose as high as the Knot Man's eyes. Blood melted into the ice, formed a crimson slurry.

'Do it quickly. While I am still live,' the Jailor gasped. His face was white, and a trickle of blood snaked down his chin.

The Jailor had proved his mettle in the end. No one could say he shirked his duty, whether or not he left those men to die those many years ago. The Knot Man felt a terrible ache in his heart; the simple faith of the Jailor's gesture moved him terribly. If only he'd taught his truest lessons to men such as this. But there was no time for regret.

The Apprentice scuttled back towards the stack. The Knot Man snatched up the Jailor's guts and pounced, fingers calling the mathematics of the Anti-Knot into being. The Jailor had pried his hands deep into cracks in the ice, his grip fastening him down as his guts reeled out.

The Knot Man attacked the Apprentice's umbilical a few metres out from the bulbous chest. He finished the last twists of the anti-knot and wedded the intestine to the dark umbilical. The Apprentice slashed at him, smoke-like contrails floating behind his strikes. But the Knot Man was out of range; it was over. The Knot Man gripped the intestine and pulled.

And his knuckles seized up – the cold, the damn cold! He tried again, ignoring the Apprentice, who was now moving towards the juncture of the umbilical and intestine. Giving up meant death, so he tried again with everything he had, spurred on by memories of crying families and hatred and a knotted ribbon thrown contemptuously before him; but his knuckles no longer wanted any part of this revenge. The Anti-knot didn't close ... and the Apprentice grasped the juncture point.

They stood eye to eye, the Knot Man and his Apprentice. The Knot Man lowered his eyes. He had failed.

Hot steam boiled off the Jailor's length of gut. Blood pattered onto the ice at the Knot Man's feet. Then, curiously, the intestine quivered. Before the Knot Man's eyes, the Anti-knot clenched, crawling forwards in a boil of tightening loops and whorls. The Anti-knot left the Jailor's living rope and segued into the umbilical.

There was a moment of absolute stillness after the Anti-knot connected with its mirror twin, and then the umbilical began to unravel. Strands of black substance slipped free; the umbilical popped from its anchorage like a snapping whip. The Apprentice stared, horrified, and then he started to lose cohesion, like a flow of hot tar. Melting arms clutched for the Knot Man, but they dissolved before reaching him.

'I'll be waiting for you,' the Apprentice said, his face collapsing into a flow of sludge.

'No you won't,' the Knot Man said. 'You're nothing. Not even the memory of a memory.'

Seconds later, only a few black splotches on the ice remained.

The Knot Man turned and followed the limp intestine back to the Jailor, who sat with both hands grasped around his guts.

'You looked like you needed help,' the Jailor said. 'It hurt like nothing else pulling that knot closed. But worth it. A show worth dying for.'

'Yes.'

The Knot Man tried to remember some biblical prayer that would fit the moment. Nothing came to mind, and in the end he simply squatted next to the Jailor and held his hand.

'Can I die now?' the Jailor said, his teeth chattering.

'No,' the Knot Man replied, and gave him a grim smile. He struggled to find the right words. He had spent so long by himself. Any words, especially the right words, did not come easily. 'You are my best apprentice.'

'I would laugh, but it hurts,' the Jailor said. 'Forgive me for saying so, but the only other contender appears to have just died for the second time. Besides, the mathematics was always beyond me.'

'What I meant was ...' Again, the Knot Man searched for the words. It was hard, but a man could only try. '... Knot Craft is about the truth, remember. I said before that in a knot, unlike in us, there is truth. I was wrong. A man's heart, his courage, is the knot that ties everything else together. It is the truth. Not the mathematics or the science. They are fallible. They can be stripped away. They are not the truth.'

'You are mad,' the Jailor said. His breath caught, he arched his back, and then he simply blew out the warm air and did not breathe again.

The Knot Man gently freed the Jailor's ghost. Afterwards, he sat there until the cold worked its way through his woollens into his old hips, and he feared getting up would be impossible. Down the length of the slope the tanker's ghosts cried out for him. Finally, the Knot Man lifted his goggles, dried the crusted tears from his cheeks, and readied his hands.

Outside, the rain came down heavier, in roaring sheets. The Lighterman shivered, and moved a little closer to the stove. As the silence stretched on, I thought perhaps the cold and the dark and the rain had stolen away the last of the bonhomie, that perhaps the stories were at an end for the night. And then, in the back of a booth, someone stirred.

He leaned forward, and the lamplight made deep, dark slashes of the lines in his face. He was a white man, but tanned dark as leather, a lifetime of harsh sun burned into his skin. His eyes were bright, and his teeth were strong and white as he smiled.

'Ghosts and plagues,' he said, his rough, strangely accented voice low and strong. 'Well, there's been plenty of both, or so I hear. Can't say I've seen any ghosts for myself, but I know plagues all right. And I know a story too, if anyone wants it. It's got no ghosts nor plagues, but it's got a dead man that was living, and a living girl that was dead, and when it's done I think you'll agree that sometimes, a sickness is the best thing that can happen.'

He sat back again, and the shadows ate up his face. A murmur went round the car, and then someone maybe the Census-taker spoke up. 'Say on! We've nothing better to do, after all.'

The old man chuckled. 'If that's your want,' he said. 'Hear me now ...'

the doctor's tale

I t was hard to drive in the waning afternoon light.I've been a doctor since I left the army in '85. I'm good at my job. I know which medicines will cure and which will kill in the wrong circumstances, and I recognise a canker when I see one.

My trade meant I never starved. Even in the dark days, there were plenty of people willing to barter for my skills. When the government reformed, so did the Australian Medical Association, and I was asked to visit some of the militias around the countryside. Many townships had not seen a doctor in fifteen years.

It takes five days of hard driving to get to Yukinbool fief. The roads were bad. It was tough out there. It still is. Hot as a barbeque, and roads that have degenerated through disuse into corrugated, muddy tracks choked with weeds. Running my beat-up Hybrid Landrover cost my new employers more than my salary.

The border was marked with the usual rusted coils of barbed wire and hand painted signs warning trespassers to stay away. It didn't concern me: most militia territories have similar warnings even now. Holdovers from the dark days, when the bush folk banded together to try to fend off the starving hordes escaping the cities.

A lanky lad in home-made trews, leaning against the stripped frame of a rusting tractor, flagged me down. Slung over his shoulder was a newish-looking automatic rifle; a gift from the new government.

The red dust billowed as I slowed to a halt. It streaked my window as I wound it down.

'You the Doc?' he asked.

'I am. I'm meant to meet with somebody called 'Ripley''

'Yeah, boss Ripley's 'spectin ya.'

'Do you want a lift?'

'That's mighty kind of you, doc.'

I unlocked the passenger side, and he clambered in.

'I'm Claude by the way.' He looked around. 'This is a bloody nice ve-hi-cle.'

'Thanks' I said warily. Some of the fiefs hadn't seen a working vehicle for twenty years. A couple had already tried to commandeer mine.

'Yeah, Ripley says we're getting a couple. I wouldn't mind having a bit of a spin.'

Over my dead body. 'Maybe. So what's it like in Yukinbool?'

'It's fucking grouse. I thought it was going to be shit, but mate, some of the pussy Ripley gets up at his place is un-fucking-believable.'

I looked around at the badlands, and back at Claude, burnt and grimy looking. Unbelievable was putting it mildly, but I didn't pay it too much mind. The world is full of Claudes who think that the most interesting thing possible is their own inflated sexual exploits.

Claude drawled on. 'The school marm? Man, she taught me a thing or two I can you. Ripley said she was fully into long dividing of the legs if ya know what I mean?' He nudged me with a greasy arm.

I grunted non-commitally.

'Then there was this other chick. Gagging for it. Me and the boys, we took her every which way.'

The conversation continued in this vein for about a half hour. By this stage, I was pretty sure reality was a place Claude visited rarely. Either that or I would need a lot more STD medication than I had. I was relieved when we pulled up to a large homestead skirted by wide verandahs.

Chained dogs barked as I slowed. Claude droned on: '... that's when Ripley says give Bonzo a go. Man he was into it I can tell you, he's a horny bastard that Bonzo, and she was moaning and screaming ... Here we are.'

I stepped out of the car, thankful for an end to Claude's pornographic anecdotes. The dogs were big, more rottweiler than kelpie. They bayed and choked themselves against their chains as they tried to jump at me. A group of armed men dressed in khakis and flannelette lounged on the verandah. They looked like wild dogs themselves. One man, slightly graying with a weather beaten and craggy face, stood and casually walked towards us, oblivious to the baying dogs.

Ripley, I guessed – the alpha male. He leaned against the sill of the open driver side window.

'I got the doc, Ripley!' Claude flashed a big grin.

Ripley nodded.

'Hi.' I held out my hand.

Ripley reached slowly into the car and pulled the keys out of the ignition. 'Glad you could come.' He didn't smile.

My stomach turned. I tried to stay calm. 'Any reason you're taking my keys?'

Ripley shrugged. 'I just want to be sure we get a full week for our coin.' He opened the driver's side door, and climbed in next to Claude, leaving me standing outside as he started the engine. 'Get in.'

I was scared and angry – I make no pretense I wasn't – but war and famine had put me in worse situations. I paused only briefly before I climbed into the back. I would roll with it and see where it took me. Three more men piled in beside me. They stank of stale sweat, cannabis and moonshine. Ripley gunned the motor, and we roared out of the station house.

I found myself staring at an ugly dark mole on the back of Ripley's neck. 'How many people will I be treating?' I asked.

'Township is about fifty odd, with another hundred or so stretched out across the countryside.'

'Plus the coons,' piped up Claude. 'There's about fifty of them.'

Ripley grunted dismissively. 'You'll be staying with Virgil Cummings, our publican. He says he knows you.'

I'd known Virgil for years. We were in the army during the resource wars, up north in the mining country. 'Yeah,' I said. 'Virgil's a good bloke.'

Claude grinned at me. 'His daughter's starting to look a bit of alright too, I can tell you.'

I did a bit of mental arithmetic. Ginny would be barely fifteen. 'Isn't she a bit young?'

He winked at me, 'Yeah, well you know what they say, doncha? "Old enough to bleed, old enough to breed"'. He laughed at his own wit.

It was only forty minutes into the town, but each kilometer seemed like a gulf, an endless chasm between civilization and me. Twilight had deepened into night by the time we reached the outskirts of Yukinbool. It wasn't really fit to be called a town. A few dilapidated buildings clustered around an old two-story brick hotel, like lepers crowded around Jesus.

I struggled out, after Ripley's men. A small cluster of people gathered on the grayed timbers of the verandah. A stranger in town was obviously a rare occurrence. I forced myself to show more cheer than I felt, looking up at those drawn faces. 'Hello!' I greeted them.

They were a sorry lot. A grimy child hid behind his equally filthy mother. I could read the story of years of disease in those faces. Here scurvy, there malnutrition, over there tuberculosis. By the smell of the street, sanitation was a rare luxury. I would have to boil my water to guard against cholera.

One face stood out in the crowd: Virgil, my friend. He smiled wanly and raised the stump of his left arm in greeting. He didn't look well. He glanced at Ripley with a haunted expression as I clasped his good hand. 'Virgil, how are you?'

'Doc, good to see you. I knew they wouldn't eat you in the city.'

'No chance., I'm too old and stringy.'

'Doc!' A girl called out to me, as she pushed out from behind Virgil. His daughter: they had the same eyes.

'Is that Ginny? Last time I saw you, you were just a baby.' I held her at arm's length. 'Now look at you!'

She was pretty, no doubt. Her shoulder length red hair was pulled back into a tight pony tail, and freckles scattered across her face. She still had the gangly awkwardness of a teenager, but I could see that she was on the verge of becoming a beautiful young woman.

She flushed and cast a glance at Ripley's men, who were staring at her like a pack of hungry dogs. 'Did Dad tell you? I'm going to be a doctor, like you!'

'Really?' A note of surprise must have crept into my voice as I looked at Virgil, because he smiled.

'She's been working hard for when you got here. It's the only thing she's been talking about for months. She's been reading 'Gray's Anatomy'. I don't know where she got her brains from, but it sure wasn't me.'

She looked flustered by his praise and hung her head. 'I haven't memorised it all, yet. Just the bones. I keep forgetting some of the Myology names.'

'Enough crap, girly.' A rough voice from beside me: Ripley.

Ginny looked at him and quieted immediately. She was frightened of Ripley; not scared and wary, like me, but truly terrified of him. He pushed in front of me and addressed the people who had gathered. 'This is the Doc, sent by the new government in Sydney. He's going to be here for a week, staying with Virgil. Try to be nice to him. Claude – Help the doc get his stuff inside.'

He stepped down from his makeshift podium, ignoring the murmurs of the crowd. I wasn't sure where stealing my car fit into the whole 'be nice' scheme, but I didn't say anything. Once again I caught myself looking at the ugly mole on the back of his neck.

Claude dutifully carried my equipment into the old kitchen that was to be my surgery. A woolen blanket lay over a wooden table. A grimy skylight would provide illumination during the day, but now a number of canola oil lamps set shadows flickering across the floor.

'That's fine.' I dismissed Claude. 'Just leave it there,. I'll set it up.'

Claude nodded, 'Sure thing Doc.' I winced as he dumped the bags and made a beeline for the taproom.

From one of my oilskin bags I unfurled a roll of plastic sheeting and gently placed it over the blanket. I wouldn't trust Claude to take it out – good, clean plastic is expensive, after all.

'Can I help?' A quiet voice from the corner – Ginny.

'Of course,' I replied, pointing at my black medical bag. It had been outdated for a hundred years, but it was a talisman to me. Somehow owning it made me a doctor more than any amount of degrees in the world. 'If you open the middle pocket, you'll find a number of implements. Find an empty space and lay them out so I can sterilise them. Be careful. Some of them are sharp.'

She carried the bag across the room and placed it on an empty bench. It was a little heavy for her small frame, but it seemed natural for her to carry it.

'Do you know what these are?' I asked her.

She named them as she carefully laid them out: 'Scalpels. Scissors. Suture needles. Swabbing. Tincture of iodine.'

'Do you know what the iodine is for?'

'It's for cleaning a wound or for cleaning the skin before you operate. It sterilises, killing the germs.' She pulled a face. 'It also stains everything brown.'

I nodded. 'You've been taught well.' I was amazed anybody was even literate out here. 'Did your father teach you all of that?'

She looked at me, and for a second I caught a glimpse of the terror I had seen when she had looked at Ripley. She shook her head, and bent to her task. 'Ether mask. Umm.' She held up an unmarked bottle.

'Ether. It's for rendering a patient unconscious during surgery. So who taught you?' I asked.

'Miss Summers.'

'She's done a good job. Is she in town?'

'No.' She wouldn't meet my eye.

'Oh.' There was more to the tale, but I didn't want to pry. 'Do you know how to sterilise the instruments?'

'No, but I guess you must either boil them, or use disinfectant, or heat them in a flame.'

'I usually boil them and then dip them in disinfectant to make doubly sure. Do any of these burners work?' I pointed at the old stove by the side of the room. It was rusted and gunky, a relic of a time when natural gas flowed to every town. The chances weren't good, but I had seen a few rigged up with biogas from livestock dung.

'No, but I could get you some boiling water from the kitchen if you want.'

'This isn't the kitchen?'

'We have a woodstove out back.'

'That would be useful. I have a small oil burner I can use to keep it boiling, but it's best if it starts hot.'

'Is she being useful?' Virgil appeared in the doorway, smiling at us both.

'She's a wonder, a real credit to her teacher.' I smiled back.

It was the wrong thing to say. Virgil's smile vanished, replaced by the haunted look I had seen on his face when I first arrived with Ripley.

Ginny glanced at him, and said, 'I'll get the water.' She hurried out of the room.

Virgil and I faced each other in silence. When I was a soldier, I stared death in the face more times than I can count, and most of those times Virgil was in the foxhole next to me. I'd never seen him like this. He looked worse than scared. He looked ... desperate, like a trapped animal. He walked over to the instruments Ginny had laid out, and picked up a scalpel, turning it about so it caught the light. He seemed to be addressing it, rather than me. 'Doc, how long have we known each other?'

'Ever since the battle of Kakadu.'

He looked me in the eye. 'Doc, I need a favour. I need it real bad.'

I nodded 'What?'

'I want you to take Ginny with you when you leave. Train her, let her help you, take her back to the city to get a real education.'

I didn't want to refuse him, but I had to be sure he knew what he was asking. 'Look, Virgil, I don't know mate. I've been out on the road for months now; I'm not due back in the city for another few months, and even then the cities are far from safe. This is pretty dangerous stuff, you know. Most of the fiefdoms can get pretty dicey. It's no place for a girl.'

'Please Doc.' His voice shook. 'She can't stay here. They'll ...' He choked and stopped.

'It's Ripley isn't it?' People are like cells: it only takes one to go bad. I recognised a canker when I saw one.

'He's not right, Doc. Not right at all. His father was a good bloke. He kept us all ok when everything was going to shit. But Ripley? He thinks he owns us. Now he makes laws up as he goes. No one can enter and no one can leave, unless Ripley lets them. He shot Hal Tucker a year ago for trying to go. Called him a traitor. Then there was Betty Summers.' He shuddered.

'What happened to Betty Summers? I asked quietly.

'She tried to stop him. Called a town meeting, asked us to petition Sydney to remove him. This was just after the government named him their representative. He took her back to his homestead, said she had broken sedition laws and would be jailed. She ... She died out there.'

'They raped her to death.' Ginny was at the doorway, carrying the water. Virgil looked mortified, but didn't stop her. 'I heard that bastard talking about it with his toadies. They took turns. They knocked out her teeth so she couldn't bite them. They chained her up outside and beat her and raped her until she died of exposure and blood loss.'

Claude's story. I felt sick.

'Take Ginny with you, don't wait. Go now' Virgil pleaded. 'Ripley's men; none of them are better than animals. I'm afraid ...' He looked at Ginny.

Old enough to bleed ...

I shook my head. 'Ripley's taken the keys to my car.'

Virgil sagged. 'Please, there has to be a way. If anything happens to me ...'

'I'd rather die than go with Ripley.' Ginny said in a low voice.

I relented. What else could I do? 'I'll try to take her with me when I go next week, but it will be dangerous.'

Hope spread across Virgil's face, pushing back the fear a little.

'In the meantime,' I went on, 'I could use her help in here. It will keep her out of the way, and I can show her what needs to be done.'

'Thank you! You won't regret it. You'll see.' Ginny hugged me. Virgil smiled.

Ginny was as good as her word. She stitched cuts and lanced boils. She was cheerful and easy with the patients. She always managed to say the right thing to calm people, and she had steady hands during surgery. In short, she was a natural.

Four days passed in quick succession. We had three tooth extractions, an amputation of a gangrenous leg, and a litany of infections and stomach upsets. We were cleaning up after the last patient on the fourth day when we were interrupted by shouts shouting coming from the tap- room. I turned to see Virgil burst in.

'Dad, what's wrong?' Ginny asked.

He stared at her with wide eyes. 'I..I..' He leaned on a bench where I had my instruments laid out. He was stammering, out of sorts. 'I hit one of Ripley's men. He was saying ...' He glanced at Ginny. I don't think that he wanted to repeat what they said. 'I just saw red, and hit him.'

I frowned. 'Is he okay?' I asked.

They looked at me in disbelief. 'Ripley hung Paul Roberts when he hit Tommy Peters.'

'Calm down' I told them. 'No one is going to hang anyone.'

The door creaked open behind me. Ripley entered the room with a low growl, head low, like a feral pig. 'I don't think it's your call, Doc.'

Claude and two more of Ripley's thugs followed hung on his heels, lethal looking rifles slung low and ready. The four of them reeked of moonshine. One of Ripley's ugly dogs slinked in behind them and flopped onto the freshly disinfected tile floor.

I tried to keep my voice level. 'Listen,' I told him, 'I'm sure all of this is just a misunderstanding. Why don't we all just go home and have a think about it?'

'There is no misunderstanding, Doc. Virgil has committed a crime, and now he is going to have to face justice.'

'And what about Ginny?' I asked.

Claude sniggered.

' She'll come to stay with me and the boys. She's going to be a ward of the state,' said Ripley.

'I don't think that's appropriate.'

'I don't think your opinion was requested Doc. You do your job, and I'll do mine.'

Ginny looked desperately between me and her father and the guns.

Virgil was crying. 'I'm sorry, Ginny, I'm sorry.'

I had my eye on Ripley. I never saw Virgil palm the scalpel from the tray beside him. All I saw was the flash of the blade as he plunged it into Ginny's belly.

'No Virgil!' I cried, but it was too late. She fell back, a look of shock on her face as blood poured from between her fingers. Even Ripley was shocked. I grabbed Ginny and eased her to the floor.

'I need one of those bandages from the table' I yelled. Nobody responded. Everybody stood around, stunned. The dog started nuzzling around Ginny's face. Virgil was still crying.

I swore. My old muscles strained as I picked her up and onto the table. I grabbed at a swab beside me, and tried to staunch the bleeding. Ginny moaned.

'You.' I pointed a blood-stained finger at Ripley. 'This is an operating theatre. Get all of your people out of here.'

He stared at me for a second, unused to orders. Then he nodded to his men, and they led Virgil out.

'And Ripley?' He turned to look at me. 'If you kill him in cold blood then you'll regret it. We've got a lot of mates in the army, him and me.' He looked at me strangely, and nodded. The dog sniffed at my shoes. 'And get that bloody dog out of here!'

Ripley sneered, and turned away. 'Bonzo! Heel,' he grunted. Bonzo scurried to his master's feet and Ripley let the door slam behind him.

... He's a horny bastard, that Bonzo.

I shuddered, and turned back to Ginny, gasping on the table. What would I be saving her for?

I scrabbled for the ether mask and the bottle, jammed the mask against her face. Forcing my hands to be still, to temper the flow, I dripped the ether onto the mask. 'Count backwards from ten' I told her.

'Let ... me ... die.' She whispered.

I grunted and ignored her. A long time ago I swore an oath. I would do my best.

'I ... don't ... want ...' She trailed off.

The cut was deep – it went all the way to the abdominal cavity. I didn't have the right equipment for that is kind of surgery. It would be touch and go.

Perhaps knowing her likely fate slowed my hand. Perhaps I didn't move as surely as once I would have on the battlefield. In my time I've saved men from bullet wounds and land mines. I'll tell you this: some of the most horrific wounds in the world can be survived if the patient has the will to live, and the best surgeon in the world may not save a patient without it.

Maybe it would be for the best if she died ...

Afterwards, I stood back from her tiny body, lying half-naked on the table. Then with a sigh, I scrubbed my hands and walked back out to the tap room. Ripley and his thugs were still there, smoking, laughing and carrying on as if nothing had happened. There was no sign of Virgil. The room fell silent as I walked in.

'She's dead.' I said simply.

Ripley pushed past me, into the surgery. I walked in behind him. He regarded her still and bloody form for a long moment, then he reached out with a hard hairy hand, and twisted her nipple roughly.

I grabbed his hand and peeled it back, so we stood face to face. I was half a head taller than him, and older or not, I definitely had more weight.

'What the hell is wrong with you?' I hissed.

He looked at me with dead eyes, then turned and walked out.

Head bowed, I started to gather my instruments. For just a moment, I paused to look at her, iodine and scissors in hand. 'I'm sorry.'

My last two days in Yukinbool passed slowly. Without Ginny and Virgil, the town seemed near-enough dead. One of Ripley's thugs delivered my car on the last day. It was battered – they had obviously taken in a few joy rides in it – but it still worked. I loaded it myself, with the help of 'Jimmy', one of Virgil's aboriginal stable boys.

Finally, Jimmy and I climbed aboard, and lumbered out of Yukinbool. I didn't bother stopping at Ripley's station. Claude flagged us down at the gate.

'Well, Doc, it's been a heck of a week hasn't it?'

'It has.' I said tightly.

'So are you coming back for the trial?'

'The trial?'

'Yeah, we're going to have a trial. A proper one, with a magistrate and everything coming in from the city. Ripley reckons now he's the governor, it's how things should be done.'

It made sense – he could use the trial to cement his position in the community. 'Yeah. I'll be back.'

Claude's brow furrowed. 'Who's in the back?'

'It's Jimmy, Virgil's stable boy. I needed someone to help me carry my stuff and he offered.'

Claude frowned. 'He's a bit yella isn't he?'

'He's got a bit of hepatitis.'

Claude drew back. 'Heh, feel free to keep him. One less coon in Yukinbool's got to be a good thing.'

I nodded. 'Well, see you later.'

'Bye doc.' He waved me on.

I drove off, wiping the sweat from my hands onto my jeans. 'Is that stuff bothering you?' I asked.

'The iodine? How long will it take to come off?' The voice was light, and soft.

'A few days. It might take your hair longer to grow back'

'Will Dad be okay?'

'I hope so. We'll talk to the magistrate. You mightn't be able to see him until Ripley is gone.'

'How long will that be?'

I thought about it. 'A year at the outside, judging by the melanoma on the back of his neck. Probably a lot less.'

'I thought so too.' Ginny said. 'I mightn't be much of a doctor yet, but I know a canker when I see one.'

*A*dead man living,' said the nun in her rough voice. 'But not for long.'
'And a living girl dead,' added the Lighterman. 'Like you said.'
The doctor nodded slowly. 'I had to try. For Virgil. For both of them. A man desperate enough to try and kill his own daughter ... I had to try, at least.'

'Brave girl,' said a dour man, with empty eyes. 'Brave man.' A mutter of voices gave assent, but the dour man seemed not to hear them. 'Lose a child: that's bad enough. But to seek the life of any child ... almost beyond imagining. I can't think what it would take ...' His eyes filled with tears then, and he dashed them away with the back of his hand.

'I'll tell you a story, then,' he said. 'About losing children, and revenge ...'

The Hunter's Tale

'm from a village called Auchindoun. My grandfather was one of the original settlers there, back during the Northern Troubles. Nine families settled themselves around an abandoned castle and hid the best they could. The years have come and gone, and we've faced more than our share of hardship, but despite the setbacks, the harsh winters and the constant threats of disease, Auchindoun has somehow managed to hold on.

This last winter was hard. A fever took two of the families from us, plus one or two children on the side. Food was hard to come by. We made sacrifices.

I did my best to help – I am a hunter, like my father and grandfather before me. Each day I went into the forest in search of deer or goats. Whatever I could find. For the last ten years I have used the same bow. My father used to use a rifle, but when the supply of bullets dried up we rediscovered the old ways. Now the rifle hangs useless above my fire.

It was winter that brought the wolf close to the village, I suppose. I was out hunting in the woods south of the castle – it's usually the best place to find deer, coming down to drink from the stream.

Kneeling in the undergrowth, well hidden from the stream, I had plenty of room to draw my bow. It's difficult work, crouched in wait among the cold and the snow, waiting for the perfect moment to loose an arrow on an unsuspecting animal.

I remember a deer had come, a young stag. Slowly I pulled back on the bowstring while it leaned down to drink. I breathed slowly but surely, calming myself, waiting for the moment to strike.

The stag bolted.

At first I couldn't work out what had happened. I was *certain* it didn't know I was there. Besides, it ran right past me, too panicked to notice me behind the branches of the undergrowth.

Then I saw it, in the trees behind where the stag had been drinking. A wolf, grey-haired and massive, staring calmly at me with brown-yellow eyes.

Walking back to the village, I thought long on the wolf. They aren't the aggressive creatures of the stories. They usually run at the sight of humans, but this one had stood its ground. It had stared at me for what felt like an age, neither of us willing to break our gaze.

In the end it was the wolf that turned and wandered off into the forest. It looked so certain of itself. It didn't run. It had no fear of me at all.

My grandfather used to talk about the wolves. They were native to the Scottish Highlands, but as the farmers took more and more land for grazing the wolves had fewer places to go. The last one they ever saw was in 1743, and it was shot for killing two children – or so they said at the time.

Sometime early last century they brought the wolves back. The old European Union had this idea of restoring indigenous species where they could, and the Scottish wolf was at the top of their list. Grandpa said nobody here wanted the wolves back, but the EU wouldn't be stopped. A reserve was set up. There wouldn't be a problem, they said. The fences would keep the wolves at bay, they said. Scientists would monitor their breeding.

I suppose those scientists didn't anticipate the Troubles. They didn't expect to be killed in the purges and the Plagues and the fall of Edinburgh. Freed, the highland wolves slowly grew in number until they became part of our stories once again.

I ate supper with my daughter that night. She was six years old, and the only family left to me in the world. Mary – that's her name – asked me if I had seen anything interesting in my day. I told her about the wolf.

'I don't like wolves,' she said, stirring her stew half-heartedly. Her poppet, a hand-stitched thing she named Sally, perched on a pile of old books in the chair next to her. It was the usual arrangement. Sally even had her own bowl, though it was empty.

'Leave them alone and they will leave you alone,' I told her. 'There's nothing to fear from a wild animal as long as you keep your distance.'

'You don't keep *your* distance,' she said, and I frowned.

'I carry a bow, and a knife. Little girls don't carry knives, so they should keep their distance.'

'Joanne McCann has a knife. She showed me last Sunday.'

I sighed. Perhaps I needed to talk with Joanne's parents. 'I don't mind what Joanne McCann may have – *you* don't have a knife, and *you* are going to keep your distance and never stray from the village. Understood?'

She nodded. The rest of the meal was eaten in silence.

'I've noticed more wolves about,' said Martin. He was the village blacksmith – a skill he learned from his father . 'I saw two yesterday down by the south wall. Young ones. They could probably smell the meat in the smokehouse.' Martin worked the bellows while I watched.

'Do you think they'll find a way to break through?' I asked. Martin shook his head.

'Unlikely,' he said, scratching his beard. 'Wolves are cunning but they're not that smart. We could lay a few traps if you're worried.'

'Something's happened,' I said. 'They're getting bolder. I've seen more of them about in the forest.' I told him about the one I had seen while hunting, about its lack of fear. 'It was big,' I said, 'more than three feet at the shoulder, I swear.'

Martin spat. 'You don't get wolves that big.'

'I've *never* seen a wolf that big,' I said. 'Never in my life. Until this one.'

He took a length of iron and pushed it into the flames. 'You should hunt it down then. A pelt that big would be worth a lot of money. We could trade it in Inverharroch, get a horse or some sheep.'

'You don't want to hunt this wolf,' I told him. 'You should have seen its eyes.' I paused, thinking. Something made me to say it again: 'You don't want to hunt this wolf.'

A few weeks later the winter took one of the Connolly children. He was a few weeks shy of his fourth birthday, but everyone knew he wouldn't make it for days beforehand. A sullen pall hung over the village until he passed, and for most of us it was a blessed relief when he finally died.

Walking out of the chapel, Mary's hand in mine, I glanced up and saw the wolf again. It stood along the treeline on the hill, beyond the village's southern wall. I watched it as we walked across the village to our cottage, and the wolf watched me.

Or was it watching her?

'Go inside,' I warned Mary. As soon as she closed the door I saw the wolf break and run. I watched the trees for several minutes, daring it to return.

I glanced back to the church and saw Martin, looking at me. I don't know if he saw the wolf as well. I never thought to ask.

I didn't see the wolf again for some weeks. Deep into the winter with supplies dwindling, I stumbled upon the body of a deer in the forest. Its death was clearly the work of the wolf, its body gutted and torn open. The remains had frozen solid in the night.

Examining the body, I heard the crunch in the snow behind me.

The wolf, mere yards away, stared at me, growling.

I stood slowly, trying not to startle the beast or provoke it to attack. It was too close: if it charged I would have no chance to draw my bow. Facing the wolf, I retreated, step by step, breathing slowly. Its ears were pricked up and alert. Its teeth, white as the snow, were bared.

I slipped.

In a moment of panic I scrambled back, scuttling away like a crab on my hands and feet. I slammed my back up against a tree, the force half-knocking the wind out of me. There I stopped, too scared to move.

The wolf didn't shift a muscle.

Then it turned, and worked its way back through the trees into darkness.

Something made me snap out of my paralysis. I drew an arrow, raised the bow and took aim at the wolf's departing form. I watched it slowly walk away. My hands trembled as I paused, trying to relax, hoping to breath, praying I could calm down.

I let off a shot. It sliced through the air inches above the wolf's head, and the beast ducked and ran out of sight.

Then I was alone, with just the dead deer for company and the lonely sound of my ragged breathing.

That night I dreamed of blood-soaked poppets and brown-yellow eyes staring at me from dark corners. I woke with a start, possibly even a yell – it's hard to tell in the moment what kind of a fool your sleeping body has made of itself.

The room was cold – *too* cold – and I rose, throwing on what clothes I could find in the darkness.

The front door of the cottage hung agape. I slammed it shut, battling the fierce wind that had blown a thick layer of snow across the floor.

It took me a moment to think of Mary. The run across the room to her bed was an eternity of terror. I remember shouting her name, praying for her to wake up.

The bed was empty. Mary was gone.

There were eight of us who lit torches and ventured out into the night. We shouted her name, wandering south from the smokehouse wall into the woods. The moon was obscured by clouds, making the darkness near-impenetrable, but still we pressed on.

I called her name until my voice froze up in my throat. I wandered through the woods until my torch was spent, and even then I pushed on, shouting hoarsely for her, staring fearfully into every nook, every hollow.

She was nowhere to be found.

The other villagers dragged me sobbing back to the camp. I slept fitfully in the front room of my cottage, the fire providing no warmth or comfort. Behind me Mary's cold, empty bed yawned accusingly, the blankets still lying where I'd thrown them open hours before.

One of McCann boys found Mary the next morning. Her body lay half-buried in the snow, her bedclothes torn and disarrayed. Her blood had frozen onto the ground, leaving the snow stained pink and red.

I carried her back to the village myself, where we wrapped her in shrouds inside the chapel.

They wanted me to stay with the body. They told me I needed time to grieve. I threw them aside, took my bow and a hand axe from the cottage and headed south into the woods.

I went for revenge.

I went for the wolf.

At mid-morning, I crossed the stream, and by noon I was deep into the forest. I crept silently from one tree to the next, always moving upwind, always scanning the ground for tracks. It wasn't long before I found some, too small for the wolf I was hunting but a wolf nonetheless.

Some twenty minutes later I was crouched in the bushes, watching a she-wolf feeding on a fox with her two cubs.

A she-wolf. Its mate.

I don't remember what went through my mind when I shot the first arrow. She yelped and stumbled to one side. The second arrow caught her in the head, killing her outright. I don't remember what I thought as she died.

What I do remember is what I thought as I leaped upon the cubs, my axe raised high. I remember what I thought as I brought the axe down hard on their skulls, and their limbs, and their bodies.

I remember thinking *this is for Mary*, over and over in my head. *This is for Mary*. By the end I was as soaked with blood as the snow that I knelt on.

I hardly remember Mary's funeral. I know we buried her. I have memories of people talking to me in hushed tones, hugging me tightly. All I remember is thinking of the wolf. All I could see were its brown-yellow eyes. The beast haunted me. Even after taking vengeance on its family the wolf still ruled my mind. It wandered among my thoughts all day, and stalked my dreams at night.

A few days later someone sounded an alarm – the wolf had been seen inside the village walls. It must have come in through the gate, slinking past when no one was looking. Everyone made a thorough check of the town, but the beast was nowhere to be seen. There were tracks in the snow, but they led nowhere useful.

The day after that it was seen again, lurking along the tree line by the south wall. By the time I fetched my bow it was gone, hidden back among the trees.

All the while I hunted the forest, alert for any sign of its presence. For days it eluded me. I never saw it, nor found its tracks. It was a ghost, seen occasionally by others but never by me.

'I don't sleep any more,' I told Martin, who used a hammer to straighten out a red-hot length of metal. 'When I close my eyes, all I see is the wolf.'

'Did you need to take something?' Martin asked. 'I had trouble sleeping once, and Mrs Connolly gave me a herbal mixture that helped.'

I shook my head. I've never put much trust in herbal remedies. My grandfather told me of the medical sciences we used to have – all diseases cured, all injuries repaired. It was a far cry from Mrs Connolly's willowbark tea.

Martin stopped banging. I glanced at him. 'We've put on extra watches,' he said, 'we're all keeping an eye out.'

'I won't help,' I replied, 'I won't help until it's dead.'

'Then you're going to have to find it,' said Martin, 'I'm just the blacksmith. *You're* the hunter.'

I looked out from Martin's shop at the village. The snows were breaking. A few more weeks and it would be spring. I watched the McCann children playing with the snow, making icy snowballs and throwing them at one another.

I started to cry. I missed Mary so much. I missed the sound of her voice, the pure joy she expressed at the simplest parts of living. She was the last thing I had left to connect me to her mother, and now she was –

Movement.

It flashed in the corner of my eye, grey-white against the dirty brown stone of the chapel. I scanned the building, the wall behind it. Nothing. But I knew what I had seen.

I broke from the shop in sprint, racing across the village's central square towards my cottage. I slammed the door open, scrabbling for my bow before running back outside again.

Nothing. No sign of the beast.

Then I saw it, charging from behind the chapel towards me.

It snarled as it ran, each foot pounding a flurry of snow into the air. Its eyes burned. Its teeth were bared.

Between us, young Joanne McCann turned away from me and screamed.

I notched an arrow, aimed in one smooth motion and fired.

The wolf ducked as it ran, the arrow tearing through its ear. It roared and leaped into the air.

Oh God.

I notched another arrow – *too slow!* – and fired as the wolf wrapped its jaws around Joanne's arm and wrenched her from the ground. The arrow shot wide. Joanne fell screaming to the ground in a spray of blood.

Around me I heard people running, shouting, screaming. The wolf continued its charge as I dropped the bow and ran. It snapped at my heels as I burst through the cottage door and slammed it shut behind me.

The door rattled as the wolf rammed into it. I stumbled back to the table and picked up my axe. Outside, people shouted, grabbing up children and running for cover, or running for weapons and returning to help. The wolf scratched viciously at the bottom of the door. Suddenly I heard yells and the smash of pottery – people throwing things at the wolf, whatever they could find. I heard it growl – and then nothing.

I threw the door back open, axe held ready, but the wolf was already running for the front gate. I hurled the axe after it with a yell, screaming obscenities.

Too late. The wolf crossed the threshold of the trees and was lost to the woods once again.

They said Joanne McCann would live, barring infection, although it was like she'd never have proper use of her arm again.

The sight of her blood, there on the snow... A group gathered. We armed ourselves, and headed out into the woods again. We went with a single purpose. We all hunted one quarry.

Spreading out among the trees, we formed a wide-spaced line that moved through the woods. We each were armed with what we could find. Some had bows and arrows, others carried axes or picks.

It was Martin who found the first sign of the wolf's tracks, and we quickly grouped together to follow it. Someone saw the wolf and raised shout. We charged after it. It darted with ease between the trees, leaving us to crash noisily between the branches.

I ran as fast as my legs could carry me, until the trees broke out and the wolf made a run for the hills. Here the stream widened to a river, its surface frozen solid. The wolf skidded on the ice, tumbling with a yelp, and I dropped to one knee to take a shot.

To my left I heard cries of alarm, and I flinched as one of the Connolly boys ran gamely onto the ice in pursuit of the wolf.

We shouted at him to stop, but he was either too stubborn or blood-thirsty to heed. The ice snapped with a crack, and the boy went tumbling into the icy water. The others tried to follow his body as it washed helplessly beneath the ice. I knew it was no use – once under the surface the lad was lost to us forever.

On the other shore, the wolf limped away towards the hills. I let off a few arrows, but they all fell far from their mark.

We returned to the village in silence: two of us now dead, a third badly injured, and the wolf still alive and free.

'It's not your fault,' said Martin, 'the boy should have known better.'

I sat at a table in Martin's shop, watching his fire crackle and burn as he worked. 'How many chances have I had to kill that wolf?' I asked him. 'How many opportunities have slipped through my fingers? And look at what's happened.'

I felt Martin's hand on my shoulder momentarily, and then heard him return to his work. 'They say the McCann girl's going to pull through. It looks like her injuries may not be as bad as we had all feared.'

I shrugged, and stared into Martin's fire. The glare of the flames burned at my eyes, leaving blue-purple whorls of colour whenever I closed them. I tried to blink it away, diverting my eyes from the flame and glancing at the ashes that piled up in the corners of the firepit. Ashes, and–

I grabbed a pair of tongs, and gingerly reached into the fire. The rags caught fire as I pulled them out, and I dropped it on the ground to stamp it out. I stared at it on the floor, then reached down and picked it up.

A child's doll, scorched and half-burned away in the fire.

'I didn't mean for it to happen,' said Martin, somewhere behind me.

I wanted to turn around, but didn't.

'She was – she was so beautiful.'

I wanted to run away, but didn't.

'I would never have hurt her. I *loved* her.'

I wanted to scream, but didn't. Visions of the wolf's mate and cubs, battered and bloody in the snow, swelled in my mind.

'You believe me, don't you? It was all a mistake.'

I heard him sobbing. Visions of the wolf were replaced with visions of her. Visions of him.

'You have to forgive me,' he begged.

My hand closed around the handles of the tongs.

'Please forgive me,' he whispered.

I turned and struck. He fell with the first blow in a rain of blood and bone. I brought the heavy iron tongs down on his head, again and again and again and again until the meat that was left stopped twitching.

I fled Auchindoun that night. I didn't pack. I didn't return to my cottage. I stole a cloak from Martin's shop before setting the building on fire. I climbed the village gate while the first villagers stumbled from their homes to seek the source of the commotion.

I followed the stream downhill until I reached the nearest town, and then I stole a horse. I've been riding ever since.

Everyone has their own reason to travel to Canterbury. Mine is absolution. Absolution for killing Martin and absolution for murdering the wolf's family.

I saw the wolf one more time, on my way south. It stood on the hill, watching me leave. I wanted to turn back and seek its forgiveness, somehow reach out to it, but there was nothing I could say that would make him understand.

He and I are the same now, I suppose. We are both hunters. We both lost our families. We both sought revenge.

I'm on my way to Canterbury to find peace. I hope to God that he finds his.

*A*fter the Hunter spoke, there was silence. People looked from one to another, wordlessly. To me, it seemed they were touched by the Hunter's story, as was I. Evidently someone else interpreted the silent stares in a different way.

'D'ye noo see the man is puirly distrackit wi' grief? Hae ye noo hairts, tha' ye'll so mock another's shame?' The voice was rough, and loud, and in a train full of accents, this one was so rich and thick that several people laughed to hear it. That only made things worse.

'Ye mullock-spawned sairpents! Y' unseely flock o' gormless gobshites!'

I won't continue in this fashion. There was more – the speaker seemed to think we didn't believe the story of the wolf's devotion to its family, and wanted to convince us that 'animals, aye, beasties o' all sairts' could feel love as well as any man. To that end, he gave us a tale in that broad, rolling tongue, and I still don't know what to think of it now.

In any case, over-riding the spellcheck system on the Vocawriter I am using to print this collection is an irritating task, and a sentence or two of that dense brogue should be enough for you, milord. Certainly, it was enough for me. I'll let the machine do its work. The word choice and punctuation may be a little odd in places, but you'll get more sense than I did from ...

τhe peατ-διɢɢeʀ's τale

Twas no ordinary horse, ye ken?
This was a beast not crafted by nature, but moulded by the hands of men. He was a mechanical beast. A robot horse. My true and faithful steed, until this very morning when I lost him.

Aye, there may be little chance of catchin' him, but chase after him I must, for he's my last hope – my only hope – of saving bonny Bluebell from sure and certain death. Without that horse, everything's been in vain. Without that horse, there's no point returning to Lewis. It never seemed cold to me, before.

Without Bluebell, it's nothing but a frozen, lifeless wasteland.

They told me I was mad to stay on, with the ice creeping down from the pole like death's dreich and dismal shadow. The new government, that King Charlie in Canterbury, sent money and soldiers to aid with our relocation. All our neighbours went south, except for the Brothers in their ancient, stone-walled Broch at Dun Carloway and the Sisters in their Hospice at the peak of Ben Barvas. They thought that God was testing them. They thought their faith would cause the ice to retreat.

At least, they said they believed it. All the while, they stocked their cellars with food and medicines, right up until the last moment when the airport at Stornoway was taken by the solid, white sea. After the big freeze, a man could walk across that sea, all the way from Lewis to Newcastle-Upon-Tyne, the nearest bastion of civilisation. That is, if he could survive the chill wind and doomed, lightless winter for three months or mair.

The birds stopped nesting on the frozen cliffs. The selkies moved away, needing open water, following the new, shifting coastline. The wind farms became strange arctic sculptures, their bladed towers now mysterious pillars of ice to replace the covered standing stones at Callanish, and the pipes and the overhead power lines cracked and failed.

But Bluebell and I had been married in the green hills, forty years ago when they were still green. I came to the isles when I was nineteen, a cattle farmer with no farm, and lost my wits for a beautiful, passionate, Gaelic-speaking lass. She tied me to her father's land stronger than anyone born and bred there. I took her family name of MacAulay as a pledge to her that we would never leave.

It would have broken her heart to abandon the isle to its cold, white grave. We ignored the government warnings. We accepted what was to come. Bluebell was always young at heart, no matter how we changed on the outside. She kept the Lewis of our youth alive. When I was with her, there was no snow; there was no ice. Only the gleaming, turquoise waters of the lochans in the sparkle of her eyes, swaying silver grasses in the fall of her long hair and red-berried rowans in the blush of her crinkled cheeks.

Aside from farming cattle, I had a special knack for cutting the peat. Bluebell called it a gift of the faeries, but only in secret, to keep her blasphemy from reaching the ears of the Brothers. When all the world was made a furnace by the burning of fuels, and cutting became a crime, they gave me the only remaining tender, for the Blackhouse Distillery with its traditional, peat-flavoured whisky. I passed the trick of digging the peat on to my son, Andrew, though he was a scholar at heart. Fearless as Olav the Black, he worked by night to compile a tome of the Clan's glorious history, never contemplating the possibility of extinction that lay before us. The MacAulays never backed away from a fight. Danger is sweet, declares our Clan motto. The MacAulays were tied to the land from the beginning, and no devil's work could undo it.

When the ice rolled over us, the distillery closed and the last occupants fled, I kennt we could still make it work. Under the ice, there was still soil. Under the ice, there was still peat, though it became a rare, secretive and cunning quarry.

The peat was our beating hearts. The peat was our life. There wasn't much of it left, ye ken, but there was enough to warm a poor man's . Enough to warm a poor family's bones. Every day, I went in search of it. Every day, I cut through the snow and the ice and the muck, and sometimes I found the black gold; sometimes I found nothing.

After a day with nothing, I could stay home and weep. There wis nothin' for it but to go out again, til my hands bled through the leather wrappings and my frozen beard turned brittle as tinder.

Meanwhile, young Andrew tended to the farm. 'Twas a fortification of dry-stone walls, with sheltered pens for the beasts and four wee greenhouses. Every day, the snow had to be cleared from the base of the walls. Every day, the snow had to be cleared from the perspex roofs of the greenhouses and melted to water the crops. In summer, bird droppings from the long-abandoned cliffs had to be scraped into buckets and brought back for fertiliser, and seeds tediously collected and stored for future plantings.

Andrew never complained. He was strong as the young bull we kept in lee of the kitchen. The boy had a sunny outlook and an easy way with the hairy cows. We kept just the three cows at any one time; the bull, the wee calf and its mother. She was a good milker, as was the daughter who replaced her. We had butter and cheese, and even veal when it was time of year for the calf to be slaughtered. The animals were bedded on oat straw, and if they ate the same good oats and turnips that went into our porridge and stew, well, we ate better than the beasts in the end, for we had modified Winterlabs lettuces and Chillzest oranges that had been delivered right before the airport was lost. Andrew's sly tabby cat, Long John Silver, hunted the mice out of the grain and made a nuisance of himself around the stable.

Bluebell kept a tidy house, of course, and tended our bay horse, Plodder. He was not as young as he used to be – none of us were – but he could still carry the weight of a man as far as the cliffs, or even to the Brothers' Broch. Bluebell did like to go to church at Christmas, to say a prayer for her mother and father and to trade onions with the Brothers for tallow candles.

A good life, ye say? A hard life? Aye, it was good, and it was hard, and if Bluebell sometimes wished for grandchildren, she never wished it hard enough to send young Andrew away. Something inside of her held stubbornly to the notion that the ice would retreat, that everything could be as it had been before, if only we held on long enough. But it wasn't just the cold we had to fight.

We never kept poultry on account of the flu. Sometimes, though, the wild geese would come, their migration sense confused by all that had happened. They landed on the greenhouse roofs and poked at the perspex with their beaks. They wanted the lettuces inside.

Andrew shot them with his longbow and buried them away from the farm. This summer, though, it wasn't enough. The cat, Long John Silver, appeared one morning with white feathers in his mouth. By noon he had left piles of vomit around the stable. When evening came he lay lifeless in the hay between Plodder's two front feet. Plodder's heavy head hung dejectedly. He made a sad, whuffing noise, like a hundred candles being extinguished by a door slamming shut. No mistake, he was mourning his furry little companion.

We didn't give him further opportunity to mourn. Cruel as it seemed, Long John Silver and the stable full of hay were immediately consigned to a hastily built bonfire.

A week later, Bluebell said the horse was strangely lethargic. When Plodder started wheezing, we knew our efforts had been in vain. The flu was ruthless and deadly. It leaped from beast to beast without pause or care.

Bluebell cried when Plodder fell down dead.

She cried, but it wasn't just because she remembered Plodder's dew-drenched spring foaling and all the years of faithful service in between. Her eyes watered and swelled up. Her hands trembled and her body spasmed when she coughed. She could barely stir from her bed.

I was sick with fear for her life, but there was little time to waste. The peat store at the farm was swallowed up in those first two weeks when we realised Bluebell had caught Plodder's flu. We needed peat to keep her warm. We needed peat to boil the water, in case it was contaminated by the virus – we could not care for her if we, too, became deathly ill. We needed peat to boil her sweaty pillow covers and sheets, and to boil the soft cloths we used to clean her wasted body.

Why did we not go out and simply cut more peat? The fresh stuff was no use, ye ken. When it comes out of the ground it's crusted with ice and holds as much water as the bog that gave it birth. Peat for fuel must be stacked and dried for months before it'll burn, see?

We did not have months to spare.

By the third week, we were trying to burn wet peat in desperation. The black smoke made Bluebell's cough even worse.

There were four places I could think of that might have dried, stored peat. The Brothers at Dun Carloway had plenty, but they did not trade in the black gold; they said it was too precious, and the penalties for cutting it on their land were severe.

The Sisters at Ben Barvis were too far away, and could not be reached without a horse. The Morrisons' abandoned homestead in the north was sure to be stocked, but it was long ago buried in an avalanche at the foot of Devil's Hill.

That left only the Blackhouse Distillery, though it lay wreathed in a seasonal fog that refused to clear, and it was swathed daily in blankets of fresh snow. That would make locating it difficult. Not to mention excavatin' the old place. When I looked at Bluebell, lying still and waxen in our old, sagging, steel-frame bed, I could hardly bear to think of leaving her.

But the fire burned low, and lower.

So low, the once-bright fire burned.

Finally, I went out into the hurtful, luminous landscape of fog-diffused sun, with Andrew right beside me. He whistled a military tune, wrapped his head in the saltire and carried the long-handled grain-shovel and ice axe resolutely over his shoulder as though they were firearms of old.

We struggled through new, hip-deep powder snow that covered the bog. The snow was as treacherous and as innocent-seeming as the white geese that had landed on the farm, bringing the flu in the first place. All the landmarks were covered, the hills obscured. We couldn't be sure if we were standing on the roof of the distillery, or just another ridge of packed snow, but we fell to with vigour, for the fire at the farm burned low.

We struck uselessly about in it for hours. The wide-bladed shovel made short work of the fresh snow, but beneath it the snow was dense and hard and layered in icy sheets. The axe and the mountain shovel with its short handle and stout metal blade were brought into play, but in every place we tunnelled down, we found no sign of the Distillery. If the needle was an awful great needle, so was the haystack an awful great haystack. Andrew and I became wet on the inside from the sweat of our toil, and wet on the outside from the melting snow, but we couldn't stop.

Sunset approached, with no success.

At last, we limped home, and fed and bathed poor Bluebell. The house was still much warmer in than out.

The next day, the house fires threatened to die. When they died, so would Bluebell. She shivered and cried out softly. It was torture to hear her. Worse than torture. I broke up our only wooden chair and set it over the smouldering coals.

Andrew stopped me as we set out desperately again in search of the elusive buried Blackhouse Distillery.

'Dad, I know where I can find some dry peat.'

'Speak up, then, lad,' I answered with surprise.

'Dun Carloway,' he said, lowering his eyes uncomfortably.

So, I thought, it comes to this. Even a MacAulay will steal to save a life. But this course was dangerous. If the Brothers at the Broch caught us breaking in and looting peat, we would be hanged. Then, who would look after Bluebell? Who would save her, if we were sent into the next life?

'No,' I said sternly. 'We cannae help yer mother by gettin' oorselves killed.'

'Danger is sweet, Dad, remember? The Brothers have a storage shed set away from the Broch, which they keep stocked with fuel. I've seen it.'

'How do ye ken it'll be unguarded?'

'The Brothers would not stir far from the Broch on a morning like this,' Andrew argued, but I kennt the Brothers lived lives of austerity and self-deprivation, and paid added homage to the Lord with every league covered by their frozen feet. 'If they catch us on their land we can pretend we're hunting rabbits. Or we can tell them about Mother, and then they won't want to come anywhere near us.'

'The Brothers don't fear the pestilence. They say God protects them from it. Come along, Andrew. We'll search out the Morrison's farm. We'll go to the sheltered side of Devil's Hill.'

Devil's Hill was northeast of the farm. Dun Carloway was southwest. Andrew stared to the southwest, kicking at the gravel path. Then, he shook his head. He set the shovel against the side of the house and picked up his unstrung longbow. Firming his grip on the bow, he said,

'I've made up my mind, Dad. I'm going to Dun Carloway. We can't risk coming back empty-handed again.'

I shook my head, too. It was a perilous plan. But the boy was, in truth, his own master. I was proud of the man that Bluebell and I had raised him to be. I gripped his forearm and pulled him into a hug, somehow sensing I would never see him again.

'May God protect you, son.'

'I'll be back before the fire has burned out, Dad,' Andrew said confidently

I took the shovel and set off alone for the sheltered side of Devil's Hill.

What happened to Andrew? Och, in the days before the ice, the law would never have stood for it. When my Bluebell is at last recovered, I'll go to the Broch to recover his frozen body. Those Brothers did arrest my son – not for theft, but for rabbit hunting. That was the story he planned to give them, and it was the story that he gave them, not realising that to them, on this particular day, it was a crime.

The crime of working on the Sabbath.

They threw him into a bleak and icy cell, and when the virus took hold of him, you can be sure there was no-one to water and warm him, or to wash his wasting body. They did send a messenger to the farm, but I was absent at the Hospice and poor Bluebell couldnae rise to answer their impertinent knocking. They left a scrawl of parchment on the front door, a missive of black death.

Will it be revenge I'm after, when I go at last to the Broch at Dun Carloway? No, never that. It's up to God, the now, to punish those Brothers as did treat my flesh and blood so poorly. I loved my son as much as any man's capable of loving his child. The best way I know to honour him is to spread this tale to all I meet.

Danger is sweet, that boy said to me. He died trying to save his ailing mother, and never was a man more worthy of the MacAulay name. Remember this tale, and Andrew MacAulay of Lewis still lives.

Ignorant of Andrew's fate, I soldiered on toward Devil's Hill. When I reached it, the wind danced with me in a flurry of snow. Hardly able to tell east from west, up from down, I started to dig in the shadow of the knoll.

For every load of snow I cast aside, the wind cast twice as much right back at me. I screamed at the wind with bared teeth, my back a rod of fire and my hands numbed past feeling.

'Give me a chance to save her!'

As my shriek died away, so did the wind, just for an instant, and I heard a sound I could scarcely credit: The sound of a horse's whinny.

It came from a lump in the hillside, not ten paces away. I dropped the shovel and took to the lump with the ice axe.

With every stroke that I struck, I heard an answering knock from within the ice. I thought it was an echo, at first, and then I thought my ears were playing tricks on me. Beneath the ice, there was a wooden crate, and my heart leaped, because I knew the wood would burn as well as any peat.

Metal-shod hooves crashed through the crate before I could move to open it. Then it wasn't just my heart leaping, but a great black horse with red eyes and steamy nostrils leaping clear of the snow.

This was no gentle Plodder, but a mad beast of war. I struggled to imagine how it could have been trapped, and who it belonged to, and all the while the proof that this was no natural beast insinuated its way before my eyes.

His hooves were not metal-shod; they were themselves a silvery metal. His velvety black hide was no living skin and hair; it was suspiciously smooth and undoubtedly synthetic. The dilated nostrils did not flare in and out with each heaving breath; they were fixed and the steam coming from them was constant and artificial.

When I looked closer at the crate, I saw the transport company's logo, and it was in no language that I could decipher; a whole lot of chicken scratchings what might have been one of the Eastern tongues.

Clearing away a wee bit more snow, I found some heavy chains and a parachute attached to the crate. It seemed the robot horse had been dropped from the sky, but it had been decades since an airborne vehicle last ventured over Lewis.

Then, I saw a symbol that sent a shiver into my very bones. 'Twas the yellow and black stamp that warned of deadly radiation. The horse's red eyes swung close to mine as it tossed its head and whinnied again. I wondered: was it a bomb? Was it some kind of spying machine? Why else build a mechanical beast with a nuclear fire inside of him? Why else build a robot horse? But he had a saddle and bridle fixed to his semblance of a body, and that could only mean he was intended to be ridden.

Somebody had made him, and somebody had packaged him, and then something had gone very wrong, for here he was, in a crate, on the sheltered side of Devil's Hill, on the Isle of Lewis in the far north-western corner of Scotland.

That mechanical beast lowered his head and put his velvet nose in my unfeeling hand. He whickered as lovingly and trustingly as Plodder had ever whickered. The red light in his eyes dimmed and darkened to deepest brown.

'Can ye help me, robot horse?' I whispered. 'Can ye help me save my Bluebell?'

I swear to almighty God, that horse nodded his head. He was shorter, leaner and finer built than a Shire horse, but he took my weight like I was a snowflake. The snowflakes that did land on him melted straight away; he was warm to the touch and the water beaded on his black flanks. I rode him around in a circle, and his great metal hooves, which should have sunk him into the snow like a stone, danced lightly over the surface. They had some amazin' power to float upwards and away.

This time, when the wind came at me, I laughed in its face. I climbed down from the horse and used the axe to break up the wooden crate. The horse made no move to leave my side. I wrapped the planks in a bundle with the parachute and tied them onto the back of the saddle. Then, I mounted again.

'Home, robot horse,' I cried, and together we soared over the white moors.

Did his joints freeze up once he got out of the box?

Och, no, he stayed supple and silent no matter how the Atlantic gales raged.

Did he ever disobey me?

No, he never fought fer his own head. He responded to my commands like the finest bred parade horse in the King's own guard.

Did he become tired or run out of fuel?

No, he was no living thing, nor was he a gas oven or a peat stove. He was invincible. He was my tireless robot horse with an unquenchable inner inferno. He was a gift from the heavens.

One thing he could not do was fight off a killer virus.

When I got back to poor Bluebell, it was plain that warmth would no longer be enough to sustain her.

There was no time to go after Andrew. After putting the wood on the fire and building it to a high blaze, I rode the robot horse to the Hospice on Ben Barvas, to beg the Sisters for help. Once, they had stocks of an anti-viral draft called Fluban. I was prepared to offer them anything and everything, in exchange for the draft.

The journey of two days now only took me two hours. The robot horse cantered up the side of Ben Barvas as though the mountain was simply not there. He did not labour for breath. He did not struggle in the snow. There was only the gentle stream of warm air from his wide nostrils and the gentle rhythm of his long strides.

The Hospice squatted like a bedraggled crow on the chilly, blanketed peak. Black smoke rose from dozens of ugly, square chimneys. Robed in black and with soot on her cheeks but spotlessly clean hands, a woman with white bristles on her chin answered the tiny, discreet front door of the Hospice.

Her name was Sister Fidelma. Her hazel eyes were warm, but she wrung her spotless hands when she learned why I was there.

'There's no more Fluban to be had, here, MacAulay,' she said, appearing as distraught at the news as I felt. 'It's only to be had at Newcastle, and there for a terrible price. Best bring your wife here to the Hospice. We can make her comfortable, until the end.'

I rebelled at the thought of giving in. When I led the robot horse out of the courtyard, I felt an overwhelming stubbornness take hold of me. God had given me the robot horse, in this, my most desperate hour. Could I not use him? Could I not ride to Newcastle? Was that not his intended purpose?

But how was I to buy the precious Fluban, even if I did reach that distant city? It was unlikely the Guild of Pharmacists would accept peat and lettuces as payment.

I dwelled on the problem, even as I wrapped Bluebell in her blankets and helped her onto the robot horse. She weighed almost nothing, but she was semi-aware of her surroundings. She leaned close to the robot horse, hugging his neck because he was so warm.

'Where are we going, James?' she asked me in a reedy, quiet voice. 'Are you taking me to the Broch? Will the Brothers say final prayers for me, before the Lord takes me into his care?'

'The Lord will have to wait,' I said firmly, smiling, trying to hide the tears in my eyes. 'We're going to the Hospice. The Sisters will nurse you back to health.'

'This is a fine horse, James. Does he belong to the Sisters?'

'No, he belongs to us.'

'What's his name, then?'

I paused. It never occurred to me to give the robot horse a name.

'He doesn't have one, my heart.'

'Then I'll name him,' she said sleepily. 'His new name is Stornoway.'

Remembering the bustling town perched on the rim of the fine-looking harbour, long since devoured by the ravenous ice, I tucked back a strand of Bluebell's wispy hair and said proudly,

'That's a perfect name for him, my heart.'

There had to be a way to find that money. There had to be a way to save her.

As I was locking up the farmhouse to leave, I found the black letter from those black-hearted Brothers at the Broch. Crumpling it up in fury, I did not say a word to Bluebell about it. It would have broken her. It would have destroyed her last remaining strength.

Effortlessly, Stornoway the robot horse carried me and my Bluebell to the Hospice on the top of Ben Barvas.

Once I'd given Bluebell over to the care of the generous and Sisters, there was no more reason for caution. Danger is sweet, Andrew had said. Nevertheless, I took water and oats and the makings of a fire in the saddlebags on the back of the robot horse.

'Come now, Stornoway,' I murmured in the horse's ear. 'It's time to test how fast you really are.'

There should have been northern lights and a full symphony to accompany our flight across the ice shelf. If I had been there, if I had felt the knives of the sleet against my face as we passed through darkness and raging storm, I would never have believed it mysel'.

No living thing could have beaten the torrents of wind and frozen water that night. Of course, my robot horse Stornoway was no living thing. He kept me alive when I should have been scoured from the face of God's earth, that horse with his hot mock-hide and the eternal flame burning in his belly.

Four hundred and thirty kilometres, we rode in night.

Oh, aye, scoff if you wish. I told ye, I could scarce believe it myself. Whether you accept it or not, is no concern of mine.

What concerns me is my Bluebell, lying so still and pale in the Hospice at Ben Barvas. It's been three days since I left her and if I don't get the horse back soon I'll never see her again.

How have I spent those three days?

Well, I've just told ye about the first day, about the leg from Lewis to Newcastle, the impossible journey made possible by God's grace. Dawn revealed the protruding lighthouse slicked with ice and the snow-covered stone shoulders of the Tynemouth Priory.

A pair of giant, black, sleek corpses gave Stornoway pause. I could have turned his head back toward the city, but even in my exhaustion I was curious to see what had startled him, so I nudged him closer to the looming silhouettes.

They were submarines, caked in rime. Once, I supposed, the same nuclear energy that gave life to my robot horse had powered them.

Stornoway called to them. It was not the whinny he'd made from inside his crate, nor the soft whicker of our first meeting, but a high-pitched trill barely within the upper limits of my hearing.

He waited, ears pricked. Fog crept up about his fetlocks. The submarines remained silent. Their time was over. I guessed they had come to save the city when the grid failed. They themselves must have fallen prey to the riots that followed the plague.

Stornoway waited a little longer. Then, his head drooped. He made a sad, whuffing noise, like a hundred candles being extinguished by a door slamming shut. No mistake, he was mourning the deaths of those vast, dormant submersibles.

I patted his neck and we rode on.

On the morning of that second day, I found myself a member of the Novocastrian Pharmacist's Guild, but do ye think he was falling over himself to help me? No, the crooked man named a fee so high the King himself could not have paid the ransom.

You, Sir, are a-smilin' at me in a way that says you're linked to that Guild yirsel'. Do ye think I did not approach the Guildsman with respect? Do ye think I made unreasonable demands? He spoke to me as though I were a simpleton, or a child. He spoke as though I'd asked him for the moon out of the sky.

Well, on the evening of the second day, I found a way to give him what he wanted.

There's no horse racing in the Hebrides. Gambling is not permitted, for it offends the eyes of the Lord. At least, that used to be the way of it, but England has changed since the early days of the Church Governances, or so it seemed as I stood in stark amazement on the barren hillside that night.

Barren until the sun went down. The punters slunk from their dens and the spirits flowed like water.

Colourful as a whore, the stands around the race track were bannered and jewelled. It was lit by a thousand lamps and watched by a thousand eyes. In the light of day, my Stornoway could never have passed for a living, breathing creature.

In the murky yellow glow, amongst the falseness and the dirty palms, in the muddy arena where the honest heavy horse had been stabled and the light, showy galloper brought to hand, my Stornoway settled as unobtrusive as a black cat in an alleyway.

I had no currency with which to wager, but I shared my porridge with a rabbit-toothed man in a felt cap and to repay the kindness he shared his winnings on the very next race. I looked at the coins in my hand and felt a surge of hope. It would be enough, when placed on my horse – a horse with such hopeless odds.

How they laughed, those weasels in their brown, stained coats, at an old Scotsman on an undersized, unknown steed. How they laughed, as I guided my Stornoway intae the gates with only the pressure of my knees. To them, a horse as battles and screams is the only, the best kind of race horse.

To me, that's a beast what's suffering. One day, I'll go back and do something about those poor, fear-crazed horses.

But I dared not hang back, after I'd claimed a prize so colossal, so vast, so mighty muckle big, that it went straight into the history books. Any scum with a bit of pipe would have clobbered me for that prize. I took my money and I took my robot horse, and I rode out of the heart of Newcastle, before the word could spread on all those wet and hungry lips.

What am I doing here, then, ye ask? Why have I not returned to Lewis with the Fluban to save my Bluebell?

When the sun came up this morning, I thought my quest was over. I broke fast in a field scattered with her namesake flower, and the clouds seemed to be parting just for me. All I had to do was take my money to the Guildsman, get the medicine and hurry back to the Hospice.

Stornoway was standing still, his only movement the stream of warm, false breath from his wide, false nostrils. A living horse would have been busy grazing the heather, but not Stornoway.

I finished my porridge, and turned to see his head high, his eyes burning bright red and his ears pointed keenly to the south. It was very peculiar indeed. I'd not seen him so alert-seeming since the morning I dug him out of the ice.

Was it policemen? Was I under arrest? Is that why I'm fleeing the authorities, on this here steam train to Canterbury?

Och, no. And shame on ye. That's no kind of question to put to an honest man. Be still and I'll tell ye what happened next.

A whistle came clear across the hills, a whistle fine and free. It was the morning train to Canterbury. The train was black and sleek in the morning sun.

Black and sleek and made of metal, just like Stornoway. Steam billowed from it in a steady, artificial stream. Just like Stornoway. When it whistled, it spoke a secret intae the heart of my robot horse.

Stornoway whistled back. The sound he made was practically identical. It made the hair stand up on the back of my neck.

Then, just like that, with almost all my prize money in his saddle-bags, he galloped away after his kindred, his soul mate. No amount of clamouring could call him back. Train and horse vanished into the distance.

So, here I am. I caught the very next train, the afternoon train, and I pray to see Stornoway before long. My Bluebell can wait forever, and without that horse, I've got no chance of crossing the sea of ice.

But, once I see him, will he come back with me? Or will he be steadfast by the side of that clanking, shuddering machine – a black steam train that speaks to his heart?

*I*f not for the coming of the baby, I think there would have been questions and protestations after the Peat-Digger's Tale. Certainly, I've never heard of any nuclear-powered robotic horses, and I wondered whether the old Scotsman was perhaps amusing himself at our expense. I did not get to ask, however, for the door to the saloon car opened, and a frantic young man burst in. It seemed he was travelling with his pregnant wife, and now of a sudden she was giving birth, and could the doctor come quickly, quickly, oh at once!

The Doctor rose with a smile, hefted his cracked black bag, and departed with a cheery wave. We waved back at him, and wished him luck, and luck and good health to the girl, and they must call the babe Charles for the King if it were a boy, or else Kylie for the ancient Queen Mother ...

In the wake of the excitement, we heard from one I had not expected to speak. A bulky man, robed in the humblest cloth, he carried with him the air of a true penitent. He had boarded late, at a stop only an hour or so before the storm brought us to a halt, and though he smiled politely, he shook his head at every offer of food and drink as though fasting.

'It's stories of love now, is it?' he said, throwing back his rough hood, and the car subsided into silence, the travellers likely surprised that the silent one had at last relented. 'This is not my first journey to Canterbury,' he said, and his voice was soft, and strangely high for such a big man. 'But I have seen a little since then, and perhaps learned, and I hope this time I have come as a true pilgrim. If so, perhaps Canterbury will be kind to me, as she was once before ...'

The Metawhore's Tale

The Metawhore's Prologue

When I was still very young, and lacked the sense to choose how I answer God's calling, it served my masters to send me on pilgrimage to the newly reclaimed city of Canterbury. In those days, enough power existed to send a single carriage down each line per day, stopping wherever and whenever it was needed in order to collect the human flotsam who flagged the driver. It was considered a marvellous way to test the faith: in those days, a priest needed to *overcome* humanity to reach holiness, not embrace it. The trip from Manchester took thirteen days. Keeping my virginity intact would count in my favour, should I return alive.

The priesthood has changed little since then.

Twelve miles from the Canterbury walls, the Manchester line met with all the other Northern Pilgrimages, and our carriage became one small part of a travelling congregation. From my window I could see the tracks converge, and in the distance, the massive walls that held back the Thames. City officials strode towards us. Not for the first time, I was struck by how rich the clothing was of those who administered the reclaimed lands, and how shabby I felt in comparison.

Having checked our paperwork, and satisfied themselves that they had collected enough bribes to make the journey worthwhile, the officials announced that we would not be entering the city that day, and would have to wait in our carriage until a suitable vacancy appeared in tomorrow's schedule. Then they left. I watched them walk away, dividing our coins between them.

'Typical,' a voice from the back of the cabin rumbled. A fat man levered himself out of his seat, thick head still bent to his own window. 'Everywhere I go it's the same. Tiny little minds running everything. Still,' He rummaged around underneath his robe, which I now saw was as rich as anything the city administrators were wearing. His hand re-emerged, bearing a heavy purse which jangled as he shook it, 'there's something to be said for experience, eh?'

He laughed at his cleverness. I tried to force my lips into a matching response. The administrators had taken every coin I was bequeathed.

'I am Magritte,' the fat man announced. 'The finest, and I admit with all due humility, the most handsome trader of meats, victuals, and small goods in the Village of Derby.' He plonked down next to me, so hard that the impact lifted me an inch or so from my seat. 'As we are destined to spend at least one more night smelling each other's farts, I suggest we get to know each other a little better, eh?' He laid a heavy hand upon my thigh. 'What do you say, pretty boy?'

I flinched, all too aware of a sudden itch in my groin. Magritte laughed, and stood, moving towards the front of the carriage.

'Gather round,' he said. 'Let us eat, and drink, and give all you nice pilgrims something to repent tomorrow.'

We gathered in the best circle we could manage, given the confines, and introductions were made: Harmon, the soldier, on pilgrimage to ask forgiveness for the deaths of his enemies; Millicent, the leatherworker, whose unborn child needed absolution; a man who introduced himself only as Best and would not reveal his purpose; Givens, and Santoro, and Braun; and myself, a poor boy who had only the priesthood to look forward to and who wished God would avert his eyes long enough for me to call this journey an adventure before I left the world behind. Over it all loomed Magritte: loud Magritte, acerbic and sarcastic, with a jibe for everyone's motivations and nothing but scorn for belief; sinful and disbelieving butcher with but one reason to make such an expedition.

'Money,' he boomed, when challenged. 'Do you think a city such as that,' he waved in the general direction of our destination, 'is happy with irradiated fish and muddy clams? A man needs meat, and I have meat to sell them.'

I rubbed a hand against my hard belly. I had not tasted meat since my father bade me take orders. 'Then why,' I found the courage to ask, 'do you travel with us?'

Magritte smiled, and it was an unpleasant thing. 'Why pay for a horse,' he said, 'when pilgrims travel for free?'

I would have turned away from him, then, but I understood suddenly that this was why I had been despatched. A priest must forgive much sin in others. Tonight, when I prayed, I would have someone for whom I could beg forgiveness. By the time I returned to the monastery, I would have a gallery to picture as I spent my nights representing their souls before God.

Whilst we related our stories, my attention was captured by a robed figure seated just outside our circle. Magritte had lit a small camp burner, and as we talked, each of us added something from our pack to his pot, until he stirred a broth quite unlike any I had smelled before. My stomach rumbled, and I was not alone. More than one of us scrabbled in our packs for bowls and cutlery. The robed figure drew a battered cup and spoon from within its bag and leaned forward. Magritte spied the motion and waggled his spoon.

'No, no,' he said, smiling like a merchant confronted with a penny less than the asking price. 'You want to eat, you contribute something.'

The figure paused.

'What?' it asked. I blinked at the voice, high and fluted, like a child. Magritte wiped a beefy hand down his tunic and held it out towards the figure.

'Food, if you please. Something for the pot.'

The figure grew even more still, as if considering its options. After a moment it dipped its head in assent, and withdrew a packet from within its robe.

'A pinch,' it said, unfolding the packet to reveal a mound of small leaves. Magritte stared at it in disdain.

'For a cupful of our contributions?'

'A pinch is all you'll need.'

Magritte snorted and snatched the packet from the stranger. He held it up to his nose and sniffed. A look of wonder crossed his face.

'Oregano?' he whispered. 'But how ... so much ...'

'Payment,' the stranger said, then 'A pinch.'

Magritte crushed the merest portion between finger and thumb, and sprinkled it into the brew. He held the roll back out to its owner.

'Thank you,' he said solemnly. The stranger reached out to take back the herb, and Magritte shot out his other hand, fast as a snake, grabbing the extended wrist. Before we could raise our voices in objection he had yanked the outsider forward, into our circle.

'Nobody in England owns this much oregano,' the butcher hissed through clenched teeth. 'Who are you?'

'A pilgrim.'

'Liar. This wealthy, nobody seeks pilgrimage. Who are you?'

They stayed that way for a tense half minute, Magritte's bulk balanced by the stress evident in the smaller figure's stance. Eventually, the stranger raised its free arm and gripped the edge of its hood. A quick tug revealed the face beneath. Magritte gasped, and let go.

'My God.'

Three of our company rose, and left without a word. The stranger turned her gaze upon the rest of us, daring us to comment. Her eyes fixed themselves upon me, and I saw how young she was. The scars made her seem older. They covered every inch of her shaved head, criss-crossing her skin so that she seemed ensnared within a white spider web. Only her eyes had escaped, and they were as hard and blue as metal.

'What happened?' I whispered. It was Magritte who answered, finding himself enough to launch a gob of spit at her feet.

'Metawhore.'

'What?'

'She's a Metawhore.' He leaned away, as if her presence might taint the air he breathed. 'A dream slut.'

'I don't understand.'

'Where are you from, boy?' He waved a fat finger at her scarred visage. 'Whatever money you have, she'll take. And in return, she'll tell you about a scar, and leave you with memories you can never get rid of. She's a dream collector. A witch.' He swivelled in his seat, turning his back between her and the pot. 'You'll get none of my food, trull.'

I coughed. 'Our food.'

'What?'

'It's our food.' I indicated the pot. 'Including hers. Give her a cup.'

He stared at me with something akin to rage, and for a moment I thought he might strike me. Instead, he flung his spoon into my lap.

'Serve her yourself.'

'All right.' I picked up the spoon and motioned for her cup. She eyed me for a few seconds, then held it out. I ladled out a fair serving, whilst the company kept their attentions fixed in every direction but ours.

'Join me.'

A space had opened up at my side. She hesitated for a moment, then shuffled over and sat down. I filled my own bowl, then lobbed the spoon back into Magritte's ample lap.

'Why do they treat you like that?' I asked her, blowing at my steaming meal. She shook her head slightly, eyes almost amused through the steam.

'You really don't know?'

I shrugged. 'This is my first time away from Nottingham. I've never even left the monastery grounds before.'

'Ah,' She sipped her broth, made a face. 'You're very young for a priest.'

'I'm still a priest's apprentice.'

'Ah.' She stared out the window, at the stationary landscape. 'So you really don't know, then.'

'Will you tell me?'

She wriggled against the softness of the seat, sniffed the warm food, considered for a moment.

'All right.'

☙

The Metawhore's Tale

'Every woman carries scars,' she said, staring deep into the blue flame of the burner. 'From the first time your Daddy sticks a finger up you while you're having a bath, to the last time you have to knife a drunk to keep what a man takes for granted, you learn that womanhood means carrying more wounds than any son of God ever had to endure.'

She blew on her broth, hard, so a small tongue of brown liquid escaped and ran down the outside of her bowl. 'I killed my father when I was six. I could tell you the story, if you like. Just point to the right scar and pay me what I ask, and I'll tell you all about it.'

Nobody moved for their purse. She didn't speak, and I began to wonder whether her invitation was genuine. Then, when I was all but set on asking her to do so, she continued.

'I spent seven years on the streets of Barcelona –'

'Horse shit!' Magritte's outburst shattered my attention. 'Barcelona's been a battleground for forty years. I've seen grown men chewed up by that place, never mind ...'

'Do you think,' the Metawhore said softly, her gaze never leaving the flame, 'that I became this scarred working in a butcher's shop?' She barely moved, but a flash of silver in her hand revealed a knife. I blinked, and it was gone. Magritte laughed, but it was an empty sound. He sank back into his seat and was quiet.

'How did you ...?'

The Metawhore glanced at me, and something that might have been a smile ghosted briefly across her features.

'How did I become a Metawhore?' she asked. I nodded, a brief, fragile movement that allowed me to shift my eyes from her gaze. She made a noise, then returned to the fire.

'I fucked my last man when I was thirteen,' she said. 'A street rat with a knife and enough pennies to buy me a meal. Except he wasn't going to waste pennies on the likes of me. He gave me this.' She raised her head slightly, so we could see the thin white line that separated the top of her throat from the bottom. 'I would have died, *should* have died.'

'What happened?'

'A whore rescued me.' She drank from the bowl, and I watched the scar at her throat shift about as she swallowed. 'A trull. A dream slut.' She looked hard at Magritte. 'Do you know what a Metawhore does?'

Magritte matched her gaze. 'Witchcraft. You snare a man's minds and make him see ... pictures, filthy pictures, pictures you keep in those wounds you treasure so much.'

The Metawhore stared at him for a long time, long enough for her listeners to peek at one another, wondering whether the tale was over already, and if Magritte had destroyed it for us. Just as I was deciding to rise and take my leave of the group, to find a secluded spot for my evening prayers, she spoke again, almost to herself.

'What a place I find myself in. A rich man flavours his meats with herbs and spices, and tells *such* lies in the name of selling dog as pork, and he meets with nothing but favour and success.'

'How dare –'

'But a woman flavours her tea with herbs, and adds a pinch of something rare and wonderful to help her customers see the images behind her words, and they call her witch and turn their backs upon her in daylight.' She shook her head. 'I've run with bulls at Pamplona. I've danced with swords in Lothian. I've gone back to Barcelona and fought with, and against, the Basques.' She looked around the group. 'I've been richer than a meat trader, and seen more death than a soldier.' Her gaze fell on me. 'I pray more often than a priest. I have lived all your lives and more.' The knife was in her hand again. With slow deliberation she held out her wrist, and drew the blade across it so that blood sprang into the light. 'I will remember this,' she said, reaching into her robe and withdrawing a scrap of cloth.

We watched in silence as she bandaged her hand. I licked my dry lips. If she was a witch, if what Magritte said was true, then what had he just forced upon us? I was afraid to ask, and yet, I was here to learn, to understand the evils I must pray for.

'What ...?' I began, then swallowed so my voice would not sound so young, so fearful. 'How?'

She glanced at me, measuring. I found the courage to look back. Perhaps that persuaded her, for she closed her eyes and sighed.

'Magda,' she said. 'When I was thirteen. She lived on the Carrer d'Amilcar in Barcelona, above the fighting. She was the one who pulled me from that alleyway. She died when I was fifteen. Nothing spectacular or sordid. She slipped and fell down the stairs. I wasn't with her. I was on my own by then, travelling, collecting.' She rubbed a spot at the top of her arm. 'But she taught me, showed me how to identify herbs and plants, what strengths produced what effects. She helped me gather and dry my first plants and sat with me while I told my first stories. She saved me. I'd be dead without her.'

'She sounds noble.'

The Metawhore laughed, a short, empty bark. 'There are nights I lie awake, hating every memory I have of her.' At my shocked blink, she opened her hands, inviting me to look at her. 'There are night when death would have been better.'

'And the stories?' Magritte's voice cut across us. 'All those tales you keep tucked behind your scars?'

'Rote learning,' she said. 'Recall. It's nothing.' She shot me a look. 'Book of John, fourth prayer.'

I blinked. 'And so this is Christmas, and what have you done?'

'Another year over, a new one just begun,' she finished for me, before turning back to the group. 'See? It's simple. Even a boy can do it.'

I flushed, but she didn't notice. 'I've collected one hundred and eighty seven scars, and each time I've remembered the circumstance, the reason, the pain. It's not magic. It's just ...' her gaze dropped, and the same sense of failure I carried flittered across her face. 'It's what I have.'

'Well,' Magritte's voice was loaded with irony, 'What gifts. I hardly begin to understand why you need to join us on our little journey.'

'I fell in love.'

'What?'

'In Milan, at the announcement of the Novo Renaissance.'

'Italy,' Magritte grunted, and the Metawhore smiled, sadly.

'The Renaissance always starts in Italy. And it always reaches England last.' She coughed into her hand, and I was suddenly embarrassed by those around me.

'What is Milan like?'

'Civilised,' she replied, her voice rich with hidden meaning.

'Who ...?'

'He was a librarian. We met at a shrine, of all places. He was taking his grandmother to pray, and I was ... well, collecting.' Her fingers moved across each other, and I saw a thin white line across the knuckles of one hand. 'He could read, and he knew history, and he wasn't –'

'Afraid?'

'No. He wasn't afraid of me. He was afraid of very little. Two days later, he came to my apartment, as a customer. He gave me a book, a collection of tales. About pilgrimages. Very old, very rare. I never asked where he got it. In return ...' she paused, gazed about herself as if momentarily unable to recall the location of a specific scar. 'I told him twenty three stories, in all, before he asked me to dinner. The first time we made love, he made me stand naked in front of him, perfectly still, wouldn't let me touch him or move even my fingers until he'd kissed the length of every scar. I spent Christmas with his family.' She looked at each of us in turn, counting us off with her eyes. 'He had a large family. For three months, I had a family too. His grandmother ... I miss her. She called me 'Brujita', and wouldn't let go of my hand. It's Spanish.' She impaled Magritte with another defiant stare. 'It means 'little witch' '.

Magritte lowered his eyes. We all did. From under his lowered gaze, Magritte asked, 'What happened?'

'He asked me to marry him.'

'But ... wasn't that what you wanted?' I asked.

'It's all I have wanted since long before he spoke the words.'

'I ... I don't understand.'

She smiled, a smile of such sadness that I bit my lip to stop from crying. 'We celebrated. A librarian does not earn much, but I could afford fresh fruit and vegetables. I spent the morning at the markets while he went to his work. I bought a feast. Apples, and pumpkin, and eggplant, and olives, and strawberries ...' She coughed, swallowed. 'I washed them, and cut them, and paid a meat trader a ransom for some spiced chicken to go with them. I walked two miles outside the city to a vintner who could supply me with the right wines. When Paulo came home, we bathed together, and I told him stories until the water turned cold and we used a week's ration of firewood to warm ourselves by his fire. We made love, and then we lay together and fed each other slices of chicken, and vegetables, and fruit, and drank wine until we fell asleep in each other's arms.'

She fell silent, and stared at our own, inadequate, flame, turned low to preserve its precious gas, sputtering at the base of the empty broth pot. I could not recall having been held by a woman, and I would never make love. I put my hands in my lap and tried not to feel base for what I knew to lie there.

'The fire had burned out by the time I awoke. We'd left the window open. I thought he was cold because we'd left the window open.'

'He ...'

'He was allergic. To something we'd eaten, something I'd made him eat. He'd died, during the night.'

'But you couldn't have –'

'I never even woke up. He died, right next to me. He hadn't even grabbed for me.' She held up her hands. The arms of the robe fell away, revealing the wounds that ran from fingertips to shoulder. 'He didn't even leave a scar.'

She lowered her face to her hands. The cabin fell silent. After a minute, she raised her head and inhaled, then looked beyond us to the darkness outside the windows.

'The family allowed me one possession, and asked me not to attend the funeral. In the end, I chose nothing. I have my memories, you see.' She tapped her head. 'And I travel light. All my money, my apartments, my customers. They can wait. It's taken me six months to get here. They can wait.'

She raised her bowl, and finished the last of her broth, cold now the tale was told, then wiped it clean with her sleeve and put it back into her bag.

'What will you do?' The whisper was Magritte's. With a start I realised that the company had returned their attentions inward to the story. How long they had listened I did not know, but the air had changed. The resentment and hatred had disappeared. Silence, respectful and humble, filled the cabin.

The Metawhore stood and shouldered her bag.

'I'm on pilgrimage,' she said.

I thought she would move back to her seat. Instead, she moved past us to the back of the carriage and through the door. Before I knew what I was doing I had jumped from my perch and was pushing through the same door. The Metawhore stood on the small platform at the carriage's rear, preparing to jump down onto the ground outside the rails. Behind her I could see into the next carriage, where a group of travellers had gathered in a circle.

'Wait.'

She glanced up at me, her eyebrows raised in enquiry.

'Where are you going?'

She dropped her bag and stretched, indicating the darkness beyond the rail station.

'I told you. I'm on pilgrimage.'

'But, in there ...' I jerked my thumb behind me, to the warmth we had just left. The Metawhore sighed, and reached into her robe. She pulled out a tattered sheaf of papers, and handed them to me.

'Have you read this?'

I glanced down at the first page, the lettering almost indecipherable under the marks and stains of long ownership. I saw the words 'Can' and 'Aucer', and a handwritten note in a language I could not read. I looked at the Metawhore in confusion.

'It's an old book,' she said, her gaze angled outwards into the night. 'A set of tales, about pilgrimages like ours. Except ...'

'What?'

'There's a tavern, in a place called Southwark. The Tabard. They start from there.' She looked back at me, and I saw a firmness in her features that had not been there before. 'You're not doing it properly,' she said. 'Unless you start from there. All this,' she waved her hand at the train, at the rail yard, at me. 'It's just a pretty train trip.'

'But ... the Bishop ...'

'Read the book.' She tapped the sheaf of papers with one finger. 'Five days walk from Southwark. Five days in April. That's what they did. That's what you *have* to do.'

I clutched the papers to my chest as she jumped down from the carriage. She glanced up at me, before striding away.

'Enjoy your train trip, apprentice.'

I watched her go, my fingers caressing the pages of her gift, my one worldly possession.

A sudden thump on the door brought me back to myself. Magritte stood behind the glass, staring out at me. He gestured, fat fingers enticing me back inside. Grease from the meal stained the lower half of his face, running into the forks of his beard. We matched stares for long heartbeats.

Then I turned from him and jumped.

The Metawhore's Epilogue

I caught up to her just outside the circle of light provided by the station towers.

'Wait.'

'What do you want?'

I held the book up.

'Where is Southwark?'

'In London.' It was not yet Londonistan in those days.

'But London's underwater.'

'I know.'

'So ...' I struggled to keep up with her. 'Wait ... what will you do?'

'I don't know. Hire a boat, find a guide, row around in circles until I find a ruin I can pretend is the right place.'

'But why?' I stopped chasing, and after a moment she ceased walking as well. 'Why is it so important to do it like this?'

She came back towards me so suddenly that I feared she was going to hit me. Instead, she stopped a step away from me and lowered her head so we looked into each other's eyes from no more than an inch apart.

'Why do you care?'

'What?'

'Why do you care? Why did you bother coming after me?'

'I ...' I hesitated. She pulled back, and looked me up and down in appraisal. 'Well?'

'I ... let me come with you.' I said the words before I really heard them. She raised her eyebrows in amusement.

'Really?'

I gulped, peered back towards the carriage where Magritte and the other travellers waited.

'Yes,' I said, and realised that I meant it.

The Metawhore crouched and extended her hand. I took it, and she drew me down so that we sat together. I felt the warmth of her skin on mine, and flushed. 'Why would you want to come with me, boy?'

I held out the book. 'You gave me ... It's all I have ...'

She squeezed my hand. 'You're welcome. Really.'

I nodded. She tilted her head, and looked at me from the corner of her eyes.

'There's more though, isn't there?'

I bit my lip.

'I saw you looking at my scars.' I bowed further, but her eyes sought mine out again. 'Do you have scars, apprentice?'

I tried to speak, and failed. My eyes stung. I wiped my tears away, regretting the need to pull my hand away from hers.

'When I joined the ... the priesthood ...'

'Yes?'

'They ... they ...' I could not speak the words. I had never wanted to cry so hard as I did at this moment, and I could not do that and speak. The Metawhore spoke for me.

'When you joined the priesthood, you took a vow, yes?'

I nodded.

'Poverty, chastity. Mainly chastity though, yes?'

I swallowed.

'They ...' I gestured towards my groin. The Metawhore raised her hands to her mouth.

'Oh, you poor boy.' I glanced at her, but there was no mockery in her expression. 'How old are you?'

'Th ... thirteen.'

She reached out, and I let her hug me until I had no more breath with which to cry.

'It must have left quite a scar,' she said as I drew away.

'I sing beautifully,' I replied, and immediately regretted the pride in my voice. She stood, and I followed.

'I'll bet you do,' she said. We turned away from the light, and faced the dark. 'It won't be easy, you know.'

'I understand.'

She shook her head and smiled. 'Oh, you really, really don't.'

'Please.'

She closed her eyes, just for a second. Then she bent to pick up her bag, and held out her hand.

'Okay,' she said. 'Come on.'

She let me hold onto her hand for as long as I needed it.

I missed the build-up to the next story, milord. As the tale of the Metawhore ended, a man pushed his way into the space next to me, and sat down. To my surprise, it was the Veteran. He turned those terrible eyes on me, and spoke softly. 'Watcher,' he said. 'The Ranger captain told me you were here. I can't stay. I'm needed out there. But you – there's a task for you.'

He told me then that the Rangers were certain someone aboard the train was broadcasting to the Londoni raiders. The broadcasts were frequency-agile microbursts, impossible to decode or triangulate, but definitely from the train. And somehow, the raiders seemed to have forewarning of the Rangers' movements.

'What do you expect me to do?' I asked. It never occurred to me to demur, or pretend. Not to him.

'Do your job,' he replied, without looking at me. Then he was gone, leaving me alone, jittery, looking at everyone in the saloon car as though they might be an enemy.

I took a deep breath, forced myself to relax, to watch – and to listen ...

The janus tale

at first I thought we were stopping so the *speciali* train could get past,' the Mummer drawled. She was a short woman in middle age, with a large head and expressive face creased white with perpetual greasepaint at the cynical corners of her mouth and the laughter lines around her heartless eyes.

Beside the Mummer was the black-cloaked, veiled woman who had not spoken yet, except by the expensive scent of her perfume which said emphatically that she was not a nun. But the Mummer's news broke her silence at last. 'A *speciali* train?' she asked. She had a low and melodious voice. 'Are you sure? You must be mistaken,' she gasped.

'I am sure. I heard the driver and the guard talk about it at the last station,' the Mummer said. 'When we stopped I thought to myself at once that that *speciali* train has caught up.' She glanced out the window at the flat fen landscape sheeted in silver water. 'I am glad we are in a good train. A *speciali* train might be fast but–' She stopped.

'What do you mean, "but"?' the veiled woman gasped. Her voice was low and breathy. But the last word flattened to an unguessed strength. She started to her feet to peer out the window, although there was no sound of train wheels, or whistle, or any sign of lights behind them.

Her sudden movement dropped her veil to her chin, where it gathered in square, even tucks before her face, while the back of her head and her hair remained covered like a nun's vestment. It was a strange coat she wore, perhaps the fashion in Londonistan but not here. It was decent black that covered her to her feet, and hid her hands and arms, but that's where decency ended. It was a rich expensive brocade.

'It is almost a mortal sin to be wearing such fine clothes,' the Peat-Digger sniffed, but fell quiet, offended, when he realised no one was listening.

The face revealed by the dropping of the veil was breathtaking, a fall of chestnut hair across a broad, coffee-coloured forehead, and clusters of curls like ripe nuts peeping out at the corner of the hood, huge amber eyes and long lashes, lips like cherries and cheeks like apples, all smooth and pampered. Mouth watering. Everyone's attention was riveted. This was some big man's plaything, that was clear at a glance. It was at once strange that she was by herself.

'Because of the llygers of course. It is after dark that they come out,' the Mummer drawled, insolently. Perhaps it was just the rivalry women display around a pretty girl, but I felt the Mummer disliked the new speaker.

'What are llygers?' the girl asked now, with enormous, eye-popping simplicity.

She must have come from a long way off, or lived a terribly sheltered life, not to have heard that tale. Both the Tingler and Mummer laughed for her folly. 'There was once a great king Whipsnade,' the Mummer told her. 'He had a huge zoo of animals, savage beasts from the far parts of the world, but that wasn't enough for him. No, he had to make them worse. That's what they do these big men. He got his genome-men to mix and match them, and then some escaped, or he let them loose on purpose. The llygers hide in the fens; they are like lions and hyenas, but with the size of a horse and the cunning of a man. They hate men and want to kill them, but worse they hate the light so we're lucky we're on a good train.'

'The genome-men,' the girl murmured and wrung her hands. Those lovely amber eyes widened.

'Now don't believe what you hear,' the Tingler put in, grinning, as the Mummer shot him a quick look to tell him to play along. 'The genome-men with bright numbers scrolling in their eyes and knives fixed to their fingers, that come out at night from the *Blitishi* Museum and snatch the children from their beds, they're just old wives tales.'

The poor girl went pale and wide-eyed. She lifted her hands from beneath her garment to clap to her mouth. She had one ring, a large square-cut amber, on the ring finger of her left hand.

Milord, primed as I was by the Veteran's warning, there was something in the girl's gesture that caught my attention, something staged, and yet real. I began to wonder if she was herself an actress, and perhaps that explained the Mummer's hostility.

I noticed, too, that the girl's fingernails were cut square, with long, strong fingers. A girl like that should have pretty painted pointed nails and small useless dainty hands laden with gems. I looked at her more carefully.

'There's no such thing as llygers,' the Nun snapped, casting an angry glance at the Tingler and the Mummer.

'There's something in the fens,' the Mummer corrected her.

'Thieves and outlaws,' the Sky-Chief sniffed.

'Maybe, but many go in and few go out again, unless they have a good bright light with them,' the Mummer said. She slapped the side of the train, affectionately. 'Once the lights are up, we'll be fine. Unlike the *speciali* train. They expected a fast journey, I guess. I don't suppose they have any lights with them. The llygers will peel off the roof of the train like an orange and–.' She made a huge gesture with both arms, as of giant jaws clamping down.

'I have not heard of any *speciali* train,' the Conductor said flat, squashing all discussion at once. He turned to the girl standing before them. 'I'm glad you've found your voice at last, and it's a voice a man likes to hear. Spin out a story until lights up,' he said.

The girl quirked an eyebrow in surprise. Everyone gazed at her expectantly. It would be entertaining either way, whether she refused or obeyed. But she gave her vestments a shake and lifted her chin.

'I'll tell you a story you won't forget. I'll tell you the story of the Janus,' she said.

'Good girl!' said the Conductor.

'The Janus! That's no such thing,' the Tingler scoffed.

'No, no it's true. I've heard of them. There are dozens of them, but they all live in Londonistan,' the Mummer said.

'There is one Janus, one alone,' the girl said, low. 'I know. A big man asked the genome-men at the *Blitishi* Museum to make the Janus, only one, just for himself alone, and when they were done, the big man took all the plans, and all the experiments, alive or dead, and destroyed them, and he took the chief genome-man, the one who had crafted the Janus, and he killed him. He wanted to be the only one with a Janus. And he was. That's the way of these big men.' The words poured out of her like smooth silk, her hands gestured in ways both artless and endlessly rehearsed.

'How do you know this?' the Mummer almost shouted.

'I lived at the *Blitishi* Museum when I was young,' she said, simply. The Mummer was chastened, for once. 'But the story of the Janus does not begin with that birth. The story began a long time ago, at least sixty-six years, six days and eight nights,' she said.

'In the name of God, the infinitely kind and infinitely cruel, God, who is wise and foolish without end,' she began. 'Once there was a village that survived the Starving Times. This was because of an old machine, the Mincer, that came from even before the *Blitishi* Museum. It was a great rectangle of rusted steel. At one end was a chute leading to two rotating cylinders of spiked steel, and at the other end was a tap. You could put anything in the chute and the Mincer would cut it up and fine it out, so nothing bad was left. The village fed it leaves, dead grass, tree boughs, shit, and dead animals, and themselves when they died. Anything they could gather or find or steal went in, except the one rule, it had to be at one time living. No rocks or stones or coins. All the wealth in the world couldn't keep you alive in the Starving Times. The rest, Mincer chopped it up and fined it out, and when you turned on the tap at the other end all that came out was a fine pink froth that hardened when it touched air so you could slice it, like ham. You could live off that pink froth all your life. It would do you no harm. When all was well it tasted of nothing. It tasted like – air made solid,' she smacked her lips as if she could taste it herself, 'but when times were hard it tasted like shit.'

'All the Mincer village lived in one long stone house, cut into rooms for each family, and one long hallway along the front – that was the main street. At the north end was the Mincer, which had two rooms to itself. The chute end of the Mincer was in the northernmost room of all, with walls of rough-cast stone and great barn doors that the dead animals and the carts full of scavenging and shit were dragged through. Dung was piled high against the walls. The Mincer was set through the wall, so that the tap was in the next room along. I suppose deep down people didn't really want to know what was going on at the mincer-end so they put the wall up, and pretended they didn't know what was on the other side.

'Families would come to the Mincer tap at dusk each evening, and take their turn. Each family would fill a pan, one for each family, and that's how they survived. As for criminals, the Mincer dealt with them, too. A thief? The Mincer took his hand. An adulterer. If a man, the Mincer took his manhood.' She paused, and everyone winced. 'A woman. It took her – hair,' she said, with a low, heartless gurgle of laughter.

The Tingler, clutching himself thoughtfully, sat straight. 'Now that is just not fair!'

'There were more men born than women for a long time so women had to be kept alive. The few girl children were born weak and most of them died. And a murderer, of course, a murderer went into the Mincer alive. That was their worst crime.

'Now the man who looked after the machine, the Mincer-man, he was a big man in the village, you can be sure. You might have thought a man with a trade like that would be a miserable sinner, but no, he was a real big man. Built like a barrel, hearty as a bull and full of good cheer, bald on top, but a great broad black beard streaked with silver. You won't believe that at this time he was almost forty, an old man, and not married. There was a touch of fear about him. The things he did with the Mincer were too much like magic perhaps, and he had a temper, a quick temper, blow through and over but nasty while it lasted. Once they had trouble piling a donkey carcass into the Mincer, and his anger blew. His face went bright red and he picked the carcass up in his two hands and heaved it in himself. His shirt ripped all down his back. You have to fear, and respect, a man as strong as that. And there were stories, too, of how some of the scraps got into the Mincer, that everyone was careful not to look too closely into. Times were hard, you shouldn't judge anyone, if sometimes a poor stranger ended up in there with the rest of the trash.

'But at last the village decided to make things right by the Mincer-man. He was after all the only man in the village who knew how to tend the Mincer. He needed sons and daughters to pass his trade on. But still no one quite liked to offer him a daughter of their own.

'Now it happened there was some villages some way off, by the shores of a long lake, that had the opposite problem. Their men were all impotent. They couldn't get it up, the poor gentlemen, and their wives were so frustrated. They blamed the water in the lake. On the far shore of the lake there was a place called the Old Stacks, where no one went, but one night Old Stacks burst into flame, and dark stuff like water came out and poured into the lake. All the fish died, and the villagers feasted for weeks, but after that the men lost interest. What could the women do? They arranged to marry their daughters far off and one married her girl to the Mincer-man. That was how the dear girl came to the Mincer village. Oh, she was a sight. Hair as yellow as ripe corn and lips like strawberries. Always bustling and singing about from dawn to dusk, and just as active after that. Oh, she was a good wife then. Glad to get some action, I guess, after all those nothing men. The Mincer-man had no complaints. No, he was delighted. Not often that a man gets such a pretty wife in the twilight of his life. But he was no fool either. He kept her busy about the house, and kept an eye on her like. But she never gave him cause to complain there. As far as he could tell she never so much looked at another. But there are few so blind as a fond husband!

'I tell you, there was something about that dear girl that some of the old wives noticed straight off. It was like there was a piece missing in her head, a moral sense. She didn't know their ways, of course, so they told her what they could, and the first time they gave her a bowl of Mincer stuff she laughed right out, but there was more than that. Perhaps this was the way things went in her village, with so few real men that what there was had to be shared about, and no one in the Mincer village thought to tell her that here things were different. Perhaps it didn't occur to her that she could do anything wrong, especially with such a fond husband.

'She took a lover almost as soon as she arrived, a young tow-haired lout, strong as an ox, full of himself, with a small beard and all his own teeth, white as white. It was her lover's caution that kept their affair going so long, not her own. Why, I believe that she would have told her husband about it at once if he had ever asked. But he never did, so she took it for granted that all was right, and went on singing like a lark from dawn to dusk, busy about the house. It was a hard time then, and the pink froth tasted like dung for the longest time, so appetites for other pleasures were strong.

'There was one time when her husband was not there to keep an eye on her, and that was when he was working the Mincer, in the late afternoon, just before dusk. So that was when she and her lover took themselves off, and here was the clever part. I think the lover worked it, the worthless sort, for she was not clever enough or cruel enough to think it for herself. They went at it in the Mincer tap room, hard up against the Mincer itself, out of sight where it ran next to the back wall, while the Mincer-man worked hard at the other end of the same machine. He'd be shovelling the scavenging into the chute, while in the next room, the lover would be shovelling something quite else into his wife, and who had more fun we all can guess. The noise the Mincer made covered their own, and they were safe enough as long as they stopped when the machine stopped. If anyone saw them, people would just think they were here to get the pink stuff.

'But all good things come to an end, and one day they were so wrapped up that they didn't stop when the machine stopped. They didn't even notice. But they noticed the silence when they finished. The worthless lover hangs back but the dear girl comes hurrying out, tucking her hair and skirts back into place. There's the whole village gawping at her, and the outraged husband standing right there, arms akimbo, face bright red.

'"What are you doing!" he thunders at her.

'"Why, fucking this man," she says, with a look of such surprise on her silly face. For, of course, what else could she be doing? I think myself she thought it was a stupid question. And I think it proves she was innocent all along, that she didn't know she was doing anything wrong, because she could have talked him around, even then. To save face he would have swallowed anything.

'Well, the Mincer-man gives a great roar and lunges forward, hands outstretched. He grabs the poor girl by her sweet throat and throttles her so hard that her dear neck snaps. It's all over in an instant, before anyone can even think to stop him. And then he drops her and stares around, like a blind bull and gives such a roar that everyone hurries off to their houses and bolts the doors. Then the Mincer-man picks his wife up again and carries her to his house, and lays her gently, so gently on the bed, and sits beside her all night with his head in his hands. For he never meant to kill her, you understand. His anger got in the way. He loved her. She could have talked him around, after a while. He loved her still, the dear sweet silly foolish thoughtless girl.

'The dear girl was twenty-two years old when she died. Twenty-two years, three days and three nights, to be precise. She was just approaching her fourth night.

'No one noticed or even cared, that during that moment of white hot anger the worthless lout has come bolting out, and hared off out of the village and out of their lives, with his hands clutched tight between his trouser legs. Some say he was killed in a bar brawl a few years later, and some say he died in the Plague, but no fate is good enough for him. God has long since sorted him out, I guess.

'The villagers talked things over that night, and the next day their big men tiptoed into the room and explained that they understand the Mincer-man did not mean to kill his wife so he did not need to go into the Mincer himself. But she did, of course. She was dead. No need to waste good clean flesh, when they'd been eating dung-tasting pink froth for months.

'The Mincer-man nodded and he picked up his own dear wife with his own hands. She still had that look of surprise on her face that he could not smooth out, no matter how much he tried. He took her down to the Mincer. He turned it on, so the mincer ground, and the machine groaned to life, and he slid her down the chute. The machine ground to a higher tone, then all was gone. Then the Mincer-man gave a great shout, and threw himself in. That was the end of him. The guilty and the innocent all ground together, all mixed up and chopped up, and tapped out in pink froth. So mixed up together that even God could not work them apart.' The story teller paused, hands to her heart.

'A dark story but I like the ending. It punishes vice,' the Census-Taker declared, before anyone else could speak.

'Only one third has been said,' the girl went on. 'But to tell the rest, I must take a different part.'

And the story-teller pulled the veil up over her face, so it became a hood, and she turned around, slowly and with an awful precision. As she turned there was a terrible sharp creaking sound, the cracking of double joints. Her arms and legs, hands and feet, stayed put, facing her audience, but now her back was to them. Everyone recoiled, instinctively. Only the Mummer leaned forward in professional appreciation. 'Fantastic,' she murmured to the Tingler. 'She must be worth a fortune.'

It was a remarkable change. The girl seemed to grow taller, squarer; she took on a jaunty air. The hooded figure expanded, seemed to suck in air. Even the perfume changed to a subtler scent. And then a hand came up, now the right hand, that had the square amber ring on the ring finger, and pulled the back of the hood down, that was now the front.

There was a man's face there, and such a man, eyes sparkling with a roguish glint, a broad determined slash of brow above, a strong nose, and slash of a red mouth, corner firmly tucked in. Such a jolly face to look upon, all fellowship and lusty good cheer. The only thing the same was that rich chestnut hair, square cut about the face in masculine style, and a square-cut beard. The veiled dress had become a monkish-style habit, but it could not be said to give him a devout air. He gave a short bow.

The Mummer could not help herself. She leaped up and applauded.

'Well done, sir! Why this is the Janus himself or such a stunt to fool the biggest of men!' she cried.

So it was, or at least so it seemed to me. And I wondered: what was the woman's face thinking now, staring into the dark of the hood – did they have separate thoughts? Did the rich brocade hide malformation? What of separate arms and legs? Of sexual organs?

'By our holy lady Margaret,' the Mathematician started.

'Did I say that was the end of them? No, not quite,' the Janus's voice was hoarse and low, intoxicating with the spice of the forbidden. All the women sat up and paid attention. 'Husband and wife were so mixed up together that even God could not work them apart, and God is the supreme worker. Men make mistakes but they are mortal mistakes. God's mistakes are infinite. God is infinitely kind and infinitely cruel. God is wise and foolish without end. So when the husband and wife appear before God, so mixed up and muddled that neither can be told apart, God throws up hands and sends them back to the world, to have another chance. "Don't mess things up this time," God warns them. So here my story starts again.'

The Mummer leaned over to the Tingler, eyes on the amber ring, and whispered. 'So which one did the big man marry?'

'The man evidently,' the Tingler whispered back, and they both sniggered.

'Once there was a Warren that survived the Freezing Time,' the Janus began. 'It was so cold that people froze in their houses. The sun never shone and no crops grew. The Warren made blankets, that was how the people survived. All day and all night the looms ran. Everyone worked. The men fed the looms from the top, the women cut the cloth as it came out the end and the children darted in under the rising shafts to snatch out the snags that would ruin the cloth. The looms must never stop or people would freeze in their houses, so if any man fell in from the top, or a child was swept in by the shaft, the looms kept going. The corpse was fed through with the rest of the thread, so the cloth came out red, and the women cut out the red cloth and gave it to the family to bury.

'The looms were dug in beneath the ground, and the people carved out their Warren below them. The poor folk lived in dormitories, hundreds of rows of three-tiered bunk beds. The better off lived in rooms deeper down, with a few families to each room, the tailors and dress makers and silver smiths and so on, deeper down were the big men that had a room to themselves, and deepest of all lived the woman who owned the factory. She had six rooms and she had the greatest luxury of all. She lived alone. But she thought she was cursed. She had never known love or what it was to be loved. She was surrounded by warmth, but it never touched her heart. She felt cold, cold all her life.

'She stared into her mirror at night, in her rich chambers, surrounded by all the warmth and solitude of wealth. She saw a woman tall and bony, all elbows and knees, with teeth like a horse and eyes like flint, and black hair streaking to grey steel. Staring into that mirror night after night she came to believe that she was cold at heart, cold as iron, and set apart, until one day when she was old, almost forty. God knows all and God sees all, God forgets all, God is blind to all. God help an old woman who falls in love with a youth.

'Every day she walked the steel bridge over the looms, where the overseers lurked making sure the loom-men were feeding the thread evenly, and no one shirking or idling or spoiling the cloth. The overseers didn't like the loom-men; "warm tools", they called them. All's fair in love and war. The loom-men called them worse. But this one day the old lady saw a young loom-man with a beard and hair like honey. He was working hard, but he glanced up as she approached and when she caught his eye he went bright red. No flush touched her cheeks. She was like iron, she believed, but she forgot that even iron can rust. That night, sitting in her fine warm rooms, she found herself thinking about that young man again, and dreaming about having him in her arms, until she came to herself with a start.

'She thought what a fool she was, dreaming of love at her age, and took herself off to bed. But the next day she woke determined to have a good look at him, and prove to herself that he was worthless.

'So the next day she stalked out over the steel bridge where the overseers lurk, and she looked down at the young man with hair and beard like honey, ready to blast him if he so much as glanced up. But word had got around to be careful, and no one dared look up, not even him. All she could see on a closer look was that he was very dirty. Never washed in his life. Probably stank of sweat and shit, she told herself. But she found she was fretting because he wouldn't meet her eye, so she took herself off.

'That night she sat in her room and didn't even glance at the mirror. No, she sat on her bed and stroked the covers and thought about how dirty and stinking he must be, and wondered what it would be like to have that filth and sweat rub off on her own self. Just because she had never loved or ever known love, didn't mean she didn't know how to enjoy herself. She had costumes, whips and chains, spurs and masks in a gilded closet in her bedroom, and she knew how to use and be used. Now, she fell back on the bed and whimpered and dived her hand between her legs, but that wasn't enough.

'The next day she summoned the youth to her antechamber. She just had to have a good look at him, poor fool. The antechamber was the poorest of the six rooms she had to herself, where she met her overseers and handled her business. It had a desk, a padded chair for herself and two bony wooden chairs for visitors, hangings and carpet.

'When the young man stepped in, the old lady drew a long, deep breath because for the first time in her life she felt warm. She was in a room deep below the earth, but sunlight came streaking in, touching her with long warm fingers. She jutted her jaw and felt angry with herself for being so weak, so angry that she must hit out at someone else or shriek.

'"Sit!" she barked at the poor youth, who is in such a hurry to obey that he tipped the chair over and landed on the floor arse first. He had to set it right and sit again, quick as quick. He was convinced he was about to be sacked, but he couldn't get over the shock of being alone with one other person, for the first time in his life. His bare toes twiddled in the carpet and he stared at the furnishings and hangings, such luxuries as he had never imagined. Frightened as he was, he was still thinking of how he'd boast to his friends of where he'd been. When he saw she was staring at him he tried a smile, but there was no response from the bony face before him so after a moment his smile winked out.

'She studied him carefully, all this time. Yes, he had hair and beard like honey and a smile that flashed out like sunlight, but he was wearing rags, his teeth were bad and broken, he was dirty, filthy with factory grime, and completely unwashed. He stank of sweat and shit and oil, and his hands were scarred from feeding the loom. He was skinny, never had a rest in his life to put on fat. Oh, but his cheeks were like apples and his eyes danced.

'So she stalked around the desk, to stare him down, and with him her own weakness. As she got nearer he tried to keep meeting her eye, so his chair tipped over and he sprawled on his back again, then jumped to his feet in haste, stammering, apologising. He really did stink. She opened her mouth to crush him, but instead she found she could not think.

'Now, all his fears drained out the soles of his feet. She wasn't the first woman to give him that look. The girls had always fancied him, although he never suspected until that moment the old lady was human enough to feel soft. As this thought flashed through his head, fear came crashing in. If he was wrong, she'd sack him, that's for sure. But if he was right ... Oh he didn't think any more. He caught her by the shoulders and gave her the best kiss he'd ever given anyone in his life.

'Then they fell backwards against the desk, which was sturdy enough, and she hissed that he was filthy and dirty while climbing aboard, and yelled "Harder, harder", and giving him a ruler. Poor youth, his head was spinning but his body didn't need his mind to be paying attention, and well, all good things come to an end sooner or later. He ended up lying there gasping and wondering what just happened, in the name of God the infinitely kind and infinitely cruel.

'"Get back to work," she snapped, then she turned back to her desk like nothing happened. He left, head still spinning, and when the overseers wanted to know what that warm tool was doing he was smart enough not to tell them.

'The old lady spent her evening marching up and down in her bedroom with fists clenched ranting to herself about what a fool she was, but there was nothing she could do. She'd let sunlight into her life and it was impossible to bar it out. The next day she got him back again, and this time she took him to her bedroom and gave him a whip and spurs. Afterwards, she sent him back to the looms again.

'That night she had a dream that he was working the looms and fell in, and the cloth fed out red at the far end. She woke in a horrible fright, knowing she could not risk that. The next morning she promoted him over the overseers.

'So, soon he was marching around in fine clothes and getting a bath once a month, whether he needed one or not, and three meals a day, with meat even. He was all gratitude, and besides he had no idea why she doted on him. The next day or the next, she might fall out with him and send him back to the looms again. So he was very careful and caring, and besides she soon started teaching him to use the costumes, whips and masks and spurs, which he found enjoyable and eye-opening.

'She couldn't believe her luck either, and fear made her jealous. She gave him good clothes, a pocket watch, diamond nose-studs and rings, then went snooping among his things to see if she could find anything incriminating. But she was wrong either way, the nosy old thing. He was too bewildered at his own luck to ever think of doing her wrong. It never occurred to him. He walked around with the righteous stupid armour of innocence drawn snug and warm around him. He was even starting to get used to his new life when one day she told him her birthday was coming soon.

'He had never had a birthday in his life. He didn't even know how old he was. It took him a little while to realise she was hinting after a birthday present, and then only because she gave him the money to buy her something. But what do you give a woman who has everything?

'At first he thought of a new dress, for he loved his new clothes. But a whole dress would take too long to make. But then he remembered the closet with the costumes, whips and chains and masks and spurs. What about another costume, he wondered. A lacy number with stays and tights. He got light headed thinking about it. But the more he turned the idea over the more he liked it.

'He hurried off to the old lady's dressmaker, who worked night and day to put the costume together, but oh! she was empty-headed, prattling young thing. Pretty enough once perhaps, and her dark hair was thick and long, but she was badly pox-scarred, poor thing. Perhaps that's why she did what she did. Perhaps she was just lonely and wanted to feel important. She boasted to some of her friends about her important customer and even showed the costume off to them, but she went one step too far and hinted at a silly little story, that he had another reason for visiting. That story had spread all over by the time she had finished the costume and boxed it and handed it over to him. Everyone had heard it, except him.

'He hurried off with his gift, absolutely delighted, but he had one problem, or so he thought, poor goose, and that was where to hide it. He knew the old lady was always snooping among his things and he didn't want her to find it ahead of time. At last he thought of the loom. She never went down to the loom floor. It was the perfect place. So he trotted down to where the children dash in under the shafts to snatch away the snarls. Watching them work he wondered if he could still do it. So he ducked in under the rising shaft, slid his present in beneath the heddles, and ducked back out as the shaft descended again. It was a smart piece of work and he felt pleased that he still had it in him, even though he'd thickened a bit around the waist and it wasn't as easy as it used to be to duck in and out in time before the shaft came hissing down. He cuffed the nearest children, told them not to touch the box and he'd bring them some food later, perhaps some meat, then he sauntered off.

'But that silly dressmaker's story had spread and spread, and finally reached the very bottom of the Warren. The old lady heard it and flew into a jealous rage. She marched off to the dressmaker to find out the truth, gave her a shake or two, and a slap. The dressmaker told her the story wasn't true, but she stuttered and hesitated while trying to talk about the gift, and raised the old lady's suspicions to such a pitch that she flew at the girl with a shriek. By the time, the young man turned up, the old lady was more than half way convinced of the worst. He was such an innocent that when she accused him he actually laughed. It was a laugh of surprise, not guilt, but it didn't help. He saw the only thing to do was to show her the present so he took her down to the loom floor, ducked under the rising shaft and snatched her gift out.

'But you can all guess what happened next, especially when I tell you how old he was. I've known how old he was then, all my life, even though he never knew it himself. He was twenty-two years, three days and just approaching his fourth night.

'He was flurried or distracted, or just plain miscalculated. The shaft came down before he was half out. He thrust the box at her, for he didn't want the poor dressmaker to get into worse trouble. That was almost his last thought. "It's your birthday present," he shouted. Then the shaft hissed down and whipped him into the loom. There was a spray of blood, and the old lady shrieked. "Get him out!" But no one budged. It was too late anyway. The shaft rose, the heddles whipped, on at a red note. Then she dived in herself, the silly old coot, and tried to haul what was left of him out, but the leg she clutched came free in her hands, then the shaft came down a second time and she was shot in herself. The cloth came out red at the other end, and the women cut it out, and buried it, all in one great sodden red loop.'

There was a pause, but this time no one spoke.

'You can't imagine how God felt when those two turned up,' the Janus said. 'The feelings of God are beyond mortal imagining. God had sent them down to get sorted out and they'd made things worse. God ranted and stormed at them. Then "One more time!" God sent them on down. "And this time I'll make sure myself that you can't fuck up!"

'God knows all and forgets all. That's how I know their stories myself. God sent them down so hopelessly mixed up that they were born with only one body between them. People say I was born at the *Blitishi* museum, that the genome-men made me, but I am of no mortal making. I am a divine mistake. And the reason I know that is all my life, all my life, deep down I have always known that I have only twenty-two years, three days and four nights. Like a heart beat, like a bell toll, every day, every night. That is how long I have to sort this out. And today is the twenty-second year, the third day, and this is the fourth night.' The Janus stared at the window, a square of blackness. But there was no sign of light. 'Tonight I hoped to be safe in Canterbury, at the tomb of the blessed martyr Margaret, to pray for strength. There I thought we would be safe.'

The story-teller pulled the veil up over his face, so it became a hood, and he turned around, slowly and with an awful precision. As he turned there was a sharp creaking sound, the cracking of double joints, until his back was to them while arms and legs stayed put. The figure seemed to lose confidence and power, the shoulders shrank. And the left hand, that had the square amber ring on the ring finger, pulled the hood down.

Everyone flinched.

The girl's downcast face peered out at them. Tears trembled in her eyes. 'The story is only two thirds told,' she said, at last. 'But I do not know how it ends. I was the plaything of a big man. At first, I thought he loved me and I was happy. I was his pet, and he made me, but then he forgot. He called me to him less and less, and then I was left by myself. Perhaps I disgusted him. Twenty-two years, three days and four nights,' she whispered. 'That's all I had and it was drawing to an end. So I fled. But the *speciali* train, the *speciali* train. That is him. Twenty-two years, three days and four nights.' The tears streaked slowly down her cheeks. 'I forgot that all along there was never just the two of us. There was always another one. What if in saving myself I have doomed him?'

Now, as the story had unfolded, the storm had crept up on us once more, though nobody had paid it any mind. But just at that moment, a sizzle of blue-white lightning brought a terrible booming roar of thunder. The night-lights flickered, and went out. Children screamed and cried, and the train shook as the thunder rolled and growled.

The rain sheeted down once again, and the lights came back on. Everyone blinked, and looked around.

The Janus was gone.

The Mummer started a slow hand clap. 'Encore! Encore!' she called.

'The end was too confusing. What does it mean?' the Census-Taker exclaimed loudly, puzzled. 'There's only the two of them in there, surely, or are there three? Two were quite enough for me!'

'Oh shut up you old fool!' The Scribbler leaped to his feet, face white. He was quite drunk by now. 'The *speciali* train!' he cried, and ran out the door. The Mummer bellowed after him. 'Stop, you fool. Come back. It was acting! Acting!'

But the Scribbler did not stop, so the Mummer and the Conductor ran after him, and brought him back.

'I couldn't see a thing. It was too dark,' the Scribbler blubbered. 'Let me out. I'll catch up.'

'Are you mad!' the Sky-Chief said. Llygers or not, no one went out in the fens after dark. The Miner grabbed the Scribbler's shoulders and shook him. 'What is this all about?'

'It wasn't just the two of them. It never was. There was always a third. The lover, the dressmaker, now the big man,' the Scribbler grabbed the Miner's coat collar and twisted the cloth in his hands, as if trying to wring out an explanation.

'You're too caught up in the story. Don't be so alarmed,' the Miner said.

'Twenty-two years, three days and four nights,' the Scribbler shouted.

'It is a time-bomb, the genome-men often plant them,' the Miner soothed him. 'It kills their experiments after a set time.'

'No! No! You don't get it!' The Scribbler's entreaty became a demand. 'We shouldn't have told her about the llygers. The Janus wasn't worried about herself. She was worried about the big man. That he'd die this time instead of them.'

The Miner threw up his hands. 'I give up. I don't like this tale,' he grumbled. 'I prefer to know how a story ends.'

'It was acting, idiots. All acting,' the Mummer shouted at both of them, waving her arms, exasperated. 'The Janus acted in the story and out of it. Didn't know when to stop. Probably didn't know how. Oh, he's brilliant he was. I'll tell you a story you won't forget, that's what he said, and this was the final touch, the vanishing. He made sure we'd remember that.'

'Are you sure there was a *speciali* train behind us?' The Scribbler turned on the Mummer.

'Of course there was. I told you. I heard,' the Mummer radiated utter outrage that her word was even doubted. 'The Janus opened this door to distract us from his real hiding place. He's a brilliant actor. He's in another disguise somewhere else on the train.'

Yet for all her certainty, it seemed none of them could quite tear their minds from a vision of that exquisite, forlorn figure, so hopelessly unsuited to its surroundings, blundering helplessly away along the flooded rails on a mission doomed to end too soon, one way or the other. They returned, arguing, and checking every carriage as they went. But no one saw the Janus again. Nor was there ever any sign of the *speciali* train.

*I*n the commotion that followed the flight of the Janus, I took the opportunity to slip away to the toilets. Not that I needed to use them. No, I had the Veteran's warning ringing in my ears – that there was someone aboard the car providing information to the Londinistan raiders. I had finally realised there was something I could do about that.

In the privacy of the jakes, I activated the multicorder's playback. Of course, the near-magical contact lens display for which it was designed is long since gone, but Technical section reconfigured the output signal for me. Now it interfaces with a standard old-style gaming visor. It's adequate for fieldwork, though not concealable, like the original contacts. Another lost technology, there.

I spun the vidfile back and forth, concentrating around the Veteran's Tale, when the first word of the Londoni raiders reached us. It took me only a few minutes to spot it, now that I was looking for it: a man sitting uneasily near the exit of the saloon car, who kept glancing at a heavy, oldstyle watch on his wrist. Shortly before the end of the Nun's Tale, the watch flashed, and the man moved quickly to cover it with his other hand. With a furtive glance around, he rose and left the saloon car.

I tucked my visor away, reset the multicorder, and went in search.

It made sense to me that my quarry would travel first class. He could not have known of the storm, any more than the rest of us. He would be, like me, an observer and something of an opportunist, looking for what he could find on this auspicious journey. Perhaps he might make new contacts. Perhaps he had a purpose of some sort. Whatever the case, when the train was forced to a halt by the storm, he signalled – and his masters answered, mobilising a team of raiders to make what they could of this opportunity.

It was pure conjecture, of course – or it would have been, except that the Veteran had seemed so very certain. Remembering the remorseless calm of his voice, I shivered as I made my way into the first class cabin-car.

With the multicorder adjusted for the seach, I found him easily. He was no longer broadcasting, but he had neglected to shield some of his equipment, I suppose. In all that darkened car, only the fourth cabin showed electromagnetic activity. Abandoning stealth, I rapped on the heavy plastic door. 'Tickets, please,' I said.

The multicorder pulsed an alert as electromagnetics spiked somewhere behind the door. Alarmed, I palmed my 'chette pistol and stood a little to one side, where I would not be seen at once.

The door opened, just a crack. A hand emerged, holding a square of paper, one corner nipped away. 'Single cabin, first class,' said a muffled voice from behind the door. 'All in order, yes?'

He was professional enough, I will say. I reached for his ticket. What else could I do? But it took no special night vision to see I wore no black gloves, as the real conductor did, and as I reached, the ticket fell away to reveal a sinister dark shape in the palm of his hand.

We shot at the same time. Because I stood to one side, he missed. Because I disregarded my training and aimed for his wrist, not his body, I did not miss. His subsonic slug buried itself in the opposite wall of the carriage, then flared in a thermite reaction which would have charred its way through my body. My nano-sharp flechettes of crystallised neurotoxin pierced his skin, dissolving instantly. He recoiled, but already it was too late. A second or two later, I heard him fall.

That, milord, is how quickly these things happen.

I stripped him of his more obvious equipment, and transferred his small travelling bag to my cabin. The heavy watch I wrapped in my own Faraday satchel. Then I washed my hands and my face. Satisfied that I didn't look like a man who had just carried out his fourteenth murder in the name of the Crown, I slipped back into the saloon car, where I was just in time to hear the Lighterman begin his tale.

The Lighterman's Tale

The tempest is spent, but there's always another.

The world hurls itself against us like a storm, with its screaming ebbs and mewling falls. The storms past were vast and cruel and these are as nothing to them, eh, but still they'll tear away our works and snatch our words out of our mouths until we're naught but gestures, and shivering; or bloody smears 'neath all that wind-brought ruin.

I've seen things come, post-storm, out of the mist, drifting dead and serene down the Stour. I've seen 'em, as I wait fer my cargo, and blessed am I that I'm still to drift myself, and sometimes my contracted ships don't come in, and I'm at a loss, because I know there'll be tears all the way along ta Canterbury proper, because the ships are the lifeblood of this island. But there's always some ships that make it and these days more often than not.

My pa was a lighterman, yes, though he came to it late, worked on them gangs that put the life back into the canals. Came to lighterage because he couldn't bear to leave that work behind. I was born to the job, and hard though it is, it's good paying, yes. Enough so's I could make the trip North and back – that such wealth could lead to me to such cold places, is hard to fathom, past the half drowned Londonistan into them icy regions perilous. Glad I am ta be returning. But let me say we earn our wage, there's none more backbreaking labour.

I've a house, four walls and all, and thick, but still those summer storms can rattle them, and those summer floods can sometimes break the levee bank.

Stories are like that, floods what transcend their boundaries, can flood your own living. Out on the river we catch a lot of tales, and see those that play them, too. And tales are good currency, aren't they. Well, we all know it.

He were younger than me, though he'd had time enough at sea to age him so he could have passed as the older of us two. I was drinking in the *Half Teat and Cupped Balls*, you fine men might know it, or not, one of Canterbury's finest dockside establishments. I was already pissed, but the sight of him, pale as bone, limbs thin, but straggling curtains of flesh beneath, one hand wrapped 'round a guitar case, and that was rare enough sight in itself.

Well, he was either a phantom or dreadful scared by one, eh. I looked at him and said, 'What you drinking?'

'Whiskey,' he said. 'None too fussy.'

But I was, and three drams of the stuff – out of St Austell, the Cornish are the masters of brewing now, and don't none of you Northern folk disagree – and he was sitting more comfortable in the chair. Jacobs, his name was Jacobs.

And he set about with this relating, and I'll pass it on to you.

Now he was never much for sailing. His father had been a musician, and a good one, Jacobs had his guitar, could play too, from all accounts. But after that Puritan Wave, eight years back, you know with the killing, all them artists left hanging on the gibbet. Well, after that the musician's life had been hard, the name itself a curse. Few dared to employ musicians except on the Holy days, those what played were clergy in the most part, and that wasn't the sort of work that Jacob's could stomach.

So he'd taken to the briny life, his father knew a man on the good ship *A.T.M.*, and it was better to have work than none, for the winters are cold for a man with idle hands, and that way's a slow death – better a fast death in the salt and the storm.

He worked the *A.T.M.*, and he played his father's guitar in the night, when he could, and for a month he'd naught been able, the work's hard on the hands. And he played careful and gentle, cause he had but a few strings, and there was few places that made them, might well be eight months (and a week's wages) till he could get a replacement.

The *A.T.M* was coming onto to Portsmouth when the storm built up, huge and fit to shake the boat from x to y. Fought that gale for three days, his captain as canny a sailor as any that ever. Still they hit a reef, on none of their maps, though by then they could have been anywhere.

The *A.T.M.* shattered, with a god-awful thunderous crack, on them rocks and he was caught in them roiling raging waters. Rosary Buddha alone knows how he ever came upon the shore, but he did in the dark, with the waves giant around him, and there he lay, in the cold, dragged halfway up the beach by chance and the beatings of the storm.

When he woke it was still dark, but there were lights, in the distance: steady, unfamiliar lights. He cast around for anyone, but no, but for some bits of the *A.T.M* he was the only thing washed upon the shore, and his guitar case. He remembered grabbing it, remembered clinging to it in the foamy sea, waiting for rocks to crush his limbs or dash open his skull, but then it had slid from his grip, and he'd been left flailing.

Now he dragged it up the shore and, well away from the water, opened it. The seals had held, the guitar was untouched. He ran his fingers cross the neck, and it was a glorious sound, and for the first time he felt less than terror.

He walked to the lights.

Wasn't far, even for a man as worn as him. He reached a circle of buildings, all lit with that strange steady light. There was noise issuing from one that must be a pub, and singing coming from it as well, a soft and sweet voice.

He stumbled to it.

The doors were locked. For all the singing, and the light. He knocked upon that door. Nothing. He knocked again, and harder. Nothing.

Third time he knocked, and his fist boomed against the door.

It opened, and he was bathed in such light that he threw his hands before his eyes, the guitar case still in one hand.

Electricity. He'd not encountered that steady luminescence outside one of those travelling shows, or them row of lights round Parliament, and this was brighter than all them lights combined. Not a head turned, 'cause all their eyes were on the stage.

'Where you from?' came a voice to his side.

'The sea,' he said. 'The storm.'

'Ain't been no storm, not for a two day or more.'

'There has, and it cast me here,' Jacob said.

'Well, be that as it may. I'll ask you this, and you think on your answer. Are you a God fearing man, Mr Jacobs?'

Jacobs laughed. 'I should be.'

'Something of an answer in that,' muttered the voice. 'You a musician are you, come to play with Eleanor?'

He shook his head.

'Don't come all elusive with me, fuckin' musicians. You had some of Eleanor's pills?'

Jacob shook his head, again, though he felt awful strange, it weren't no pill, but the sea. The sea was all that had battered him. He looked down at his clothes, not a crust of salt, nor a drop of the storm remained upon them, not even a memory of a mark. And for a moment, he was frightened, and then caught sight of Eleanor, proper, and she was a beauty. With lips as full as though she'd had em bruised, but she hadn't, not a single hand had touched 'em. And she could sing, and she could dance.

'That's our Eleanor. We all love her. Sometimes she'd find a handful of them glam pills that the Spanish sell. She'd pass em out, one by one, to all her paramours, and they would tumble or rise to the occasion, they'd never know with her, never know just what she might have passed off, but we'd risk it for a kiss and the promises contained within such favours. You tell her your heart, you tell her the truth, or it will go ill for you.'

He looked down for the source of that voice. There was naught, but the air at his elbow, and the door closing behind him.

Now we lightermen and sailors, we see things for what they are. We understand the ephemeral, the river and its Mistress the sea brings with one hand and snatches mad with the other. It kisses then it bites.

You've seen them towers of art, them installations that survived the storms of the past. You know about them ironic stacks of old useless stuff; the Ipods still in their cases, silent, I've heard they could sing, plug em in and you could hear all the noises and beats of them anthems, the Beatles, the Stones, the Queens, and the several varieties of Roses.

Well, she knew the old songs, and there 'ain't a man of the river, or the sea – and what's the river anyway, but a generous finger of the sea – that doesn't live by the songs, the beats that pass the time, that make it generous rather than cruel, even if it's a lament.

That place, warm and song crowded was like those installations. Something out of time, out of place. Here there was song, pure, but not pious, and steady light, and voices amplified in ways that only the government and the clergy possess, though not half as well as what he heard in that pub.

And there, out of time, probably dead, or mad, or cursed, he grew brazen. Jacobs pulled out his guitar, careworn but cared for, and strummed a few bars; all melancholy, and loud.

The singing stopped, every eyes turned on him, including, and most wonderfully, Eleanor's. She was all mock, and it was the mockery of a woman who knows what she is, and don't care. 'So you play,' she said.

He grinned. 'Like the fuckin' bands of old.'

He started on some Hendrix, the old dead, drew the strings with his hard fingers. And then he played *Eleanor Rigby* and she grinned, at his cheek, and started singing too. And that voice struck up hard against the music and every one of them (men, or faerie things, or beasts born out of longings and the sea and the past) knew that they'd lost this lovely: like in them stories out of the tattered books, when there was models and singers, and c'lebrities. That she'd fallen for the oldest thing in the world, a man with a fuckin' guitar.

But not really, they were both matched; they both lost themselves to each other.

When he was done, he smiled and went off for a piss.

Another paramour came at him with a knife. You don't fight a lighterman or a sailor. You don't interrupt his stream. He slapped that knife away and broke the bastard's hand in three places afore he'd even shaken himself at the trough. Come have a go at me, if you don't believe it. Ah, but enough, eh. It's the story not the boasts, and we've all done enough of that.

He returned from the violence of the head, and Eleanor called him up onto that stage, and as he bent to pick up his guitar, she stayed his hand, and passed him something else.

Oh, and then he was afeared and delirious with joy.

You ever seen those photos of the Old time bands, with their electric instruments, their keyboards and their drums? She'd put a Stratocaster in his hand, wood and gloss and iron, and polished to a ruddy sheen. She had given him the true voice of rock, and he ran his fingers along its strings, and it roared. And she grinned, and they played, and they played.

God know's what it was he played, some of it he knew, some of it he didn't, but the notes pulled him along, and his fingers followed. He rocked, and he was as a god.

When Jacobs played that crowd lifted, as the notes rose, as he strangled them, or let them fall away like death and the absolution and the glory after. But when she started singing.

Oh.

Shit, man, it was rough and sweet at once, it was mad grinning sex, it was like this train, but set alight and hurled, fairly hurled, trailing fire through the fucking sky.

His eyes were only for hers and the voice she brought to his song, and the few times he turned into the audience, all he could see was some luminous dark, some roaring silkiness. He played, into the night, and then, when his fingers were raw. Eleanor stopped him. The pub was clearing out.

'Where are they going?' Jacob's demanded.

'There's hours to dawn,' Eleanor said. 'They're leaving us alone.'

She brought those bruised lips against his and kissed him with a fury that only the storm could match, or a storm-tossed boy.

Well, you need not doubt that he and Eleanor found no loneliness that night, they fucked, and wound themselves inside each other. He dipped his fingers into her beauty, and she dipped back. Jacob's wasn't lax in the ways of love, fucked for country and all, but they were wild.

And there was the song. For they sang, he in his rough voice, her in that sweetness and fire. And when they were done, still they murmured to each other, still they lay their voices and laments against each other's skin.

He'd been gentle as the sun drew near, bathed her, and she him. And they'd kissed fierce too. From tit, to lip, to toe and puss. Cat and cock had seen out the night and now there was just talk and weary satisfied glances.

'You're a sailor,' she said, as the sun was rising, and she slipping all that wonderful into her clothes.

'Yes,' he said.

And that was his mistake.

He said to me, as he took another dram. That was his cruellest moment, for if he'd but said, no. Or answered, I'm a musician, things would have turned different. For the rules are different for sailors.

Like the voice had said, at the door, where he had knocked thrice. You speak true to the lady, and he hadn't.

Or maybe not.

The thing is, there's no way of knowing.

Her face hollowed, and the stars filled the spaces between her flesh. Her eyes widened, and then she was gone. The sun fled, the dark came, all of this at once, and plummeting, and he fell with it.

The crew of the *New Labor* found him on the shore; lips cracked, barely alive, arms wrapped around his guitar case. He would not leave it at first. Even though it were nought but a sliver of beach off a reef, more like to be blown away in the next storm, or wash away with the tide.

Seems they'd heard singing the night before, and the captain a hale, rational fellow, keen on illumining those dark superstitions what have flared up since all the deaths and bleak days, had set about finding it's source. No siren call, just him, and the shore.

He'd asked: what sort of singing? And the captain had smiled. 'Sweet as angels, and pitched right high. You still got your balls?'

'Aye, and then some,' he'd croaked.

So that would have been that, but for two things.

Seems there were new guitar strings in his case, metal ones and they never wore down, never broke, nor went out of tune .He showed me a small box, one of them players of old, I put the buds into my ear, worn as they were, and he played me two songs, turning the key in its side.

Sweetest sounds I've ever heard. Eleanor Rigby, and something else, something I'd not heard before, beautiful, but behind it, in the background all I could hear was the sea, the crashing waves. 'I don't know what it is either, but I played it,' he said, and snatched it away before I was done. 'You've had your listen.'

I asked him about that sound, the waves crashing or the static, like what you might hear on one of those old radios.

'The mechanism's wearing down,' he said. 'The static gets louder every time I play it. Sometimes I close my eyes, and I can hear the sea or time, or whatever it is, drawing nearer, drowning out her voice.'

'Maybe, she's waiting for you,' I said. 'Maybe she's just waiting for you to admit what you are to her?'

Jacobs looked at me, and grinned. 'Fricken romantic Lightermen. Maybe the sun shine's out mae arse, too, eh?'

He finished his last dram, and thanked me for it, and I thanked him for the story.

Now, that was the last I heard from, or of, him, but for this.

A man what bought a passage to Spain, cast himself in the sea, by a thin nail of reef. He'd leaped into the briny dark, with his guitar. Screaming and singing, and laughing. 'Musician, I'm a fuckin' musician.'

Well, they'd searched for hours, but the sea was getting higher, and darker, and they'd never found no body. Which doesn't mean nothing, but

I'd like to think it does. I'd like to think he found his Eleanor.

There's things out there, powers and memories of when we were gods, and music was everywhere. Seen none of it myself, but I've heard it, in that box and in his words, and it was the past brought back, and like the past everywhere, it was sad and potent, and already starting to fade. And in the background, behind the music, was the storm, the raging sea, which will outlive us all.

And you know, sometimes out on the canals, waiting for the ships to come in, in the quiet and the dark just before dawn, I'll close me eyes. And I can hear it. That distant crackling, oceanic static, and the strong, pure voice of Eleanor.

'Maybe it was one of the old machines,' came a woman's voice. 'An entertainment device. I have heard of such.'

I peered into the gloom. The speaker was a small, busy woman, dressed very practically in cast-off military fatigues. She was of those they call 'carbon-knitters', who fashion knitted bandages of linen or wool, and then turn them to sterile carbon-fabric with a portable solar device. Once we could turn out such battlefield dressings by the tens of thousands, in automated factories. Now – I can only imagine the number of soldiers who owe their lives to such as she, and whose healed wounds still bear the patterns of her fabrics.

'Old machines? I never heard of no such,' growled the Lighterman. 'Not such as they'd waste in a lighthouse. They were rich, them old-time men, and stupid somewise. But not so's to build a haunt for nobody to see.'

'Even so,' said the carbon-knitter cheerfully. 'Stranger things have been known. I could tell you a thing or two, I guess.' She knitted as she spoke, her voice mild and even, but with her eyes flashing when she looked up from her work.

The Lighterman stirred, then, but the Scribbler leaned across and passed him a bottle, and he took a long pull, then subsided with a noisy belch, and a sigh. As he passed the bottle back, the carbon-knitter nodded to herself, and began to speak ...

the carbon-knitter's tale

We from the Stoke villages like to tell the story of Ram whom the Lady took into her heart at the end of his labours. Stoke being the city that many people believe to be an apparition projected onto the clouds above the Trent by a machinery from the past.

Ram Pan began life as a yellow-angel-addled child.

In Stoke country the angels are remembered in a finger counting rhyme: the first four fingers fold over, one by one, with the red angel thumb under the others. 'The red angel takes with war. The black angel with ash. The grey one takes with water and the green one with pus.' The bad finger remains upright. 'Long after the rest are gone will the yellow angel still bide with us.'

We tell our children in the season of rain thundering down and flooding the land, that if you stare into a water-curtain long enough, you'll see Ram Pan Rain-Hero inkling among the rain-staves; leaping to save the next victim of injustice.

Ram, as he was then, meant only to save the children of his village from the monster in the hell in Stoke; by being that monster, and then by his stealth to allow the others to escape.

The stone and glass towers of Stoke suffered neither fire nor flood. It lasted into the new times as a beacon for warmongers who liked to test their warriors on machine-projected monsters before casting them onto a battle field.

Stoke's gameshell was a monstrous cube covered with lights and mirror shards spangling and starry in every sort of weather, named 'the Temple' and which stood at the centre of the city.

However, though Stoke survived and though the gameshell survived, its entire workings did not. Time and use corrupts and gameshell technicians were often stolen away from their livelihoods – perhaps to repair war machinery here and there. Who knows?

Ram grew up in one of the villages tithed to supply Stoke with grain and fruit; wool and flax yarns; stone and wood and salvaged goods. When the gaming machinery ceased to supply avatars because the program generating them was unable to be restored, Stoke required the countryside also to provide youths to be trained for that purpose.

In the weeks following an impressment, when parents were prostrate with grief, people would say, 'It's too much. They're taking them younger and younger. Someone should do something to stop it.'

But then life went on with new children being born to help the forgetting. Such as Ram was after his family's first son was taken. Ram was born yellow-angel-addled with wide shoulders, no neck and no voice beyond the roar of a bull, and with the eyes of a cat even to seeing in the dark.

The family rejoiced because he didn't fulfil avatar requirements.

For Juttie, born the year before, Ram's addlement was a disaster. She and Ram should've been wed, but her parents broke the agreement. Her mother took her early to learn trading in an attempt to keep Juttie and Ram apart. To no avail. Juttie would escape as soon as she returned from a journey and run to find Ram up in the pastures. She would help him look after his father's sheep and he'd teach her the new hand-talk-signs he'd learned.

The year Ram turned twelve, the impressers began to take the yellow-angel-addled too.

Mother Honey was the village wise-woman and a returned avatar, a rare treasure. She thought it likely that Stoke had now also lost the facility for making monsters. Guessing Ram's future, she made an agreement with his father to take the boy into her sword-fighting school.

In his sixteenth year, Mother Honey felted Ram a coat. Coloured-side-out, it would hide him in a flock of Lady-lovers. The black-and-grey side was for loitering in shadows.

Ram showed Juttie everything when she returned that autumn. In one coat-pocket was a bale hook such as carters use to shift wool. In a secret fold over Ram's heart lay a gadget any salvager would be glad to take from him. Mother Honey, according to Ram's signing, called it a "remuhtee".

'A what?'

Ram signed a hooky index on the palm of the other hand for "r"; right index to left index for "e"; three right middle fingers on left palm for "m"; right index to left pinkie for "u"; right hand wiping left hand for "h"; right index to left hand's side for "t"; and right index to left index twice. Remuhtee.

Juttie tried the sounds every which way and the word they most resembled was "remedy".

Mother Honey told Ram she stole it when she was avatar, before she escaped from the place to where he would be taken when the impressers came for him. The remedy would open doors without handles; shift walls; cut down forests and pulverise rock.

'Dangerous,' Juttie said.

'Not here,' Ram signed. 'Mother Honey said, 'Press this to activate it. Use only in the hell. Its power is not unending.'

'The hell?'

He nodded.

Juttie said, 'On our way home we passed the impressers at Juniol. If you and I travel the opposite way, through the ruins, we can miss them.'

'What about food?'

'Secret food stores in trader camps: flour and dried fruit. Nuts in the forest of Mayde. Water in old cisterns.'

They had their clothes and boots. Ram had the coat of many colours for sleeping under. They were afraid to say goodbye. What if they were stopped? All they knew of the world beyond was that it continued in every direction.

Travelling with her mother, Juttie had learned old roads and new tracks. She pinned her hopes on a north-easterly directioned one, to the mountains, that turned off somewhere along the paved road into Stoke. To escape the impressers they would have to circle the ruins at the centre of Stoke county.

It was the end of the travelling year. Most of the stores were near-to-empty. The traders were easy-going about the food customs. If there was no bread they'd snare rabbits. Needs must, Juttie's mother always said. But Ram refused to eat flesh. Sometimes Juttie ate and Ram went hungry.

The morning they intended to cross the paved road, they heard bells jangling and a drum drumming. A pipe as sharply fifing as birds crying.

Ram pulled Juttie down behind a brace of oak saplings.

They heard the creaking of a cart. A driver shouting and whipping haul-ponies. Drumming and fifing loud enough to cover most of a moaning.

The impresser cavalcade jerked into view with soldiers lounging on a roofed dray. Harnessed in two lines, the impressed youths pulled the cart as if they were beasts. The smaller, younger youths were chained to the back and sides of the vehicle, to push.

The musicians played their instruments while they skipped about, keeping out of the reach of the driver, who snapped about himself with the end of a rope.

Ram signed urgently. 'I see Aril at the front. Hardy and Ilo at the back. The flesh-eating driver is whipping them though they are doing their best. I'm going in to stop it.'

'I'll wait here.' Juttie still believed they would escape.

'No. Here is the hook. It's for climbing the outside of the hell.' Ram smiled uncertainly. 'Please come to see my story afterwards.' He shrugged out of his coat, and his woollen shirt which he thrust at her. His coat went back on.

Then he hugged her. Crunching her arms against her ribs hard, so tears sprang from her eyes. He licked them from her cheek; mouthed his love against her mouth.

But then he ran after the procession, on silent feet and with his coat billowing stiffly behind him.

The soldiers scattered from the platform as Ram sprang over the children at the back of the cart, grinning like a demon, taking special note of the scared little faces under his stride.

He stood swaying with his hands on the dray's supports by the time the kids who didn't know him raised an outcry. 'A monster!' 'The monster!'

The driver turned with thunder to shout them down. He recovered quickly from his amazement. 'Chain him! Get the chains on him!'

Ram growled as if he was a bear dressed up in clothes.

The impresser gabbled. 'Don't anger him! He's here by choice. What if he's other-worldly?'

The driver laughed and the soldiers laughed.

Ram winked at the kids. None of them deserved what awaited them. Mother Honey had told him stories he'd never tell anyone he loved.

The road arrowed towards the silver towers.

Alongside were two dykes of dirt and stones and building rubble as though a huge pointed plough had cut the base of the road through the suburbs that once surrounded Stoke's towers.

Only Ram was high enough to see Juttie running through the ruins along the other side of the barrows.

When the rubble dyke stopped, Ram worried that she'd be left behind.

Along both sides of the road now, there were patches of colour as if someone was growing Crossmassy ice-flowers to sell.

As the cavalcade approached, the fields erupted and became donkey-masked and rainbow-clad Lady-lovers skipping and jangling bells and throwing flower petals.

Ram put on a show by acting fierce so that Juttie might scuttle unseen into the crowd. He wished he'd given her the coat.

The whole mess of people, with figures leaping in and out and round-about, tripled in confusion when, reflected by the glassy walls on each side of the gateway, the cheekier among them ran up onto the dray to kiss and drape Ram with flowers.

The soldiers fisted and kicked at them.

The driver shouted for the musicians to start a hauling shanty to rouse up the avatars, while he slashed donkeys and haul-ponies without favour.

By and by the procession reached a wide place where four roads met.

Ram was blinded by mirror light refracting and reflecting off a silver, straight-edged, spangled, shining monument in the road meet.

A raucous and rough shouting issued from behind it.

'The knights, and about time.' The driver threw a cloth over Ram's head and shoulders and lashed it tight before Ram had the chance to fight it off.

A couple of strong arms hustled Ram from the dray.

The clamour died suddenly as his captors took him inside what he suspected might be the glittering place.

'Let's put him in the shell right away.'

'My money is on the man-eater.'

'You're on. Search the trickster?'

'Nah. Look at his coat. He's a Lady-lover. He'll be mince meat by sunrise.'

Ram's heart touched the remedy for comfort. He heard a whoosh in front. Smelled a meld of airs, ancient and fresh.

'Here will do. We don't want any nasty surprises ourselves, do we? You!'

'Remember that the yellow angel has got his tongue.'

The first speaker shook Ram. 'This thing on your head is your flag. Haul it up the flagpole on the roof when you've tidied up the one you're replacing.'

The men laughed raucously.

The braying laughter ended on a whoosh.

Ram dragged off the flag. He stayed put to allow his eyes to adjust and to hear what the temple might tell him.

A long way opposite, the afternoon sun sent light spearing through high holes in the end wall. Refracted many times by intervening see-through walls, the spears were multiplied until they hedged the western wall with fire. The wall at Ram's back was made of ordinary concrete. The north and south walls at either hand had struts and webs and other features to explore.

But sound was what Ram had to attend to now. The low never-ending burr of machinery could easily be accustomed to and then ignored. The other noises came irregularly: now low, a mumble; now a shout – the rough voice of a monster. A dark sweet stink of rotting flesh pervaded the air.

The floor was sand. Scuffed everywhere with foot traffic, never raked.

Three metres in front a see-through partition stretched from north to south and high to a fogged ceiling and thick and smooth enough that there was no climbing it.

Ram stood up close to look at the substance; and look through it. His eyes were very accurate in the half dark. He turned his head and stared cross-eyed and aslant.

All Mother Honey's explanations hadn't prepared him for a wall that seemed to be made of twinkling dust motes, but with a two-layered effect. As if a different strength of light shone into each side. This side plain, see-through, with the moiled floor beyond plainly visible. The back with patterns reminding him of …

Finally he dared touch the substance.

Crackle. Bzzzttt. A blue light enveloped him as though he'd become part of the wall.

The monster stopped his chatter.

Ram withdrew his finger and the wall took on its former mossy colour.

After a long breathless minute, the monster's burbling continued in the same general area as before, as if it had decided the crackling wasn't a danger.

Walking south along the wonder wall, not touching it, Ram came to an opening, one pace across.

He turned to face the gap and stepped forward.

His nose almost touched another of the walls.

Ditto his left hand.

This side, the walls were patterned with trees and shrubs; ferns at ground level; vines above his head. As he had imagined.

A trail of depressions in the sand were probably the tracks of the monster's comings and goings. If most lately it had gone to the place where its noises came from, these depressions in the sand signified northward travel.

Mind you, Ram admonished himself, that applied only to this one passage between only these pace-apart substance-less walls.

How many of these walls and passages could the hell contain?

The sky above the forest along all the walls whitened in increments while shadows increased in the east. The hidden machinery appeared to be doing 'night'.

No way did he want to get caught in the maze in the dark. Not with a flesh-eater of some sort on the loose. Ram returned to where he'd entered. He'd check out the remedy while there was still light enough to see, then find a safe place to spend the night. He pressed 'O' while pointing the remedy at the doors, as taught by Mother Honey long ago and far away.

Nothing.

Oh yeah. POWER UP was first.

Yes! The whole remedy lit up. Ram thrust it into his coat, though it was faint. No sense in warning the monster.

He pressed "O" again and the doors in front of him slid open. Light from beyond flooded into the big space.

Ram stepped through smartly, begging the doors to close behind him. Was that the monster roaring or his own blood rushing past his own ears? Mother Honey said the doors would close by themselves. Expecting his nemesis to arrive in a wall-burst of blue light, Ram retreated and so discovered the sensing mat.

The doors slid shut and he was safe from that direction.

Bright lights sprang into life wherever he turned.

Quickly he checked each room against the lay-out in his memory. No one. He could breathe again.

The hum of the machinery was much louder here because the machines resided here, in UTILITIES, according to a sign on the door.

In the kitchen there was water in the taps. No food. But never mind, Juttie had given him all the bread. A couple of mouthfuls a day would keep the angel of starvation away. Why hadn't that angel a place in the rhyme?

He investigated the dunnies and showers. Benches and mirrors. Just as well he'd been warned or he would've punched his own reflection. A shower of beer would've been good.

On both sides of the IN/OUT doors was a set of stairs. The left one went up to a pair of double doors not sensitive to the remedy. The right hand set descended.

Mother Honey always refused to say what was down there, but said Ram should take a look if he had the time.

Although low of ceiling, the room might be the size of the hell above it, with rows and rows of pedestals each installed with a virtual of a man, a knight and a monster. Each pair of fighters was always killing the yellow-angel-addled one, be it he or be it she. Real weaponry at their feet. Ram didn't like to be in a place with so much evil against his kind.

The only place dark enough for sleeping was with his head under the table in the kitchen. Though he worried over Juttie. What if she came while the cannibal was still in residence?

Ram punched himself. He was the one with seeing-in-the-dark-eyes.

For the sake of Juttie he had to start a war with his brother.

He approached the doors without touching the sensory mat. Where was that little monitor screen Mother Honey told him about?

Left hand side, on the doorjamb. Beside the doors.

Button under it.

He reached for it with the tip of the sword he'd borrowed from a joker in the basement.

A little map glowed in the jamb.

He knew such maps. Mother Honey had been thorough.

A red dot hovered in the maze, one light-wall away. Did the fellow know to jump through the wall? Should Ram test him by opening the doors and closing them in his face? No. Likely the flesh-eater wouldn't be tricked twice.

Instead Ram roared from the doorway, cutting left at once, and leaping for the zig-zag he saw earlier.

The flesh-eater laughed!

Ram half-fell over the balustrade; ran and gained a bit of height.

Runnggg! The monster's sword dented the place Ram left a couple of seconds earlier.

The place to run, he saw with a wild glance, was the top of the utility block, an intrusion that reached all the way to the north wall. In the north east corner a glow reached half way down a set of carpeted stairs.

The moon?

Ram slid the corner and risked a backward glance and saw the glint of a sword and his adversary's eyes approaching steadily along the same bit of the ramp Ram was on.

Ram jumped up the stairs for the moonlight.

Coming suddenly to a pair of glass doors.

"O" marked the spot.

He grabbled for the remedy.

The doors slid apart.

He jumped out and away.

The doors did not snap shut even when he was outside; off any sense mat; or while pressing the "O" button flat to the remedy's casing.

A wild reconnoitre of the roof.

The western wall, the one with the holes in it, probably where people climbed down. A fearsome cliff of knives it looked from the top, but, yes, various foot-and-handholds. A climb he'd overbalance the second he set foot on the first tread because he wasn't built to slink down narrow pathways. If only he hadn't given Juttie the hook.

The flesh eater was cagey. He did not appear at the doors.

Ram waited with apprehension high in his throat. He should be planning a battle for when the fellow did show.

He rocked back, sick in his heart.

Any kind of battling played right into the hands of the frikking city management! He was here to *save* the avatars. He'd only allowed himself to learn everything Mother Honey had wanted to teach him, by swearing to himself he'd never use her tricks to kill! How could he forget so quick? It wasn't the poor sod inside who was his enemy!

Ram sized up the shed covering the stairwell.

He ran at it and grabbed its roof's edge. The wall allowed him just enough friction for a boost. Most worrying was the noise of it all. Once on the little roof, he waited with bated breath.

But the flesh eater was still shy.

Ram's heart calmed. The roof was big enough to lie flat. His black-and-grey coat would break up his outline for any spy eyes.

A long time, yes, a long time later the moon shone more directly down into the stairwell and maybe that's what the poor angel-addled monster saw. Or smelled: the white light with freedom on it breezing down along with the night air. For at last, he came shuffling out not more than an arm's length from where Ram lay as still as a shadow.

The flesh-eater advanced hesitantly, as if he hardly believed each step towards freedom. He was bent. His hair was grey. Who knew how long he'd ruled the hell? He found the piece torn from Ram's coat suggestively placed as if Ram had already wended his way down the wall and he'd used the scrap to protect his hand from the first shard. Slowly the monster dropped below the roof's edge.

Ram slid off the shed and stole back inside where he could watch the monster's hands and feet shadowing now this slot, now that hole, down to street level. There the monster studied the scene before disappearing down a nearby alley.

Now Ram could begin his work.

First, a close examination of the temple.

Ram pressed FORWARD on the remedy and the forest turned into a labyrinth inside a mountain.

He pressed it again and the maze became the war-torn rubble of a smashed city.

Again and the rubble became a battlefield with silent fire falling and flashing.

Again and the light-walls cleared.

Then there were only the four distant walls and a vast field of moiled sand. The ceiling was a mosaic of all the possible maze-patterns waiting to be drawn down in turn.

Next, Ram took the poor bones of the fallen avatars from the flesh-eater's den and shared them among the fights in the basement.

He scuffed as much of the sand as he had energy for; rubbing out the clues and marks of the flesh eater's travels. He cycled the remedy back to the forest maze and went to haul up his flag.

He slept until it was daylight.

'Hallo?' A man approached with an object the twin of Ram's remedy loosely in his hand. He also backpacked a sack of things clunking together.

His shadow preceding him, Ram shambled forward.

The man jumped back in fright. 'You!' He glanced about quickly as if expecting to find a corpse before dropping the load from his back. *Clank, clatter.* 'I'm the temple keeper.' He stood up straighter and prouder. He pointed at the bag with a toe. 'Weapons, and beer for later. Now come with me.'

Aiming his remedy at the ceiling, he led the way through the light-walls. He pressed the FORWARD button.

The cave-cut labyrinth took the place of the forest.

Ram was interested to see him then pressing buttons in the bottom third of his remedy.

A red sun appeared low in the east of the maze. Magnified each time its image passed through a light-wall, a huge bloody orb appeared to shine directly into the mouth of a virtual cave situated in the south west corner of the maze.

From the cave a dark bottom-lit passage led to a tall space filled with a column of golden light pouring down from overhead when the real sun, outside, was still hidden by the city's eastern towers.

'Be a good fellow and learn the new layout. You'll have the first prince to fight tomorrow. He's very sure of his avatar so he's having a live audience. Luck of the draw, or so he says, that he scored a real swordsman.'

The keeper walked away without waiting for comment.

When Ram heard the doors whoosh shut he went to investigate the sack.

No food. A couple of bladders of beer. A belt with scabbard and a *short* sword. Didn't the man just say the avatar was a regular swordsman?

Ram ignored the angel of fear wanting to step into his thoughts. He'd been trained in both long and short swords. For a real surprise all around he could come out with the long sword borrowed from the basement.

Only he wasn't ready to let anyone know he had a remedy.

The floor plan of the new maze was almost the same as the jungle's, except that different stretches of the light-walls were lit up, this time with rocks and shadows. Walking through a wall, *bzzzttt,* was not an unpleasant experience.

The gold-glowing sand in the passage was the source of the light in there. The chamber that had the golden column shining straight down into it had no ceiling that Ram could see.

He dare not experiment with the remedy in case he couldn't retrieve what was meant to be. Instead, he walked through a couple of walls until he was outside the maze, between the maze and the south wall.

One of its ramps led to a balcony about half way along, level with the golden column.

Ram sat down in the front row of the lushly cushioned seats. People sitting there would have a good view of anything happening in the golden well. At the moment a very good view of golden dust motes dancing.

Then there was the rest of the day to wait, with Ram getting hungrier and hungrier until he weakened and started in on the beer.

Some time in the evening, by his woozy reckoning, the entry doors whooshed apart smartly.

He'd better have a look.

It was the keeper, leading two fighters swishing along the sandy paths of the maze. One of them completely enclosed in a suit of armour. The green plume on his helmet swept in and out of the light-walls, disrupting the code with blue electrical charges. The avatar was Aril, a class mate in Mother Honey's fight school.

Gladness flooded Ram's heart. He hardly heard the excited entry of the audience along the south wall. Aril was his best fighting buddy. He'd enlisted with the impressers for the adventure of it. They'd surely each save the other's butt. They'd spar and feint and make like something real was happening.

Ram ran to get armed. He jogged through all the intervening walls, *bzzzttt, bzzzttt, bzzzttt,* and arrived in the golden well sooner than expected.

Ram winked to forestall Aril calling a greeting. Signed at him with his hand close to his chest. 'Shut your mouth, Aril. Let's do our stage fight.'

Aril cracked one of his sarky little smiles and was ready, blade up.

Ram started into him straightaway. Clash and parry, feint and follow.

Aril shouted his usual encouragements. 'Eat my steel you dastardly sheep stealer!'

Ram grinned and made a lot of noise with his sword clashing and skittering against Aril's.

The knight terriered around Aril, yelling and attempting to direct Aril's thrusts.

Aril and Ram ignored him as best as they could. They were into one of their entertainment pieces, intricate and impressive to the inexperienced eye.

Harmless if bystanders kept out of the way.

Ram signed that he was ready for the dis-arming flourish in which Aril would hook Ram's sword from his hand and send it spinning towards the golden fog ceiling.

The knight just then took leave of his sense of self-preservation and stepped between them.

Aril's blade shimmied between the knight's helmet and armour.

The knight's sideways thrust continued. His head in the helmet dropped like a stone and his neck gouted blood. The armour froze and the body fell like a pole.

Aril threw down his sword. 'Now you're supposed to kill me.'

'Why?'

'If you take too long about it, Ram, the keeper will come and goad you.'

'Why bring in me when the old monster would've killed you as soon as he looked at you?'

'He only killed when he was hungry. Though apparently he had a mighty appetite.'

'I opened the roof doors for him. Watch out for his appetite when you're out.'

'Here comes the goad. I'll keep to the middle of the street.'

Ram slung an arm around Aril's neck and took a grip on his shirt with his other hand to drag him through the nearest wall, *bzzzttt*.

The labyrinth instantly disappeared, leaving them as perilous as a rabbits in the sight of an eagle. Due to the temple keeper and his remedy, or the temple's toiling to re-digitise after two bodies parted the walls? Whatever, for they had an acre of sand all around them. They were like one of the tableaus of a fighter in the grip of the resident monster.

The spectators in their balcony sat stunned.

Out of sight of both keeper and audience Ram slipped his hand into his pocket, pressed FORWARD.

The temple-machinery booted up the canyons.

Keeping his thumb on the button, Ram pulled Aril back towards their swords. Scooping up their weapons, they stabbed and clattered their blades at the top of the balcony's balustrade.

The spectators fell back with a howl of communal terror. Scrambling over the seats, they ran towards the exit.

Ram gingerly took his thumb off the remedy.

Suddenly they were in the forest.

Ram and Aril cat-and-moused through the jungle with always one or the other on the look-out. Cupping his ear, Ram listened for unwanted company.

Nothing within the walls. Only the excited rumouring outside, at the front of the temple, at street level. The sandy surrounds of the maze, the doors into the utilities and the catwalks all seemed deserted.

With their swords constantly at the ready, they clambered over the barriers and up the ramps in the south east corner to gain the stairs leading to the roof house.

Would the temple keeper and his cronies be waiting up there?

Ram broke into a sweating quandary. As soon as they climbed higher than halfway they couldn't also watch the doors below. He threw Aril the remedy and signed for him to continue up the stairs.

Aril quickly returned, signing the all clear. They shrugged the inexplicability at each other.

Ram signed, 'So go, Aril, so I can do it all again.'

Aril watched Ram hide the remedy, then hugged him, 'The last one out is the champion.' What they used to say among their friends to stay in the winter-river longer than anyone.

Ram closed the roof doors and ghosted back to his lair behind the flesh eater's den, to wait for the next thing to happen. When he put his nose near one of the holes in the western wall, he smelled the rains a-coming.

Please Lady, let them come sooner.

He woke to a whoosh. First thing he noticed was a couple of sun spears, almost upright. Noon. Was it the doors that made that noise?

Right on. The keeper accompanied by two figures.

The one in the suit of armour moved awkwardly and not in full control of his helmet's visor.

The avatar was a thin short youth with a long sword in his left hand. His belt was too big and the scabbard brushed the ground and threatened to trip him.

The keeper stopped them at the maze entrance opposite the utility doors. He straightened the avatar's belt and smacked the suit of armour on its head.

Exit the keeper.

The boy led by half a step. He guarded the armoured player with a trembling sword.

Once they arrived in the cave, the steel suit bade the avatar guard the entrance, while it toddled over to every wall in turn and with its helmet millimetrically close to the virtual partition, tried to see out.

Ram kept pace, eye to eye, on the other side of the light-wall, waiting sardonically for the knight's accidental touch. But only the plume touched the wall, *bzzzttt, bzzzttt,* well above both their heads.

Finishing his reconnoitre, the prince went to the avatar and swiped him over the head with his gauntlet.

The boy almost fell. Blood dripped down his face.

Ram stuck his two fists through the cave's light-wall and roared lividly through the hole between.

The knight shouted with fear and ran into the passage. 'Guard my rear! Make a stand!'

Ram's mind's eye burned with the scenes in the basement. Every one of them said that the armoured figure was supposed to help the third man by encouragement and talk. Some of the armoured figures had even taken a hand themselves destroying their monster.

When the knight and the avatar were properly in the passage, Ram entered the cave through the wall. Three paces took him to the knight. Setting the youth aside, Ram pulled the knight round to face him.

The knight dragged the avatar back by the jerkin-neck to stand between him and his monster. The youth's head bonged against the breast plate.

Ram grinned at the hollowness of the knight's pretences. His roar seemed to rattle the armoured one's brains.

The knight screamed at the avatar. 'Kill the bastard! Go on, poke him in the gut! Do it and you'll live!'

The youth stepped out of the confinement of the stand-off and unbuckled his sword belt. He kicked it from underfoot. His eyes bulged with staring fear as he faced Ram and the knight.

Ram tossed his own steel to the ground.

The avatar sagged with relief and the knight stabbed the youth in the back with his gauntlet fingers. Then he pushed the avatar onto Ram and fell to his bloody hands and knees and crawled away.

Ram roared with such grief the light-walls shuddered as he lifted the dead avatar and carried him to the unsullied sand of the cave.

Ram closed the avatar's frightened eyes. Crossed the arms. There was nothing to put in the youth's hands for the Lady because Ram wouldn't grieve her with a weapon. Instead he finger-combed the avatar's hair and the sand around him so that the boy lay as if on a river; in the way ancient heroes were sent to their after-lives.

At the western wall the sun's staves stood aslant and faint, the sun shining through a low level haze. The moist golden glow bathed Ram with the knowledge that to save the avatars, the temple must be destroyed.

When he'd planned his campaign, he FORWARDed the labyrinth to oblivion and made his way to the roof where, with his sword, he unhinged the doors permanently.

Low clouds advanced among the towers, pink and grey.

Ram carried the stones of the flesh-eater's lair to the roof and constructed dams and banks to channel water to the stair house.

Tearing his coat into pieces, he wrapped each bit around a quantity of sand to stuff the downpipes.

He was on his way to disable the downstairs doors when the temple keeper appeared, backpacking a kit with a hose and nozzle.

'Ha! Thought you were alone, didn't you?' The keeper stared all around the bare temple. 'Of course! The missing remote has returned home! Is that a cremation job in the south-west?'

The west wall was patterned with blocks of drizzle backlit by street lighting but the temple keeper kept on with his farce. 'This flame sweeper is for disinfecting the temple. And my favourite tool for resolving any little problem I might have with the monsters.'

Ram stayed on the bottom step of the staircase to the roof.

The temple keeper worked his way around the east, then north edges of the temple, sweeping the flames over the sand towards the west wall. 'I regret Red Plume wasn't up to the job but the consequences would have been happier if you'd allowed him his honour.' He stopped. 'Where's the den?'

Ram grinned widely.

'I said, where is the den!'

Zing! Crump! Boom!

The temple keeper's final syllables were lost in the light and sound of a lightning bolt earthing on the temple.

With a niagara-like roar, the clouds opened and rain descended in an unbroken fabric of water which sheeted down the stairs, almost taking Ram off his feet.

The temple keeper screamed. 'No! Not water in the temple! It's a treasure, the only one still remaining.' He clambered over a rail onto the ramp up to the stair house, flame dribbling undirectedly from the flame thrower. 'Stay there! Let me at you!'

The stairs gushed with water as the channels slung their load at the temple keeper, dousing the flames and bowling him haphazardly down the ramp.

More water flowed in than could spurt from the holes in the west wall and the level rose quickly.

Ram fought his way up to the roof to wait for Juttie.

But the deluge continued. For a month, a week and a day. Ram drowned. The downpour was followed by unimaginable cold. Spouts became buttresses and the lake inside the temple froze. The unnatural cold separated Ram's fibres from his fundament.

In Spring, the melt licked away his skin, shred by shred, and mixed his flesh into the lake in the temple. The holes in the west wall spurted with his elements which in the summer were taken up by the life in the earth and the water in the sky.

The Lady harvested his soul-dove, feather by feather, and launches it into every storm ever and again, to be, in soft rain or surge, Ram Pan the Rain-Hero.

This is the story Juttie made of Ram's life after death. The story she told up and down the villages and that led to their revolt against Stoke's rule. Though Stoke still lives, it is now like a rotten tooth, hollow in the centre. Its people now are Lady-lovers.

*A*lmost before the Carbon-Knitter ceased to speak, another voice was raised. A man – by his voice – in shapeless grey robes, he wore a traveller's hood pulled low over his eyes, leaving only his pale-skinned, lightly-bearded mouth and chin showing. His English was excellent, though strongly accented, and he spoke with a kind of amused, self-deprecating drawl that somehow made his words seem more important. He was a practiced speaker, and quickly it became apparent that he had told his story many times before.

'Lovers of the Lady?' he said. 'Why, by chance I may know some little upon that subject myself. Indeed, I fancy I am well acquainted with one of her greatest devotees, a man who loved Her so that he traded his vision of this humble world for the memory of a vision of Her glory. Shall I speak of him?' The question, evidently was rhetorical. The speaker went on quickly, his voice raised as though to discourage any who might wish to dissent. 'I shall speak of Oule, then, and the vision that transfigured him forever ...'

The evangelist's tale

Oule the hunter. Oule of Oulu, that rust-wrecked steel skeleton of a city on the shores of the Gulf of Bothnia. Oule who might have been Gällivari once, if only they had let him. It was he who found Her, deep in the tangled belly of the old city where Oule's faint-hearted Gällivari kin never ventured, one day as he sought rabbits and squirrels for the stew-pot.

It was the building that drew his attention.

Its walls had been stained by fifteen feet of mud, its windows permanently shuttered by the flood's residue. There was a sign, once, which used to herald this building's purpose; now it was half mute. Oule could read, 'M-o-t-h-e-r ...' emblazoned in defunct neon tubing above the door, but all subsequent letters were gone, rendering any extended meaning indecipherable. A rectangular steel placard was fastened beneath the surviving letters and supported the handful of rivets that would have held the second half of the broken word. This steel plate read *Emolevy* in reflective blue paint. Oule didn't know what the word meant, and since he wasn't equipped with the kind of patience decoding defunct languages required, he turned his attention to a more pertinent, more attainable task. He reached for the door, tested his strength against it. The door was silent, but combat-strong; it easily won the arm-wrestle between Oule and itself. It wasn't a fair fight, really. Oule had to resort to underhanded techniques in order to beat it, but who can blame him? I'm sure we would all agree that the end justified the means. He walked back to the curb, to the disintegrating vehicle that waited there for the elements to reclaim it. Its front bumper was nearly detached, so Oule encouraged its imminent separation by stomping on it until the car's chrome smile clattered to the ground.

A flock of startled pigeons launched themselves like miniature cooing rockets as this chrome projectile sailed through the front door's single pane of glass. Oule followed soon after it.

'Everything must go,' he read from the side of a faded paper fish that dangled from the ceiling on a dusty filament. 'Flooding you with savi ...' claimed another flyer – a finless flounder, perhaps, or a tailless tuna? Oule couldn't tell – while a shark's silhouette promised him enchanting eternal guarantees.

The room was plastered with these cloned paper sea creatures. Across each fibrous fillet was inscribed in diminuendo promises of wealth and goodness to come.

Oule couldn't resist the glittering foil goldfish that fluttered above him. Within seconds, he had climbed up a stack of sturdy boxes, and had gotten a hold of it in all its googly-eyed glory. He pulled down on it, leaning his full weight into the motion, and tried to snap the string that anchored his prize to the rafters. The line gave on the third tug; the released kinetic energy sent Oule sprawling to the floor, taking a column of boxes with him.

Sparks flew as these boxes hit the tiles; a high-pitched whine simultaneously pierced Oule's eardrums. When he righted himself he saw that the remaining cubes, which lined all of the walls and other prominent spots in the cavernous room, had sputtered to life.

Oule was spellbound as silent images traipsed across the panels in front of him. Hundreds of tiny pictures, all identical, were repeated across the grid of glass panels. Flabbergasted and utterly rapt by the miraculous visions before him, Oule sent his hands out behind his back to search for a place to sit down. He moved away from the dazzling wall of light and colour, and the backs of his thighs were soon greeted by a solid table. As he shifted himself up onto its cluttered surface, Oule's life changed forever. His left hand came in contact with a small rectangular device when he hoisted himself up onto the table; he was instantly buffeted by a cacophony of sound. These unexpected soundwaves propelled Oule into uncoordinated motion; his body did its best tangled marionette impression, which sent the device skittering across the tabletop.

When it crashed to the floor, the hundreds of segregated images merged into one, and Oule saw Her.

'Greetings, and welcome,' she said, and smiled broadly at her audience. Her twenty-by-twenty foot features glowed down at Oule, marred only by the fine lines that travelled across them. The grid that segregated her face at measured intervals did nothing to detract from her larger-than-life beauty.

She was breathtaking. Not for the first time that day, Oule was transfixed by what he saw.

A nimbus of whispery hair framed a face that looked like the sun had melted on it, then had decided to stay there for joy. Her voice was mellifluous, her phrases were pushed out by perfectly-formed lips, and her words were separately by unimaginably white teeth. *White teeth* – can you conceive of such a phenomenon?

'It's my pleasure to show you the best 2037 has to offer. Upgrades, new models, vintage; we've got it all. Perhaps you're searching for something special? Well, we've got special.' She paused long enough to wink at the viewers. 'Tired of the same old drab entertainment? Spend twenty minutes with us today, and you'll see what Mother ...' Oule tuned out while he came to terms with the wisdom she had just imparted, especially for him.

How could she know that? Oule wondered. *She speaks from the distant past, but somehow she's all-seeing.*

Her colours can communicate, Oule thought, entranced by the visions before him. The realisation reformed him, and he was reborn in its kaleidoscopic flames. *I think I'm beginning to comprehend Her message ...*

But he didn't, my friends; not yet.

She speaks in code, he despaired. *Mirroring? Microchips? Plasma? Pixellation? She wraps mysteries within mysteries; but I'm a hunter, not a sleuth ...*

'You don't believe me?' she asked, a coy expression on her fractured face.

'Of course I do,' Oule replied, 'I just need to know more!'

'You want to see more?' she quipped.

'Yes! Yes!' he cried, beside himself with relief.

'Well then hold on to your hats, 'cause power like this is really going to blow you away.'

And such power it was! The icon of Her Ladyship was replaced by a torrent of gyrating images, all accompanied by frenzied orchestras, and frantic drumbeats that urged the visions along at dervish pace:

'Jylle Hilton hosts Hedonist Holiday – Vintage Big Bro is Back to Back to Back! Live Housemate InterAction 24/7 x 52 weeks! – Avatar Apparatus; Avoid Identity Abduction – Club Prime Time, 7-2-9! Forget passive viewing; See and Be Seen! – Holocasting for New Year's 2038; when the Big Apple drops, where will your 3D be? – Biowarriors: Are you a Survivor? – Join the JayWatchers; Justice at its Juiciest: It's Live ...'

On and on the delirium reeled.

On and on the music throbbed.

Oule's heart kept pulsating time, his eyelids gave ground while his pupils dilated and contracted in response to this technicolour assault.

'How's that for resolution? And the sound quality is unsurpassed. I know what you're thinking ...' she began.

Oule replied, 'Truly it ought to be said that there is nothing more perfect than this work, in which the whole of universal knowledge is contained.'

'... it's more real than reality! So if you do want to experience what it's like to Go Live, stay tuned; see Mother –'

Blackness. Oule's eardrums hummed in memory of the lost sound; his retinas repelled the luminescent jellyfish that clogged his vision the instant the wall went blank.

'Come back!' shouted Oule. Devastation sculpted a grotesquery out of his features.

'I pray to you – Mother! Do not deny me – please! I know not how to Go Live, even though you've chosen me to unravel your mysteries. Such communities you've revealed – such sights! Oh, how those small shining beings rejoiced in one another's reflections – such magic is endowed along with the task of Viewing!'

No response from the speechless screen.

'I will be your most devoted Viewer, Mother – please! Come back!'

Outside, a grey-squirrel's muffled chittering added a staccato harmony to Oule's ragged weeping. The wall's burnished surface stared mutely down at him while Oule rocked with woe.

I will Stay Tuned, Mother, until we can see and be seen once again.

He glanced up at the wall, hopefully. Nothing.

He looked down at the crumpled metallic fish still clasped in his hands. A skewed representation of himself squinted up at him through a mirror of uneven amber.

And then, he had it.

Oule knew, then, that the visions he'd seen were real, you see. Our Mother, bless her in her wisdom and foresight, had given him all of the guidance he sought – and she waved it in front of his dripping nose, in the form of a foil goldfish.

Mirrors.

Tiny – no, infinitesimal – mirrors.

They'd have to be small, wouldn't they, he thought, if they are to reflect the miniature people's actions. Reflect and refract, that's it, then reassemble them. That's it. That's it!

She's real – it's real – they're real – and they're alive. Out there, somewhere. With Her.

But where?

Somehow, I've contorted the conduit, sent the signal off-kilter. The visions are there, they're just scrambled like my face on the fins of this fish. But I'll set it aright, reconnect the channels. It'll be a Great Realignment. Yes, a Realignment. That's what will rescue their society, and help us reclaim ours.

Such dreams Oule had while he waited in the shrine for Our Mother's return. In them, civilisations were threatened by a sickness far more frightening than the plagues that had ravaged the earth. The plagues – the then that was now – The Doom Year ... The past and the present both saw Her trapped in visions and reflections. In his sleeping mind's eye, Oule watched as men hid themselves from other men; women deprived their children of fresh air; children became shades that slithered around sightless men. It was a madness that only Oule seemed equipped to quell in these nightmares; he would release Her; he would shine Her radiant light on the hordes of purblind peoples; he would save them from self-destruction.

Beams of molten sunshine streamed from his outstretched hands, prismatic shards of salvation that were directed at the damned. But all of his ministrations only seemed to lull the depraved masses for a fleeting moment; and at the moment of epiphany, his visions would be coated in blood; endless geysers of blood; blood and devastation. When he awoke, after seven successive nights of horror, he knew he'd been sent a sign.

Oule returned to New Gällivare an enlightened being. His encounter with Our Mother had transformed him; he had transcended; he was cleansed and baptised into a new way of living. He did his best to share his visions, to save the Gällivari from the horrors he had witnessed in his night fevers. He collected and distributed shards of mirror so that they could all participate in the Great Realignment; he removed their window panes so that each and every citizen of New Gällivare could really see – would have to see – one another at all times. Oule preserved the eyes from the rabbits and squirrels he hunted, and he scattered collections of them across doorframes and windowsills, and he laced the eaves of each building with dozens of these disembodied orbs. He had read the signs; he knew that their path to salvation, and the key to the Great Realignment, lay in their communal co-viewing. Only by being completely exposed to one another would they learn their strengths, and avoid their weaknesses. Only by truly being together, a multitude of cells co-existing in support of a singular display, could they Go Live and receive Our Mother's transmissions.

Oule knew that we must all be open before we can learn how to be closed; like flowers that throw back their petals in the morning to embrace the live stream of day, the Gällivari needed to show their broad faces and welcome Her fortifying light, so that when night fell, they would be all the stronger to confront it.

But the Gällivari, may She find a way to save their souls, were a closed people. They said that they hardly recognised Oule upon his homecoming, said that he'd been possessed by the same spirits that had turned the Scots into wode-clad *zombi*. Embracing and exposing were fine for flowers with roots planted firmly in the soil, they said, but who amongst us has ever seen such a garden in any part of the steel-clad city that surrounds us?

His father shunned him the day that Oule removed the glass from his front-room window; he claimed the govreps had gotten to him. A daft theory that one was, but it was the only story Sol could concoct that might explain the blessed change in Oule's behaviour. Oule wasn't *his* boy, Sol had said, *his* boy wouldn't be so reckless, *his* boy wouldn't endanger his people with these freakish flights of insanity, his boy would've brought him some reinforced steel like he had asked instead of smashing his precious shelter apart like some raving lunatic.

But none of them know anything –

Or so Oule thought.

Somewhat encouraged by the Spring Assembly's decision to declare him an outlaw, Oule decided to steal one of Sol's more legible maps (a necessary theft, condoned and made possible by Our Mother) so that he could broaden the scope of his project. Bedecked in his warmest leathers, wearing his indispensible mirror-shard helm, and accompanied by a brigade of foil fish, Oule bade New Gällivare farewell and turned his gaze toward more amenable horizons.

South, he went, and further south. To Helsinki, where the ferryman mocked him as the shrill seabirds swarmed him, snatching the mirrored helm off his head. Enraged and embarrassed, Oule's mood only worsened when the ferryman offered him a pail, and assured him that his landlubber's legs weren't suited for the sea. His spirits sank through the depths of the Gulf of Finland and watched him from its sandy floor as Oule spewed and spat in his seasickness, wiping his soiled lips on his shirtsleeve after each wave initiated another bout of retching.

His luck seemed to have plunged into the sea along with his lunch. Oule was decidedly out of place on the water, but he did not fare much better on land. Through Eesti he toiled; his lagging energy only just led him through Latvija and Lietuva. In these regions summer raged unabated, much to poor Oule's surprise and detriment. Naturally, he had equipped himself with Gällivari gear; his squirrel skins and hare boots were ideal for Finnwegian autumn, but he had not considered how incompatible these garments would be with the warmer weather he encountered on his way south. His pants were slick with sweat, his stained sleeves were torn from the torso of his shirt and stashed in his satchel for future use, and his newly constructed mirror-shard helm (with reinforced chinstrap) was sodden and stank to the high heavens. By the time he reached Bydgoszcz, Oule felt that his luck would have to be forced to change for the better.

But the Polska were pitiless.

Eyes glittered out at him from behind barely-cracked shutters. He called out – for help, for food, for shelter – and he heard no response.

'Please,' he cried to the silent watchers, 'I can see you there looking at me, and I desperately need something to eat. I have furs to trade, and news from afar!' He had realised that he would have to be stealthy in his dissemination of Our Mother's message, and since he was sure he could mask her meanings behind pretence and verbal camouflage, he had decided to disguise her revelations as 'news'.

The foreigners were clearly not interested in Oule's news, disguised or otherwise.

'You've missed yer opportunity, mate,' came an English voice from behind him. 'I've already done the trade for this town; with the underhanded swindles they just struck with me, they'll be set for the next century, I reckon. So holler all you like, but they won't answer,' the man continued, 'specially if y'aren't speaking their tongue.'

Oule followed as the man walked over to water his horses; he tagged along as the trader adjusted the belts that fastened his cargo to the back of a wrought-iron wagon. The trader was a few years older than Oule; his skin was a weathered nut-brown, and his voice was abyss-deep and somehow reassuring, despite the bleak words it had imparted only moments ago.

'What I am to do, then?' asked Oule.

'Looks like yer buggered,' was the trader's response. 'Unless,' he added, 'you help me make this next delivery – got to go down to Bratislava, that's one hell of a journey, that one, and a nuisance ever since Austria and Slovakia joined forces in the 80s. Anyway, you can help me by tending these two beasts,' he gestured toward the horses hitched in front of the water trough. 'You carry what I tell you to carry, you load what I tell you to load – do these things well, then I'll feed yer sorry self on the way down to the Brats in Slovösterreich.'

It's humiliating to have to share this with you, as I'm sure you'll agree, but Oule thanked the trader for his generous offer by promptly passing out with relief.

When he came to, Oule found himself jostling around in the back of the trader's wagon, his head knocking up against the corner of a steel crate. He felt the cold metal against his cheek, and an instant later he sat bolt upright. His mirrored helm was nowhere to be found. He called up to the trader, and explained that he'd have to go back, that he'd lost his most prized possession.

'You mean this fool thing?' the trader asked, holding Oule's battered helm up from the driver's seat. 'Thought you were going to slice yourself open on those damned shards, so I took it off yer head while you were, uh, resting. I gotta tell ya though, mate, you look like a right idiot with that thing on yer noggin'.'

Oule climbed out of the wagon's bed, and sat down next to the trader. *My first opportunity*, he thought, and launched into the inaugural defence of Our Mother. He explained the significance of the mirrors, and his role in the Great Realignment. When they stopped at the banks of a swift river a few hours' drive out of Brno, Oule used his miniature mirrors to cast a spectacle of reflections off of the water's surface in an attempt to generate the necessary wattage for one of Our Mother's broadcasts.

The trader shaded his eyes against the glare, and kept silent while Oule struggled with his mirrors by the riverbank. After twenty minutes or so, he beckoned Oule over to the wagon. The pair rode in silence all the way down to Bratislava.

When they arrived later that evening, Oule helped the trader unload the wagon's cargo at the city's main storehouse. He tried to engage the trader in some light conversation, but the man silenced the boy with a sharp stare. After the last crate was unloaded, Oule came around to the front of the storehouse in time to see the dust settle in the ruts the trader's wagon wheels had left on their way out of town.

Downcast at this betrayal, but not deterred in his mission, Oule returned to the storehouse and sought out its elderly manager. All deals had been done, as far as the manager was concerned, and Oule had nothing he wanted. Trying a different tack, Oule began to relate his life-changing experience with Our Mother, and to explain how suitable his great warehouse would be for a meeting place for her Viewers.

He had hardly opened his mouth when the ignorant Brat closed it for him.

Oule lost his footing as the impact from the man's fist threw him off balance; he turned and scurried out of the warehouse, knocking jars and crates over in his uncoordinated wake. The manager pursued him, calling for support as he gained on his prey, and soon Oule found himself surrounded by a circle of Slavic scowls. An audience of frowning onlookers gathered, immediately causing Oule to exceed his anxiety quota for the next decade. He felt stripped bare and put on display for the benefit of his assailants' sadistic pleasure, and his heart pounded like the heart of a man about to have his face bashed in for entertainment. Sensibly, Oule did the only thing knew he could do successfully, and I'm sure you would have done the same if you were in his position.

He ran.

Beneath the outstretched arms of the storehouse manager; between a twin-set of flannel-wearing thugs; beyond the warehouse that lurked across the street. Over the road with its wagon wheel grooves still warm; out of the city centre and into the illuminated rail yard; and finally onto an abandoned train car, where he hid, petrified, until he fell into a fitful sleep.

When he awoke, our hero discovered that he had become a stowaway on a cargo train headed for Brussels. What luck, he thought, what a boon!

What a lark! What a plunge! echoed an old woman from the front of the pilgrims' train car. Her interruption threw the Evangelist from his narrative; it had been so long since he had heard more than a whisper from any of his fellow travellers, he had assumed they had all fallen asleep long ago. It wasn't until he heard the woman's hoarse voice that he realised that he still held some of his audience's attention.

A lark it wasn't, I'm afraid. The journey was long; the food, nonexistent. By the time he reached his next destination, he was half-starved and half-mad with deprivation. He abandoned all thoughts of luck; no use thinking about good luck, he thought, when all it does is plunge you head first into the bad stuff. Instead, he turned his thoughts to Our Mother, and continued to think of her mysteries as he wandered aimlessly around Brussels' vacant streets.

A few moments later She appeared before him, and saved him from tribulation.

The woman was beautiful. Gentle. Kind. Tears came to Oule's eyes when he looked blearily up at her, at the refracted golden glow she seemed to emanate.

She wasn't Our Mother, he quickly realised, but she could have been Her agent, escaped from the mirrored realms to console the wretched of this world.

Confronted by her concern, Oule began to feel wanted, even accepted, for the first time in all of the months and all of the miles that separated him from New Gällivare. The woman slid her arm under his, and led him away from the dank alley he had contemplated sleeping in for the night. She introduced herself as Lilah, but Oule was in no position to exchange niceties. Not the least bit nonplussed, Lilah accepted Oule's behaviour and brought him to her tiny home in the city.

She shuffled him into a room that contained too many people for its paltry size. After sweeping a pair of calico cats off of its moth-eaten headrest, Lilah ushered Oule onto the room's only chaise lounge. There he rested that evening; and the next; and for several nights after that one. Lilah helped him regain physical strength by supplying endless vats of watery soup; but it was her constant presence, and that of other people, that really nursed Oule back to health.

They smiled, these people. Unexpectedly, and frequently; the discoloured whites of their teeth and eyes gleamed like exit signs that promised a way out of the filth in which they lived. And Oule found himself smiling, too. His jaw cracked, and his cheek muscles ached from years of disuse, but he practiced this manoeuvre daily, and was delighted at how easy he found it to simply be happy.

At the centre of his joy, at the centre of all of their lives, was Lilah. When he looked at her, Oule understood why so many people were content to squat down in that drafty, dingy, Belgian apartment. She fed their spirits, that's what it was, even though she couldn't always feed their wasting bodies. The Residents, as Oule liked to think of them, rewarded Lilah for her efforts by recovering from their varied woes, and when they were sufficiently fit by patrolling the neighbourhood each evening. She always sent them to the same sector – to the Rue de l'Aveugle and around the main warehouse there – and she kept a wide-eyed vigil each night until they returned with no news to speak of. Only then would her smile return; only then could she know that the warehouse was secure.

Oule wondered why Lilah worried so about a single storehouse. He broached the subject with a few of the Residents – he was still too shy to ask Lilah herself about it – but their explanations were disjointed and obscure.

'Plague spawn squats therein,' said the brawny Spaniard in response to Oule's query. The next night, the Lombardo claimed that it wasn't the plague that was secreted in the cavernous hold, but enough forbidden fuel to earn them a fortune on the black market if the Chinese ever came calling.

'They're both wrong,' countered the Bratislavan. 'There's nothing of interest in there. The structure's unsound, simple as that. Lilah just wants to ensure that everyone's ... safe. So stop asking about things that don't concern you. Be glad you've got someone like Lilah willing to bear the burden of worry for all of us, and leave it at that.'

No matter what their reasons were for setting out each evening for a stroll along the Rue, at the end of their rounds the Residents always came back to Lilah's. It's hard to explain why, really. But they always did come back, and you would have too, if you had been there at the time. Under Lilah's care, the Residents created a new commune of the rejected – at least, that's the way Oule saw it. Occasionally, those that could speak English would share stories from *before*; from the times of Old Indo-Europa. They shared anecdotes and horrors; adventures and sadness; peregrinations and captivities. A gamut of narratives unfolded nightly, but they were too frequently bleak. As you'd expect, I suppose. Yet they told these tales ... not for sympathy, no. Not even for catharsis. They weren't asked to speak; they didn't force others to open up, neither. But share they did, much as we're doing today, in dribs and drabs, so that there would be a living record of their trials, a repository for their troubles.

And there was something troublesome hanging in the atmosphere on Oule's final night in the house. It seemed as though no one was in a divulging mood, but there was an air of expectation nonetheless. The Ruskan and the Bratislavan had returned from their turn on duty, and were whispering in the corner like dried leaves across concrete. Oule sat on the chaise with his head against the peeling wallpaper, stroking C.1 and C.2, who had grown quite attached to him over the past few days. Oule tried to decipher the men's murmured message while the cats nestled into his lap, fully prepared to wait out the night in his company. While two sets of feline eyelids drooped to half mast, Oule's senses were heightened. Lilah joined the muted discussion on the other side of the room as Oule looked on unobserved.

Feeling excluded for the first time in days, Oule decided to distract himself by adjusting his mirrors. During his stay with the Residents, he had accumulated an impressive collection of shards from the upper levels of the apartment block. He'd spent many hours positioning them: shards were placed in window wells, they were balanced on balustrades, and some were tucked into travel cases in order to prepare the others to meet Our Mother.

Tonight, Oule decided, *is the night.*

These people, he thought. *They paint painful pictures of their pasts, and yet; and yet. They survive the telling of their tales, only to be dragged down by the shackles of isolation, by the misery of mistrust. Oh, the woe of this segregated world! The yearning to be reconnected lies latent in them – I just know it – but they have lost the ability to truly see and to* be seen. *They cling fast to the shame they have felt; the thrills they've experienced; the sorrows they carry; the secrets that can't wait to be unburdened. And if it weren't for Lilah, these people would implode from the weight of it all.* Oule looked at Lilah, who sat beside the Ruskan on the other side of the common room, her hand placed gently on his twitching knee. Oule knew he couldn't leave the consolation of souls up to her; Our Mother had given him a gift, and the time had come for it to be distributed amongst the oblivious masses. As the silence grew in the wake of the Bratislavan's abrupt exit from the room, Oule prepared his first sermon.

'Ah-hem. Excuse me, Lilah; excuse me, friends. Thank you – thank you for your attention.' Lilah looked over at Oule. Her gaze flicked back to the Ruskan at her left, it jumped toward the front door, and skipped back to Oule. She blinked, and opened her mouth as if to speak, but Oule forged ahead before he could lose his nerve to speak.

'I've seen a message of hope, my friends, written in electric light. Our Mother has broken through pixellated barriers; the screens have exuded her plasmic greetings – greetings that I joyfully pass on to you. Do not despair: we have fallen, my friends, our transmissions have darkened, but I have seen our way back. With Our Mother's help, we can recapture the peace and prosperity of the past; we can Go Live once more.'

Oule began his tale; he told it to them much as I've told it to you today. He spoke of masks, music, and broken glass; the Residents grew uneasy. Seeing their discomfort, Oule adjusted his approach and focussed on flying foil fish and magic projection boxes; yet his audience's nervous shuffling and anxious giggling seemed to increase with every word he spoke. *I am no orator*, Oule acknowledged to himself. *But surely, once they've heard Our Mother's message, surely they will see ...* He continued with his account, and turned to Lilah for the support she'd unfailingly provided since he had arrived in Brussels.

Lilah's face was ashen; her hand was frozen midway between her lap and her mouth. Tears streamed down her face, and Oule thought she must have temporarily forgotten how to blink.

He was rattled by Lilah's appearance, but only for a moment. When Oule thought of how he himself must have looked when he had first encountered Our Mother, he felt reassured; and he became even more determined to communicate every precious phrase from Her gospel to Lilah and the other Residents.

And so he closed his eyes to shut out their beguiling stares. Behind the armour of his eyelids, he battled his way to the end of his sermon. He removed this protection only when he felt it was safe to see them once more.

Lilah was the first to break the silence that threatened to overpower Oule's final words.

'Come with me,' she said, gesturing at Oule.

Lilah's tear-stained cheeks lost their former glow, and her mouth settled into a firm line as she turned and strode out of the room, following the same path the Bratislavan had taken earlier. Confused, and more than a little dismayed at her reaction, Oule trailed behind until the Ruskan pushed him out the door. Our poor hero hadn't been outside in days, and it took him a few seconds to get his bearings. As his eyes adjusted to the darkness, Oule realised that Lilah was already several yards away; she marched determinedly down the street, and didn't spare a glance behind her to see if Oule followed. She knew he would come; he knew he would never go against her wishes.

'They say the Owl is a prophet of misery,' said the Ruskan as he materialised at Oule's side.

Perplexed, Oule's steps lagged. 'What is that supposed to mean?' he asked.

'Only that the crying of the Owl by night betokeneth death,' the Ruskan continued, 'and I'm sure I heard one hooting earlier.'

'I didn't hear anything,' Oule replied.

'Pardon me, then; perhaps my use of English is no good for such matters.' He shrugged, and urged Oule along the midnight path. 'Come now: Lilenska is waiting.'

The pair had arrived at the annex. Oule could see Lilah moving through its darkened door ahead of them.

'So this is the infamous warehouse,' Oule said to the Ruskan. The Ruskan ignored Oule and his observations, and walked around the side of the building. Oule heard the click of a switch being flipped; the sound was soon accompanied by the low hum of a generator growling to life.

'You've got electric power? Enough for this place?'

Again, the Ruskan didn't dignify Oule's comments with a response. Instead, he directed Oule back to the warehouse entrance, dragged him through it, and then locked the door behind them.

'Lilah?' Oule called out her name, but his words were weak. His voice struggled like a fledgling under a tiger's paw as it tried to penetrate the gloom inside the warehouse. Behind him, the Ruskan found the light switch. Oule was temporarily blinded as the room was flooded with fluorescence. Pain tore through his head as his pupils contracted to pinpoints; when they dilated to the point where vision was again possible, shock stepped in and took a turn at making Oule's head reel.

Lilah stood in the centre of the room, a clench-fisted figure of fury, flanked by the largest stack of screens and magic boxes that Oule had ever seen.

In the space of one breath, Oule thought, *Our Mother!* while aloud he said, 'You *do* understand!' Indescribable elation coursed through Oule's veins as he fell to his knees before Our Mother's majestic altar.

'Understand, Oule?' spat Lilah, her voice quavering with rage. 'Yes, I *understand* things you couldn't possibly imagine. I *understand* that you and your half-baked delusions have been sent to destroy everything we've created – everything we've salvaged!'

Lilah turned to the nearest tottering stack of monitors. Anger supplied the propellant she needed to launch herself against this ten-foot tower; with her shaking arms outstretched, Lilah pushed with all of her might until an avalanche of screens came crashing down in front of her.

Still seething, she spun around to face Oule's horrified expression.

'Have you lost your mind?' whispered Oule.

'Have I lost *my* mind?' she retorted. 'If only I had known – if only I had *known!* I would have left you and your crazy mirrors to rot near the railways. If I've lost my mind, Oule, it is only because I let you near us. But I won't let you ruin us, not after all we've done to survive. You don't know what dangers your words hold – mirrors and Mothers, reconnected broadcasts ... and using filthy power! You're the insane one here, to think of going near that foulness.' Lilah punctuated *foulness* by toppling another column of priceless transmitters.

'What are you doing, Lilah?' Oule squeaked. 'You're severing us from Her! We've got another chance to see Her, and be saved!'

'Saved? I'm saving us now. I have been saving us from these poisonous products for the past two decades. Why do you think this warehouse is so important, Oule? Why do you think we've been working to keep people – people like you – out of here these past twenty years? These –'

crash

'– cursed –'

smash

'– conduits –'

crash, crash

'– caused the end of civilisation!'

'But ... but ...? We need these screens,' Oule mewled, 'if we can ever hope to see or be seen ...'

'See?' howled Lilah. 'Be seen? Your mad beliefs have blinded you to reality,' she continued. She crouched down as she said these words. With her eyes locked on his, Lilah's hand foraged around in the detritus until it curled around a jagged fragment of glass. She loped toward Oule while the fierceness of her tirade against him grew.

'You want to expose all of these people to the world? You want their every movement tracked, their families traced, their security threatened? You want to undermine a generation's rebuilding, and for what? So that an illusory woman can hypnotise you with talk of togetherness?'

The Bratislavan appeared at Oule's side; his appearance was mirrored by the Ruskan's. The two burly men knelt down beside Oule, and pinned his transfixed form more firmly to the warehouse's littered floor. Lilah stalked over to the threesome, and straddled Oule where he lay sprawled on the ground. She settled her weight on his chest, and pronounced her judgement.

'You want to see, Oule? And yet you refuse to open your eyes to the world that surrounds you. You are more than oblivious, Oule; you're willingly blind. Sightless, and stupid. We can't let you spread your disease; you've got to stop ...'

An idea illuminated Lilah's face, so that it regained some of its former glow. 'So you want to pursue this blind path of yours, do you? Fine. Let's see,' she purred, as she raised the glass shard up to the level of Oule's eyes, 'how well you can hallucinate visions of that whore you revere when your eyes are as blinded as your black spirit.'

Lilah's fist pressed into his cheekbone, and her face became warped and twisted as Oule looked up at it through the sharp fragment. *I'll gladly be a martyr for you, Mother*, Oule thought, as the point of glass pierced his right pupil.

'Oule made his choice,' the Evangelist said, as he adjusted the ragged kerchief that bisected his face. 'See and be seen. And you may determine the wisdom of Oule's decision for yourself, in time. Blind he may be, but he can still see one thing clearly: Our Mother's radiance will be revealed to us all. I know this as well as I know the sound of my own voice; for I saw Her brilliance, if only that once.

'With that, my friends, I'll end my tale. Now if one of you would be so kind as to help me ... it's been a long day, and I am dying for a drink.'

*H*ardly had the blind evangelist finished speaking when the most extraordinary person jumped up and raised a furious outcry. It took more than a second glance to determine that this new person was a woman, for she was aged, and wrinkled like a sun-dried apple, and swathed like a newborn in a truly astonishing collection of hides, furs and mismatched clothing. Her head was bound and swaddled in a length of rough cloth so that only her round, wrinkled face could be seen, and from every possible part of her hung gimcracks and gewgaws, necklaces of teeth and stones and spines and scales, leather thongs with mysterious bags on them, bones, sea-shells, feathers and the like. Unlike the blind man, there was not a scrap of plastic nor the smallest sliver of metal about her person that I could see.

Her voice was as remarkable as her appearance: rough, shrill and astonishingly penetrating. She railed at us for at least a minute in a language nobody appeared to understand, full of hard sounds from the back of the throat. Then, perhaps seeing the puzzled looks being exchanged, she threw her brown hands in the air and stamped one foot.

'Ai! Stories it is! Stories you want! Listening to this *durak*, this *bolvan!* Story I give you then. Here, you. Take this! ...'

The Gnomogist's Tale

You lost children of Sapien-Ape, listen now to the Lay of Mamont: When Aerth was still small and unformed, without any grasses for folk, Mamont journeyed to the bottom of the sea, and tossed up vast clumps of dirt, which grew bigger and bigger until Aerth was large. And wherever Mamont trod, there was a lake; and wherever Mamont gored the ground, there sprung up a river; and wherever Mamont threw dirt with his tusks, there swelled a mountain. And Aerth grew grasses, and folk came, and they grassed and ate each other and ranged where they pleased.

In those days the ice was still hard, and Moon sang sweetly to Aerth, and Mamont ranged through all Beria, all Merica, all Europa. He grassed in Neyorkgrad when grasses still grew. He marched through the steppe, deep in research, and sang his song with deep bellows from his trunk. He lazed along the Seine's hazy banks. His tusks grew long, and his wool thick; the snows came and went, and Mamont thrived.

In those days, Sapien-ape was still within himself. He ate folk, and folk ate him, and he ranged about, from Africa to Sralia, but he was just one of the folk, like Mamont and Tickbird and Bison and Wulf.

But one night, as Sapien-ape lay by his firesticks and listened to Moon's song, he thought to himself: I might step up and tread on Moon, just like that. And in his dream Sapien-ape was no longer one of the folk but a mighty creature who looked down on all the lowly folk from his Moon-perch. After that Sapien-ape looked every day for things that might make him strong enough to trample Moon's song.

A day came when Sapien-ape gazed upon Mamont's mighty curved tusks and was jealous. Sapien-ape took up a firestick and drew near Mamont, but Tickbird, who lived in Mamont's wool eating ticks, was startled and flew away; and Mamont saw Sapien-ape, and rose up to trample him, and Sapien-ape fled.

So Sapien-ape collected ticks in his hand, and showed them to Tickbird; and when Tickbird came to eat the ticks, Sapien-ape strangled him. Sapien-ape again took up a firestick, and he chased after Mamont, who was surprised and fled until he fell in a boggy hole. Mamont struggled greatly, and begged Sapien-ape to dig him out, but Sapien-ape would not; and snow fell, and the tundra hardened, until Mamont was frozen. Sapien-ape cut off Mamont's tusks, and sharpened them, and he used them on his women and his enemies.

When the tundra thawed, and Mamont could move his head, he looked all about Aerth where Sapien-ape now ranged, but he still could not rise from his eck-stinky hole. So Mamont dug deep beneath the ground with his broken tusks, burrowing tunnels like he had once seen Mole do, until he came to Underaerth, where the dead live. And Mamont lived among the dead many snows. His tusks stayed broken, and his wool fell off, and the snows came and went, many many times, and Mamont grew afraid of the surface, so that if he even saw the sun's light he would die of his fright, like Pike on a riverbank.

Sapien-ape became proud of his victory over Mamont, and forgot that he was folk. He chased after Bison and Elk with firesticks and spears made from Mamont's tusks, and he ate all the folk who he saw, over and over he killed them, until none were left who could eat him. And Sapien-ape burned fire where he ranged till no more folk could grass there and they died. In Beria, the grasses of Mamont's steppe frosted away, and mosses grew that few folk could eat; the firm ground turned to boggy tundra, and the plentiful scenery became hollow.

In those days Sapien-ape ranged through all Beria, all Merica, all Europa, all Africa, all Azia, all Sralia. And he took tusks from all the folk, hard tusks and soft, took tusks from all the ground, sharp tusks and heavy, and he made things with them: things that tore apart the ground, things that flew like birds, things that made terrible noises and took away all the grasses. And Sapien-ape took the tusks he had taken from all the folk and the ground and he put them inside himself and made himself into what he had dreamed.

And he forgot forever that he was folk, and he treasured his strength. I am Teck-sapien-ape, he said.

And Teck-sapien-ape did step on Moon, and trampled her song.

Thus it came about that Teck-sapien-ape ranged through all Aerth, who was sad that she could no longer hear Moon's song, or Mamont's, or the songs of many other folk. And Teck-sapien-ape lay down upon Aerth and she could not move and he took her tusks and she wanted to die. And Mamont ranged only through Underaerth with the dead, until he fell asleep, and could not wake.

In those days there were some of Teck-sapien-ape's children who put tusks inside themselves until they became biogists. And they researched and researched until they remembered that Teck-sapien-ape was folk; and they saw what he had done to Mamont, and they grieved greatly. And they asked Moon what they could do, but she did not answer.

But they still took heart, and journeyed to the hole in Beria where Mamont had fled into Underaerth. They called to him, but he was sleeping, and could not hear them. And they saw where some of Mamont's children had come too close to the surface and died of fright from seeing the sun.

And one who was among them that day, who knew both science and magic, stepped over to Mamont's child who lay buried in the thawing tundra. Some of Teck-sapien-ape's children had taken her left tusk; and now enough ice had melted to uncover her right tusk; but this fellow who knew both science and magic did not take her tusk. Instead he reached into her trunk, from where she had once sung her song so deeply through the plains of the steppe, and he searched until he found the sequin, and he pulled it out, all glittery and sparkling, and was bedazzled. Then he pulled another sequin from her trunk, and another, all strung together, sequin after sequin, until he had them all, and he put them in a book.

This book is the Gnome, in whose song is the thriving of Mamont.

And this fellow of science and magic, who was the first gnomogist, and the other biogists, they took the Gnome-book to Merica. And they researched and researched until they could sing Mamont's song. Then they journeyed back to Beria, and stood around the hole in the ground where Mamont had fled, and they sang Mamont's song. Day and night they sang, reciting the string of sequins, until they tranced as deep as Mamont ranged, and between them created the most powerful Gnomogy.

And Mamont woke from his slumber, and heard their singing, and was heartened. Mamont dug away from Underaerth, back up his tunnels, and climbed out of his eck-stinky hole, and once more Aerth heard his deep bellow as he sang with the biogists.

The biogists led Mamont to a park where they had grown grasses again, and brought once more Bison and Horse and Hare and Saiga and other folk, all Mamont's friends, except Tickbird, who they could not find. They taught Mamont to no longer fear the sun. And Mamont ranged through all the park, grassing with Reindeer and Muskox and Elk, so the grasses grew. His tusks grew back, and his wool grew thick once more; the snows came and went, and Mamont thrived.

And the biogists said to Teck-sapien-ape, who was smothering Aerth: Look what we have achieved! We have undone your evil; come and see that Mamont has returned! They thought that when Teck-sapien-ape saw that Mamont had risen from Underaerth, he would remember that he was folk, would abandon his tusks and come and grass with Mamont.

But Teck-sapien-ape did not listen to the biogists. He ripped great holes in the ground. He tore down mountains and filled in lakes. He blocked up rivers, and burned fires until the sky filled with smoke. And still he took tusks from all the folk and all the ground, and turned them against Aerth. The biogists pleaded, but Teck-sapien-ape went on strangling Aerth, until she became angry and drowned his children with her rains and kept her grasses from them until they starved.

And Teck-sapien-ape feared greatly, and he thought, shall I burrow into Underaerth like Mamont did? There I can go to sleep and never wake up, until some other folk come, and find my sequins in me, and return me to the surface. And some of Teck-sapien-ape's children did flee into the ground; and others journeyed to Can'bury to protect their tusks; and those that remained Mamont chased and gored and trampled, over and over he killed them, until none were left. But others renounced the tusks they had taken from Aerth, and returned them to her. These became once more merely Sapien-ape's children. And though they were few, they ranged from Merica to Africa, trying to remember how to be folk. They took no more tusks from folk or the ground, but just grassed, and listened for when Moon would sing again.

But Moon did not sing, and Aerth was still angry. The waters rose. Neyorkgrad became grassy again, and the Seine's banks broke open. In Beria the ice was soft, and the tundra melted.

In those days the biogists ranged through the park to remind Mamont not to be afraid of the sunlight. And they gave each his task, according to ability, so that together they could watch over Mamont's needs. Some made sure their firesticks always burned. Some followed Bison, and took his small children, and some made meat from them with firesticks, so they could eat. Some took trees and bones and made shelter from the snows. And the gnomogist researched and researched the Gnome-book, to remember Mamont's song, so that if Mamont became sick, she could sing it.

After Mamont had returned from Underaerth, he journeyed far searching for Tickbird, but could not find him. A day came when some of Sapien-ape's lost children who ranged through Beria drew near the park wanting to spear Mamont, who was surprised and fled. They chased after him with firesticks and tusk-spears, until Mamont came to a boggy hole, and had nowhere to run, and bellowed loudly, for he had come to love the sun's light again, and did not want to return to the deep dark of Underaerth. And the biogists heard Mamont, and remembered when Teck-sapien-ape drove Mamont into the ground, and they came and speared the hunters, and put them in the hole. And Mamont saw that the biogists were not like Teck-sapien-ape, but knew they were folk.

When more came wanting to eat Mamont, or to take him to their cages in Novosibirsk to stare at him, the biogists, who now ranged close by Mamont, saw that they were coming, and they made a great noise and alerted Mamont, who fled.

And Mamont gave to the biogists the tusks of his dead children, for them to put in their body. And the biogists made a horn-beak from the tusks, which made a great squawking noise; and when danger approached, they warned Mamont with their cries.

And so they became Tickbird-sapien-ape, who ranged with Mamont, and Mamont thrived.

In those days Mamont ranged through not only the park but all of Beria. And Mamont re-formed Aerth again: he pushed down trees and trampled shrubs; he cleared the snow and tore up the mosses. Wherever Mamont grassed, there grasses grew. And though Aerth was still angry, and the waters still rose, wherever Mamont ranged, the boggy ground became firm again, and the hollow scenery was once more plentiful.

Other children of Sapien-ape who saw this came and ranged together with them. Tickbird-sapien-ape warned Mamont of danger, and Mamont gave the bones of his long dead children to Tickbird-sapien-ape, who built huts from them, pulling hides over the bones to shelter from the snows. And Tickbird-sapien-ape burned Mamont's shit, so that his fires became great. When one of Mamont's children died, he would give them to Tickbird-sapien-ape to eat, and to use their tusks. And Tickbird-sapien-ape made great knives and spears and statues from them, and needles to sew cloaks, and bracelets for his arms. And Tickbird-sapien-ape made great red pictures of Mamont, on stones and on his body.

And few dared hunt Mamont, for fear that Tickbird-sapien-ape's great cries from his horn-beak would see them trampled and gored and tusk-speared through. But some would still journey to Mamontgrad, wherever the season saw it rest, to wonder at the bone-huts and shit-fires.

A day came when Tickbird-sapien-ape's children became jealous, and wanted to be with Mamont always, to ride on his hump and pick ticks from his wool. And when they came to Mamont, he would trample them mostly, unless he chose one, who came to live among Mamont.

This one, who was called the mamontogist, ranged with Mamont all his days. And if he tried to climb onto Mamont's hump, Mamont would gore him mostly, unless he bore him.

When one of Tickbird-sapien-ape's children died, they were buried in the ground with their tusk-statues, and Mamont's dead children would burrow up to ferry them to Underaerth. When the gnomogist died, she too was buried, with her powerful pendants on her cloak; and another was given this task, so that there would always be a gnomogist who knew both science and magic, and could research the Gnome, and sing Mamont's song, and heal him when he was sick.

So it was that I became gnomogist, according to my ability, that I could watch over Mamont's needs.

And though Aerth was still angry, and the waters rose, and the ice was soft, still the grasses grew, wherever Mamont grassed. Tickbird-sapien-ape remembered always that he was folk. From his mounds Mamont looked over his plenty-scenery, and with Tickbird-sapien-ape he ranged through not only all Beria but even through Merica, across the frozen sea. And he sang his song with deep bellows from his trunk; and the snows came and went, and together they thrived.

Then it came about that when the mamontogist ranged through Beria on Mamont's hump, deep in research, he came upon a lost child of Teck-sapien-ape who parleyed with him. This one told a tale of when the biogists pulled sequins from Mamont's child's trunk, and sang Mamont back to the surface from the deep dark eck-stinky hole. And he told of the Gnome-book, which had been copied in Merica and Azia and Europa, and taken to Can'bury, where the last of Teck-sapien-ape's children now ranged, protecting their stolen tusks. The mamontogist worried that Mamont's song would be forgotten again, if Teck-sapien-ape had the Gnome; and he became angry at the child, and wanted to trample him, but the child fled. And the mamontogist journeyed to Mamontgrad, where I was deep in trance, researching the Gnome-song.

And the mamontogist said, your song is weak, and Mamont shall die, for I parleyed with Teck-sapien-ape, and he has the Gnome in Can'bury.

But I rebuked him, saying that my song thrived. And I brought forth the Gnome-book, and showed him the sequins within, all glittery and sparkling, and he took comfort, and forgot about his meeting, and returned to Mamont to ride on his hump.

In those days many of Mamont's dead children, who ferried Tickbird-sapien-ape's buried children to Underaerth, and were still afraid of the sun's light, would accidentally burrow to the surface and die of their fear, like Pike on a lake's shore. And Wulf and Bear would come to eat them where they were not frozen; and Mamont would come, and frighten the other folk away, and he would mourn. In those days Aerth was still angry, and the ice still melted, and more and more of Mamont's dead children dug up through the ground to die on the surface, and Mamont grieved greatly.

Then a day came when Mamont, who was mourning with his trunk over his dead thawing children, became sick, and could not range far. And Mamont bellowed loudly with woe, and Tickbird-sapien-ape came, and I sang and sang, trancing deep in the Gnome, to heal Mamont. But he grew weak, and his trunk filled with slime, and his wool fell out, and his hide wept with pus. And Mamont began to die, just like his children.

I feared greatly, for my task and ability were to sing the Gnome and heal Mamont, but I could not, for my song was weak. Perhaps some of the sequins had fallen out and been lost in the snow. But then I remembered what the mamontogist had said about Teck-sapien-ape's lost child, who had the Gnome-book in Can'bury. And I said to Tickbird-sapien-ape, I shall journey to Can'bury, and find the Gnome-book, which has all the sequins, and research and research, until I can sing Mamont's song again, and stop him from dying.

And so I journeyed across Beria to Europa. Mamont agreed to bear me on his hump, until there were too many of Sapien-ape's children, and I went on foot. I passed from plentiful scenery to hollow, wherever Teck-sapien-ape had once ranged; and Sapien-ape ranged there now, still trying to remember how to be folk. I came upon the Beria-train, which Sapien-ape had built from sharp tusks and boiling water, and rode upon it until I came to St. Leninburg. When the children of Sapien-ape who ranged there saw me, they were much astonished, and took me to some who said they were biogists, and had researched Mamont and the Gnome; and they took me to a great hut, in which the bones of Mamont were placed, but not in a useful way, to give refuge from the snows, but in a mockery of Mamont, as if he still stood upright when dead, but without flesh or hide. And I sat beneath Mamont's bones and rebuked the false biogists, saying they must use the bones for shelter, not their forged spectacle.

And I left St. Leninburg, and walked through Europa, and rode upon trains, and saw many of Sapien-ape's children, and many strange and wonderful things they had made from the tusks of the ground and the folk. I came to the Seine, and smiled upon its hazy banks, and asked those who ranged there where Can'bury lay. They took me to a great tusk with white steam breath that went upon the sea, swift as fishes, and I crossed the cold water to the place of the New Castle, which was old and had no castle.

Then I came upon the Can'bury-train, which screeched mightily of boiling water, and rode upon it. And we journeyed to Can'bury, where the last of Teck-sapien-ape's children had fled with their stolen tusks. And inside the train I saw some of these sickly children; their nails were short, their hair had fallen out, and their muscles were weak. And outside the train I saw vast dirty holes in the ground and mounds of wasted broken tusks, and straight huts that gave shelter not from snows but from the sun. And I knew that Teck-sapien-ape was afraid, and had forgotten how to live, and was building himself a great eck-stinky mound in Can'bury.

And you other lost children of Sapien-ape journeyed with me upon the Can'bury-train, and begged for stories, so I stood, and in my best voice, full of the spirit of Tickbird-sapien-ape, sang the Lay of Mamont.

But now as I finish and look around at you pilgrims, I see the mockery in your eyes. I know that you see Tickbird-sapien-ape like bones dug up from the ground. I have heard others journeying on the Beria-train speak of me as Mamont's pet, a curse in my tongue. So I rebuke you! Do not become once more like Teck-sapien-ape, who hides behind straight huts, so afraid of the sun that he tries to build a new Underaerth on the surface in Can'bury. Open your eyes and see: Tickbird-sapien-ape has forged a new contract with Mamont, with all folk, and with Aerth. Soon she will forget her anger, the waters will no longer rise, the ice will be hard, and together we will thrive.

So listen now, as I sing what will come to pass.

When I arrive at Can'bury, I will seek out the lost child of Teck-sapien-ape who has stolen the Gnome-book. I will find him, and stick him with my strongest tusk-spear, and take the Gnome-book back to Beria. I will research and research as I journey to Mamontgrad, until I can once again sing Mamont's song, so that he will no longer be made sick by his frozen children from Underaerth, but will range through the steppe, deep in research, grassing so the grass grows, and sing his song with great bellows from his trunk, listening for when Moon will sing again. And I will teach Tickbird-sapien-ape to sing the ancient Gnome-song of Mamont to all folk of Aerth with all our breaths of the day, and between us we will create the most powerful Gnomogy: attacgacatagtacagatacgatcagatcactatgaggacatcaggagagactagattacatacga ..."

At least, that's how the transcriber has chosen to render what I recorded. (There was more, but I edited the file.)

It was quite a performance. She fell into a kind of trance, I swear. Her eyes rolled up into her head, and her limbs trembled, and from her mouth the syllables poured, quick and staccato like the rattle of drumsticks.

I see now, of course, there may have been some sense to her. The four letters, repeated over and over – seeing them in print, I remember the significance of those letters. And the word which the transcriber has rendered as 'gnome', she pronounced with a hard G, almost like 'guh-nome', or even 'geh-nome'. Intriguing, isn't it?

Still, I will not be able to follow up my suspicions further. You will understand why, milord, when you read what happened next.

*A*t the conclusion of the little shaman's tale – the 'Gnomogist' that she called herself – while the audience was laughing and calling to one another, I felt a hand on my shoulder. I looked up: somehow, the conductor had made his way through the press unseen, and found me. 'Ticket, sir, if you please,' he said, his bland face unreadable.

I frowned, for I knew he'd already checked my ticket, and I said so. 'Not long outside Newcastle itself,' I told him. 'I distinctly remember.'

'Nevertheless,' he said. 'If you would step this way ...' He moved aside and gestured for me to go ahead of him. Seeing little choice, and much puzzled, I did so.

The conductor escorted me to the front of the saloon, and through the security door which he carefully relocked behind us. Only then did he turn and face me, and I saw his face was white with strain. 'The guard captain tells me you can be trusted,' he said. 'He said that in an emergency, if the guard were not available, I might turn to you.'

I made a mental note to have Captain Anglestone's clearance pulled. The man spoke too freely. 'I'm not sure what you mean,' I hedged.

'I think there may be a bomb,' he said simply.

I won't put my reply into print. The conductor opened a door to the night, and I followed him into the rain and bitter chill.

As we stumbled along beside the stilled train, he told me the little he knew. The guards had been drawn to the rear of the train during the encounter with the Londonis. 'Not all, of course,' said the conductor, his breath steaming in the white glow of his ledlight. 'But perhaps enough so that a single man could slip through the protection at the other end. That's what I thought, anyway. So I came out to check the engine.' He stopped so quickly I blundered into him, and I put my hand on the great, sleek steel side of the beast to steady myself. It was cool to the touch, but there was a hint of vibration that spoke of the life and power inside.

'Here,' said the conductor. He reached past me, and pulled at a handle recessed into a panel below the curve of the great tank. There was a noise of metal scraping metal, and the panel opened. 'It was locked, but I have an inspection key.'

'Give me your light,' I said, and with the little ledlight in hand, I looked inside, and lord, lord help me, I near to filled my boots with shit from fear.

The conductor must have glimpsed my face. 'What shall we do?' he quavered.

I looked again. There, anchored magnetically to the undercurve of the great tank that held both water – and unbeknownst to all but a handful, a large number of uranium pellets wrapped in graphite spheres – was an ugly, electronic device. Insectile and threatening, it was armoured with a beetle-shell of woven ferrocarb. There was no glowing display of led numbers, naturally, but a single blinking light told me it was active, and hostile. I took a closer look, trying to remember everything the Department ever taught me about such things.

'Light,' I said finally. 'I need you to keep that panel open, and keep your light on this thing.'

His eyes widened as he took the meaning of my words. 'Shouldn't we – get help? Someone?'

'Who?' I said. 'I think this is a timed device. The panel was locked, so most likely it was placed back in Newcastle, by someone complicit. Probably it's meant to do as much harm as possible.' While I spoke, I handed him back his light and fished in my pockets for the heirloom Swiss Army Tool my grandfather gave me. I didn't know whether to bless the old man's memory or curse him. Without that precision tool, made better than anything we can manage today, I wouldn't have dared attempt to touch the device. 'I think it's timed to go off when we were due to reach Canterbury.'

'An hour? That's all?'

'If we're lucky,' I said. 'Hold that light still!'

His hand shook so that the shadows jumped and leaped. 'I cannot, sir,' he said. 'Call someone else!'

'Damn you,' I said, not unkindly. 'If I get it wrong, neither of us will ever know.'

'That's cold comfort,' he said.

I shrugged. 'Call the engineer. Have the train emptied – no.' My mind raced. Even if we emptied the train, a bomb that ruptured the nuclear fuel supply would likely still kill everyone, albeit more slowly. Better to – to what? 'Have them move everyone to the back of the train. We can't put people out into this, with those raiders still out there somewhere.' And the sealed carriages might offer protection from any contamination. For a time.

The conductor spoke briefly into his hand-unit. There was a short exchange, and then he nodded. 'It is being done,' he said.

'Fine. And now, if you're ready, I need the light. I can't hold it, and keep the panel open, and work all at once. Will you help me?'

'I – I'm not certain, sir.'

I turned away from him, and focused on the device. 'Tell me a story, then.'

'A – a story?'

No way to pull the device off the metal tank. The magnetic clamps were almost certainly trapped. Could I slide another sheet of metal underneath? 'Yes, a story, dammit. Take your mind off what we're doing.'

What if there was some kind of a magnetosensor? That would be simple enough. And if I moved the damned thing, we'd be blown to hell.

'I don't know ... any stories.' The conductor's voice was almost lost in the wind.

'Tell me your story, then,' I said. 'Your life, the life of a friend, or a friend of a friend. Whatever. Just – talk, and keep the light steady.'

There was a long silence, and I ground my teeth as the shadows flickered, and jumped – and then, miraculously, grew steady. 'A friend of a friend? Hmmm. All right then,' said the conductor. 'All right. I think I can do that. Yes ...'

As he began to speak, I unfolded the tool my grandfather left me, and with a prayer on my lips I went to work ...

The Conductor's Tale

The Conductor's Prologue

The train jounces over the wet track, tossing the passengers like corn in a pan, but the conductor never misses a beat, his black-booted feet landing exactly where he intends.

'Tickets, please,' he calls.

His eyes sweep from left to right, scanning the ink-filled cards that show both starting point and destination. Pilgrim, businessman or sightseer, the destination is always the same. They are all headed to Canterbury.

Lightning brightens the interior of the train, the accompanying thunder following close enough to crease more than a few foreheads.

All is in order, just as it was the last time he checked and the time before that. He makes his inspection at every stop until he knows every face and has witnessed every mood.

There are four.

First, there is willing compliance as the passenger dutifully hunts through their luggage. Once found the ticket is raised in victory as if the conductor and the passenger share a bond.

Annoyance follows as they once again make the search. It doesn't take as long, but the inconvenience breaks the flimsy trust the passenger has placed in this lone man.

The third time brings anger and a few unkind words questioning the conductor's intellect and heritage. The ticket is thrust in his face so as to imprint the memory of it upon his mind.

Finally they grudgingly accept their lot. The ticket hasn't even made it back into the bag at this point, but is held snug in the hand, the pocket or the front cover of the book being read. It is held aloft even before he approaches the seat, while the passenger continues on with whatever they're doing at the time.

Throughout the display the conductor says only two words. 'Tickets please.' He doesn't respond to their overtures, not the happy-to-please smiles, not the glare, not the murmured insults, and not the bland disinterest.

The train stops at Cambridge to pick up new pilgrims. The conductor pulls open the large doors and swings the step into place. A storm is in full swing and rain lashes itself against his thin cotton uniform. Yet another nun bounds away from the storm and up the single step that takes her from platform to carriage. She raises the hem of her habit and sweeps it away from the slick rust that lines all metallic edges. Sweeping the drops from her face she searches the carriage. It is full so she moves along the corridor and through the connecting doors. She'll locate the other nuns soon enough, giving her a ready made community which the other passengers will try to emulate.

Three others follow in her wake, all trying desperately to escape a drenching. They, like the nun, move along and through the train until they find a place to sit. The conductor raises the step, grinds the doors back into place and steadies himself as the train shunts into motion.

'Tickets, please.'

They have not travelled more than a mile when the train wails and slows down. The conductor reaches for a hand strap and hangs on. Soon enough they come to a complete stop and he is free to look out the teeming windows.

'It's flooded again,' he tells the worried folk. 'They'll send a crew along soon enough, but we won't be moving for a while.'

The conductor ignores the grumbles. He moves down the train, delivering the message and dodging questions. His job is to check tickets and warn of delays, not hold their hands. Once completed he returns to the main carriage and waits. Sure enough eye contact is being made and personal situations judged. Now they are ready to forge a temporary kinship based on isolation and boredom.

And so the stories start.

They all think they're special, unique, as if they are the first to pass the hours this way. Lives are shared, secrets revealed, as each traveller endeavours to paint with words the world they left behind and the one they hope to come.

The conductor surveys the group as it forms. A girl, no more than fourteen and heavily pregnant is asked when the baby is due. She is shy at first, a little reticent, but a shared block of carob soon gets her talking.

It is always like this. Sharing is never free. A price must be paid, either in food, drink or 'other' services. The only aspect that changes is how the price is worked out. Sometimes the story-teller pays, other times they are paid. Such is the case with this particular group. As each new story begins the teller is rewarded with a square of the bitter treat. Once the dynamic is in place the conductor moves on. He is not interested in what they have to say. He has heard each story a thousand times or more.

He returns an hour later to find the main carriage shrouded in silence. One woman, a pilgrim judging by the sightless boy in her arms, sniffles and wipes her nose upon her sleeve. A moving tale has been told here and the participants are pondering its impact upon their own meagre existences. The conductor briefly wonders which passenger delivered the tale of woe.

This is a group in need of distraction, a way to re-enter the world as it had existed moments before.

'Tickets, please.'

One by one the passengers look up at his approach and proffer their ticket.

They begin to converse again in low tones. The conductor catches the odd word, all dealing with the weather, the hold up and when they'll be on their way. They could ask him, but he has become invisible to them and he is comfortable with that.

'Can you tell us a story?' the blind child asks. 'A story about working on the train?'

The conductor draws in his breath and shakes his head. He's never been asked before and now the invitation leaves him feeling unnerved. He shakes his head again.

Nobody presses him. What life experience can a mere conductor have to offer? He cuts short his inspection and heads through the four carriages to the observation platform. Truth is, there's nothing they can offer to make it worth his while. The only ear fit to hear his story is God's and they speak of the matter often enough.

The conductor stands on the platform and glares at the fleeing storm.

And there, for God's sake, he begins to pray for his life.

The Conductor's Tale

Call me I. I once carried a citizen's name, a name that could open doors within society. I gave up that name along with the other detritus of community life.

Do You hear me? I am but one voice among millions, offering nothing more than words and asking nothing beyond deliverance.

I am a sinner, true and through, raised in the name of God, but educated by the Devil. It is his hands that snatched me from the path my parents set me upon, his boots that bound my feet to his.

Satan is with me still, whispering in my ear as I walk the narrow corridors that carry me from one carriage to another. It is his voice I hear as we head toward Canterbury, his words that remind me of my shame.

Groups form, groups dissolve, taking shape long enough to impart some bloated wisdom before disappearing into the crowds that line the streets of the Capital. The voice in the dark reminds me I'm a bystander, affecting to be part of their world, but invisible to these mini-societies that form for the sake of an entertaining yarn or two.

Time and again I beg for release, an end to the torment, but it never comes. And so You leave me to wonder, am I beyond redemption?

The first sin I remember committing was theft. I stole a bottle of peaches that were being kept for The End Times. We were fundamental to the core, believing in Christ and the reproach he would soon visit upon the world. While other religions teach of peace and love and forgiveness, we were taught to live in fear. Fear of the world and its influence, fear of Satan and his temptations, fear of You and Your proven ability to cast Your followers aside.

I was so intent upon fearing You, I forgot to fear the community.

There were four hundred and thirty nine jars of peaches being kept in the cellar. Every member had helped in the preserving process. That way we would all have a stake in the coming Judgement. I did not think anyone would notice one missing jar, but I was wrong.

I was cast from the congregation for four weeks. In all that time not one word was spoken to me by the members, not even my own mother. No one spoke to me, no one provided for me. School work was left on the door step so my class mates wouldn't have to suffer my presence. Shunning made me invisible, left to fend for myself in a world that refused to see me.

Happy are the invisible, for they will learn free-will.

It took seven years for sin to resurface and this time it was my developing body that let me down. A brief touch of Aggie Cartwright's left nipple saw me publicly flogged and cast out for two weeks. By now I could cook and clean and sew the tears in my clothing, but the pain of my flesh stopped me from enjoying any of these freedoms. For two weeks I slowly starved in my bed as my family carried on their lives without me. The only provision made was a kettle holding a litre of warm water and a dirty cup, placed at my bedside each day.

My father didn't fully observe my punishment. At night he stole into my room and whispered any scriptures he could find foretelling my descent into hell-fire, when even God would refuse to acknowledge my presence.

By the third shunning I was prepared. I didn't stick around for a beating, or starvation or sermons from on high. I packed up my bags and stole out into the night before anyone had a chance to know what I had done. By then my invisibility was so complete the community didn't think to search me out when I ran.

You know what I did. You were there when Cain beat his brother's head in with a rock. Did it never occur to You to step in, to stop Cain before he destroyed that which you loved most? You didn't stop Cain. And you didn't stop me.

Out of the mouths of babes. How many times have I made the pilgrimage? Ten years I've followed these tracks. Ten years of journeys, one week south, one week north. That's twenty six round trips each year. Two hundred and sixty? You do the maths.

Sorry.

That was uncalled for.

But pilgrimages?

None.

Not once have I stepped off the train and entered the city of redemption.

It just seems too hard.

The people in the trains, they have it worked out. They have their lives and they want better. They visit Canterbury to make new contacts, to ogle the Clergy, to attain a miracle. It doesn't matter why they make the journey, they're on a personal pilgrimage, a way of understanding the life they lead.

I want to ask forgiveness but I'm afraid.

I'm afraid that once I start asking I won't be able to stop.

The community wasn't all sermonising and punishment. We were valued members of society and earned citizenship by our conduct. Our people produced two great skills for the world.

First, we had books. We had many books, shelves and shelves of all sorts of books on every type of subject. From an early age we were taught the art of copying and providing books to an education-starved world. As a result we had the best schooling in the land.

Sure, we were taught about the Kingdom but we also knew how to read and to write and to interpret music and computer code and blueprints and many other wonders of the bygone age, all of which made us a valuable commodity.

I was a young man, remember? Barely out of my teens. Such a crucial age when friends are family and family are the enemy. The only hope a young man has is a mentor and I found mine in Brian.

I loved him, as best friends do. The community loved him, as those with a need will.

Our second skill was in coffee. We didn't just brew the best cups in our cafes, we grew the most magnificent berries. Brian was Master of the Bean and I was his apprentice. While the rest of the planet sank untold euros, dollars and yen into the ground trying to coax *Robusta* cherries from reclaimed soil, Brian was able to command *Coffea Arabica* from near-dead land as if by Royal Decree.

Which, in a way, it was. The young Prince Charles himself was said to drink at least one cup of the community blend a day. Not even Brian could afford such luxury which added shine to his already great prestige.

Men of the world would have killed for the secret of Brian's success with the bean but in the end it was his brother that got him.

And we know the secret, don't we? It's the one thing we share.

You grew man from mud. I grew coffee from men. Blood and bone. Fresh blood, ground bone. There's nothing like it. Brian taught me that.

Ten years. And not one cup of coffee shared. Don't You find that strange? Carob, olives, medicines, they've all done the rounds, but I am yet to see a steaming thermos passed around a group. I think it's the one item I'd sell my story for if offered. Just to engulf a cup in my two hands, lift it to my nose, inhale the growing region through the scents of citrus, dark soil, berries or chocolate.

Then, and only then, would I caress the *crema* with my lips, drawing the pale froth over my tongue and letting it evaporate there in its own time.

Oh God, oh God, I miss Brian so.

See? Talking to You always make me cry.

What were Cain's first words to You after the event? Did he ask You to forgive him or did he laugh in Your face?

I remember my last sin as clearly as my first. It was not Brian's crushed head, or the breaking from the community or the theft of this uniform. They were mere symptoms of the greater evil lurking inside me. Pride, jealousy, anger, evil as they were, could not be accounted as my last and most deadly sin. They were the impetus that propelled me forward.

Brian was my mentor. I was supposed to be worthy of his tutelage, to eventually meet his skill. And I was good, in my own way and we would have prospered nicely enough on what I knew.

I had the knowledge. I had the skills. All I needed was the talent, the passion, to bring it all together. Everyone trusted I'd get my act together and develop the craft of real coffee growing.

But I never could.

I never could.

I never could.

Not while Brian was around. Does the apostle Luke not say that the pupil can not outrank his teacher?

And so I put him away from me. And from You. And from the world. They all had to pay. You all had to pay. We all had to pay for loving him so much.

I loved him more than I love You.

And that was my greatest sin, the stain upon my soul. He had to die. I did it for You.

And so, You see, You have to forgive me. You have to guide my footsteps from this train and into Canterbury. You have to love me. It's the law.

I hear the King is in his castle, counting out his money. Maybe I'll call on him there, remember the community to him and the good days. Maybe we'll even raise a cup in Brian's honour. It won't be the same though.

It won't be the same.

We'll be at the West Station soon. I could do it. With Your help I could make the journey, meet the tests and renew myself within You.

I refuse to be Cain, marked by sin and shunned by the world. I'll be David, wise and repentant. I'll be Abraham, ready to face any challenge, no matter the price. I'll be Daniel, reliant upon the grace of God to lead him to safety.

Get behind me, Satan. I am ready, ready to be reborn in your name. Prepare me God for what lies ahead. I am ready.

Amen.

Amen.

(He paused then. Drew a long, shuddering breath.

'But if I did,' he said. 'If I did ...')

The floor vibrates beneath the conductor's feet. He braces himself, not missing a beat as the train shudders, stalls, then slowly begins to crawl along the sodden track toward Canterbury. Muffled cheers erupt behind him. It is time to make a last inspection. He opens the connecting door and re-enters the confines of the carriage. The mood is lighter and the pilgrims chat easily now. They are on their way.

They are two hours from their destination and the conductor is congratulating himself on the decision made. He is a pilgrim now, intent on facing the challenges God has set, ready to overcome them with a willing heart.

A quiet hush has settled over the four carriages, as if, like the conductor, the travellers are bracing themselves for journey's end. They have heard many tales this day, tales of love lost and found, friendships betrayed, enemies smote, businesses plundered and ruined. They've all made their confessions and feel stronger for the experience. Some even feel a little smug, judging by the deprecating smiles here and there.

He smiles with them, bonded to the group by their spiritual solidarity. Like the community of his past they have alienated him, but he forgives them this debt as he hopes they'll forgive his.

He takes a seat on the floor of the main carriage near the mother of the blind child.

'Are you seeking a miracle?' he asks. 'For your son?'

The woman startles and looks down to the boy upon her lap.

'Oh no. We accept Saul as the miracle he is. Didn't St Paul suffer a similar fate on the road to Damascus? Yet it empowered him more fully to do God's work.' She brushes the hair from Saul's forehead and gives him a little squeeze. 'We're going sightseeing. We hear Canterbury is very beautiful this time of year.'

'Oh. Ah, well. I hear the King is in residence, maybe you'll get a chance to see him.'

The woman smiles. She strokes the boy's hair away from his unblinking eyes. 'We hope so.'

'Did you, ahh,' he clears his throat. 'Did you tell your story?' For the first time the conductor is interested in another human being. He wonders about this woman and her child. Was his condition genetic, a leave over from the plague, a freak accident?

'Nothing to tell really. Life is good and I'm happy with my lot.'

'And the boy's father?'

The woman flashes him an apologetic smile. 'Waiting for us, just ahead. He came up last week on business.'

'Oh.' She has mistaken his interest for something more but the conductor doesn't care. He'll never see either one of them again, not once he's back with God.

They lapse into silence and soon her gaze has drifted away from him and over to the window. Her eyes are glazed and he knows she no longer registers his presence. Invisible, he gets up and moves to the carriage door, watching for the tell-tale spire. The last few miles pass in a blur until the train begins to slow once more. The tracks bend and turn and finally the city comes into view.

'West Station,' the conductor calls. 'This train terminates at West Station.'

He moves up and down the carriages, making the announcement and stepping out of the way as passengers bustle to retrieve bags, packs and children.

Order is achieved and the conductor moves into position. The train groans to a standstill and the doors open with the barest of tugs. The conductor lowers the step. The passengers surge forward, eager to be away from the cramped confines and onto the buses waiting to take them to the city. The conductor, defying his invisibility, is the first to take the step towards redemption. He turns his back on the train and heads toward St Dunstan's Street. Several pilgrims follow, eager to take Henry's Walk, the route demanded of the truly repentant.

A decrepit sign post announces the street. A white shingle proclaims its historical significance. The conductor stops in the middle of the road and makes his plea.

'Help me face this test with fortitude and integrity so I may once more tread the path to salvation. Amen.'

He takes a deep breath and, with a slight wobble, steps toward the waiting city. One, two, three, four. He stumbles but one of his fellow pilgrims steadies him. He shakes the hand away and continues. The way to salvation lies with God, not man.

Wrapping invisibility around him he moves away from the pack.

The silence of the group is sliced open by the growing clamour erupting from the city.

'Ooh,' they exclaim with one voice. Around them waft the heady scents of pork sausages for the rich, and potato stew for the poor. They split up and wander the stalls, picking up and discarding rosaries, postcards and authentic pieces of the one true cross. Roughened hands caress the town's brickwork as if God can be found within the cracked mortar.

The conductor ignores them all. His eye is on the greater prize, solace for his weary soul. He looks around for guards, or priests, or the military to stop him and ask his business, but so far he remains unaccosted. Surely repentance will be demanded? The way ahead is clear and the conductor continues walking on all the way to Westgate Towers.

There he stops at the arch and waits. Tourists jostle past him and a dog sniffs his leg, but nobody gives him a second glance as he searches for a place to rest his troubles.

A bus toots impatience and the conductor stumbles into the heart of the Tower. A set of stairs beckons and the conductor climbs to the top.

And from there he views the beauty that is Canterbury. Streets that he has only heard of but never seen spread out in all directions. His eye roves along High Street, along the route taken by King Henry II, into Mercery Lane and past the Buttermarket to the main entrance of the Cathedral itself.

God is mere steps away and the conductor can't wait to rekindle their acquaintance. He searches for a priest or monk but it is finally a nun that notices his confusion.

'Are you lost, sir?'

'I, I want to make the pilgrimage, but I don't know what God requires of me.'

The nun smiles and presses his hand.

'Why, you simply walk down the steps and into the city.'

'No, you don't understand. I, uh, have a lot to make up for. A lot,' he adds in whispered embarrassment.

'Don't we all? Now, off you go, just follow St Peter's Road and head toward the spires. You can't go wrong.'

She nods and moves away, just one more body in the crowd.

The conductor shakes his head. 'Impossible.' It can't be that easy.

He knows God. He's read both testaments, lived life in the community. He is a demanding God, a God of retribution and torment. He'd want a heavy price paid in ransom for a life taken.

The conductor raises his face to the cloud laden sky. 'What do you want from me?' he shouts to Heaven, but God remains silent on the matter.

He looks around at the other people on the roof.

They have, as expected, ignored the outburst. They are on their own journey and his words mean nothing to them.

He is still invisible.

So many times. So many times he has turned to God, opened his heart and made his pain known. Others sat warm and comfortable in the carriage, sharing their secrets as well as their treats with strangers before entering the city unencumbered. He'd stood alone on the platform in all weathers, keeping his conversations private, just between himself and God, determined to confess all to the one who promised eternal forgiveness.

And for what? To be ignored during his hour of need?

'Where is my test? Am I so insignificant in Your eyes? Am I not worthy?'

The conductor wipes a tired hand over stinging eyes. 'Am I to be forsaken? Am I not redeemable?'

He shudders and makes little deals with God. 'If I climb to the top of the Tower and find a Guard I'll make my confession.'

'If I climb down from the Tower and find a priest I'll take that as sign of redemption.'

'If I circle the Tower to the left ...'

'If I circle it to the right ...'

In the end it is the woman, the one taking her blind son sightseeing, that finds him. 'We're on our way to the Cathedral. Would you like to walk with us?'

The conductor stares at her for long moments then shakes his head. 'I can't. I have to wait.'

'Wait? For who?'

'For God. For His test.'

The woman looks around and bites her lip.

'I don't think there is one. Far as I can tell you just head over to the cathedral and join the other pilgrims.'

The conductor groans with the stupidity of it all. 'Since when has 'easy' been God's way? Don't you see you're being misled? God demands penance and pain. You can't just walk in and take salvation for granted.'

'Why not? It's what the Lord offered when he died for our sins.'

The conductor glares at the woman and shakes his head. 'And you wonder why your son is blind. I'd say he inherited it from his mother.'

The conductor growls and turns away, away from the woman, away from the Tower, away from the cathedral and its empty promise.

Too easy. He stomps back to the station and steps onto the waiting train. They have another hour before the journey north begins. The conductor wanders the corridors, making sure all is ready before they begin. Returning pilgrims take up the main carriage, their excited chatter underscoring the glow that lights their cheeks.

'Fools,' the conductor mutters as he closes the door and takes his place.

Raising his head he steps forward as the train shunts into action. 'Tickets, please.'

And there, for God's sake, he begins his journey again.

He opened his eyes then, coming back from wherever he'd been, surprised to meet my gaze. And for my part, I was just as surprised. Sometime during the Conductor's storytelling, I had isolated the detonator from the timer circuit, found the secondary actuator and shorted that, clipped the feeds from the magneto-sensors, and finally lifted the heavy block of bitter-smelling plastique from inside the casing of the bomb.

It wasn't Londonistan work. If it had been, I would not be here to scribe this for you, milord. If Mohammed MacTavish and his people had crafted that device, I would now be shreds and rags at best, and half the damned train with me. But it was almost a simple thing, needing only a steady hand, strong nerve, and adequate knowledge of electric circuits to pull it apart.

And so I sat, cradling that inert lump of death in my lap, staring vacantly into the distance, emptiness in my head and heart, while the poor Conductor bared his soul to me. I wish, now that I've reviewed the multicorder file, that I'd paid more attention, listened more carefully. I don't know what I might have done for him, but he deserves something, surely.

I can only hope that in holding the light and staying by my side in the face of death that he found the test he wanted. I've found records of him since, though the community of which he spoke has long since expunged him and denies his very existence.

It doesn't matter. Sitting there with the rain falling about me, shivering with cold, numb within and without, there was nothing I could have said, nothing I could have done. There was no strength in me at all. And so, when the Conductor met my gaze and gasped, and sobbed once, and fled back along the tracks, I did not even think to call out to him.

I let him go.

Some time later, a pair of Rangers found me, still sitting. They were understandably suspicious, but by then I was too tired, too mentally shattered to dissemble. I showed them my identification, and gave them the emergency password, demanding their utmost aid in the name of the Crown.

Laughable, really. The bomb was disarmed, and a detailed search revealed no other. By that time, the rain had stopped, the clouds had parted, and dawn had come. In the growing light of morning, all the nights fears and trials seemed faintly ridiculous, and as soon as we got word that the track was clear, the engineer got up steam and we made our way onward, without incident, to Canterbury.

I wish there was some stirring finale, some grand triumph with which to finish this account. It would be fine to relate that the Doctor heroically brought a healthy baby boy into the world, to be named for the King – but in fact, he simply kept the woman clean and comfortable, and as soon as we drew into West Station, she was bundled into a waiting ambulance. I have heard she was delivered of a daughter at the King's Mercy Hospital some hours later.

In the aftermath of my own trials, I lost track of my fellow travellers, I fear. Not that I had any great interest in them to begin with. Still, after labouring in the dark and cold to save all their lives – and mine – I wanted ... something. Acknowledgement? Fellowship? I don't know.

I did see some of them disembarking at the station, while I looked for deSoto from Technical to take charge of the device. The old Scotsman, long-faced, searching the crowd as though his robot horse might be waiting for him. The blind evangelist and the mad little mammoth-shaman from the far East, now apparently become travelling companions: they argued volubly with each other even as they crossed the platform. They'll kill each other within a fortnight, if they don't get married first.

I don't know. I'm haunted by the feeling I missed something. I tell myself that it's only the stress of the night. Raiders, and murder in the dark. The madness of taking apart that bomb in the rain, with only the Conductor's light and my old Swiss Army Tool. If not for those things, surely it would have been nothing but a banal train ride delayed by a flood. Even the storytelling and the queer characters would have been no more than an amusing footnote. Now?

Now I wish I'd had time to tell a story of my own. Never mind that I have no idea what I might say. Never mind that I probably wouldn't be allowed to tell any of my best stories in any case, what with the Crown Secrets Decree. I don't fully understand why -- but I wish I had been able to speak up and be part of what went on there, instead of having to stay outside.

I think that may be the real reason why I've made my report in this manner, milord. I know what you will say: you will tell me that it's natural, that anyone would be shaken after such an experience. You'll say I need some time to rest, and perhaps you'll arrange for passage to one of our holdings on the Free Coast in the south of France.

I'm not so certain, myself. How could I be? I know only what I feel, and like the good spy and servant that I am, I analyse those feelings and give you the summary: I feel empty.

I think I've passed my usefulness in this job. I don't believe I can keep doing what I have done; watching, analysing, refining data, and treating people – our people, the people who are this country that the King is trying so hard to rebuild – like points on a graph, like numbers.

Then there's the killing. I don't even know the name of the man I killed in the dark. I'm not cleared. I don't have 'need to know'. I know if I had not killed him he would likely have killed me. It's true that he was guiding the raiders who were attacking the train, and likely I saved a number of lives by killing him. It changes nothing. I don't even know his name.

I doubt I can keep doing this. In fact, I've come to believe it's not sane, or healthy to live this way. Perhaps, for the sake of the safety and security of many, some few have to think and live the kind of lives you and I have led these long years, milord – but I am beginning to believe that the longer we lead such lives, the less fit we are to guide and rule the people who do not.

In short, milord, I'd be obliged if you would accept this last report as my resignation from active duty. Butterworth is ready, and able, and so much younger than I. He can take my place, I'm sure. Or if not Butterworth, then Rostov. You'll find someone.

I will be good, of course. I will accept my debriefing. Like as not, I'll accept a week or two on the Free Coast, and the inevitable sessions with the psych crowd. But I doubt my decision will change, and for your peace of mind, I will tell you why.

I believe, milord, that I've understood something. It seems to me that the old world, that halcyon era of marvels and miracles, broke down and fell apart because the people that owned it and ran it stopped believing they were part of it. I suspect those all-powerful men of a century ago forgot that underneath, they were no different from all the billions they ruled. They made their decisions to benefit fewer and fewer, until at last all that power and might and strength was bent to the whim of just a tiny handful. They forgot that everyone else had a stake too.

They stopped listening.

People like you and I, milord – like I used to be, anyway – we should listen to more stories. The King, and his son that will be king after; them too. Didn't they used to do that with the royalty? Send them off to the army, the navy, whatever, so that they'd learn what it meant to serve, and be part of something? Put them into a story of their own, a story shared not just by kings and rulers, but by commoners and soldiers and ordinary train passengers?

It's easy to forget, when you have power, what it means to live without that power. But take a night, and a storm, put your life in the balance along with a score of others and suddenly, perhaps, you may find yourself listening to their stories again. Listening, and wondering what you missed.

I'm done with power, now. I'd like to think that my last act in your service is this report, milord. I want to believe you'll read it, and consider it, and perhaps even pass it to those who might need it all the more.

Perhaps you will. Perhaps not. I can't do better than try.

So that's all there is. I'm finished stealing other people's stories. Next time I take the Canterbury train, I hope to have a story of my own to share.

Cordially yours,
Geoffrey Tailor

afterword

I can't offer enough thanks to the writers who took part in this. Small press doesn't pay worth a damn. The writers in here are here because the project intrigued them, and it was a real delight and a privilege to work with them. It was much more difficult than most, calling for a high degree of negotiation and co-operation, and everyone in this thing, from our newcomers to our seasoned professionals, were incredibly giving, and forgiving. Editors, publishers everywhere take note: you want to work with writers like this.

Beyond that, there's Cat Sparks. There's simply no way to thank her adequately, not just for this volume, but for the last half-dozen years or so. If you're not aware of the role Cat Sparks has played in recent Australian SF, then you should probably just skip this book and head down to the Romance section of the bookstore. The only thing I can hope to say about Cat is that I'm proud to call her a good friend: the greatest compliment I can offer, no matter how inadequate.

Special mention goes to the proof-readers, people who take time out of their lives to straighten up the edges on a half-finished project – the amazing Kathryn Linge, the irrepressible Tansy Rayner-Roberts, the delightful Tehani Wessely, and Simon 'The Rock' Petrie. (Couldn't resist the religious reference and the pun rolled into one, Simon. How good was that?) Without folk like these – and in particular, without these folk! – Australian SF would be a lot poorer, and much less professional.

Can I thank my long-suffering wife and children too? I'd better. And I can promise I'll be coming out of my study more often now, too.

Dirk F. September 2008

authors

Geoffrey Maloney – The Tingler's Tale
Geoffrey Maloney was the hangman at the infamous Newtown gaol where he was responsible for the execution of over 180 criminals. He pioneered the clean-break technique and the use of the suede slip-knot. In 2102 he was awarded the prestigious 'Long Drop' award by the Canterbury Hangmen's Guild for his services to the industry. Today he describes himself as a scribbler, penning articles for the *Hangmen's Review*, and working on a revised edition of 'The Hangmen's Lore'.

Angela Slatter – The Nun's Tale
The problem with writing a bio for storyteller Angela Slatter is her stubborn refusal to shuffle off the mortal coil. At the age of 142, she still haunts the spec-fic scene even though she's old enough to know better. Having survived plagues, purges and the abolition of hair-straighteners, it has become apparent that she may be immortal. She refuses all writing awards, citing her belief that writers, like politicians, are professional liars and should not be rewarded. Her early work appeared in publications such as *Shimmer*, *Lady Churchill's Rosebud Wristlet*, and the *Dreaming Again, Strange Tales II* and *2012 anthologies*.

Martin Livings – The Dead Priest's Tale
Martin Livings was a late twentieth and early twenty first century fabulist author from Australia. Before his premature (and, according to leading historians, spectacular) death in 2017, he published eight novels including the critically-reviled *Werewolves! Werewolves! Werewolves!* and over a hundred short stories. He never won a Ditmar, Aurealis, Hugo or Nebula

award in his lifetime, but he *did* win the Darwin Award in the year of his death, apparently a very prestigious prize indeed. He maintained an Internet web page, a popular method of disseminating vital information in his era, still archived at the following address: www.martinlivings.com

Stephen Dedman – The Veteran's Tale
Stephen Dedman was liquidated in the purge, along with all his works. Attempts to erase his existence from history have been mostly successful, but he is rumoured to have been the author of at least four novels and more than 100 short stories, as well as having been a teacher, actor, experimental subject, used dinosaur parts salesman, and part-time bookpimp. His application for sainthood is still pending.

Laura Goodin – The Miner's Tale
The literary world knew little of Laura E. Goodin until the first decade of last century, when her name began appearing in online publications and anthologies. Diligent postgraduate students have unearthed information that suggests she was born and raised in America and moved at length to Australia, possibly in the company of a husband and child (although records are ambiguous on this point). She led an unobtrusive life as an editor, public-relations hack, martial artist, and trophy wife before, it seems, suffering what used to be known as a mid-life crisis and beginning a new career as a writer.

Sue Isle – The Sky Chief's Tale
Sue Isle was born in Perth, Western Australia and worked as a scribe for the law courts. Her interest in environmental politics led to a Senate post and after the Evacuation, a term as Premier-in-Exile. During the Plague Years, she joined a remote community and turned her creative attention to oral storytelling tradition as the high-tech trappings of the Old World fell in upon themselves. Only a few scant copies of her written works are believed to have found their way by ship to the northern hemisphere. Little of this writer's final years are known but she witnessed the reformation of a government in the west in 2063.

Kaaron Warren – The Census-Taker's Tale
Kaaron Warren, now considered to be one of the 21st Century's most over-rated writers, was chiefly known as the oldest woman to publish a volume of rhymed erotica. She did this at 97, five years before her death of suspected food poisoning. Her eighth husband blamed the salmon mousse.

Durand Welsh – The Mathematician's Tale
Durand Welsh lived in Sydney, Australia. He drank beer, not wine, and preferred his friends to do likewise. He liked dogs, but no more than any man should. Cats, he despised as unfaithful and slovenly. He was a graduate of

Clarion 2008 San Diego, during which he disgraced his country and proved to the numerous Americans present that not every Australian can hold his liquour. He won the Apex Digest Halloween Competition in 2007.

Grant Watson – The Hunter's Tale
Grant Watson was born in Whyalla, South Australia, in 1976. He had a varied creative career, including acting, directing for the theatre, and writing plays, comic books, television scripts, short stories and film criticism. His short stories were published in *Andromeda Spaceways, Antipodean SF, Shadowbox, Potato Monkey* and *Fables and Reflections*. In 2008 a general societal anxiety over the launch of the CERN hadron supercollider created a quantum event and caused Grant to cease to exist. Today his works both exist and do not exist, until you open a book and check.

Thoraiya Dyer – The Peat-Digger's Tale
Thoraiya DYER, circa 2000. Notable Achievements: While representing her State at a National archery competition, she was first to destroy her arrows in an attempt to shoot through a small hole in an iron turkey. Criminal Record: Found guilty by fashion police of dressing her newborn in a yoda costume. Occupation: Ms Dyer is said to have enjoyed her dual roles as storyteller and veterinarian, although on the whole she was rumoured to have found it more enjoyable to make up entertaining lies than to apply scientific fact.

Lee Battersby – The Metawhore's Love Story
Lee Battersby (11 November 1970 to 2nd February 2047). Considered by many to be Australia's foremost exponent of the Unknown school of writing, Battersby wrote over 1500 short stories before his death, several of which were read by more than a dozen people. In his later years, he taught trans-amdental meditation, a form of spirituality concerned with the relative speed of the practitioner's teeth. After his death, he was spread across the beaches of his hometown, Clarkson, despite not having been cremated. He is survived by nobody who will own up to it.

Penny Love – The Janus' Tale
Penelope Love is thought to have been born in Melbourne, Australia, sometime between the assassination of John F Kennedy and the abduction of Harold Holt. Her work appeared in a number of Australian anthologies of the early 21st century, notably the Aurealis-award winning *Daikaiju* (Agog Press, 2005), *Fantastic Wonder Stories* (Ticonderoga Press, 2007) and a 2007 Aurealis Awards 'Best Science Fiction Short Story' finalist, 'Whitey', in *Shadow Plays* (Ed. E. Bunter, 2007). Like most Australians of the time, the author could read and write both English and a Chinese dialect, however only one extract of her Mandarin writing survives, the terse yet eloquent, 'Going to the shops to buy some things.'

Trent Jamieson – The Lighterman's Tale

Trent Jamieson was believed to have lived in the Brisbane area, though there is little evidence that he actually spent time there. A writer of fictions he started his own cult in 2011, but it was not popular, described variously as tedious, and just making no sense. It was in his later life that he made a real name for himself, as a purveyor of carpets and sundry goods. Trent's corner shops exist all across the country, and still do a brisk trade. The river Trent is erroneously believed among the general population to have been named after him. His death, consumed by rats in the Dire Plague of 2040, is not apocryphal, the photographic evidence both compelling and stomach churning.

Rita de Heer – The Carbon-Knitter's Tale

This story was written down for posterity by Rita de Heer, sometime refugee in England from the flooded Lowlands, now pattern scribe in the Knitting Guild House in the Australia Archipelago, sister house to the Guild House in Canterbury, Old England. When she is not engaged in the work of the guild, making up patterns deeded to the House by past knitters to keep them in use, Rita travels the country to record legends about the touchdown in the Australia Archipelago of an alien from the Procyon Star System. She is finding that every island has an ' alien' story.

L.L. Hannett – The Evangelist's Tale

Social historians have been unable to pinpoint the precise year that L.L. Hannett was cloned. We do know that by late 2010, L.L.version.1 had completed a PhD, while in early 2009 L.L.version.2 was a graduate of the Clarion South Writers Workshop. Rumour has it that the two L.L.s went their separate ways in 2021, when Version.1 refused to quit publishing obscure academic essays that were of little interest to anyone (apart from a pocket of Ancient Icelandic scholars). Recently, a Canadian collector discovered Version.2's earliest speculative work in a priceless paper copy of *On Spec*.

Matthew Chrulew – The Gnomogist's Tale

The grandson of a Siberian-born veterinarian, Matthew Chrulew closely followed the scientific drama surrounding the resurrection of the extinct mammoth. In 2026, he travelled to the Republic of Sakha-Yakutia to witness the reintroduction of the mammoths to their ancestral home. According to witness reports, he strode towards the grazing herd, which then gored and trampled him. A quick-thinking scientist placed Chrulew's dying body in a nearby ice cave, alongside other excavated mammoth remains. It's noteworthy that the cave meets the basic conditions for cryogenic storage. Recent visitors report that Chrulew's head – complete with frozen ecstatic grin – is remarkably intact.

Lyn Battersby – The Conductor's Tale
Lyn Battersby spent most of her adult life barefoot, pregnant and in the kitchen. She did, however, manage to steal time on her husbands' computers and type out the odd word. The results of her life include two broken toes, five wonderful children and the title of 'muffin queen of the universe'. She had short stories published, of which 'The Conductor's Tale' was the last. Lyn's life changed one warm Sunday afternoon in November 2045 when her husband Lee finally bought her a pair of shoes and told her to get out of the kitchen. She hasn't been seen since.

Dirk Flinthart – Editor
Dirk Flinthart appears as a colourful, possibly mythical figure associated with the First, Second and Third Tasmanian Republics during the chaotic years after the 2012 Event. A number of obscure books and stories are linked with the name, usually in the Australian small press. Reports of his hand-to-hand struggle with the proto-fascist Malcolm Turnbull are almost certainly exaggerated, but there is a growing body of evidence to suggest that Flinthart may have triggered the nuclear incident which eliminated the Singapore Concordiat. Nothing further is known of him after that point.